Death Trap

Death Trap

Patrice Chaplin

Duckworth

First published in 2003 by
Gerald Duckworth and Co. Ltd
61 Frith Street, London W1D 3JL
Tel: 020 7434 4242
Fax: 020 7434 4420
Email: enquiries@duckworth-publishers.co.uk
www.ducknet.co.uk

© 2003 by Patrice Chaplin

The moral right of Patrice Chaplin to be identified as the
Author of the Work has been asserted by her in accordance
with the Copyright, Designs and Patents Act 1988.

All rights reserved. No part of this publication
may be reproduced, stored in a retrieval system, or
transmitted, in any form or by any means, electronic,
mechanical, photocopying, recording or otherwise,
without the prior permission of the publisher.

All characters in this publication are fictitious and
any resemblance to real persons, living or dead,
is purely coincidental.

A CIP catalogue record for this book is available
from the British Library

ISBN 0 7156 3215 9

Typeset by E-Type, Liverpool
Printed in Great Britain by
Biddles Ltd, *www.biddles.co.uk*

1

I was having a drink outside the locals' bar. The purple sky, turning to gold where it met the sea, was too vibrant and seemed to belong to another existence altogether. A dome of dense purple, it covered us like a lid, holding in the goings-on of that patch of Northern Spain. A dog crossing the street was endowed with a mystery, an importance impossible in normal light.

The English girl, Lily, said, 'It's the "Green Hour". Or maybe the "Blue Hour". In the green they used to drink absinthe. It was called the Green Fairy. In the blue they drank anything.'

Stars as big as plates switched on above the castle. The sea, a sheet of gold and silver, glimmered as far as the French coast. Flowers I took to be honeysuckle breathed out their scent in a sudden breeze and added to the seduction. Leaves tinkled like tiny bells.

Over the years visitors had murdered the coast but they couldn't ruin the natural atmosphere. God hadn't quite abandoned it. Fairy lights came on around the terrace of Claudette's hotel and the Thirties dance music she loved started up.

The light made the fortress village spectacular, a stage set for the dramas to come.

'People come here and that's it,' Lily said. 'Why leave?' She was one of them. She had recognised me as a Londoner, offered me a drink and suggested we meet again tomorrow. But I wouldn't be here tomorrow. I'd finished an assignment with two more reels of film left. I thought I'd use them up on the village in the morning and then take the plane to London.

The bar perched in the middle of a precipice the locals called a hill. It started up at the castle and plunged in a sheer drop to the low-life district below. It was a mad hill, thin and broken, and the cars jolted down like a fairground ride. Only drunks survived that hill. It was not for the average person.

'I've never actually walked up it,' Lily said. 'I take the bus. There's one at midday. Or Serge drives down to get me.' She had another glass of the light rosé wine. She said it was so inoffensive and natural it could do no harm. Later, I discovered she put away a couple of bottles of it a day and never touched red except with dinner. The wine drinking began just after the early morning beers down at the market and perhaps was why her husband Serge didn't rely on a bus to bring her out of a bar. 'He needs his meals. Mad about lunch. What a carry on if I should miss that bus.'

I learnt that Lily was a good and practical cook. She dealt in antiques, found things for the expatriates. Her everyday life was ordered. The wine flowed like a distant river, not interfering, yet. Sometimes on hangover mornings it roared in her ears. Her face now had the same blush as the rosé wine.

'At nine you go down the hill for the morning coffee and a newspaper and you have a quick one before you do your shopping. And then a few in the market. And certainly something before you get on the bus.' She hated the fact I was drinking Coca-Cola. 'Everyone drinks. That's what Les Frontières is about.' She waited for me to become sensible and let her order me a proper drink. I stayed with the Coke. 'The regulars have got half a pancreas between them, new livers and plastic veins in their legs. The last thing they give up is the drink.' Her voice was attractive and clear with a similar resonance to the chapel bell. She looked again at my glass and didn't like it. And they wouldn't like it, the villagers. They were prepared to change their bodies to accommodate drink's effect. What the hell was a non-drinker doing in their bar?

The shop opposite with its noisy bead curtains might save villagers that perilous journey down to the real shops. For the only shop in the village, it was remarkably under-stocked. A few tins and packets, some cheese, a sweating salami and, out front, a crate of green vegetables turning yellow as I watched them. Why didn't the grocer have more food?

'He doesn't like it,' Lily said, and made a gesture indicating he did like drink. 'I wish he'd start selling bread. We've all asked him. But he's always in here.' She pointed at the bar full of flies and, further back, the bar flies. Then she asked about my job that took me everywhere and I remembered later the word 'lucky' came into it. She said it twice and I thought it odd. I couldn't see how being a photographer had much to do with luck. A bird laughed that raucous mocking laugh that I originally thought came from a madman. Someone told me it was a pigeon. Someone else said it was a magpie. Lily said the bird was only found round here. Another broken octave of mirth and I looked upwards.

The woman came over the hill in that medieval frontier village like a galleon in full sail. Behind her followed the moneyed group of admirers and hangers-on but she was all you saw. Her shoes clicked rhythmically on the stones and the sound was familiar. She held her head beautifully. The bird laughed, a jarring sound, and with a thumping of heavy wings was off. Lily stirred, excited. 'That's her. The Russian. They call her Elle.'

As the woman came nearer her face was more and ever more familiar. Yet I'd never met her. She came to a stop by the bar and every eye in the place was looking her way. For a moment they forgot to drink. At the back of the group, a tall willowy girl with flaming yellow hair clutched an exotic cat that cried. She was stylishly turned out in clothes the prices of which could only be guessed at. The girl was striking and wild and the many bracelets gonged expensively as she grappled with the cat.

'A top model?' I asked Lily.

'A top girlfriend,' she hissed.

'Whose?'

'Hers of course.'

'Who is she?' I was looking at the woman.

'Have you got all night?' Lily kept her voice down, indicating the group understood English.

The woman's eyes, hazel not unlike the cat's, moved across my face casually. I was a stranger. That was all. She was about to follow the men into the bar but something made her look back at me. Another meaningful nudge from Lily. 'She likes you.'

It was 22 September 1984 at 8.50 p.m., unless the hands of the bar clock lied.

Like everyone else, I couldn't take my eyes off her. Her companions were less than a blur as they came out and asked what she wanted. I knew her, I just had to remember where from. A piercing scream from the cat as it tried to hide in the girl's long white-gold hair frightened even the dogs, and they started barking on all sides. I could see a lot of attention went into that hair, brushing, nourishing, rendering it silky. Laser treatments thickened it, capsules gave it sheen. There was nothing casual about it. Or her. This girl was cared for, tuned up, turned out, and money and effort were not spared. She got the best. Her grooming and self-care were light-years away from Lily's and, I had to recognise, mine. The woman spoke to the girl in a language which turned out to be Finnish. As the girl turned I saw her face clearly. All the make-up in the world couldn't do a thing about the expression in her eyes. I thought: I don't ever want to feel pain like that.

The girl and the cat were sent home and the woman decided to acknowledge Lily. They agreed they were neighbours. Lily paid a compliment to the evening. She said the sky was so colourful, she'd never seen it like that before. Lily moved along the low wall, making room in case the woman chose to sit down. Lily made some kind of introduction and we all spoke English. The woman fitted into the small space next to me and smiled right into my eyes. Of course I knew her, had known her all my life. I think she asked what I was doing in the village and I mumbled something about photography. Actually I felt as though I'd slipped through time into another reality altogether. The woman sat with that special poise the French describe as 'good in her skin'.

Lily whispered, 'Careful,' and raised her eyes in warning. I wasn't sure which particular danger I should avoid. Even if I had known, what good would it have done me?

'Is she gay?'

'She's everything.' Lily was serious.

The visiting group stood apart from the locals, drank wholeheartedly, spoke in an unrecognisable language spliced with American. Their clothes were probably Versace. Somehow these rich people needed labels. The money didn't quite do it for them. But not her. She would look good whatever she wore. Hers was an inner elegance, a classiness she was born with.

The after-dinner light of this particular evening suited everybody and for that short hour I felt I was, by trespass or chance, in some exalted reality. It was like watching a much-loved movie, except I was playing a part.

She asked me where I stayed. At least that's what I thought I heard. She was surprised to discover this was my first visit to Les Frontières. My voice answering her question was quiet. Words stumbling, face hot, I wasn't used to being shy.

'You look as though you've been stung,' said Lily. How she enjoyed all this!

Saturday night and the bar was full, but then it was always full. Writers, painters, housepainters, a musician, the plumber, the castle guardians and people with a past they didn't have to bother with here. No one challenged their identity. This was the reason Lily had settled here. She'd had a turbulent life: up, down and then really down. Famous, well off, scandalous, then she ended up with a new name and a roomful of what she described as antiques. I came to understand that many foreigners residing in Les Frontières had left behind quite out-of-the-ordinary lives.

I said something about the atmosphere of the district, which during my short stay had been languid, off-key, disconcerting, joyous and disappointingly commercial in places.

'Oh yes,' said Elle. 'It's beautiful here but as beautiful as it is, so it is bad.' She looked at Lily. 'You have to distrust beauty sometimes. We learn that here, don't we?' She sat casual, effortless, elbows resting on her knees like a young boy. 'It might suit you here.'

'That doesn't sound like a compliment,' and my voice shook and surprised me.

'It would suit you because you're paradoxical.'

Of course I'd known her deeply. When? Where? This meeting was a collision, not on a conscious level. She liked my name, Catherine, and decided it sounded serene.

The bead curtains opposite rattled. 'Jo Jo,' shouted Lily. 'You've got a customer.' Men filled our hands with drinks. I changed mine for citron pressé.

'Why?' asked Elle.

'I don't drink.'

'Don't or can't?'

I wasn't about to open the book at every page and stuck to the 'don't'. I asked her what she did.

Eyes looking too intently into mine, she said, 'Nothing.'

Lily passed me the bag of crisps.

'Do you live in the village?' I asked.

'Now and then.' She reached across for a crisp and her arm touched my thigh. How graceful and well formed her wrist was. For the first time I really understood what was meant by inherited breeding, class. That slender, shapely wrist said it all. 'I'm one of those the true villagers disapprove of. I'm just part-time.'

I felt that what she said had little to do with what she was thinking. I was actually excited. No. I'd been that from the first moment she came over the hill. I was transformed. I realised, although I'd talked about myself, I'd got nothing out of her.

The men ganged up in front of her, ready to go. She was not ready. They wanted to go into France, to the casino. She ignored all that and took one of Lily's cigarettes. Her hair was glossy, streaked and cut in a boyish style, swept back at the sides like Robert Redford's. Her face, exquisitely made and tanned, needed no make-up. She was boyish, female, dazzling, sought-after, daring, sexual, rich. She was made up of bits and pieces and elements of Les Frontières. It was more than her natural habitat. It was her.

Where had I seen her? Who was she? I recognised her too well for it to be some distant acquaintanceship. I believed her imprint had been inside me all my life, waiting for the time she would eventually appear in the flesh. Finally I said, 'Have I met you before?'

'Possibly,' her tone casual.

Lily was thrilled. This, the stuff of real village gossip, would be in every bar by nightfall.

The woman sat so easily beside me, her hand, as it almost touched mine, so known. How could I have forgotten her? And the fact it didn't quite touch mine set up a definite longing. Provocative, dangerous, her eyes grazed across my face and then she was gone.

I'd been one thing before I met her. Afterwards, another altogether.

'You should see her house.' Lily was star-struck once she'd left. 'It's the best in the village. Rich? You couldn't even imagine it.'

The last look she'd allowed herself before leaving ... It was as though she owned me. The dome of opaque sky boomed, as though in warning.

'Don't jump,' laughed Lily. 'It's only the last plane coming in.'

I didn't have to ask about her. Lily was going to tell me everything. 'She's married to the richest man in Finland. Or is it Denmark? She's friends with royalty. She's got political connections everywhere. Visitors come here who we never get to see. We're the unfortunates at the gate. And she's got her girlfriend living with her. Calls her the Princess. Apparently they're so scandalous they can't go back to their own country.' Lily was jubilant, also resentful. She wasn't quite good enough to get in that gate. Or was it bad enough?

And I remembered one thing Elle didn't have. As she'd stood in the ray of light from the bar, I had not seen her shadow.

2

The next morning as I walked around the village I was no longer looking at the way the light fell at the end of a stone alleyway. Or at the squat farmer's wife fanning herself on a chair outside her house where a painter had stayed and painted landscapes mauled by the terror of too much seeing. They said starvation caused that and the farmer's wife had given him soup. I didn't really look at the club a French chanteuse had made famous in the Sixties. The day was a jigsaw puzzle with one piece missing. Elle was more like a beautiful boy than a woman. Yet the silk of her shirt had emphasised quite lavish breasts. Her voice had disappointed me. It was ordinary and belonged to someone else altogether. It was strange that she had no trace of an accent.

The village windows were not what they were yesterday. Full of eyes, they watched as I sped isolated through those too-narrow streets. I felt tainted, as though infected by some disease that might spread. The village seemed to know it and its eyes widened with mockery and its doorways shook and laughed. I was caught and contagious. And then the feeling was gone and the buildings were still and innocent.

Lily shouted down from one of the windows. 'What's your hurry?'

I asked where Elle lived.

'It's only eleven o'clock. They were in town last night. Probably didn't get back till seven or eight.' Lily, however, liked a bit of sport. She came down into the street and led me along cobbled passageways, across courtyards, up crumbling stairways to a cul-de-sac fringed with trees, private, unnoticed from the square. The tall house was one of the oldest, shadowed and impressive. It had been built when pirates attacked the coast during the fifteenth century and had an underground passage leading to the sea. The iron gate was locked. Lily rang the bell then, giggling, bent down and hid.

'What's it like in there?'

'I've never been inside,' she whispered. 'We're only the villagers.'

The willowy yellow-haired girl from the night before leaned over the terrace and asked who was there. Her hair fell forward. She looked like a princess from a fairytale, longing to escape. Behind her, I could see at least three men sitting at a table eating. The girl went inside for advice and came back with a short answer. The polite version was, 'It's not convenient just now.' She'd been told to get rid of me. She stood up and her hair swung out of sight. Now she looked straight, young and strong, but not quite of this world, like a male angel visiting bad places. She didn't so much leave the terrace as dissolve.

'You don't want to know them,' said Lily, suddenly serious. 'They've got it and they let you know you can't have it.'

We had breakfast on the square in the sun and Lily described the village. All kinds of people came here. The one thing they had in common, it seemed, was that none of them were ordinary.

'The thing about this place – it doesn't let anything go. It's as though time holds on to everything that's happened here, so it's as if it all happened a minute ago. Yet go a few kilometres further and it's all moving on normally. It's as if the village chose me rather than I chose it. But I was desperate when I came here and I met Serge and found I could buy and sell things. That was a surprise. We get by. We have four dogs. They're our children. I'll never leave here. I just have to make it work.'

Later I saw Elle at the wheel of a splendid open car speeding down the sharp hill to the sea. The girl sat in the front beside her. A tanned man sat in the back with his hair blown straight up by the wind or else sheer fright. Elle, I could see, was enjoying the speed, the steep drop and the danger. They were all smiling widely. It looked not unlike a scene from a Fifties movie.

'They're going to France.' Lily was beside me. 'They go down there for lunch. The man's the son of her old husband, Olav. Olav only comes here for the horse racing. They've spent a fortune on that house and restoring it. They get it decorated in one style and then the Princess wants it differently so they do it all over again. And then that isn't quite right either so they do it once more. I'm supposed to find the curtains for the guest rooms when they make up their minds.'

'Will they be back later?' Was I prepared to miss my plane for a chance of seeing her again?

'Oh no. They've got another place. Right on the sea.'

No one could say destiny wasn't on my side. I didn't see her again and I shouldn't have seen her again.

I took two last shots of the bay from the top of the hill and that was the end of the assignment.

My husband met me at Heathrow. 'You've changed, Catherine. Something happened over there.'

I couldn't think what.

3

The following spring a legendary performer married a girl forty years younger than himself and I was sent to photograph the wedding. The assignment took me back to Les Frontières. The photos were bland but the American magazine was paying a fee that would allow me at last to concentrate on my own work and perhaps mount the exhibition that the need for financial survival always delayed.

On the way back to the airport I had to pass around the base of the fortress village where I had been in the previous September. The horrendous main road that led from the sea past the railway station was choked with exhaust fumes from a thousand vehicles, and this toxic fug roasting in the sun stung people's eyes, nostrils, skin. The tar on the road had started to melt in the heat and spat up face-high. Then we got stuck in a traffic jam. It was at this point the cab driver decided to go mad, becoming so restless and anxious I thought he was about to leave the cab and run off. I was very pleased to see Lily crossing the street, a long loaf protruding from under her arm. Hers was the only happy face on that street, a dozen drinks happy. She opened the cab door.

'No good sitting in there. You can't go anywhere. Not just before lunchtime.' She told the driver he was crazy. He didn't deny it. 'The plane? Forget it. Get the next one.' She took my bag and pulled me out of the cab and together we started running for the small village bus.

The bus, full of villagers, started to inch up that terrible hill so that the oldest passenger, Dolores, could get out in front of her door. Dolores had modelled for Renoir and Matisse. The bus clung to the hill like an insect, buzzing and scrabbling until Dolores returned with a huge frosted glass of white wine for the driver. No one seemed to pay for a ticket. Dolores had penetrating eyes, a bone structure that defied age, a strong full-blown body: a town-pale orphan at twelve, she'd handed out towels to the prostitutes in a Parisian brothel. She'd seen everything.

Lily looked at the sample photographs I'd developed to send to the newly-weds as a present. 'They're ludicrous. Those two never stand together and smile. I've never seen them smile. They fight all the time. How could you get them to look like that? You should have come to me. My husband plays boules with him most afternoons. We call him Star. The pictures would at least have been realistic.'

'So the marriage is already in trouble?'

'It's never been anything else. He's sexually jealous as hell of her and she keeps it that way. It's perhaps the one way to keep him. And he's bored because he has to play house and can't rage around the Riviera with his gang.'

I felt almost ashamed I'd got it so wrong and hid the smiling, lying pictures back in the envelope.

'They're a true Riviera couple,' Lily continued. 'Jaded, bad, fun-loving, pleasure-crazy, and now I'm being nice. Think what you could have got on film.' She sounded sad. I agreed with her, but I had to produce what the magazine wanted. That's how I got paid.

The wine had given the driver a hit and the bus lurched left down an alley into dark roads, so narrow their bulging medieval walls grazed the metal sides.

'He always does detours. Likes to improvise the journey. If he drinks too much we can just end up anywhere.' The bus stopped at every passenger's house and he was given a drink for his trouble. Lily assured me if he got 'tired' she'd do the driving. I couldn't be less assured.

Finally, after curling, curving and screeching in the maze of back streets, the bus shot blindly out of a stone tunnel into a square full of brilliant light. Restaurant tables stood under the trees.

'A day like this, a gift from God,' said the driver.

Lily bought him a drink.

She took us to the locals' restaurant for lunch. The others were for the tourists. 'They come and go and think they've seen something.' She ordered tapas, chicken from the spit, fresh crisp salad and the obligatory litre bottle of rosé wine, for her. 'You can't know this village by snapping photographs and reading the guidebooks. It has a certain magnetism, so that things impossible elsewhere could be done here. And it adds a touch of sin from a previous time that is still present. Like a stubborn ghost refusing to be snuffed out. In the past you could have a very good time with sin. You live on the edge here. No half-measures, I can tell you. That's why these creative and starry people stay. You can be sure you are really living life. Some people take it further than that – I mean the local cemetery. A grave keeps being dug up. They buried some Russian there a long time ago. What's wrong with a Russian? They've got everything else in there.'

She was about to order another bottle but spotted her husband, Serge, crossing the square. Instant telepathy had his eyes fixed on the empty litre bottle of wine on the table in front of us. 'Say you drank half if he asks,' Lily whispered.

He had a style which didn't suit the sensitive. He liked to provoke and joke, using a quick stand-up comic patter and you couldn't tell if it was in fun or not. His eyes were unmoving; there was no fun in them. The idea was to unsettle his audience. He could cross from banter to cruelty and back again so fast you had to question your own perception. Did he really mean that? He made sure everything was on you so nothing landed on him. When she wanted, Lily had a streak of sarcasm like a cat clawing. She could draw blood and he didn't mess with her.

'Serge is on his way to play boules with Star. He'll take you to his house after the game and you can photograph what you like. Star is very easy after he's won at boules so Serge will see he wins.'

'Providing you don't take my picture, chérie, though I'm the best-looking of that lot.'

Serge was younger than Lily and had come from the north of France. Like her, he had his reasons to leave. They'd found each other during the necessary business of creating new lives. Their fresh identities began the minute they started climbing the hill. What went on before was, according to village custom, no one's business except their own. And God's. The baptism took place in the locals' bar. He'd got work looking after the art collection in the castle. He was small, sturdy and fast moving. His pale face was good-looking and secretive. His small, tricky mouth knew when to stay shut. He quickly made me see that personal photographs of Star would fetch a bigger fee. I'd already seen that and offered him a cut. He didn't want it. He'd only have wanted it if I hadn't offered.

After the in-depth photograph session which Serge had manipulated, even directed – he certainly knew how to get a result from people – I headed for Claudette's hotel. 'You sell the original spread to the magazine and the real ones to the French gutter press,' said Serge. 'You'll be able to afford to stay at Claudette's for a month.' Again I offered him a cut. He shrugged. 'Buy me a drink sometime.' Later, someone said, I think it was Claudette, that Serge was really very kind but didn't dare show it. Not in this village.

The crumbling hotel was halfway down the hill, next to the bar, with a terrace overlooking the coast. It had seen better times, even splendid times. At night Claudette turned on the fairy lights and played Thirties dance music on old 78 records. Her permanent guests, a singer from the Toulouse opera, a footballer from the Toulouse team and an exotic prince fallen on hard times, ate dinner at separate tables on the terrace.

I'd forgotten about Elle until I heard the music. I asked if she was still in the village. 'She lives in a tall house near the castle with a girl ...'

'I may have seen these people but I do not know them.'

If Claudette knew her she wasn't letting on. It was one conversation she would not continue. What had they done, Elle and the Princess, to be denied existence in this village where the only crime was to be boring? Boring people perished from some extra punishment for daring to set foot in this territory reserved for fallen angels and those who could enchant.

Claudette knew the village but its mysteries eluded her. She believed she could never feel satisfied anywhere else but her husband hated it. He was standing in the kitchen on legs filled with those plastic veins Lily had mentioned before. He'd weathered his bankruptcy, obesity, gambling, but not the stuff that came in the frosted glasses the bus driver liked. He was present somewhere between reality and black-out, his eyes were scarlet and unfocused, his face ruddy and huge like a sun that refused to set. He looked as though at any minute some organ might implode.

'He's got gout,' Claudette explained. 'The air doesn't suit him here. Too humid.'

I asked what he did.

'He's the cook.'

I decided on a cold dinner.

Like Lily, Claudette believed the place had an essential personality of its own that you either loved or hated. You didn't just deal with your own life. You had to deal with the atmosphere as well. 'It doesn't move on or evaporate, so what happened back then is still here now and visible on the air. You get all these sensations and feelings that aren't modern at all.'

The opera singer interrupted. 'People say when you die here you don't pass on but live amongst us invisibly. They say you leave a bit of yourself, your imprint like a negative.'

'It makes it kind of crowded,' said the prince. 'Four hundred people, forty thousand ghosts.'

I mentioned the desecrated grave but no one seemed to hear me.

Claudette put another Thirties ballad on the turntable. Her clothes seemed to belong to that era and her hairstyle too. Further down the hill, a man sang in a high-toned voice with a catch in it, that reverberated, full of nostalgia.

'Bel canto,' the opera singer told me. 'Turn of the century. Hear the vibrato in his voice.'

He was singing from an opera, *La Dame Blanche*. Every night he sang songs from that time, only from that time. The most modern was from 1916.

So, here and there in the village, those misfits were happy living in the past. Move them to some modern place and they would not survive.

4

'While you're here you must see the views.' And so Lily took care of another day.

I asked questions. I wanted to know all about Elle. I understood the village. Its inhabitants wanted me to know they weren't just living anywhere. I wasn't asked to photograph anything. Word had got round I did tabloid work. I'd made Star and his girl bride insultingly normal. They looked like any other couple in it together for the wrong reasons. I was commercial. A hack. If I stayed in the village long enough I could shake all that off and be someone else altogether. But I was also a visitor and that was what they talked to.

Lily said the village had always been agricultural and in trouble from invaders. She couldn't remember which ones. Then came the drug trade. She knew the dealers, even their names. 'There was a shooting at the bottom of the hill by the drinking fountain. They got the chemist, the dentist and the anaesthetist. The Mafia did. Someone hadn't paid up for some morphine. It was years ago before the First World War. Dolores says she remembers it, but she's clairvoyant.'

Who were the invaders now? 'The tourists,' said Lily. 'But they're merciful. And the foreigners who buy the houses and live in them for two weeks a year.' There were no stars. Just memories.

I understood that the village thrived on its past of attractive sin, outrageous pleasures and pure glamour.

Lily invited Serge's friend René, a house painter, for dinner. Most of the work in the village came from restoring and looking after the foreigners' houses. René's other talent, according to Lily, was undiluted gossip in several languages. Languages seemed to come easily to him. His English was fluent.

'You can be sure everything he tells you he's actually seen. He gets it all first-hand standing on those ladders.'

I showed Serge the new photographs of his starry boules companion. I was far from sure about offering them to the gutter press. It didn't fit well with some instinctive moral sense I still had. I wasn't particularly aware of it, but was sure I would feel its loss.

Lily grabbed them up and looked closely at the bride. 'Her eyes aren't young.'

'They've never been young,' said Serge.

And then the conversation changed gear as impulsively as the bus driver after a glass of wine.

'She doesn't let her out,' said René.

'Who?' I asked.

'The Russian keeps the girl indoors.'

Serge laughed, a hard brief laugh. 'I see you like understatement tonight. It goes with your shirt.'

Serge and Lily teased the house painter about his clothes and the Princess was forgotten.

'They're his best,' said Serge. 'But they can't be best together. That shirt should be worn with jeans. No, on second thoughts it shouldn't be worn at all. Have one of mine.' He tossed René a white shirt. 'They're his number ones and he's put them on for you, Catherine.' He pretended to kiss my hair then went to the stove and started cooking.

I brought the conversation back to the Princess.

'The things that have been going on over there,' said Lily. 'The police came and an ambulance and she was taken away.'

René had just the right facial gestures to keep her going.

'Three o'clock in the morning.'

'She?' I asked.

'Mia. The Princess. They'd had a fight. You could hear her screaming. You could hear it as far as the coast. Of course Madame said she'd had a turn. Something she'd eaten. An allergy I think she called it.'

René's eyebrows arched, making his eyes dramatic. 'Not for the first time.'

'But of course not,' said Lily. 'And now you're going to tell us about the first time.'

René lowered his voice. Gossip was more effective when properly presented. 'The girl, Mia, is terrified. I used to do some work for them.'

Serge banged pans on the stove.

'She was shaking so much she couldn't speak. She stays in that house for days. Won't or can't go out.'

Oil hissed in the pan.

'That'll change,' said Lily, sharply. 'She's inherited money. Real money. Family. That will change the balance.'

'Money won't do it. She's terrified of Elle,' said René. 'She's tied up.'

'Literally,' laughed Lily. 'I wonder what they do together?'

Serge was impatient. 'What do any two people do together?'

'They don't scream the place down.' Her voice had an edge.

Chopped vegetables spat in the pan. He stirred in a sauce. Lily leaned close to her guest. 'Are you sure she shakes with fear, or is it the shakes? We see enough of that around here.'

'She shakes with fear.'

'Oh, my wife is disappointed.' Serge heated some plates.

'Elle sleeps with the old man's will under her pillow,' said Lily.

'Old man?' I was drawn in again.

'The husband,' said Lily. 'So she remembers why he's in the bed.'

'I heard he's got a sexually transmitted disease,' said René.

'She takes a risk. That's why the will's there. Makes it worth it,' said Lily.

'Who told you about a disease?' Serge asked him.

'The nurse in the doctor's down below.'

'You don't want to get ill in this place,' said Serge. 'The Hippocratic Oath can't get up the hill.'

'It's never been a lucky house,' said René. 'The owner before the last went mad. They said it was the clap. Called a restaurant after him. El Clap. They had a dish of the day, Spotted Dick.'

Serge cut in, 'You get no sympathy up here, Catherine.'

Lily was puffed up with laughter like a pink balloon. 'Oh, René, I should have married you.'

Serge quickly eased the hot plates in front of us. The food was good. It was better than that. It was light, crisp and tasty. 'It's so good,' I said again. 'Were you a professional cook?'

All conversation stopped. In the dark corner near the stove his face seemed disembodied, a pale moon face above the saucepans. 'I don't like direct questions.' His tone made it clear he didn't expect any more.

Lily rescued me. 'I cook the everyday stuff but I'm not allowed to upset the guests. I once made hamburgers and Serge gave them to the dogs. D'you remember, René?'

I was wondering what I should do to rebalance my social esteem. I decided on silence but felt awkward. Serge ate quickly then switched on the television which was at the end of the table. It was like another guest. One he wanted.

'I know what their screams remind me of,' said Lily.

'The last owner,' said René.

'Of course. She died screaming from the window. You must remember, Serge.'

If he did he wasn't telling her.

'The top floor,' she said.

'No, the first,' said René.

'It was awful,' she told me. 'The woman wouldn't let anyone in. She had cancer and shut herself away. Then in agony she hung out of the window screaming. Serge broke the door down and rushed in but the woman fell out of the window. She was bones and skin. Weighed no more than a child. I'll never forget those screams. I heard them again the other night. Even my friend Amber down on the coast heard it.'

'Impossible,' said Serge.

'Not the way the wind blew that night,' said René. 'You could hear the chapel bell as far as the coast.'

'It's not a lucky house.' Lily lit a cigarette.

'Nor is this one if you keep on,' said Serge.

'A demonic house.' She poured herself a sizeable glass of wine.

'Why d'you spend your life trying to get in there then?' said Serge.

She ignored his anger. 'Because I'm curious. I want to know why they made such a point of buying that house. No one else would set foot in it after – have they changed it again, René?'

'Every time the wind changes.'

'Why?'

Serge jumped up and placed the dessert on the table. A home-made apple tart. I didn't think I should comment too much on its excellence. I didn't think I should say anything more to him.

'Why?' said René. 'They're special people. They want it special.'

'In what way?'

'She likes privacy.'

'She's got that.'

'Doesn't like people looking in or … She likes it cold. And not too much light.'

'Then why does she buy a house here? It doesn't make sense.'

They were talking about Elle.

'It's obvious. She's from the north and is used to the dark and the cold and can't adapt.' For Serge there was no mystery.

'It's a bad house because it is too dark,' said Lily. 'All those lower floors. You don't get the light and the sun until you're up at the top. And then it's magnificent. You feel you're in the sky. It's like a stalk with a flower at the top. They paid a lot of money for a stalk.'

Serge said again that was what Elle wanted.

'She wants to recapture a Finnish life. It's dark and cold most of the year,' agreed René. And that was that.

Lily was struck by a new thought. 'Does she make the Princess sleep with the old man?'

'Are you crazy?' said René. 'There's only one partner that girl gets in bed with. Elle makes sure of that. But actually – no, I shouldn't –'

Lily gasped. He shouldn't but he would. Serge, not a fan of gossip, dared to turn the television volume up.

'If you're bored,' she said sarcastically, 'why don't you go to bed so you don't hear what you shouldn't and get your little soul all in a muddle?'

'Perhaps he likes the Princess,' suggested René. It wasn't said altogether in fun.

'I don't have to bring people's lives into my own house. I've got enough with my own,' said Serge.

'What's the fucking matter with you?' said Lily. 'Is it the Mistral coming? They say it drives certain people mad.' She emphasised the 'certain' and one of the dogs barked. She was going to get away with it because company was in the room.

What had brought him to the village? Who was he? A disgraced chef? I was now playing the local game. What were you before you were you?

Lily was nudging her guest. 'Get on with it.'

'The Princess has had men. I know of two in this area.' He blurted it out suddenly as though under investigation.

'Don't look at me,' said Serge, underplaying it, trying for laughs now.

'A local who works in the castle.'

'Not true,' said Serge.

Lily flicked the top off the next litre bottle. 'But there's only one other in the castle and he's gay,' she said.

'He leaves me alone,' said Serge promptly.

René spread his hands helplessly. 'So the Princess has tricks for every occasion. She's had a good tutor after all. We know where Elle started out. She's stood on a few street corners before old Olav happened to pass by.'

Lily didn't agree.

'Well, that's what I've heard,' said René.

'And since when do you rely on *heard*?' asked Lily. 'You're letting me down.'

'It's where I heard it,' he said, smoothly. 'I was in the guest bedroom, out of sight, fixing the windows, and the guests on the bed knew plenty about her past and where it started.'

'But not that you were there,' said Serge. 'They sound really smart.'

'Are you doing the Princess's PR or something?' Lily was irritated.

'He's gone religious,' said René. 'Or he wants to work for her. She's got plenty of jobs to offer.' He winked at me.

Suddenly I wanted to see her, the woman from that last September evening. To see if she was all I'd thought she was and if I still believed I'd known her. I stood up. 'Are they over there?'

Lily screamed. 'Now you've got her excited.'

'You won't get in, my love,' said Serge. 'Not even your glossy magazine could open that gate. Only by invitation.'

'Or if you're a workman,' said René.

'What's it about in there really?' said Lily.

René tried to decide. 'Perfection.'

Serge got the brandy and put the coffee percolator on the table. 'Perhaps that's why they keep changing it.' There was no mystery.

'I changed the tiles in the main bathroom three, no four, times.'

'Weren't you fed up with it?' I asked.

'Not as long as they paid me.'

'So who'll change them fifth time around?' asked Serge.

Lily was looking at him. The lover in the castle had made her thoughtful.

'They never keep anyone long,' said René. 'They don't want you knowing too much.'

'They should get the deaf mute from Nice. He'd suit them.' Serge fed the dogs, all ruffians from the village that no one wanted. He loved those dogs.

René was pausing before the next golden titbit. 'If it was just a question of what you heard –'

'Go on,' said Lily, thrilled.

'She drinks.'

'Not Madame. Too controlling,' said Lily.

'The Princess. And she's not a lesbian. I promise you she's had men. I know one who's put her right.'

'I'm not that good.' Serge looked at me expecting I'd smile. He was definitely one of those who made me uncomfortable. I didn't know what to do with his jokes if that's what they were. After a while I did as everyone else. I ignored them.

They agreed Mia was pretty but needed a job and a healthy life. The duo made Lily uneasy and she couldn't get the information she needed. René found them a sumptuous hive of activity he could dine out on. Serge seemed to think his wife and René were making something out of nothing. I wanted to see Elle. Again I asked if she was at home.

'I haven't seen them since the ambulance took Mia away,' said Lily. 'They come and go. They've got an apartment in Monaco. The old man likes the golf there.'

'And to stroke his money,' said Serge. 'He's got it hidden in five banks. He doesn't even trust them, not enough to keep it in one.'

'Why do they fight?' I asked.

'Lesbians fight.' Serge was cut and dried. 'That's part of the deal.'

'Oh, she's a lesbian now,' said Lily and the jealousy showed. 'And I had you all fitted out for the lover from the castle. After all, you're the only straight one.' She played the pause well. 'Aren't you?'

René laughed. 'I've never been up his ladder so I can't tell you.'

Lily wasn't playing. She was looking at her husband. 'Am I going to get another surprise this evening?' The wine didn't seem to get to her, no matter how much she drank.

She got a thousand-volt glare from his unblinking eyes. 'This is exactly why I hate the chitchat. Someone sooner or later takes it seriously. You don't watch enough television.' He pointed at the Western which had replaced the football. 'Watch that and René's cute games won't even register.' Looking at René he added, 'You're worse than the women who sell fish.'

'The girl sleeps with men,' René insisted. The drink was getting to him. He said he'd walk me back to my hotel.

'Don't leave with him,' said Serge, 'or you'll be next. You can see what this village does to a person's reputation.'

I said I'd go over and see how the Princess was getting on.

Lily laughed and hugged me. 'Oh, I love you.'

That night I dreamt about a princess locked in an ivory tower screaming unheard, long hair hanging yellow in the moonlight. She was denied life, love, youth. I could see she was leaning too far. Wait, I cried. I'll get you out. She overbalanced and fell and took a long time to reach the ground. The thump was too loud. I lifted up the body. It was skin and bone, no heavier than a child.

I was glad to wake up that morning.

5

Of course I wouldn't get away. I walked in those narrow dark streets, their medieval buildings leaning towards each other, allowing a mere strip of sky above, like a blue ribbon. I was stuck to those cobbled, clattering passageways like a buzzing insect thrilled by the smell of mimosa. I almost whirred and droned with the high joy of the morning. The locals plunged down the hill for their first public drink of the day.

Claudette, carrying a shopping basket, opened the rusty gate and, for a moment, looked hopefully at the shop across the street. Same old crates of green things going yellow. The hope went out of her face and she started down towards the market. Then she saw me and said I should wait in the hotel. I'd had a phone call and the person would ring back.

My bag was packed, bill paid, cameras and tripod in the case. I wrote a card thanking Lily and Serge for dinner. Claudette's husband said he'd get a local taxi to take me to the airport. I explained I wanted to get out before the pre-lunch traffic. He thought I wanted to get out.

'I don't blame you. You're right not to be here. It's a graveyard painted pretty colours. It's a fake. Even the walls of the houses. They're done up to look old. René does it to put the prices up and fleece the foreigners. You're still young and healthy and you work and have a profession. You'd lose everything in this village. It's a dark, merciless creditor. It'll take the lot.'

It made me almost regretful to leave such a powerful place.

My agent phoned back and suggested as I was in Les Frontières, I should do a quick coverage of some architecture. Nothing elaborate. I could do it in an hour and still get the plane. I could include a reel of the local cemetery and desecrated grave.

Carrying the tripod and cameras I did something unusual. I hurried up the hill. I met Lily at the top. My clothes, wet with sweat, clung to my skin. My face was streaming, hair damp. My breath came and went uncertainly.

'Do you always shower with your clothes on?' she asked.

And then I learned this was the castle's weekly closing day. I hadn't counted on that. I needed that set of photographs. I needed all the work I could get. I was at the beginning of what might one day be called a profession. I needed to please the agent. So Lily sent Serge for the key while I sat on a stone and waited for my pulse to come back down from the hundreds. Lily looked down the hill with a certain respect.

'The only things that hurry up that are the dogs, occasionally.'

Serge did get the key but returned via the bar so everything was now late. I was strangely nervous and thought I should get away quickly from this village. He helped me light the pictures I needed and said he'd take me in his truck to the airport.

'What d'you mean you're not going to sell the latest photographs of Star and the bride? Let's call them candid photographs. A professional photographer never takes photographs they're not going to try and place. You don't take photographs to put in the drawer.'

I agreed with that. They belonged several levels up in 'art' photography. I'd exhibit them when and if I got an exhibition.

Then he mentioned Elle and advised me to ignore the ridiculous and childish stories of the night before.

'What is she like?' I asked.

'Like you or me.'

That told me nothing.

'She's generous. She's offered to back me in a business. The grocer's shop. She'll put up the money and I can run it. She can see what people are about. Can see that I should be doing better things than dusting pictures. I could turn that shop into the real food store for the village.'

He waited for me to approve of Elle and her – was it generosity?

'She can also see that there are a lot of backbiters up here. That's why she keeps to herself.'

I could see the reason Serge defended her reputation so fervently. Self-interest.

'Elle is just ordinary. Nothing to get excited about.'

Suddenly I needed to get home. Even I was surprised by the desperation in my voice. He said we'd go straight to his truck, pick up my bag, take short cuts to the airport. The chapel bell rang noon. Most people would be at lunch. The roads would be clear. He carried my equipment, and we hurried towards the square.

Lily was in their doorway, fizzing with excitement, the willowy Princess beside her.

'You are special. Didn't I say you'd be the one to get in that house? I must be clairvoyant. Tonight you're to go for dinner.'

Tonight I'd be in London. I tried to kiss her goodbye.

'You can't.' Lily was firm.

Serge rattled his keys. 'Come on.' He continued towards the truck.

Lily got in front of me and the Princess took my arm.

'You can't do this,' said Lily. 'Not to me. I'm invited too.'

'Then you go.'

'She'll cancel it. She doesn't want me. You're my way into that world.' She'd forgotten or didn't care that the Princess spoke English. 'Come and have a drink or one of those sensible colas and –'

'No.'

The Princess shook my arm playfully. 'You're a free spirit. I can see that. That's a gift. Yet you go on as though you're some little secretary living by the minutes on the clock, existing by permission. Ellie wants to see your photographs.' And she took my other arm, her breath already thick with beer. I could hear Serge shout and the engine starting. The Princess lifted me through Lily's doorway.

She said prosaically, 'Ellie wants to know if you eat chicken livers.'

*

At some point during that stolen afternoon in Lily's house the Princess said, 'I am so in love.'

I said I was pleased for her and wondered which of the wooing workmen had got lucky, had, to quote René, 'put her right'.

'I am in love with her as madly as the day I saw her.'

'Her.'

'Ellie. Yes, I love a woman.'

'You need to get a job, said Lily, brusquely. 'And get your mind off all that.' She couldn't do justice to the immensity of 'all that'.

'I had a job. I was an actress. And I got a place in the National Theatre school in Helsinki. And then I met Ellie.'

'Of course,' said Lily, not without sarcasm.

'What is she doing now? Right now?' I had to get back to the present, the Russian and this unsettling invitation.

The Princess gulped. Did she too dislike direct questions?

'Doing?' It was not a state she was familiar with. 'Ellie just is.' And she tugged the focus back onto herself. 'Do I look thinner, Lily? I know you'll tell me the truth.'

'Absolutely. To both questions.'

'Does she want to see my photographs?'

The Princess hesitated. 'Well, she must. Why else would she ask you for dinner?'

Lily got up and asked me to follow her into the bedroom. 'I want you to try on a dress for tonight.' She shut the door and whispered, 'Whatever you do, don't mention the screaming. Or René and the workmen. Don't tell her we talk about their sex life. And don't keep asking questions. She doesn't know anything. And don't, whatever you do, call her Princess.'

There were so many things I wasn't to say I found it hard to speak at all. The door opened and the Princess came in. When she asked me where I lived, my mouth opened and stayed that way. No sound came out.

She looked at Lily and said, 'Has she a problem about where she comes from?'

'A million, darling. We all have.' Lily chucked me a slim, black cocktail dress.

The Princess looked at her body in the long dressmaker's mirror. 'Ellie took me to a spa in Italy. For my nerves. I worked day and night doing the exercises, the diet, the baths. I had massage and electric massage for my face and –'

'Can you move? You're blocking my light.' And Lily shooed her away from the beam of sunlight.

She sat on the sofa with the dogs and told me her life story. She'd been born in Finland, a Danish mother, Finnish father. She'd acted as a child and been spotted in a talent contest. The family moved to Helsinki and she worked in 'little theatre' and television. Then came the scholarship at the top drama school. But Ellie was already there. Someone she'd known she'd meet.

I realised I didn't know her name. I assumed Mia was another nickname like the one I mustn't mention.

'Elizabeth, but we say it differently. Everyone calls me Mia.'

The hair saved her, and the eyes. The clothes did their bit. She was too tall, too thin in parts, too large in others. Heavy make-up did its best to give her a good skin. She was disconcerting because she was a bit of many things. Fearless, show-off, intuitive, bright, self-centred, sensitive. I thought she'd have made a wonderful music hall artist, done up to the nines, singing with her raucous voice and telling, with quick malice, the 'in' scandals of the moment. Anarchic, dramatic and, I sensed, destructive. I wouldn't put being pleasant past her either.

'Even my mother finally understands I love Ellie.' With disarming charm she added, 'You're just like her. My mother.'

'Thanks a lot.' And I cancelled 'pleasant' from her list of assets. I said I was not yet thirty-five. Looking again at her tired face lit by the ray of sun from the doorway, I thought thirty, for her, had passed.

'You don't seem young,' she assured me.

Lily made sure she got my attention and tapped her head. 'Simple.'

I asked the Princess how old she was, knowing she'd lie. She mentioned something with twenty in it. I asked how she'd known she'd meet Elle. Was it a thing of destiny? It seemed too similar to what I was feeling.

'Because I'd seen her photograph in the society pages. I knew one day I'd meet her. Nobody suited me but I didn't think I was gay. And then I saw her walking along a Helsinki street.'

Unlike most of the village, hiding behind a wise diplomacy, she couldn't wait to reveal her life. It spilled out in that dark room with its one shaft of light and the fans whirring, dogs snoring. Her assessment of the village, she'd got that right. She was the proud partner, perhaps 'partner' was putting it too high, 'lover' of a being I was drawn to and believed I'd known intimately at some previous but hidden time. Perhaps I met her during my sleeping hours? Was that possible? Did I float out to some other sphere and live a disembodied life with this being while my physical self snoozed faithfully beside my husband? I thought the heat was not doing my thinking any good. I knew I should leave.

Lily stopped polishing a battered lamp bracket. 'Why can't you just do something different, out of the ordinary? Take a risk for once.'

'Take Serge,' I said.

The Princess was alarmed. 'I'd have to ask Ellie.'

'Perhaps Madame wants you to photograph her house,' said Lily. She even looked cunning. 'You get a big fee photographing houses.'

The Princess was even more startled. 'I'd have to ask.'

'No you don't,' said Lily. And she mentioned my previous assignments and the magazine.

'Perhaps you could photograph me.' The Princess looked enthusiastic. 'I mean if you've done him. He's the biggest star in the south. Ellie knows him. But I'd have to ask Ellie.' The enthusiasm went away as fast as it came. 'But she's very fussy.'

'So am I,' I started to say.

'Don't bother.' Lily touched her head again. 'There are some things you just have to let pass. They're too silly. Just think, exhibition, exhibition, money, money.' She held up the bracket and frowned at it.

'I don't photograph weddings or do drama students' photographs.' I hoped I sounded proud.

'You should photograph Dolores. She lies in the sun naked all day on her terrace. Brown as a nut. Still got a good body. She goes dancing on the coast with young men. Really enjoys life. Just being with her I enjoy it too.'

Many of the old village women had been models for painters. They said they had paintings hidden in their basements, art works not dreamed of.

'You should stay on here,' Lily advised. 'You'd have something to photograph, I promise you.' The old women had either secured their futures by marrying money, sleeping with those who had it, opening a business such as a perfumery or bar. Or they ended up as cleaners. Lily thought there was a moral in this. 'Imagine getting to ninety and having to cook and clean for yourself and then go out and do it for foreigners.' She put the bracket aside. She said Serge just made enough for the rent and essentials. Doing casual work helped him pay off his truck. Her dealings put something in the bank. 'We don't own a thing. We don't have pensions, either of us. If anything happened to him –' She didn't like that thought.

A woman wearing an apron knocked on the door. She'd come for someone's key. Lily leaned across to the wall on which a hook held a dozen keys. She chose one and handed it to the woman. 'Tell them I watered their plants.' Again she turned to me and said she was worried. 'I keep an eye on the foreigners' houses while they're away but it's nickels and dimes.' Here in a sort of paradise a woman had the same worries as if she was in some uncaring city.

The Princess slipped out, as Lily put it, to fill up for the evening. 'She likes beer. It calms her. She can't drink in front of her keeper.'

'Why not?'

'Because Madame can't bear guilt. After all she's turned the girl into a drunk.'

It seemed this was a place where three-quarters of the population drank excessively and kept it away from the quarter that just drank.

I could see the Princess's long shadow outside the door. I could smell the beer as she breathed. She was listening. Lily seemed not to care.

'Come on, let's get dressed up. I've been waiting for this night for years.'

6

I made her laugh. That's the thing I remembered. And also, how she was unlike anybody I'd seen. In New York it seemed people turned to gaze after her – she was that good. The Princess made a joke of it. How the crowds, even on Fifth Avenue, thought she must be a famous person. But who? Some even stopped and asked her.

Dressed in silk trousers, a long-sleeved blouse, the colours muted, style played down, she stayed like a guest at the table waiting for the food to be served. The Princess was in a dither. Nothing would go right. She was trying to fork life into some hors d'oeuvre that had been left in the wrong temperature. Elle remained aloof from this unexpected chaos. It had nothing to do with her. In fact, on reflection, she seemed separate from everything, even her house. I couldn't remember what she said. Later I realised there had been other people present. Had I spoken to them? Yes, I made her laugh and she seemed to need the funny side of things.

'So you're photographing this sinful village again.' She looked into my eyes and it was the look of a lover. I was lost. Apparently the Princess had to ask me twice about the chicken livers. 'Are you sure you like them? You do know what they are? We do them the Russian style.'

'Chicken livers?' Lily prodded me. 'Yes or no?'

I could say that evening split my life. Before the look and after.

The chicken livers weren't up to much after all because the Princess, in the chaos of the evening, forgot about them and after being burned they were then too cold. Something happened in that house that was most unusual and its ripples of drama spread amongst the other guests and unnerved them. They felt the effects without knowing what it was or to whom it was happening. Lily got the giggles. The Princess wept. The spoilt cat jumped through the window. A guest dropped a plate. Was the Mistral coming? Elle looked at me and I at her. We knew. She did and I thought I did.

Lily cut the chicken livers in pieces and spread them around on her plate. She got my attention. 'I'm not too sure about them,' she said quietly. She made a display of enjoying the salad. Elle didn't eat.

'But you're not eating,' said Lily.

'She never eats,' said the Princess.

Elle poured a glass of wine and seemed to drink it. Her hair was swept back on each side as it had been the first time, sun-streaked, glossy, plenty of it. She had the head of a proud bird. Her hands were small and strong. The only odd note, too many rings. I didn't know anything about jewellery, but I thought they were cheap. I was right about that. It turned out they were presents from her various admirers, the ones who didn't have money.

I waited for Elle to ask me to photograph her. I was dying for her to ask but Lily pulled me away so the Princess could give the longed-for tour of her territory. 'Don't eat anything,' said Lily firmly.

'Not fresh?'

'She wouldn't know.'

The house, an Aladdin's cave, offered the unexpected and was strong on effects. Splendid furnishings, unexpected salons, walls created like sculptures, huge original fireplaces, sofas on engraved bases, circular leather seats that turned into beds, exotic lights and lamps, glowing bowls of light, showed one thing. They had money.

The objets d'art scrupulously selected and placed to create this world of magical onslaught thrilled Lily. The Princess explained how the sculpted walls had had to be redone. Who'd done them? She had. Herself? Her mind had, she said, but the hands had been Jo Jo the plasterer's.

'I wanted a curving feminine division between the bedrooms. Not something strict and rigid. Walls can be punishing things.' She shivered. Then she took Lily's hand and ran it along the femaleness of the wall. Lily started giggling and turned away.

I asked a couple of questions while Lily pulled round. I knew nothing about renovation. My house was the complete opposite to this one. Lily was eager to know where they'd got the antiques. The Princess gave an antique collector's fun story, how they'd combed the countryside, discovered out of the way shops and markets but the reality was that most of it came easily from a big-name collector.

'That's real money,' Lily told me.

A lot of the furniture seemed nailed down. Huge chests were created from the wood of the floor. The Princess said, 'But they are part of the floor. The wood of the floor rises up in the shape of a box and flows back down the other side. So there is no join. A lid is made.'

I pointed to a chest. 'What's in there?'

'Our possessions.'

The circular seat that turned into a bed was also, on inspection, created from the plaster of the wall. I could see no join. I'd never seen anything like that.

'The whole room is sculpted,' said the Princess. Lily thought it was very clever. I thought the furniture looked walled-in.

Behind a wall of mirrors, rail upon rail of clothes that even a princess might find overwhelming, all with brand labels, placed according to season and colour. Antique chests held the shoe collection.

'How do you two wear all this?' asked Lily.

'No, this is mine. Ellie's clothes are in her dressing room.'

A weathered door was shoved open and we were in a series of apartments, an Alice in Wonderland territory that shrank and expanded, slipped and sloped with the help of mirrors, lights, steps, screens and passageways. I had no idea where I was. Was I actually in the village?

There was even this famous underground passage down to the sea. The door opened easily and she showed me where it began. There was a well, a secret courtyard with a shrine. The house had an extraordinary number of bathrooms. 'And this is the blue bathroom,' and she pushed open another groaning door. It was one bathroom too many for Lily and she started to become hysterical.

'What's so funny?' asked the Princess.

Lily tried to blame the Mistral but choked and squealed with the unreleased mirth of decades. She was another who needed to see the funny side. The final master bathroom with its magnificent circular tub had her weeping with laughter.

She tried to pull herself together and whispered she must think of something sad, all those plastic veins running with alcohol suddenly leaking, the new livers bursting, the inflamed pancreases that killed faster then anything, the strokes, wet brain. Or Serge lifting one of those foreigners' sofas for two hundred pesetas and falling to the ground with a heart attack. She thought of it all and then realised she was in another bathroom and a new fit of laughter swelled up and she fell back in the bath helpless. The Princess said she looked like a rubber duck and went away to get her a glass of wine.

'I'm sorry,' said Lily. 'Really I am. But there are just too many bathrooms. They've made a mistake.' Then she choked out another cause for hysteria. Would they try it on with us? She said she'd never been so close to gay women. 'Stay close to me.' She dabbed at her eyes from which black make-up ran in rivulets. 'We mustn't get separated. Do they jump on us like guys do? Maybe they're worse?'

We realised we didn't know much about lesbianism. What do they do? I had an idea. She had no idea. I knew women who loved women but neither I nor they talked about their sexuality.

'She'll just grab us and we'll have no chance. And there'll be even more screaming from this house.' Her laughter was worn out. She'd be crying next.

The Princess, overhearing her incautious remarks, held the wine just out of reach. 'But you're a rubber duck. Who'd want to try it on with a duck?'

I wanted to get back to the dining room and to her. I thought she was the most exciting person I'd seen.

Later I realised the house wasn't an Aladdin's cave at all but a mausoleum, as cold, as rigidly ordered. And Lily said, 'Don't you mean a museum?'

'No. Worse.'

Elle didn't ask about my photographs. Had she even heard about them? I decided she was bored and that's why I was there. She was looking me over. It took care of another evening.

Then Serge was shouting up at the windows. 'I want my wife back. What are you doing with my wife?' And Lily was giggling again. 'It's two in the morning. Give me back my wife.' He was drunker than anyone round that table.

'Why does he have to let the whole village know I'm here? My reputation will never be the same again.' Lily crept to the window and shouted to him to shut up.

The Princess took her arm and we started down flight after flight of polished stone stairs to the gate. The Princess was laughing with Lily but her eyes didn't join in. I didn't think she was going to let villagers visit again. And suddenly Elle was behind me. I waited for her to say something. She said, 'What is that liquid on the stairs?' She pointed at the small puddle.

'Cat pee,' I said.

'Well, I didn't think you'd done it.' And she laughed and said my name and its syllables resounded back through my past and raced into my future. This was my baptism. I longed for her to touch me because it should happen. That's what it was about, the meeting of the known but not identified. And through the wild and euphoric lovemaking we'd recognise ourselves as we had once been. What was I thinking about? I wasn't gay, and she was already spoken for, it seemed. Not to mention the wife of the old shipping magnate, Olav. I still longed for just one touch. She did say, 'I'm worried about Mia. I have to find something for her to do.'

And so, eager to keep in contact, I said, 'Photography?'

That brought them to England and my life was never the same. I was in the 'after'.

7

The Princess was treated like all princesses get treated, at least in fairy tales. She was watched over, doted on, applauded. What Mia wanted she got. I thought she must be suffocating with gratification. Even the pain in her eyes looked less or I was getting used to it. I saw no sign of discord between them, and Lily's story of police and ambulances didn't fit.

They invited me to lunch the day after the chicken liver dinner to show me the real frontier. I could spend a lot of time in the wrong places. They chose a traditional restaurant in the old part of an inland town. The food was cooked on the open wood fire. Here was a part of their world, the dark calm restaurant with good house wine, splendid simple food, regular customers. It was family-run, nothing pretentious.

The owner made a fuss of Mia and said how beautiful she was. He knew on which side his bread was buttered. Elle looked as satisfied as if the compliments were for her. It became clear their days followed a trail of pleasure and they lapped up the good things still on offer on that exhausted coast. Olav came by from time to time to settle the bills, play golf, go to the races.

'He doesn't like it here,' said Mia. 'For him it's burnt out.'

I asked about his health, remembering the rumour that he was suffering from a contagious and mortal sexually transmitted disease. She described someone fitter than most. He got up at 5 a.m., ran, swam and was in his office by six. He did the sauna ritual daily and in the winter came out of the hot hut to roll in the snow and beat himself with twigs. He cycled, skied, sailed boats up the coast beyond the Arctic Circle. There seemed nothing he couldn't do in the stamina department except, perhaps, look after his wife. And live in a frontier village.

Mia said too much and Elle not enough. I did notice once or twice that Elle corrected her. A nudge under the table, a quick warning shake of the head and the sentence Mia had started hung unfinished in the air. Or she would put a wrong emphasis on an English word and again she'd be corrected. Or a name would be mispronounced. She was reprimanded for eating bread before the meal.

'You just fill up your stomach with nothing.'

And when Mia ate the bread with the food that was wrong too. What did Elle want? Carbohydrate and protein did not go together. The gut did not like it. I wondered if the Princess was being put down for my benefit.

Elle picked at a piece of chicken and green leaf salad. She liked perfection. She only liked perfection. I suspected that once she'd got over the turbulence of novelty, the helplessness of passion, she liked her conquest to be her ambassador, to represent her perfectly in a chaotic world.

Mia, after a few drinks, was like an enormous young dog, too big for the owner and the restaurant. But the owner loved the pet. And I – I was jealous. Mia jumped around the crowded tables, flirted with waiters, got attention and just managed to pull it off. Elle watched the show and I thought it pleased her. She talked about Mia quite openly and Mia even joined in. Life for her was marvellous, she said, but Ellie said she was a young girl and girls had to do something. Young? How young? I still thought she'd seen thirty.

'Ellie thinks I should be a film actress.'

They both looked at me as though photography would give the answer. I asked polite questions. Yes, Mia had been given a screen test in that cold country I knew nothing about. It was a long way away. I was surprised to hear they all spoke English.

'It's our second language,' said Elle.

Then Mia got involved with the man at the next table and Elle put all her attention on me. 'How do you become a successful photographer?'

'Forget about trying to be a name. Just do the work. Keep doing it.' I told her I preferred working in black and white on thirty-five millimetre. I liked photographing a city at night. Then she asked about the dinner at Lily's. I said the television became the fifth guest.

'They need it there. It stops the aggression. To avoid a confrontation they watch TV.'

Did she have confrontations? She seemed so cool. Yet ready to heat up.

What did I think of Serge? For some reason, I said I found him kind.

'Oh no. He's dangerous. That pale moon face. They're always the worst. Moon types. Give me a face like the sun, boiling hot. Angry and out with it. You know what you're dealing with then.' This did not sound like the talk of someone who was going to back him in a little business affair.

Mia was on the guy's lap. She took off his tie and put it on herself. After that, they exchanged shirts.

'She never goes too far,' said Elle. Then admitted, 'I hope.'

The more Mia frolicked with the man the more I collapsed inwardly. The zest, if that was what it was, went out of me like air from a party balloon. Where was Elle's excitement of the night before? I looked at her eyes. She returned the look. We did not connect. By the time we'd got to the home-made crème caramel speciality I believed I'd read the signs wrong. I must have been off my head. This place certainly did not suit me. I was filled with the wrong conclusions.

Mia started on some Dietrich songs and had a strong voice in the low register. To keep comfortable I asked Elle some general questions. She told me where she'd travelled, where she'd lived.

'I prefer Les Frontières. I don't like anywhere as much as here.' It had created her. Before she came here who was she?

The proprietor brought her a speciality he knew she enjoyed and they gossiped about the locals, then gave some time to Star and the bride. He said Star had had a face-lift. He mentioned the surgeon and the price. Then he went away and left us in silence.

Mia had worn out the man at the neighbouring table and was now playing with the people in the kitchen.

'We must save her,' said Elle.

Save is a big word.

They had to get ready for a private show in Nice. A painter friend's first exhibition and Elle was going to buy a picture.

'I like artists. I collect art.'

'So you do do something,' I said, not entirely able to hide sudden inappropriate anger.

Her tone was provocative as she said, 'Did you think I didn't?'

I reminded her of our first meeting outside the locals' bar the previous year, and when I asked what she did she'd replied 'Nothing.'

They drove me back to Claudette's hotel. She looked young and boyish. I wished she'd been male. I'd have known how to deal with that. I couldn't bear to think of her woman's body. Still angry, I said, 'Do you want to see my photographs? I've got the contacts from the last job.' Did I really have to crawl to her?

They waited on the terrace while I went in to get them. Claudette and her husband were peering unashamedly through the shutters. When I got inside Claudette hissed, 'They never wear the same clothes twice. That older one – she's left a lot behind.'

'So you know her?'

'Know her? She's polite and charming but whenever I see her I think for some reason of those signs my mother used to believe in. Crossed knives, spilt salt, don't bring flowering May into the house. My mother never liked the number five. She said bad people used it for invisibility. She was a country girl, my mother, and read fortunes. Why should that Russian make me think of those signs?'

We went back to their house so Elle could look at the contacts while they got ready. The Princess made tea, then put her hair up in an exotic style. The make-up came out next and she painted eyes an ancient Egyptian would have approved of. Elle told her to take down the hair and reduce the face paint. She finished looking through the contacts of Star and his wife and handed them back. 'Where are you in these?'

She was disappointed. I couldn't say they were work, that I had to do that boring thing, earn money. That would make them so bored I'd ruin their evening.

'They don't have your perception. You aren't represented here. And you have a perception all right. You're creative. They're not.'

The only good thing was she didn't hand them to her girlfriend to proffer an opinion. The Princess lay at the end of Elle's long sofa and put her head in her lap. She'd done what she was told and the hair fell in a dollop on Elle's thighs. The carnival outfit, although it would only be worn once, had cost more than my entire clothes for the season. Cinderella hour for these fabrics was 4 a.m. and then the ripples, streamers and gossamer wings would die gracefully. The outfit was a hothouse flower. She might still keep the feather headdress. Elle's hand moved to the yellow strands of lustrous hair and started stroking it. 'Silky,' Elle murmured to the Princess. Another nickname.

I took my unloved self across to Lily's.

Star's wife had just left. She was doing a lot of leaving, including her home and husband.

'It must be bad,' said Lily, still in her doorway to do honour to the visit. 'For her to come slumming up here. She'll be back in Marseilles next.' She waited for René to turn up before saying anything further. Gossip told twice got stale.

The sewing machine whirred as she renovated some curtains for an American couple. She asked about Elle and I said I'd seen her. I didn't mention the lunch. I felt dismissed. Yes, that was it. Lacklustre and empty.

'Is she gay? Has she actually come out?'

Lily's eyes left the curtain and the machine slowed. 'Now I come to think of it … I've never heard or seen anything directly. They don't walk arm in arm exactly. It was hearsay, I suppose. And Mia is obviously mad about her.' The machine gathered speed. The curtains were a rich old gold that the sun would make glorious. She assured me they cost a fortune but the Americans had money. 'I wish I had half of it.'

Four dogs panted into the room, heralding the arrival of Serge. Lily said again, 'I wish I had half the money they've got. Leave out wish. I need it. We need it.'

Serge dumped a crate of unusable vegetables from the grocer's shop on the floor.

'No pensions or insurance or savings. You can't live on air or sunlight.' Her voice was tight.

Sighing, he tugged off his jacket and poured a glass of wine.

'We rent this place. That's dead money. If they close the castle, Serge loses his job and we're on the street. He carries that furniture for the foreigners on his own. What if he had a heart attack? He's not young.'

In Spanish he told her to shut up.

'We have to do something. Something has to be done.' She looked shaky in a way I didn't think was possible. 'Because it's such a beautiful place doesn't mean … A park bench is still a park bench.'

'How many times do I have to hear it?'

I knew his eyes would be unblinking and detached from the rest of his face. I didn't dare look at him. I could feel the – was it anger?

Then René came to the door and Serge stood up. She said, 'Do something.'

Serge nodded. 'You don't give me much choice.' He grabbed his jacket and left.

'Is he going to kill himself?' René laughed.

'We have to have security. How many times do I say it?' Lily was bright red and not even drinking.

'Absolutely. But it's natural.' He sniffed into the crate. 'He'll die if he tries eating these.'

'I left England to find another way of being alive. But you take yourself wherever you go.'

René poured her a drink. 'But it's normal to want a base.'

Had Serge crossed the road to his possible backer? I thought it was likely.

And I thought you didn't have to see people hold hands to know they were gay. It wasn't about seeing or hearing. It was a feeling, and the feeling I had was Elle was gay.

René picked up a stringy vegetable decayed beyond identity. 'You're not really this hard up are you?'

Lily, irritated, said, 'He uses them on someone's allotment he looks after. Don't keep on with it.' I knew she was struggling but she wouldn't cry. She'd looked into a lot of crates of vegetables to get that dry-eyed.

'All you have to do is put down a deposit and pay off a mortgage with the rent you pay for this place, or let it for more than you pay here. Stay here and use the rent –'

'Oh René, fuck off. If I wanted to get more depressed, I'd talk to my bank manager. We don't have the money for the down payment. But we do have the story of the Star's cheer-up present. Ready?'

René pushed the main door shut.

'The wife is fed up with everyone saying she took him for his money. Also she may one day need to support herself again. We know his time-span with young girls.'

'They grow up. So she went and got a job and I bet it was –' René let her have the next bit.

'Modelling. The tabloids and magazines want her because of him.'

'Now comes the real test of marriage,' said René.

'Not what you think. A fashion editor tells her she's too fat.'

'Loses the job?'

'She fights back. She fights. There was a nasty half hour. She comes home and is honest with Star. She lets him see how upset she is and cries. After a while, a short while, Star says, Oh, come on, cheer up –'

'Fairly quickly he says that,' René cut in. 'He hates crying.'

'He tells her to go and buy herself something nice. "Go out and get a really expensive thing. Money no object." So she buys a Calvin Klein outfit and when he comes home she puts it on. Does he like it? "As long as you do," he says. And something occurs to her. Very nasty little thought. "It is a present?" she asks him. "That's what you meant, wasn't it?" "Not at all," he says. "It's not what I said. I suggested you cheer up by buying yourself something nice. I'm not paying for it. You've got money of your own now." '

'Having a go at women's independence,' said René. 'I bet she's stopped that job.'

Lily hadn't got the reaction she'd hoped for. Their gossip was like jazz. It took off, took them to unexpected wonderful places. Today it was just clumps of information deader than the vegetables in the crate.

'Somehow this loses in the telling,' said Lily. 'Let's just say he's fed up with her.'

I thought René was right.

René started up another tune. 'This place is full of alcoholics.'

'I think we all know that.' She stroked the gold of the curtain, all the gold she so wanted and might never have.

'This is the only place where you can be one and yet not be allowed to be one. Most places they say, you're an alcoholic, and you're condemned. The end of the line. You have to do something about it. Here, you're stripped of the name, the idea, immediately.'

'Are you suggesting we start up AA or what?' She was irritated.

'The postman, the young one, not the old one, came out of hospital. They told him never to drink again. Another one would kill him. The patron of the bar was offended he didn't come in any more. Was he drinking down the hill? The postman told him what the hospital had said.

"Don't be so stupid," said the *patron*. "They don't mean beer or wine. They mean the strong stuff." The postman wasn't sure so he went to Dolores.'

'She knows everything,' said Lily.

'She said, "Don't be crazy. You'd be dead without it." So he said, "They tell me I'm an alcoholic." She said, "You can't be because you drink openly in front of everyone. Alcoholics don't do that." So the postman went to Claudette. She said, "You're definitely not alky because you eat. Alkys don't eat." So he saw the grocer who said, "You're not an alcoholic because you couldn't drink all that and live." Very confused, he asked the schoolteacher. She said, "Alcoholics always drink alone. I've never seen you do that. And you don't drink in the morning. That's the big sign. You're just a heavy drinker." The mayor said, "Alcoholic? Doesn't exist." So he went on drinking.'

'And?'

'I've just been to his funeral.'

'I could see that coming,' I said. It reminded me of something I hadn't done.

René came with me while I shot the cemetery and the contested grave from several angles.

8

I was glad to get back to London. I established a routine that kept me busy. There was no loose time for wayward ideas to take hold and become dangerous realities. I used to justify the ideas by saying they heightened my creativity which could only exist on the edge. Justification nearly killed me. I preferred the routine.

I walked and sometimes managed to run on Hampstead Heath, then went to the gym, then to yoga and meditation classes. The fitter I was, the better I felt. I did the shopping, cooked the meals, took an additional course in lighting at the college, went to films and exhibitions. I worked at photography and wanted to be as good as I could be. I wanted it to take me on a journey into realities I couldn't even imagine otherwise. Photography was my lifeline to that realm of light and intensity I'd only glimpsed but had to reach. I needed to be attached to that place or state, otherwise I'd be forever restless and uprooted.

There was never enough money. I took all the commissions I could get and secretly did weddings. I'd learned early on how the professionals despised those. I added to my portfolio by getting friends to sit, filming urban locations, especially around King's Cross, and, in contrast, the Heath at dawn. My friend Lou, an established photographer, said I was wrong to do commercial assignments. It tainted the creative work I was capable of. If I needed money, which I did, I should stack shelves in the supermarkets or drive lady cabs. Don't put at risk the real work. We argued about that, but I felt safer taking commercial work because it put me in touch with what I wanted to do. Lou had always been 'pure' but she knew how to get money from her family. She had done shelf-stacking briefly once, but made sure the family knew about it. They weren't keen for one of theirs to sink that fast.

I got a temporary job as a photographer's assistant for the money and experience. He made me promise that I wouldn't resent him or the money he earned, and think I could do it all better. I broke that promise.

Lou had worked her way up patiently, insistently, getting her photographs in exhibitions, local then national, preparing a book and publishing it, getting a one-woman show. It had taken years. Now she was going in for the prizes. She photographed dancers in rehearsal, in the dressing room, leaving the theatre, at auditions. Occasionally she captured a dancer in performance leaping in the air, flying. These flying pictures made me excited, uplifted, took me away to a vibrant undreamed-of place.

'You're always escaping,' said my husband James.

There was one picture of hers I loved especially. In it the dancer seemed to be flying, soaring in the night towards a city lit up, far off. Lou never used colour. I'd always loved black and white. Love. I could use the word easily about photography.

I described the village to James and, as I did so, I realised it was an oasis, unspoilt, full of its own kind, not even paying lip service to the rest of that coast. How far down the line did you have to go, to turn up there for your baptism into secrecy? You'd need the bank account. I did not mention Elle.

James taught English Literature and I understood he was a good and popular teacher. He got his message across but not always to me. The photography bothered him because we were paying a heavy mortgage on the early Victorian house in Kentish Town. We both loved the house. It was solid, generous with original moulding, rosettes, marble fireplaces, stained glass windows, oil lamps. The solid wood of the banister always gave me pleasure. I had, and I remembered it, agreed to do my share towards the mortgage. That was why he finally purchased this house and not some cheaper horror he'd seen on the main road. He didn't actually say I had let him down. He said I shouldn't rely on photography as a career. I laughed and said he sounded like a disapproving parent. He did not laugh.

Friends said we had a good marriage. But James and I had gone past the 'in love' phase. Suddenly I couldn't have sex with him any more. We were too intimate. It would be like going to bed with my best friend. We were close and comfortable like two old cushions in front of the fire. I didn't expect this marriage would last because he would definitely not go on accepting a chaste life.

I had to stop thinking about Elle. The life-death passion was not unknown to me. It took a few moments to track it down to my schooldays in Kent. Remembering those was not something I went in for. The first thing I did when I got out of school was forget it. I disappeared into the nightlife of London, and the grown-up glamour of being fifteen in those nightclubs and jazz basements soon made up for the years of being an outsider. Cities at night, my natural habitat. I wasn't my right self at school age. I made up for it soon enough. I'd negotiated myself out of school a year early. I realised even then that survival, although not on the school timetable, was a life necessity and something you practised and got good at.

Once I allowed the memories of those schooldays to surface – had I really spent five years in that unhappy place? – I remembered the woman who came once a week to teach piano and I had had a crush on her but she went away. Trying to recall that time was like fishing on a bad day.

I might never again have thought of her if I hadn't met Elle. It must have been some aspect of her face or expression I'd fallen for. I was thirteen. This unexpected attraction to the Russian/Finnish woman twenty-five years later was probably an upchuck from that past and would be forgotten as easily.

I'd forget Elle like I forgot the piano teacher. I did however phone Lily.

'They're going away,' she said, and my heart sank like a sun into blackness. 'Elle looks happier.' The inside of me, a funeral procession.

I asked where they were going. I did not have their phone number.

'The cases have been put in the car. They're probably going to Russia or Finland, or the Middle East, or all three.'

A funeral? Twenty funerals. That was what I was full of. In my mind a draped coffin and black and gold crosses, incense, deadliness.

'Are you crying?' Lily sounded surprised.

I said I had a cold. Crying, I was beyond that.

'They go to and fro all the time. Not like us. She's got real money and power. I was surprised you didn't ask to take her photograph.'

I hadn't asked. It turned out to be the one thing I did right.

Days later when I was developing film in the darkroom the call came. Elle said, 'We're in a place called Hampshire. Come and join us.'

9

The hotel provided a health and beauty service and the Princess spent her days being transformed. There was an indoor and outdoor pool, a low calorie restaurant, a juice bar, underwater spa treatments. She stepped into a gaggle of masseurs, personal trainers and skin soothers and was lost from view. It gave Elle and me the opportunity to spend the waiting time together. There was boating on the lake, sightseeing, bowling, but she was more interested in the golf course. Elsewhere in the hotel there was a gourmet restaurant and piano bar where businessmen hung out and Elle would appear for a short hour each evening.

They shared a room with a huge canopied bed and I, on a lower floor in my chintzy single bed, wondered what they were doing. I was uneasy, perhaps jealous, and imagined them in some sexual embrace.

Seeing Elle gave me an uncomfortable lift of excitement that sent the blood to my face. She made me ascend to a preferable level of being and it linked up with all the good moments of the past. Being with her was like a glorious summer day. Someone once asked what I most wanted to do. Fly. With her that was possible. It linked me to Lou's photographs of the flying dancers. And then I was aware of the tall figure beside her and realised I had to show some enthusiasm. The Princess was all over me like a young dog happy I was back. She led me off to the exclusive treatment zone. 'Elle can't be bothered with all this but I know you'll like it. By the way, we're inviting you, so just have what you want.'

They got her submerged in a mud bath and I ran upstairs in search of Elle. She was standing outside the golf shop. Just coming across her like that gave me a jolt. I was full of questions. Why was she here? What had she been doing? Was she hiding? Who was she? I kept them to myself.

'Do you putt?' she asked.

I didn't think so.

'I've decided Mia needs to get her confidence back and act again. She'll need an agent and photographs. I think the health programme or whatever it is here will get her ready.'

I asked where the acting would take place. In which country? Which media?

'She's got a strong presence. And she's right for certain roles other women wouldn't remotely approach. Fellini's *La Dolce Vita*. The party scene. Orgy scenes. Any of those Roman epics. Historical or modern.'

'So you'll go to Rome?'

'Or gay films. Costume stuff. Operatic roles.'

I agreed she was a big person and belonged perhaps in pageants. I think I even mentioned Boadicea. I had no idea if the Princess could act. And so the conversation clung to the career possibilities of the absent woman. Like two casting directors we plotted where she would fit in. It was agreed she should take singing lessons.

Elle was wearing a green tweed jacket, tailored trousers and soft moccasins. The colour of the jacket brought out the hazel green of her eyes. I hadn't been able to look at her properly. Like an adolescent, I hung my head. 'It's good you're here,' she said. 'I'll take care of the bill of course.' The Princess had already made this clear. I wondered whose money it was and hoped it was Elle's. That would make me feel loved.

She looked away at the men starting out for a game of golf and shouted encouragement. Laughing, they asked if she'd join them. I sincerely hoped she wouldn't. She hesitated. 'Later.'

'What's your handicap?' one asked.

She shouted a figure which they found good. I realised I was suddenly invisible. For them I did not exist.

A limo pulled up and she joked with the businessmen getting out. She had no fear. That's what it was. Not a scrap. The hotel manager came in for some attention. The up and down of the leisure industry shares. Yes, she knew about business. He looked only at her, spoke only to her. I was next. The helper. She said they'd come on impulse to England because they needed help.

'Help for what?'

'To get Mia right for today's market. She hasn't worked for years. You know what the trends are. What they go for.' It was about Mia again. It always had been.

'In your job you have to know that.' Her voice was suddenly flat and tired but she was still smiling. She was made up of charm and cat-like grace, very much in the moment. She never showed tiredness or any change. Just her voice gave it away, whatever it was.

She watched the golf and told of hangover mornings at the nineteenth hole and how the ball always got lost in the rough.

'Do you play?' She turned her friendly jungle-cat eyes on me and could see I didn't. It had never occurred to me to play golf. She moved nearer the green to see the start of the game and I began to speak. The golfer was about to do whatever it is golfers do at the first hole and she told me to shut up. One sound could ruin the shot. I think she didn't know what to do with me so suggested tea. I suggested a walk. I was filled with the kind of longing I'd had for the piano teacher and more. It was an alarming surprise. As though condemned, I was forced to face the truth. I wanted to make love with this woman. I was in the grip of this strange state, as out of control as if it was an acute illness. I couldn't understand what had happened to me or what I should do.

I hurried her off between the trees in case the Princess should rise from the mud bath and find us. I couldn't think about the bodily aspect of making love to her. To encounter breasts would be a forlorn moment. What did I do with them, with the rest of her?

We rushed through the trees and out onto the heathland. If I did it just once I'd get it over with. Take her in my arms, crush her. And then? Then it occurred to me she would know what to do. As Elle and I stepped over low gorse bushes I wondered if I was gay. Was that it? So intense was the state of longing I could feel my body tighten and pulsate, needing to be brought to the necessary pleasure and release. I could feel the sweat drop, my heart leap. I looked for a hill to climb so I could take her hand. No hill, just mile after mile of low flat bushes. No hand holding for that.

I sank to the ground and she took off her jacket and offered it to me to sit on. I lay back, my eyes full of sky. I could see how cats felt on heat. I was like an unfucked cat. She sat beside me and I waited. I felt she was not unaware of my excitement as she said, 'So who are you exactly?'

Should I ask her to do it? Should I tell her, 'This is the first time and I want it to be with you'? She leaned nearer, looking at my body, taking her time like a confident lover. I couldn't answer and closed my eyes. The heightened feeling stayed heightened, neither decreasing nor reaching the obvious conclusion, an inner firework display, a blast of electric shocks of pleasure. My head turned with hot lewd images, I thought, this is how an animal feels when it is aroused by some creature or presence a long way off, unseen, unheard, yet sensed. I was spread out, available, yet she did not take advantage.

'Perhaps we should think of you and not so much about Mia,' she said. It was a strange voice, without energy. What she said made me open my eyes. I was preferred. Was I pleased! She was chewing a piece of grass. A wind was starting up.

'It'll be night soon,' she said.

I almost reached up and touched her and would have grasped whatever my hand found. And yet I didn't do it. It seemed such a huge act, intrusive, reckless, it could go badly wrong, leading to all kinds of humiliation, rejection, hostility, even violence. During that short hour I realised how difficult it was to draw someone into my sexual state even if they seemed to want to be included.

She asked questions and I couldn't answer or speak. I wanted the one thing she was apparently not providing.

The expression whenever she laughed was intense, beautiful, not easily forgotten. She hinted at worlds beyond sexuality. Sex was just the doorway to what she offered, to what pleased her. The eyes were jungled-up now, flashing bits of yellow. I'd expected them to be tender but I never saw tenderness, not in those eyes.

Then she said, 'Shall I lie beside you?' Her voice was purring now.

Oh Jesus, yes.

Then another voice called across the heath. 'Ellie. Where are you, Ellie?'

And Elle waved an arm, the fool. 'Over here.'

The Princess plunged towards us, out of breath. 'Don't be out here.'

'Why not?' I was furious.

'Because – because it's nearly night.'

It must have been the first thing that came into her head. So stupid.

On the way back, Elle dragged behind and I changed pace to keep up with her. Suddenly her hand was in mine, a strong well-shaped hand, cool and dry. 'You will help Mia, won't you?'

I didn't know whether to tug my hand back and run. Run for the rest of the day, through the night, run out this terrible feeling which obviously could not be fulfilled.

'You could do her photographs. I trust you.'

My hand stayed where it was but, when the Princess turned round, Elle slid hers away and into a pocket.

The moment Elle left, the heightened excitement left too. Like a balloon deflating, my body became a still-dry, slightly tired entity that was mine, calm and without needs. I thought it odd that such an intense feeling could disappear so quickly. It seemed to depend for its existence on her being there. No, it was as though a soundless call from her stirred up a previously unknown part of me causing this molten-hot response.

I lay across the bed, too limp to get up. Like a sea shrub on a beach stranded when the tide went out, dying, drying, unnourished. I thought of the story I'd heard many times with variations, of the two strangers meeting in the lift. By the fifth floor their desire for each other was so strong that when one got out the other had to follow and they could hardly wait to unlock a door and get inside. That's how I'd felt with her. A player in a story I'd heard already.

The Princess brought a tray to my room. 'You seem tired. Are you ill?' She looked at me closely. 'No, you're not ill.' While I ate the dieter's salad she sat on the bed and talked about the parties they'd given on the Côte d'Azur, how, for her last birthday, Elle had hired a boat with a dance band to sail along the Italian coast. It sounded sort of innocent. Mia assured me it was not innocent. To celebrate their anniversary, for they had been together seven years, Elle had held a ball at the Hôtel de Paris, Monaco.

'What does her husband say about all this?'

The Princess stole a large lettuce leaf. 'What should he say?' She crunched some nuts. 'You haven't any chocolate?' While I shook my head she took half of my low calorie dessert. 'Ellie likes parties. It's one long party and a collection of hangers-on. We're going to the Red Cross Ball in Monaco and to Prince Rainier –'

I cut in and asked about her career plans. She looked puzzled and then decided life was better as a sacrificial offering to her lover than doing the same thing on stage with other people's words. 'It's all about love or the lack of it.' She gave me a quick look. 'You don't come over as someone who is loved.' I told her about my marriage and I could have told her many things because she had a certain receptiveness which was unexpected in someone so self-centred and she could translate what she heard into perceptive helpful comment. It wasn't all about her all the time. It just seemed as though it was.

Before she left she gave me a kiss on the cheek. 'Nothing is how it seems. Don't be too trusting.'

I dreamt that night of a horse in a paddock shivering and alarmed, eyes bulging. Out there, hidden on the heath, was this essence that took shape, changed shape until it became the figure of a rider in an immaculate habit. As the rider started towards the paddock, the horse rose up in panic. The people around seemed not to notice and I tried to tell them the rider was not real as it strode amongst them. I had to save the horse before this fake rider got on its back and took it away.

The next day I told Elle about the dream and she said, of course it made sense that I would dream about a horse, because there was one neighing outside early in the morning. She went to the window and pointed to horses eating in the field. 'They have a riding stable here. Mia wants to ride.'

'Oh yes,' said Mia. 'I just need the clothes.'

Elle half laughed. 'Let's see if you like riding first.' Then she looked at me. Before she even said it, I knew what she was going to ask.

'I do not ride,' I said quickly.

'Mia hasn't ridden since she was a child.'

'But I love horses.' Mia was determined.

'Stop it,' Elle laughed. 'You're beginning to sound like her dream.'

10

Her name was Elian von Zoelen and she was not married to Olav the ship-owner. She had been married to Stephan von Zoelen and had one adult stepson. Lily had not got everything right. She'd been the mistress of the ship-owner ever since her divorce in the early Seventies. She accompanied him on his world tours as he bought and sold ships. There was no warmth when she talked about him.

She'd been born in Helsinki on the smart side of town, the only child of a Finnish professor of medicine and a Russian émigré socialite who supported the arts. Her father made a discovery about blood which won him renown and sponsorship. Her tone when she talked about him was not warm but charged with a certain pride. Her mother had filled the house with visiting actors and painters. There was an energy in her voice when she spoke of her.

'She just let herself die.'

I asked why.

'I expect being with my father had something to do with it.'

Was the energy I'd noticed only anger? Elle had not started out sophisticated or worldly. She'd lived an outdoor life, swimming, skiing, skating, rowing, and spent the short summers in the summerhouse by the lake. There was a constant mention of summerhouses and I understood they were a vital part of Finnish culture.

'Throughout those dark months we long for the summertime. The berries, flowers, smell of the moss. You can't imagine how good nature makes me feel.' She'd sailed boats over lakes and out to sea in all weathers, but best of all she loved the icy winter nights, skiing from house to house, the snow so high the buildings weren't visible. 'You had to guess each location. When and if you arrived you were asked in to warm up by the fire. But it was the aquavit that got you warm. That is strong liquor.' She left out her schooldays. A lot was left out. It appeared she was in her mid-forties. She didn't say all this in one piece and her background was lifted from the various remarks she made during our stay in the luxury country hotel.

She was descended on her mother's side from a Russian collector of art, a nineteenth-century aristocrat remembered for his eccentricity, travel, fragile nerves and setting a fashion for the drinking of spa water. I'd never heard of him. She said no one had so not to worry about it. Elle resembled his only daughter, her great-grandmother, who'd been one of the Bohemians in Helsinki in the mid-nineteenth century. She'd had strong political ideas in direct contrast to the rigid Lutheran beliefs of the time, wrote an anarchic manifesto stating the artist's way of life. She was a friend of painters and the Bohemian group. Artists painted her, wrote poems about her and fell in love with her. Elle was proud of her great-grandmother, of how she was a unique pioneering spirit in a closed and pious world.

'She inherited her father's fortune but even she couldn't spend it all. She ended up in America.'

'Will you?' I asked, impulsively.

'If you will.' She looked at me with a certain challenge.

I felt a shock, then a warmth spreading out from my solar plexus. Before I got too happy she was back on the subject of Mia.

Mia cut in, 'The great-grandmother wore amazing clothes. That's where Elle gets her sense of style. I'll show you some photographs of her. One day. They're in our house in Helsinki.'

It was so different from what Lily described, not to mention Serge and René. I could see you could be badly misinterpreted living in a Spanish village.

She has bad nerves and I look after her. That was how Elle described her friend, lover, partner, whatever she was. Why was I asked to help? It occurred to me then that just as Lily could invent a colourful life for these women so she could for me. I'd been painted with the village brush.

When we were alone I asked Elle what Lily had said about me.

'Nothing you couldn't tell me.'

When I didn't answer she said, 'I'm sure you could tell it better.'

I guessed it was the Coca-Cola. Lily would have a reason for that. And Mia had a drink problem. 'I drink Coca-Cola, is that it?'

'You make people look the way they want to look in photographs. That's it.' She wanted me to do a set of outdoor photographs that Mia could present to agents and casting directors. We should wait one more day until the treatments had done their utmost. On the final day I should do studio portraits using good lighting effects and as many tricks as I knew. 'Do they still put gauze over the lens?'

'Only if you want to tell people you're worried about your age.' I explained I could do most of the improvements by touching up in the darkroom.

*

Whenever I saw her, I felt a lift of happiness, even joy that she was in the world. The world became an enchanted place because of her, just as it should be. She would turn to me with that penetrating look, familiar, tantalising, that had nothing to do with what was going on or being said. And then our eyes would lock suddenly and I could feel the effect of it in every part of me. Realistically, I knew all this could have no expression or outcome. I'd misread what was her natural provocativeness, taken it personally. Any six golfers probably got the same look. Seeing her caused that raging addictive sexual longing that left me the moment she did.

Did Mia notice the locking of the eyes, the glances that went on a little too long? Mostly she was with the fitness trainer, jogging across the heath or out riding in the newly purchased jodhpurs and jacket. She spent a fortune in the boutique. Elle approved as long as she didn't have to do it. She was always fully dressed, I noticed, as though ready for a journey. Her collars were high, sleeves long, and I commented on the fact she never showed her arms.

'Arms? Arms went out at twenty. Or are you suggesting I have a heroin habit?'

'Then I won't photograph you.'

'You won't,' she agreed.

She spent her time reading the newspapers, checking shares, watching the news on television, making long-distance phone-calls in several languages. Occasionally she played golf. She talked mostly about Mia.

'It's good for Mia to get out of that village. It's like a stage set. Every time you go out you're too visible. If you buy a lettuce everybody knows about it.'

'They will if you go to that shop. What does he do with all those dead vegetables?'

She agreed the grocer's on the hill was a waste of a shop and I almost asked if she was going to back Serge in taking it over but I remembered him asking for discretion. I did ask if she would stay on in the village.

'I like privacy. You're so on show there.'

More than she knew.

'Let's see if Mia needs to be in a city,' she concluded.

She'd been reconsidering the career strategy. Was it wise to put her up for parts so suddenly? How about a term or two at drama school to get in training?

I told her most courses took three years. She couldn't be bothered fitting in with some timetable and asked for the names of the best schools worldwide. I explained the competition to get a place was a little more than she might anticipate. You couldn't create scholarships, whatever the bankroll, as far as I knew.

I got no thanks for that.

'You are an ordinary little person, abiding by the rules,' she replied.

Did she know what the rules were? I doubted it. I suggested Mia be coached by a drama teacher to help her present the best possible audition pieces. London was the obvious place.

She smiled so attractively she got the attention of a gang of returning golfers.

'You live in London, Catherine?'

I nodded.

'Then we'll go to London.'

The golfers thought she must be famous but couldn't place her. She accepted their offer of a drink.

I saw Mia again in the boutique buying with a frenzy. She seemed to gulp up the boxes of creams, the cartons of lotion, their promises exciting her, offering a different, perhaps hopeful, life. She asked me to help choose between an expensive facial massaging kit and a simple device suitable for travelling. Either would tone her skin. Choice was not a problem regarding the ailing career we'd mapped out for her. She didn't want it. It would take her too much away from Elle. She decided on the expensive facial kit and added a lace nightgown to the pile.

'Last night, Ellie came up with another solution. A baby.'

'Who's going to have that?' Shock sat me in the box of unsold nightdresses.

'She doesn't want to deprive me of anything and thinks by being with her I sacrifice myself. She said it's natural I should have a baby.'

The sales girl tugged me up from the nightdress box. 'It's not a chair, madam.'

'Ellie said we just have to find the right man.'

'Man? We?'

'We'll sleep with him together and –'

'Together?' I was back in the nightdress box.

'So I agreed. You look shocked, Catherine. You must be old-fashioned. Lots of men like sleeping with two women and –'

And James phoned and the call was put through to the shop. He wanted to know how to work the repaired stove, where was his better jacket, when was the dog's appointment for the yearly shot. I thought he was lonely. The sales girl wrenched the box from under my buttocks. 'So when are you coming back?' James asked.

'We'll find a man. It won't be the first time. And I'll conceive what will be our child. Ellie's and mine. I'm so happy,' said the Princess.

'Do you want to buy anything in here, madam, because this is a shop. The hotel is not short of places to sit,' said the sales girl.

'Daisy misses you. She's wagging her tail –' said James.

'I think I'm going mad.' I jumped up and ran to the stairs, one stray green nightdress somehow attached to my shoe.

I tracked her down, the lying imposter, in her bedroom. As large as it was it could hardly contain the mountain of luggage. She was hiding behind the opened pages of a huge financial newspaper.

'So you're going to have a baby together. Should I congratulate you?'

'You seem very concerned.' She was looking at me over the printed page. 'I wonder why that is?'

I could have thrown myself on top of her, clamped my lips to hers. I moved backwards until I felt the door and opened it for safety.

'You look as though you've seen a spider. What's the matter with you?'

Near her I was full of unusual impulses. Usually choice came into things.

'You keep fluttering about. You're like a butterfly.' She looked back at the paper, turned a page, the noise horrible.

'You said you wanted to save her and I should help. I can't see how I can be of assistance impregnating her.'

'So chastising. My!'

'A child. Is that a help?'

'It seems a popular idea. Otherwise why would people keep having them? You don't mention any.'

'Don't change the subject.'

'Mia is wonderful with children. I didn't say when she should have a child. Only that she could.'

She was never short of an answer.

'Don't you have any fun, Catherine?'

I supposed compared with them I didn't. I had to worry about the equation: one and one make a living. Zero could be a park bench. I didn't have an Olav to change the sums, fix the result or the style of behaviour that could do things on impulse without consideration. Except in my work.

Laid out on the bed she seemed relaxed but she still had her shoes on. She could leave at a moment's notice. Always giving the impression of not belonging where she was, I wondered where in fact she did belong.

'I have a lot of work to do. This acting idea has no reality suddenly.'

I felt she was laughing at me. She sat up. 'Let's go to London and find out.'

11

She became Mia and not the Princess when I saw the amount of substances she needed to take in order to get through the day. She took uppers, downers, sleepers and painkillers, washed down with wine whenever consciousness became too much. She had to get fixed and it was getting harder. Out of control, the pendulum had swung too far chemically and she admitted she needed help. Retail therapy didn't work and the sheer volume of purchases frightened her. Shopping left a hollow dissatisfaction.

The hairdresser finished nourishing her roots and combed through the strands. 'Fab.' He said it again. 'Fab condition.' He put her under the dryer to soak in the unguents. I made room for the next process. The Knightsbridge salon was full of models and I felt as out of place as in the hotel boutique. A lot could go wrong in here. 'But you had it done yesterday,' I said and nearly knocked down the tray of brushes.

'It needs to be at its best. Ellie likes it at its best.'

I was surprised to discover its flaming yellow colour was natural. A manicurist painted her nails which were not in such good condition. They were bitten to the quick. We were due to meet the drama coach and I said again that our appointment was the other side of Hyde Park.

'He's being paid whether I'm there or not. I'm sure he can handle a few lonely minutes.' She was on a down and took a handful of mixed pills and I don't think she knew what they were.

They were staying at an expensive hotel near Hyde Park Corner, had taken a suite so Mia could practise the audition speeches.

'I need a doctor, not a drama teacher.' She sat very still trying to suppress the shakes, waiting to see if the pills would work. Then she reached into her pocket and I thought she was trying another dose but out came a twenty-pound note which she thrust into my hand.

'Get some beer.'

I got up.

'Don't let Ellie see it.' She tried to wink but her nerves weren't up to it. Her face teetered on complete collapse.

'I think you should tell her to find you a doctor.'

'God no. Don't let her know I even mentioned it.' She grabbed at my hand. I assured her I would say nothing but agreed a doctor came before a drama coach. She sounded bleak as she said, 'A doctor won't even get near it.'

'I think you need a doctor.'

'I need a priest.'

Elle appeared at the door, a taxi waiting behind her. As we were leaving the salon, Mia said, 'Sometimes I don't know how to get through the next five minutes.' She pulled me back so Elle got into the taxi first. 'Get the beer, a six-pack. If she finds out, say it's for you.'

In the wine shop I asked for the drink to be placed in a plain bag and stuck a sparkling mineral water bottle on top. Twice Mia interrupted the ride supposedly to pop into a shop and each time the off-licence bag went with her. By the time we arrived at the drama teacher's flat, beer and pills had wrought a strange change. She was no longer shaking but looked proud and statuesque like the figurehead on the prow of a ship. But the drama teacher looked only at Elle. She was the star on his doorstep.

'I've seen you. Of course we've met. Visconti's? La Scala, Milan?' Her smile let him think that was it. She introduced Mia but he gave the pupil scant attention. He was so taken with Elle he even forgot to invite us in.

'Gustav Klimt painted you, Madame.'

'How old do you think I am?' she asked.

Mia looked mournful as the substance mixture lost effect. Was she jealous of the attention her lover received?

'In another life, Madame, you were the woman with the veil and those amazing eyes offering sin, power. The temptress.'

Elle said she knew the picture, then got his attention back to Mia.

'We'll make her good,' he promised quickly, then back to the real excitement. 'Klimt didn't even have to meet you. He'd met your spirit before he picked up a paintbrush.'

Behind Elle's back Mia was busy in the drinks bag and the smell of beer spread thickly into the room. He turned and gave his pupil and the soggy bag a bit more attention. He couldn't put her together with the elegant Klimt creation leaning nonchalantly against his grand piano. I was already having trouble with that and it seemed the more the one fell apart, the other blossomed.

'Your protégée has a definite quality for film, Madame.' Then he whispered something in Elle's ear that made her laugh. He knew where the money was coming from.

Mia wanted us to stay and watch her and Elle softened and thought we should because it was like leaving a child on the first day at school. I definitely wanted to go, and I wanted Elle to come with me. Mia could more than look after herself. The last beer had got the chemicals right for now and she was smiling. She also had her transitional object, the pill bottle. The teacher decided an audience was not required.

Along by the park and Elle was there beside me, talking, listening, but her presence had no weight. It was as though she was in my head, a daydream, and I'd turn round between one word and the next and she'd not be there. She was impossible to retain. She was like, no, it wasn't slippery soap, what was she like? I could hear the click of her shoes. I tried to gather her into my life by planning a future. I chose the drama classes. The auditions were six weeks away in June. She said yes and no in all the right places but I could not get hold of her.

'Mia drank at least two bottles of wine last night and then started on the brandy, so don't go and buy her more alcohol, Catherine. And please don't think it's a secret.'

'She seems to be very …' I was going to mention the priest and thought better of it. Needing a priest indicated something serious going on and, like Serge, Mia had spoken in confidence.

'Very disturbed.' She finished the sentence for me.

'Why?'

'I told you. She's got bad nerves. She has mood swings. And hallucinations. Don't take too much notice of what she says –'

'She needs help.'

'Isn't that what the drama classes are for? She needs a career.'

It occurred to me then that Elle found her protégée medically dangerous and was going to offload her. The thought pleased me, because I wanted all the love and care she gave Mia.

We were going towards the hotel and again she seemed not to be there. Terrified of losing her I said, 'But you will stay for Mia's audition?'

She didn't answer but continued with that light effortless walk and I understood she didn't like having to give unpleasant answers. I also understood she hardly ever needed anything. Unlike Mia and, to a lesser extent, me, Elle wasn't rushing into shops, restaurants, hairdressers. She didn't have moods and weaknesses. What were her needs?

'I'd like to see where you live, Catherine.'

Should I let her in? What if James was there? Perhaps that would make it easier. And if I didn't let her in? Seeing where I lived would say too much about me, the part I didn't want people to know. I aspired to something more Bohemian and glamorous than a ramshackle house in an ordinary street. Once through that door she would know me. I would no longer be the adventurous, turn-up-for-life person, travelling light. My possessions and the atmosphere of those rooms would give me away. I'd lose all sense of the person I wished to present, the one I wanted her to see. So I put it off for another time.

'You don't give much away,' she said. 'I don't remember hearing much about Catherine.'

I put that off for another time too.

She got my life story eventually. Everybody has a story they need to tell, she knew that. All she had to do was make me confident and for that she used flattery.

I told her how at fifteen I'd been a showgirl and modelled for artists. At sixteen I'd become a fashion model. No, I'd started much earlier than that. Make-up and clothes let me pass for sixteen. I couldn't wait to grow up, couldn't bear being a child and thought I was missing something that would not return.

Eventually I stayed in Paris and started painting, especially themes from the city at night. And then I found photography did it better. The modelling paid for the photography course. I photographed at night, modelled in the day. I didn't tell her how I started to use substances to keep going. I was driven, that was it. I talked a lot about the low budget film I'd made of night in the city. I'd got it to the festivals.

'You're not exactly chronological, are you?' she said at one point.

I was trying to remember things and keep other things out.

After the low-budget movie everything stopped. I was too old and too ruined to model but I could be a film maker. I was in my late twenties. Then I lost my money, my independence and nearly my own life. No, it didn't go up my nose. My substance of choice was wine and beer and I drank to live, not to die. That's what they couldn't understand and I was offered a smart detox on the last of my bank overdraft but I got off it on the street. Hand to mouth, sleeping on floors, taking photographs, more photographs; I think it kept me alive. I told her how five years later, clean and sober, I met James.

'Now I've a career as a photographer, a husband, a home, my health and freedom from addiction.'

'Perhaps you could make the film of the night again. How you really want to make it this time.'

Had she got it, the dissatisfaction in my voice?

As though reading my thoughts she said, 'After what you've been through you'd have a different perspective, wouldn't you?'

If only she knew what I'd been through.

12

Mia would do a scene from *Miss Julie* by Strindberg for her drama school audition. The obligatory Shakespeare piece was more troublesome and she was considering Portia from *The Merchant of Venice* or, if that didn't work, one of the comic characters from *A Midsummer Night's Dream*. Maybe she'd do all of the comic characters at once.

Elle and I sat in the hotel suite with a plate of smoked salmon sandwiches and a jug of lemon juice between us. Mia continued to outline her plans and I could sense Elle was restless, bored even, and the text of the play she was supposed to hold in case Mia forgot her lines slid insultingly to the floor. Mia scooped up the pages, swiped them against Elle's cheek, not altogether in fun, and gave them to me. The well-bitten fingernail pointed at the speech's beginning and she advised me, if she stopped, to allow a pause for her memory to return.

Elle cut in, 'Oh, do get on with it. Can't you go back to circus performing? At least we didn't have all these words.'

Mia stamped and shouted, the real stuff now. Why couldn't this ill-educated, middle-aged slothful bitch at least pretend to take an interest? I lingered on 'ill-educated'. Was she? It hadn't occurred to me.

Elle, who had long given up trying to grasp the concept of three characters at once, said, 'Why can't you just do it and keep it simple and get it over with?' She looked longingly at the television set. 'Why do you need three? It's not shopping.'

Mia sulkily moved off to the end of the room and started a warm-up exercise which made Elle even more impatient. 'Is this part of it? The three goblins you're talking about? You'll never get in anywhere with that.'

Mia turned to me and did the *Merchant of Venice* speech and made sense of Shakespeare. She knew what she was doing and I was surprised. In the middle of *Miss Julie* I realised Elle was looking, not at her protégée but at me. It was a look I had seen on men who fancied me. There was no doubt. I looked back at her and knew that we would be lovers.

Because I was suddenly happy, I was generous to Mia and agreed to read in the other characters but when Elle crept off to the bedroom, on a pretext, I followed her. I was wild with excitement. She was about to make a phone call but I walked up to her, stood in front of her, closed my eyes and waited. I was shaking and I realised again how like illness acute sexual arousal was in my case. It was altogether a too-heady, mad state. Of all the things she could have done she chose something mild. She took my hand. Our hands wound around and writhed together, as our bodies would, given the chance. I looked at her face and there was an expression in her eyes like a distant heat and the cold ridges of the various rings dug into my fingers, an unwelcome obstacle interrupting any pleasure.

She indicated the other room which had gone suddenly quiet and wrenched her hand away. Yes, there was a lapse in the warm-up voice exercises and no outburst from *Miss Julie*.

'What's this?' And Mia was behind me. 'Ellie, you're all flushed. I wonder why? Guilt, Ellie?'

I thought the evening could take a bad turn and I didn't like standing in the middle, so I tried to laugh and say Ellie was stretching out the cramp in my fingers.

'I bet.' Her eyes were flashing so violently I thought I could actually see sparks darting out of them, small daggers of ice. It wasn't a good sight and I considered running past her and out. Elle stood up and looked at her rings. 'Mia always teases me about these. Says they're cheap.'

'I said they're crap. You look like some superannuated punk wearing those.'

Elle ventured back into the sitting room and I followed. It wasn't much fun passing Mia, not because she was bigger than me and also unpredictable, but because of her threatening, disquieting air. The screaming, Lily had mentioned, could start any time. Elle knew what she was dealing with and got her back on stage, held both scripts herself to prompt any shortcomings, even applauded the next round of *Miss Julie*, but the actress was not to be placated.

'There's more drama in the audience.' She was looking at me. 'What am I? Some kind of interval entertainment to give you a cover?'

Elle was going to take care of it. 'Stage nerves. Do it again. I think it needs to be more.'

'Piss off.'

Elle polished her rings. So far she'd shown no sign of fear. 'She must be more inviting. If she's got the hots for the chauffeur –'

'The butler.' Mia sat rebellious on the opposite sofa. 'I think I'll drop it and do rebirthing.'

Elle looked up from the rings. 'Having a baby, you mean? You're back to that?'

'Rebirthing will get me back to the cause of all my problems.' Staring at Elle, she said sharply, 'I won't have to go that far back.' Then she rang down to the desk and asked for a taxi.

'Are you going to start this rebirthing now?' said Elle.

'The taxi's for Catherine. It's time she remembered she has a husband.'

We all sat in silence, then I spoke. 'Where is the rebirthing?'

'You would ask that.' She got up and flung the scripts into the bin.

I looked at Elle on my way out, my eyes clung to her, my hand reached for hers.

'I'll call you,' she whispered.

*

The next day at the hotel Elle said Mia was upset and wanted to go home.

'But you won't go.'

She looked away, at other things, the florist freshening up the foyer display, the costume jewellery in glass cases along the wall.

I changed the 'won't' to 'can't', my mouth dry with fear.

'She misses the village, the cat.'

'You must not go back.'

She didn't answer. She was going back. I wanted to plead with her, tell her I couldn't live without her. But I realised it wasn't her wish to go back but Mia's. I simply had to change Mia's wish.

I rushed up to the suite and got the cleaning girl to open the door. Inside, their cases were packed, the lids still open in case of spontaneous and necessary luxury purchases. The cleaning girl waited until Mia acknowledged my presence and didn't disagree with it being in her room. Mia was strewn across the bed, an arm dangling to the floor, a lifeless leg abandoned against the wall, her head hung back over the bed's corner. Light from the window running through the tumbled hair made it look like a waterfall. She seemed flat and dead. I said the first thing that came into my head.

'You're too good an actress to swan about in that village.' I realised I believed it.

'That's a heap of shit from you, Catherine, and you don't know what you're getting into. Go back to your husband.' Tired, depressed, she drained a beer bottle. She was wearing one of the new lace nightgowns, stained with drink and yesterday's make-up. If she went, Elle went too. That was the deal. Somehow I didn't think I would be invited to join them. I knew why Mia was going and it had nothing to do with acting except the sort I was doing, trying to look as though I wasn't infatuated with her partner. I so wanted her to change her mind I even took myself out of the picture and said I was leaving London for an exhibition, to see some friends, to get some air. I brought my husband into all of it. I gave her another beer bottle and said I'd do her photographs. She told me she had nothing against me and asked for a full beer bottle. Again she talked about how well she'd acted years ago in Finland and how proud her mother had been. How she'd given it up to be with her lover and couldn't go back into it. The proud mother left the story at this point. Acting would take her away from Elle. The village was constricting but preferable. Nobody took anybody away there.

I talked about how unhappy she'd seemed in the village and how she'd admitted she needed help and what better place to get it than London, a shrink on every corner. I told her all she'd get in that flea-bitten village was false friends and that she'd be pulled down by gossip.

The beer gave her enough energy to grab the new Strindberg book which included a text of *Miss Julie* and hurl it across the room. Then she collapsed back amongst the pillows. I offered to get her tea, water, toast, but I knew, only too well, how the intensity of that hangover would only be soothed by beer. I tried again to offer her a career while she emptied the beer bottle and put it by the bed. It had plenty of company. I finally suggested she go away and get well.

'And who'll look after Ellie?' She laughed, not the pleasantest sound I'd heard. And then she asked for a priest. There was a whole oratory of them up the road in South Kensington. I said I'd go with her.

Another bottle of beer and she was talking. 'I am scared. I know things.' She stopped herself from elaborating on those. 'And Ellie keeps saying it's because I'm sick.' She touched her head. 'So I should get treatment but she doesn't want that.'

'Do you think you are sick?'

She paused and thought for a long time. 'I don't know. I would have said no.'

'Why does she insist you're sick yet stop you getting help?'

'That's one story I'm not telling.' She was full of stories she wasn't telling. She reached for another bottle but then thought better of it. 'She's afraid things could get out, I suppose.'

And I thought of the battering stories I'd heard at Lily's.

'I never know when I get up if I'll make it through the day. I'm terrified.'

'Of?'

'Of shadows.'

I could see the treatment idea made sense. The shadow thing didn't sound too good. It made it easier for me if she was sick. What the hell was I doing wanting an abusive batterer? But Elle wouldn't be like that with me. Something in Mia, her wild lack of continuity, disturbed her. I told her she must stay in London and get off the drink.

She took a handful of pills. What were they? She said vitamins. I told her they'd have to go too.

'I am the one person who can look after Ellie.'

Elle had not followed me upstairs. Who was looking after her now? A businessman? A golfer? A Gustav Klimt enthusiast? I'd made no dent in their travel arrangements. Desperate, I started towards the door.

'So you don't exhaust yourself running all over the hotel, Elle will be buying newspapers.'

She was cold and hard. 'Be careful.' I thought she'd say that.

*

Elle was coming in through the revolving door and I noticed how light and free she seemed. It came partly from the fact she never carried anything, not a handbag, purse or shopping bag. There was no money belt round her waist, her clothes were easily worn and chosen to accentuate her air of lightness. There were no fripperies and, apart from the rings, no jewellery. She always looked as though she was wearing green even when she wasn't. It almost occurred to me what she was but her eyes swerved, saw me, stayed on me and I rushed up to her, obedient to that gaze. I nudged her back out into the street around the corner, out of sight of the doorman and up against the wall.

'You can't go.' I'd never behaved so absurdly in my life. And to a woman.

'I have to take Mia back.' It was a small voice, with no colour or conviction.

'You can't leave me.' And I finally got hold of her. It was going from one continent to another, it was turning from white to black, it was a change with no return. I locked her into the necessary embrace and then I was dropping into another place, falling through darkness, whirling, spiralling – was this how dying was? The closeness, delicious, forbidden, becoming sexual. I had never done something so forbidden. I dissolved in the savage, hungry holding, her arms tight around me in a long embrace. All around us were shoppers coming back with Harrods green bags and I felt a roaring in my ears and a gushing sweetness going from her being to mine. It was a sweetness like honey, like wine, endless, entering my body, as ecstatic as an orgasm but without the drop. There was no end – it went on and on, high, unearthly. This was how angels felt when they embraced. It was being filled up with an endless essence, a sweet supply of ecstasy. It came into me from her and then I realised how odd it was. I expected the same rising and falling of passion and hunger that I felt with a man. This filling with sweet light belonged to dreams. And then she pulled away. I still felt higher than high, out of reality, like the time I'd had the morphine shots. It was as though I'd taken every drug in every orifice. I was filled up and carefree. I'd done something erotic, crazed, exquisite, dangerous, yet all we'd really done was embrace. Was it possible? I'd held her so tightly my arms ached.

'I'll come back.' Her cheeks were flushed, eyes glowing.

I knew she wouldn't.

This feeling was love. I'd never known real love before. That's what I decided. I tried to hold her again but she got out of the embrace in spite of me and I was surprised by her strength. Sweeping back her hair she re-entered the hotel, cool and contained, crossing the foyer as though nothing was wrong and as though it never would be. She had no connection with what was lying across the bed upstairs or what was five paces behind her. Two women, both desperate. We arrived at the lift.

'I can't –' I was going to say something true but it sounded so over-used and hackneyed.

Once inside the lift I fell against her, pressed into her. We got out and she dabbed at her lips before starting along the carpeted passage to the suite.

'You can make her stay.' I was pleading now.

'Mia thinks there's something between you and me.' She half-laughed. 'She's not wrong.'

I was beginning to dislike – no, dislike was a luxury – hate that spoilt would-be actress brat.

'I'll come back through London on my way to Washington.' She squeezed my hand.

Back in the suite I again tried to persuade Mia to try for drama school in London. She was in a bad mood but oddly not with me. She'd taken enough substances to be chatty and she described the roles she'd played in Helsinki, the scholarship, the various actors she'd worked with. Drink made them all famous. I'd never heard of any of them but then I wasn't up on Finland. Elle did things in the background, rewound her watch, wrote a note with a tip for the maid. 'Have you cancelled the drama teacher?'

'Just send him a cheque,' sighed Mia.

Elle snapped shut the last case and phoned for a porter.

I was going to have to say goodbye but, beyond speech, I just stared at Elle, at everything she was and did. What did it matter any more? I felt like a condemned prisoner about to die and she was life. Perhaps if Mia did go to a psychiatrist I should book the next session. Mia all of a sudden laughed. 'I hope that waiter doesn't carry bags in his spare time. You should have seen Ellie at breakfast. Was it yesterday? He didn't want to serve us because it was after breakfast hours but we're paying enough and what the hell do these waiters do all day? To really upset him I ordered a vast amount of cooked food and when he wheeled the trolley in here he was in such a sulk. So Elle jumped up, took the coffeepot from him and mimicked his actions. She said, "How would you like to be served like that? Such a face. Would you pay money for it?" And she did his face and gestures. She'd got him. He didn't like it but the service got crisper.' She tried to get Elle's attention. 'Show her how you do the waiter.'

Elle caught the slur in her voice and looked up. 'Watch the top-ups. You're not even at the airport and you know that's your black spot. And then we've some way to go.'

I was surprised by the waiter story. Elle had gone ever so slightly down in my estimation. She'd left the pedestal. I could not imagine anyone mimicking a waiter. It was quite a surprise. But then they were always joking around and familiar with staff, taxi-drivers, doormen. They had a brazen fearless approach and obviously could handle rejection. They could certainly dish it out.

I said goodbye to Mia and, looking hard at Elle, left the room. I'd got almost to the lift when she crept up lightly behind me.

'Here's my number in Spain.' She'd scribbled it on a hotel matchbox.

'Don't you think she should go back to acting?' This was my very last try.

'Good God, no.' She pressed the lift button.

'She's a good actress.'

'I paid for her to be a good actress.' In case I didn't believe her, she said, 'It wasn't like she says. I got her into that Finnish drama school, paid for the scholarship. She was unwell and acting seemed to be the answer. Then.'

'But she worked with those top actors –'

'Small parts, with scripts commissioned by me. I put investment into the productions.'

The lift stopped and the doors opened. She was going out of my life. If I got into that lift I'd never see her again. The lift doors, ever merciful, slowly closed and the lift went on up without me. Further along the corridor the porter was getting their luggage. For a mad moment I even considered going to Spain with them. A visit to Lily. Yes, that was it. I turned and faced her and she took my hands and pulled me to her and again the embrace and it went on and on until the end of time.

*

I said I'd see them off at the airport and the limo started towards the Cromwell Road and got caught in traffic. No one spoke. Mia looked strained, Elle carefree and smiling. I said something about going to Scotland for a fashion shoot and would they like to come with me? No one answered and then Elle started joking with the driver. I asked Mia what she thought about Scotland and she turned away and took a large drink. Beer had been replaced with something stronger.

'Perhaps you should do what you really ought to do,' said Elle.

I looked up as expectant as a puppy hearing the sound of the biscuit bag.

'Forget all that snap snap stuff. Anyone can do that. Make the film about night in the city.'

'The night,' said Mia. 'That figures.'

'Make it in Hollywood.' Something in her voice was different. Dare I hope?

Mia put on sunglasses and slumped against the window. Elle assured us all it was the pollution. Desperate to get her attention I touched her leg. Everything in my face said 'Please'. This scene had been played out thousands of times by thousands of lovers and still there were so few words.

The loved one would either leave their original partner or not. Her eyes were moving around. She was thinking. Then a small flat bottle fell from somewhere on Mia's body and smacked to the floor. Mia had passed out. Elle's eyes stayed still. A decision was made.

'Mia's exhausted. She's allergic to these petrol fumes. We'll book her into a hotel near the airport so she can rest.' Elle told her they'd get the evening plane, then reached down, picked up the whisky bottle and pocketed it.

The driver waited while the huge quantity of luggage was checked into the best of the airport hotels, further out in the country so Mia could benefit from fresh unpolluted air, then he turned the car round and Elle said, 'Just one day.'

*

She wanted to see my photographs so I said they were at home.

'Then let's go to your home.' She was back on that one.

I didn't like this at all.

'Tell the driver where you live and he'll come and pick me up later. We'll let Mia sleep it off.'

I suggested a walk by the Thames or lunch in Soho. What about visiting Hampstead Heath?

She smiled, she was mesmerising. I would have done anything for her. 'I'm not interested in the state of your place. It's you I'm interested in.'

13

The pressure of walking with her to my door forced me to decide on the sort of place I should live in. An old apartment in New Orleans, a boat moored on the Seine, a palazzo in Venice, a loft in the Village, New York. Being where I lived would also show that I'd only just started getting commissions. I wasn't sought after, hard to get, or recognised. What had I told her? Now I didn't want her in there at all, everything was too obvious, nothing hidden in that house. So I lied to her. 'The house doesn't represent me at all.'

The hedge decided it, uncut, bulging and somehow dusty, suggesting the dust that was to come. I walked right past the house for I couldn't own that hedge. Daisy the dog started barking eagerly by the front door. An unwelcome twinge of snobbery made me say, 'It's not convenient. I'm sorry.' I suggested a coffee and turned towards the main street and then I remembered, not all I'd been through, but some of it, and I had come out the other side so why did I worry what this spoilt, rich, shallow creature thought? I'd had to fight for my life. I earned my money. I loved James. Now I was proud of what I'd done. Remembering what I'd heard on the street. 'Christians fear they'll go to hell when they die, alcoholics have already been there.' I turned her back towards the hedge.

She entered the house with ease, even grace, and stepped over James's delivery of books, still unpacked. Thank God James wasn't in. Then he was in. He shouted from upstairs something about a message from my agent. He was in his workroom, the disorder of which could only be imagined. She concentrated on the dog. Her visit was badly timed. I should have made sure he was teaching. He ran downstairs, something he never did, to give me the agent's message and joined us in the kitchen. His expression was serious as he greeted her. I realised I hadn't mentioned her or Mia. She sat at the table as I made tea and looked at my photographs. That was safe.

The house was a mess, not at all what she was used to, the opposite of her property in Spain, of her property anywhere. I gestured to James to send her up to the first floor lavatory if she needed to use one because the leaking pipe in the ground floor bathroom produced a smell of rot and I wasn't sure she'd understand that smell. I could see the house through her eyes. Nothing put away, overfull shelves, cupboard doors open, unopened bills, dog hairs. James was asking questions, his pale face taut, dark eyes sombre. They were strong eyes and she stood up to them. He was good-looking but I'd got used to it, that was the trouble. He explained he was marking the final year exams and they were then sent to an external examiner. This year he anticipated a significant number of firsts. She made sure she knew exactly where his university building was on the pretext of believing she'd passed it on an earlier visit. It didn't quite ring true and I believed this was the first false thing she'd said. Stick with photography, I thought, and get them apart, get out of here. God, I was jittery. She was interested in the darkroom. This was my kingdom and I explained the trays, the tanks, the chemicals, the lights. Again James said I'd had a call from the agency and they wanted the film for the weekend supplement now. I said I'd do it and get it biked over.

She said, 'You're a chrysalis. You'll come out a wild butterfly.'
Would I fly?

*

I was beginning to understand that she liked power. The smile stopped people in their tracks and it stopped the business of questions. She said, 'I don't like direct questions,' and for once her tone had an edge. What had I asked?

We walked to the local shops and suddenly they were all new as though an extra light had been switched on. They were stripped of the daily grind of countless economical visits. The assistants were lifted from the grey pall of habit and I actually saw what they looked like. Being with her did that.

She still didn't carry a handbag and her lipstick and credit cards were carried in trouser pockets that she had made extra deep. She didn't bother with a mirror and simply moved the lipstick over her full lips. The skin, the flesh, was all it had to be, a dewy loveliness I'd only seen on photographs of brides on their wedding day. She looked the same both morning and night and took two minutes to get ready while Mia took two hours. Yes, she agreed, she did have a wonderful constitution. She made it clear that she was there for the person she was with and that she'd give them anything. She seemed to expect nothing herself and did not make demands. I took this smiling detachment to be a mature calm and I thought she had an extraordinary life sufficiency.

'The house is a mess,' I said, eventually.

'At least you don't try to do anything with it. I can't stand places that are half-done or badly covered up.'

From time to time during that afternoon she would suddenly look at me and I'd feel the glances burn inside me. When she could she pressed my hand, caressed my face. All I wanted was to go to bed with her. I supposed I was now a lesbian. But although I could sense her excitement she kept its manifestation at the extremities and not the intimate parts of my body. I ached to be sexually joined to her and could visualise with difficulty some of what would happen.

Shall we go to a hotel? That was the obvious outcome. When should I say it?

She got me talking by setting up a vacuum I was only too eager to fill. I told her about the celebrities I was starting to photograph and their jokes and gossip. She liked to know about people. Yes, she liked knowledge. That was why she wanted to see where I lived. It left me with no chance to be mysterious or even interesting. She now knew my reality. Meeting James had helped and then the photographs. Many were experimental and could be perceived as failures. James would not let one shred of deception near him. He was what you saw. How he despised pretension!

We walked to Hampstead Heath and all the while she gave me the fullest attention. How green her eyes were, jungle cat's eyes! And, when she was laughing, how they could heat up and glow! She walked without pause, tireless. She just had to find out why I hadn't had children and she'd have me placed. I did not tell her about the addiction, the inner skid row. Believing it to be genetic, I wouldn't risk putting a child into the world who could suffer as I had.

She asked about my parents. How I wished I could say I was an orphan. Dad worked in the civil service and Mum looked after the house. How simple it could sound. Upbringing? Suburban, middle-class, relentless. I rebelled and escaped. What the hell were those poor people doing with a wild Bohemian child like me?

I found the cluster of trees and pulled Elle into the centre where we could not be seen from the path. I started to take down my jeans, lift my sweater. I had to have the nearest I could to sexual intercourse with her. But she clamped me as she had that morning and the feeling, honey sweet, flowed from her to me, a non-stop gush of dizzying energy, better than sex with its rising peak and subsequent falling. I was aware of an unusual sensation: my body quickly became one unit, rather than erotic zones inflamed and needing. There was no effort and my clothes stayed on. I felt that this was how it was done in the higher states of being. She didn't wear perfume. In fact she didn't smell of anything. We left the trees high as though on an endless drug.

But then there was the car to take her back to her other lover.

It didn't seem possible that she would leave me but the door shut neatly, the car started, was gone. Nothing was sadder than that empty street and I became unhooked from the high state and fell like a piece of clothing off a hanger. Somehow I got home and James said he'd fed Daisy. At some point I asked what he thought of Elle. He sounded off-hand. 'Charismatic.'

I left in the middle of the night and went out to the airport hotel. The night looked remarkably vivid, every part of it individual, available, not a dark blur, keeping its secrets as it usually did. I could see someone walking across the grass. The moon full and bright lit up her face.

'Aren't you scared, walking alone at night?' I asked.

'I love the night.' The way she looked at me I knew I was loved too. We sat on the grass which she said was country grass and it smelt sweet. 'I had to get a doctor for Mia.'

'She's not –' and out of all the states she could be in I chose, 'overdosed?'

'Alcohol poisoning.'

I suggested going in for detox.

'She becomes frail and exhausted and that's why she drinks. To keep going. He's given her something to make her sleep.'

'What did he say is wrong?'

'Doctors! What do they know!' She couldn't sound contemptuous enough. I remembered her father had been a doctor. 'I'll get her back to Spain on the first plane.'

We spent the rest of what was left of the short night lying in each other's arms on the country grass and she was so sturdy and beautiful and we didn't speak or ask questions of the future. It was a sweet night, smelling of sweet grass that I would remember. I truly belonged to her.

*

The same journey, the same cast, even the same driver, but we were coming from a different direction. The driver was part of the gang and told jokes and Elle and I found we never could remember any joke however funny, and if Mia did she wasn't saying because she wasn't saying anything. I could see she detested the attention I was getting. She had to be the centre of everything. When Elle wasn't speaking to her or looking at her, her face fell and became lifeless and weak.

'Wasn't this where we talked about you making a film of the night?' asked Elle. 'Let's go to Hollywood.' And she told the driver to stop.

'What about –' I looked at Mia.

Mia shrugged, resigned.

'Let's get the tickets.' Elle was out of the car. Nothing was faster than me getting out after her. I didn't want anyone realising we could get all the tickets we needed by just continuing to our destination, the airport.

Elle leaned in the car window, looking at Mia. 'You could be in it. We'll go and set it up, then you can fly out when you're better.' It was all settled.

I was watching Mia, her eyes. And suddenly the pain cleared. It was like looking into someone else's eyes altogether. Their expression was now decisive. Yes, she'd made a decision and was relieved. 'You go,' she said to Elle.

Elle slapped the car as though it was a horse. 'I'll see you back in Spain.'

As the car started up, about to take the very changed Mia and all the luggage to the airport, Mia turned to me. 'Catherine, you don't understand.' I thought she looked sad. The car was gone. Even the rush hour was on my side because the traffic had cleared.

She stood in the sun in a country street with nothing except the clothes she wore, her lipstick, Vaseline and credit card in her trouser pocket. Her passport and comb were in her jacket.

'A hand-held camera. That's how we'll make the film. We'll go to the top and set it up out there.'

I explained you had to know people to do that.

'I know people who know people. Let's go. You've got to make a film and dedicate it to impetuous love.' She took my arm and we crossed the street. I'd never done anything like it, not even in dreams.

There was one shadow: Mia had decided to let her go. Why?

And then I realised I hadn't biked the film for the weekend supplement. I'd even forgotten to print it.

14

Sitting on the plane to LA we were just two women, not familiar exactly, neither friends nor relatives but somehow together. Perhaps we'd met just before take-off, not having seen each other for some time, and found we were travelling to the same destination. From this point I started being concerned with how people saw us, a consideration I'd not encountered before. Who could possibly guess the dramas of our liaison as we sat casually sharing an in-flight magazine? Elle pointed to the page of perfumes and asked if I wanted anything. In my mind the glossy display was replaced with a cauldron, brand-new and untried like a just-delivered kitchen appliance, and in it would boil lust, licentiousness, deceit, jealousy and joy, unacceptable all of it.

'I think I'm going fucking mad,' I said, and back came the glossy page and her finger on a perfume bottle.

The excitement of being near her was just covered by a veneer of respectability as false as the fabric of the seats we sat on. Under the sheets of her newspaper our hands met and grappled and dug for more intimacy. My hand slid free and felt her thigh, a caress she allowed, her face immobile, and then the hostess hovered over us with menus and Elle's hands had to come up from under the newspaper. A difficult moment. What did the woman think we'd been doing? Elle asked for a complicated drink and got her attention away from the missing hands. Did we look like a couple? She so extrovert and very much part of what was going on around, and me, seemingly beyond speech, staring with, I hoped, disguised fascination at her face.

Her eyes made sure they met mine, then flicked to the toilet sign, and

I got up and followed her. In that cramped, lurching space I clawed off her clothes and grasped her hand and shoved it against my body. I brought her face against mine to kiss her and she again clasped me in such a manner that whatever I would have done could not be done. All longing was absorbed by this other state, the fill-up of sweetness, an anaesthetic putting out all mere sexual impulses to make way for the big blast so delicious, so exquisite it took away even thought. Her blouse undone, breasts visible, trousers half down, had no part in this. They were the untidiness of a sexual act abandoned in favour of the drugged gush, unstoppable, going into my body as hers pressed against mine. She spoke caressing words as a man would and a tongue of flame leapt out of her eyes.

She pulled back out of the embrace and I was surprised by how unchanged her face was. It looked as composed as when she was reading the menu, even her lipstick was unaltered.

'What is this?' I asked.

'An affair.' She smoothed my hair, straightened my collar, eager to tidy up disarray.

Someone was banging on the lavatory door and she pulled up her clothes, all the while smiling into my eyes, tantalising.

'You go out first. They'll think we've had a joint.'

I left the lavatory and the man about to go in was taken aback when the sign clicked to 'Engaged'.

Then she slid into the seat beside me and gave me a light caress almost of ownership. She was my lover.

'I've never been to bed with a woman,' I told her.

She was looking at the menu again. She chose the dish with the least description.

'Don't have the chicken.'

'Did you hear what I said?'

'No, I'm sure you haven't.'

'I don't know anything about it.' And I realised the women I knew did not talk about their sex lives, the explicit details. I heard much more from gay men. I knew the stories of well-known lesbian affairs but not the bedroom details.

I told her I would have the chicken.

She looked surprised. 'But I told you the other choice is better, if "better" is a word one can use about airplane food.' She flipped the menu on to the pile of newspapers. 'I was only trying to save you from a lousy meal.'

I didn't like the description of her preferred dish but of course I could eat it. I didn't want to offend her, so decided against the chicken. I did wonder why it mattered to her what I ate.

She talked about Casper, a businessman who occasionally put money into the film business and might go for the subject of the city at night, depending how we angled it. I thought we should try a producer but she couldn't be bothered with that.

'They're in the same position as us. Looking for money. We'll need a line producer, that's all.' She knew Hollywood from visits she'd made over the years with Olav and his circle. A top movie actress had been a sort of friend and a director or two were mentioned. She'd already decided where we should stay and I could see her experience of Hollywood was very different from mine. All at once I felt nervous of the distance between our worlds. I'd have to be very sure of my identity and talent to deal with the set she frequented. I'd shoot the film in black and white 38 mill. Thinking about it gave the plan a reliable reality. I asked how long we'd be there.

Another jolt of insecurity. 'I have no idea.'

After a pause I said, 'A week? A month?'

'I just live with the moment.'

Nervous now, I touched her arm and was distracted by the material of the freshly purchased denim suit chosen for the journey. I didn't like it. It was wrong for her, too stiff, restricting, masculine – she belonged in silks and soft textures.

After the meal she covered us with a blanket and pulled me into her arms to sleep and again I was worried about how we looked. Two sisters, mother and daughter, two gays. I couldn't sleep and my head filled up with images, sharp-edged, too clear – Mia lying with her head in Elle's lap and, slowly and with pleasure, Elle's fingers stroking the yellow tresses, fingers filled with cheap and differing rings and yet on her they found a symmetry. Nothing about her was out of proportion, not part of the dance of subtlety and seduction she needed as I needed make-up. That first meeting outside the bar on the hill, what had she said? 'This village would suit you. As it is beautiful, so it is bad.' What was it that was odd about her that I should remember? And then the great wave of love and desire came rolling back and I whispered the well-worn declarations of love and meant them.

What could we do with this passion? Stamp it to death? Slay it in the corridors of the next luxury hotel, run from it in the cobbled streets of the next Mediterranean town? Then I remembered Mia perched on that mountain of luggage in the middle of an unknown place, abandoned. Did Elle think of her? Miss her? Whatever happened she must not think of her and I stroked her hair, her neck, and the threat of loss made it less difficult to visualise acts of intimacy unthinkable a day ago. I realised on that droning plane with its false air that I was determined to keep her. I would do quite a lot for that. Jealousy was the fuel. Yes, I'd go to bed with her. When we arrived? Bathed? Unpacked? Would there be separate rooms? A suite? Yes, I did have a husband and she had a lover and a girlfriend and a stepson, and a husband who wasn't altogether out of the picture.

'Are you asleep?' She knew I wasn't. She turned her watch back six hours. 'You'll see the Rockies in a minute.'

I'd been seeing Rockies all night. In what was now morning I noticed that the cabin staff, when looking at us, did so with a certain interest. They knew. I put on dark glasses, unsure what I was doing. The alertness in their expression had not been there at the beginning of the flight.

Elle gave me her scone and coffee. I told her about the places and people I knew in LA and what we must visit and where we should eat. 'Hamburger Hamlet. On the Strip.' She didn't know it. She knew the exclusive places. I wanted old Hollywood: the Château Marmont, Swabbs Drugstore, Barney's Beanery. Yes, I'd show her my Hollywood. And I was all of a sudden happy. I was in love, about to create a marvellous film, I was travelling, beginning an adventure. This was everything I'd ever wanted. There were no shadows. And then I recalled what had evaded me during the night hours. The evening I first met her, standing against the light of the bar, she'd had no shadow.

A more ordinary odd note I didn't like occurred as we were about to land. She began a sort of smiling banter with the crew.

'But she knows the rich and famous and she's a famous photographer.' Then she said my name. Even they couldn't pretend they knew me so she gave my credits. 'You must know that magazine. It's the most read magazine in America. And she's just photographed the best known star in Spain.' I felt deeply uncomfortable. 'And she got a scoop. How they are at home with the blinds drawn and the make-up off.' She talked about Star's wife and the house and the success I'd had with that. So now they'd got it. One of them asked what Star was really like.

'A famous photographer is what I should have been,' Elle cut in. 'But I never paid attention to anything at school. Except to the boys perhaps, and too much.'

She'd got them on her side. The odd note? The showing off. The 'famous'. It was so cheap.

15

A problem arose as we presented ourselves at the reception of the exclusive hotel in Bel Air. Did we want two rooms or a double room? Had she thought about this? The clerk filled the pause by flicking his fingers showily at the computer screen. His impatience was meant to be obvious.

'What is he?' said Elle, not bothering to lower her voice. 'A wannabe flamenco dancer or what?'

'If you take a double room you'll want two beds and –'

'Not necessarily,' said Elle.

'Two ladies sharing usually take twin beds and –'

'Exactly when did I ask you to take over my sleeping arrangements?' she snarled.

'So is it a double bed or king-size bed, madam?'

He dealt with Elle, only with her. I wasn't even in the picture. I was suddenly embarrassed. I wanted to be with her but I didn't want the whole world to know about it. 'Make it one bed,' she said. 'King-size.'

The clerk noticeably changed. I thought contemptuous summed it up. She leaned towards him provocatively. 'What's your interest? Is being gay a crime?' She was off on the rude-waiter-serving-breakfast kick and I was dying inside. I could see this unexpected temper took her into bad places. She was losing face. Her mimicking might stick for a while but the memory of her beautiful mouth suddenly brutal and cheeks scarlet with rage would take some erasing.

I was burning with jet lag, exhaustion and embarrassment but she was on a roll with anger and wanted the manager and this prissy clerk out of a job. We had the full attention of people passing through the foyer. I nudged her. 'Let's get out of here.' I did not exist. It was her, the clerk and now the manager, and the quarrel raged along the corridors to the room. Although I tried to join in with advice and hopefully placating comments, I had no part of it. We had little luggage and they didn't like that. It was a bad start, but then Olav must have come into it somewhere because the manager sent flowers and champagne and visited us in person to make sure she had everything she wanted.

'I might if you got proper staff. What kind of hotel is this suddenly? What's a little shit like that doing here? He doesn't go with the prices or the reputation.' And she shooed the manager out.

I felt she was in the wrong and would apologise to me for the unpleasantness but this did not happen. The bed seemed to fill the room and I wasn't sure about being so continually intimate with this half-stranger. A sexual episode was one thing but being at my best night and day for a new lover was not something I could handle. For me, a short interlude was always more successful. I made an entrance, all my lights on, giving a performance they'd want again, and then off, anonymous into the dark streets where I could be anything, wiping off make-up as I walked. It was like being on stage. I supposed it was to do with the fear of getting too close and failing.

While I was worrying about this step into lesbianism she picked up the phone and called Mia in Spain. Now this did surprise me. She sat on the bed and talked and laughed in this foreign language for over twenty minutes. I cleaned my teeth, hung up my clothes, lay down, got up, put film in the cameras, and the conversation showed no sign of ending. I thought she was impolite, uncaring and I should move, not just to another room but another hotel, one I felt comfortable in over on West Hollywood. Her eyes as she spoke occasionally flicked my way but showed no warmth or interest. There was no gesture to assure me this conversation was appallingly long and out of place and she couldn't wait for it to finish. Should I go out, lie down, sleep, scream?

Finally she put down the phone and smiled at me. Her eyes were mesmerising, and her smile assured me I was all that mattered in her world.

Playfully, boyishly, she jerked up her foot and hooked me behind the leg, pulling me to her. 'Lie down with me. Come on.' She leaned forward, touched my face and I could feel the effect in every part of me. She lifted my hand to her lips and the unpleasantness of the arrival was forgotten. I was still half bent over her. Should I lie down beside her and be lost in the lovemaking that would follow? Or perhaps not be lost. I might not like it.

'So what do you want to photograph? I see you've loaded the cameras. But you'd rather wait for the night.' With the same foot she pulled me nearer. 'That's something we share.' I almost toppled over onto the bed. 'Oh, you are standoffish. I thought you couldn't wait to get your hands on me.' Looking into my eyes now, challenging. This was going to be the moment of making love and I wasn't sure, not at all, that I wanted to be a lover of women. I wasn't sure where I really was with her or if it would work technically at the most basic level. Or if it should work. And the girlfriend far from dropped – why did I assume she had been? – was a mere laughing phone call away. The boyfriend, Olav, would be next. I was in love, no doubt about that, but could sense pain in a thousand guises just one caress away. What if I got hooked on her? I'd been hooked on lesser things. What if she just left me? Mia had been left. As she said, she lived in the moment. That thought had plenty of company. They were all there, the fears, doubt, panic, suspicion.

'So shy?' She shook free of the denim jacket and undid the shirt.

'I've not been with a woman, I told you.'

'I promise you it's very nice.' She pulled me, arms flailing, across the bed. And then we just lay and waited.

'It's all such a surprise.' I included disinclination to do all the things I did with men.

'But you have such passion. That's what I like about you.'

She started to slide down my trousers and complimented me on my hips.

The trousers stopped at my knees while she looked at my thighs and stomach. I knew if we just rushed into it, into the action, got lost in passion and lust it might be all right, but this was slow, leaving too much time for thought and then doubt and the daylight was glaring and showed too clearly our skin, its pores, the small hairs. How healthy she looked, cheeks like apples. Next would come pubic hair, nipples, and I didn't know how I'd react. I slid away from her. I had never had trouble making love, not at the beginning, when the need, the infatuation, was still there.

Although I sat away from her there was so much room on every side, the bed vast, a continent, bleached white, making me feel small and infantile. 'I just can't do this.'

She got me back beside her and again pulled at my trousers and they fell to my ankles. Another pause. What she expected I couldn't guess. It was stop, start, lurching like a car in trouble. I hoped she wasn't going to attempt oral sex and I kept my underclothes pressed against me. 'I need time, Elle. What I feel for you – I can't put into this physical –' If I'd been with a man he'd have jumped on me and that would have ended all the talk.

She made one last try to get me undressed but I was like a bad doll whose clothes get stuck on the jointed bits, whose leg comes loose with a change of shoe, whose hair falls to one side at the touch of a hat. She gave up and lay on her side, eyes closed, a beautiful slender hand lying across my thighs.

'You'll get to like it,' she said.

I had no idea what time it was, what day. I felt separate, flat, and a million miles from that dizzying feeling. I missed James and felt frightened without him. Then she got up, closed the shutters, drank from the mineral water bottle and got dressed. 'So you've never wanted a woman?'

I said no and then decided I would tell her the truth, something I did not necessarily do with men, and that pleased her. I felt there was no point even trying to be her lover if the liaison didn't have the benefit of complete openness. For some reason I believed being totally open to this woman was the one way into the relationship. She liked it, my recounting scenes from the past, the schooldays and the piano teacher.

'What did she do to you?'

'Nothing.'

She seemed disappointed. I told her my doubts about sex with a woman. 'To touch a woman's body – it's like masturbation.'

'It's unending with another woman. You can get such an intense closeness and it doesn't drop as it does with a man. It's much better with a woman.'

Not that afternoon.

'Have you had many?'

'Enough to know that.' She pulled me against her and said softly, 'I love being with you.'

Did she love me?

*

Elle couldn't be bothered with sleep, not while there were shops still open. She knew she had to lose the denim suit, that quick necessary purchase when all her luggage had been abandoned along with her abandoned girlfriend.

'I bought it for you. I thought you would want me to look like your guy.'

A dash of lipstick, the flip of a comb lifting the sides of her hair, made her ready for anything Bel Air had to offer.

The foyer was staffed by docile people with lowered eyes. The prissy clerk whose looks had reminded me of Marcel Proust was not on show. In this hotel I felt sure I was stepping into old dramas. 'So you stayed here with Olav?'

'Occasionally.'

'And Mia?'

'Occasionally also.'

Then I remembered I had to phone James.

'Not now,' she said. 'Let's have a good time. What have husbands to do with that?'

'Soon it'll be too late. It'll be the middle of the night over there.'

She decided to smile. 'You cling to what you know. Don't you?'

She made me feel ordinary. My conversation with James was even more so but fortunately she didn't hear it. I told him I was here to do the film and there'd be money for the mortgage. I mentioned the mortgage several times. The clinging, mundane ordinariness would have made Elle scoff but I thought a chunk of mortgage repayment was the one thing that would please James and make up for my absence.

The movie star, Jewel, made an entrance as we were going out. Elle stared at her and the woman's eyes swivelled round to meet hers, almost hypnotically. Elle pulled a tomboy 'up yours' expression and the woman laughed and turned to watch as Elle took my arm and walked lightly into the street.

'You should photograph her,' Elle suggested. 'What about a spread in the *LA Times*?'

She made everything sound so easy. There wasn't a chance that I could get a session with Jewel and then offer the result to the top newspaper here, which had the pick of photographers. My reasoning made her laugh. 'Then I'll do it for you.' She obviously liked a challenge. She also liked the shops on Rodeo Drive and although I was exhausted and dazed by the sun and heat I went along because I didn't want to lose one minute that I could have with her.

Although the denim suit was quite horrible it didn't diminish her sexual charm, a charm that had an edge, could be dangerous and caught the eye of a passing woman whose stare alerted Elle. She spun round and their eyes fully met and in the woman's there was a definite invitation. Elle half smiled and turned to look at the boutique window, no doubt looking at the reflection of this woman who continued regretfully up the street. I wasn't wrong because she turned and, if I hadn't been there, would certainly have returned.

'You obviously know her?' I said.

'Who?'

'The woman you looked at just now.'

'Oh, her. I've seen her at some party, I think.' She didn't even try to make it sound like the truth.

'And the movie star in the foyer?'

'Oh, her. I've seen her in some film, I think.' She was mocking or teasing me but she hadn't answered the question.

She bought the necessary clothes quickly, all in beautiful fabrics, and then found a shoe shop with moccasins in all colours. She'd got everything she wanted in less than an hour.

'What do you want to buy, Catherine?'

I assured her I had all I needed. I was suddenly worried, not about money but by the contrast between me and the rest of Rodeo Drive. I had no idea what time it was, their time or my time, and the shops were shutting. Then Elle saw an assertive-looking tweed jacket and rushed in before the shop door closed.

'I have to have something to make Casper think we're serious.'

The sleeves would have to be let down and she wanted the pockets deepened and of course she'd need trousers to go with it. The shop stayed open for her benefit and I sank, flattened by exhaustion, on a leather chair. I didn't want her to know quite how terrible I was feeling, thought I should keep it to myself, and said I was simply hungry. I hadn't, I realised, slept the night I'd spent with her on the hotel lawn near the airport or the one on the plane. It was now coming up for evening in California which meant I was in the middle of my third sleepless night. She wanted to buy me a belt so I had to get up and the contents of my body shifted dramatically to my feet. The egg timer feeling made me sink back on the chair.

'Stand up and let them pierce another hole.'

It was the hardest thing I'd done since the bad old days. The assistants marvelled at the smallness of my waist, the toned-up stomach muscles, the long lines of my body. I marvelled I could keep it all vertical.

'I'll have to go and lie down,' I admitted finally.

'Why? Are you tired?' Perhaps she thought I meant a sexual lying down.

'Aren't you?'

She shrugged and chose a credit card from a small case in her pocket and arranged for the jacket to be delivered to the hotel. Tiredness made no dent in her style and she was as energised as at all the other times I'd seen her. I could not understand how she kept going.

'I control my body. Not the other way round.'

The starving jet lag hollowness sat me in the nearest deli, where I ate and drank until the shaky feeling was gone. She had something small and insignificant and watched me, not without surprise. 'Now you won't want dinner.'

'Of course I will.' What I wanted was to lie down and soothe the jet lag and drink hot milk and not think and eventually lose myself in a long, selfish sleep. I hadn't, I realised, changed any money.

'Don't worry about that. You're my guest.' She got the bill.

Although I said I felt altogether better having money of my own she turned away from the nearby cash dispenser and took my arm. 'Let's choose a car.' She was ready for walking, a lot of walking. Again I asked if she was tired.

'Not at all.'

'How do you manage?'

'I catnap, I can sleep for two minutes, less, and I wake up refreshed.' She'd learned the trick from Olav who, when travelling, could go without sleep altogether. She described LA as her playground, smart dinners with Olav, business meetings with Olav, weekends at Palm Springs and golf with Olav, and bars, clubs and parties without Olav. About movies she knew and cared very little. For her, Hollywood belonged to the Forties and Fifties. Now this town was Olav-town, otherwise she'd have left it alone. Then she mentioned Mia and how she should get an agent here and I realised I'd been behaving as though Mia was over and done with and I was the replacement. And then someone in the street asked for her autograph and I became depressed. In comparison, tiredness was a luxury. I asked how far the car hire firm was, and could we take a taxi?

'You can't just hire one. It's not New York. We'll call for one.' She turned into a coffee shop near the Beverly Wilshire Hotel and I sat on the first thing I saw and got a Coke and an aspirin. I felt boring and earthbound, assassinated by tiredness. I needed to talk to James, to cuddle Daisy, to be back where I belonged.

She was laughing with the waiter, who tried to guess where she came from, and I saw she could make plenty out of very little.

'Let's get that car.' She almost danced, light and free, out into the street where the rich and famous paraded their wealth, their status, and I had to acknowledge she took every eye. The street was hers, and she so simple and unadorned.

She asked the taxi driver about the clubs and nightlife. 'There's never much,' she promised me. 'But I'll take you to a club after dinner. They all go to bed before sundown in this city.'

Lucky them, I thought.

She wanted me to choose the car but I was overwhelmed with exhaustion and decided to go back to the hotel.

'You are a slave to your body.' She laughed so I couldn't possibly think it was a criticism. She chose a different credit card to pay for the car.

'If you go to bed now you'll be awake before dawn. That's why I'm trying to keep you going. We'll get some more Cokes and go to Malibu –'

'I'm going to the hotel.'

She spun the car round and it purred under her control along the freeway where she chose the turn-off for Malibu. 'The sea air will freshen you up. Or you sleep on the beach. Why lie in a hotel room?'

She was a good, smooth driver and allowed no surprises. She ruffled my hair.

I didn't normally feel so tired or go on about it. I did wonder about that.

16

Sometimes she had a wildness that probably belonged to the time when she loved the elements – skiing dangerously through glacial nights, taking boats through rough seas – and then the wildness would subside because there was nowhere for it to go and she'd become cool and smiling and sophisticated. She also had a way of making just an ordinary statement moving, even thrilling. 'I drove by the ocean and the colours – they're so beautiful.' A million people could say that and it would be unremarkable. Why, when she said it, was the essence so powerful? The statement came from a place of bereavement, of sadness, because the beauty and the colours were soon to be out of reach and always would be. Out of this sense of dying was an explosion of life and the desire for all it offered. Later she said, 'I come from such a dark place, so the colours are precious to me.'

'Finland, you mean? It's always dark?'

'No, I meant the night.'

I thought it an odd thing to say. But she came alive at night. She enjoyed dressing up, who knew what the night would bring? Into the bar, free and confident, not for the drink but for the effect she made and who she could attract. I came to realise putting things into her body had no importance – not food, alcohol, stimulants, water. She never said, 'I really long for a drink,' or, 'This food is great.' Where was the word 'more'? I never heard it. She liked to challenge the absolute 'in' places and, magically, a table became available for her in establishments that demanded weeks of booking ahead or no booking, just fame. Did they know her or think they knew her? Possibly they remembered Olav doing some effective tipping.

Sometimes she preferred to dine simply by the ocean and then take a boat along the coast until it was time to go dancing, clubbing, meeting strangers – yes, she liked that. She never wanted to go to bed and we'd drive along the coast waiting for the dawn. Again she said she decided life, not her body. 'I'm in control.'

'Is that what you mainline on? Control?'

She smiled and I'd begun to notice the smile was always the same, full on, lights blazing. She gave it everything. It didn't grow, it was there, as though switched on. 'Love. That's what I mainline on,' she whispered. I wanted to believe it. I thought I'd got it right, the controlling, because not only did she hardly drink, eat, sleep, but she didn't change mood and, apart from the statement about the colour of the ocean, expressed nothing. She just was. The mocking temper outburst at the beginning of the visit was not repeated and if it wasn't that I remembered the brutal mouth and crimson face, I would have doubted it had happened. It would have belonged to the vivid dream state I sank into before sleeping, where activities occurred with slight distortion. I believed it was because I was over-tired.

She was alternately very close to me, there only for me, or off on the phone, long-distance in many languages. Or she'd be deep in conversation with people she'd just met in a foyer or bar and I didn't exist. Sometimes she'd point out subjects I should photograph and in what light, and interiors and exteriors we should use in our film. The photographer was now 'we'. She'd ask about light, exposure, how to use a lens, the latest equipment, setting up a darkroom. Also she did what she said she'd do and the meeting with the financier Casper was arranged for the following week.

The best time was in the bedroom and I had no doubt we were locked in a love affair and soon the language of gay love would be available to me. The original awkwardness of trying to manipulate a sexual act was over. I would hold her in my arms waiting for passion to rise and she would clasp me with her thin strong arms and it seemed we would at last make love but then would come that other-world transfusion, which seemed to depend on the stillness of our bodies. In that moment I realised I was helpless.

I sat with her on the bed and told her I'd never felt anything like that strange high, and what was it?

'It sounds pleasant,' she said.

'But you feel it. Don't you?'

She expressed, with a rough body gesture, total ignorance. So I went through it again, the fill-up of sweetness that deadened and soothed and also exhilarated like a drug.

'If you get all that from a simple hug from me, why want anything else?'

I asked if she'd had many female lovers and she dived onto the bed and threw a pillow at my head. 'So serious, Catherine. All this Sherlock Holmes suddenly.'

I was too serious in another sense when I resisted her touching me in public.

'Why can't you accept love?' She sounded sharp.

'Not in public.'

She didn't get it.

I told her I didn't want to draw attention to the fact I was with a woman. For once she didn't answer. I explained I wasn't gay, had never been gay, and now I was confused.

'Confused?'

'Because I want to be with you.'

She pushed me away firmly. 'Well, you're not with anybody if you won't let them touch your hair.' She picked up the car keys and was going to leave on her own. She did not like to be resisted. And I said the worst thing in the world, the words I thought I'd never say.

'I need to talk about it.'

'Talk?' She was almost amused.

The touching me in public showed she owned me and I did not want to be owned or taken for granted. It was very different to being loved. I didn't tell her this because her sudden irritation with me was not pleasant. I said how difficult it was to suddenly find I might be gay. She didn't quite shrug. For me it was a talking point, perhaps a problem, a life change. She couldn't wait to get away and buy a newspaper. I had to know what she felt about me and bluntly asked her. Talking about it was not her thing either and she said if I didn't know what she felt, words wouldn't help. I ran after her and waited while she chose an armful of newspapers. The togetherness with her was unlike anything I'd experienced and was something I could not lose. I'd known her forever, before I was born.

*

An agent I knew came into town and asked if she could show my portfolio to the studios and PR companies. The magazine spread on Star and his wife was in the current issue and the agent thought this was enough to build on. I went to see her in one of the small chain hotels in West Hollywood, below the Strip. I walked in and out again. I couldn't, I realised, bear to be apart from Elle. This, a surprising and unwelcome development, was verging on panic. I rushed back into the foyer in search of a phone box as though there was some calamity. Would she be in our bedroom, in the bar, at the newspaper stand, driving by the sea? She had only to go out to pick up a quick new life. I insisted the switchboard let the phone go on ringing, but she wasn't there. All the lights of my life went out. I just didn't slump to the floor.

In the agent's suite I showed the latest photographs with only a quarter of my mind working. I didn't want to talk to this woman because she wasn't Elle. I didn't want to see her, be with her. She could never be Elle. Life without Elle? Unthinkable. I wanted to use the phone. I wanted Elle to be back in the hotel. I wanted to hurry into her presence, her arms, her bed. Why couldn't I make love to her? Just take off her clothes and do to her what had been done to me by a man, innumerable times? Just get my mind above and away from the genital contact, on to her lovely breasts and face? Elle had presence radiating as strongly as perfume. The agent had none.

She was just a dull, lightless human being, two-dimensional, as I had been before Elle. I didn't even want to acknowledge her existence.

Again she asked if I wanted coffee. 'You look...' She stopped. However I looked it wasn't going to be flattering. She took a deep breath. '...Drained.'

I explained it was a sort of jet lag that hung around like flu. I hadn't, I realised, got over that first massive exhaustion.

'No. Different.' Of course she thought I'd started drinking and using, and was in the throes of a hangover.

She asked the prices of the photographs and I asked to use her phone. Elle was still out. The skin on my body started to creep and burn. I was as vulnerable as an abandoned child. I asked for the message desk. Nothing. Was she angry with me because I'd come to this meeting alone? It hadn't occurred to me to include her because this was work. I'd told her the agent's name.

'You mean, you want a thousand for this but only five hundred for the two?' The agent tried to get my attention. I wasn't getting the figures right, anything right.

'You obviously need an agent.'

Had she gone back to Mia? A simple minute could offer her freedom, the next joy. She didn't have a half-starved existence scraping up bits of emotion, making do. I was now heart-jumping terrified. Unable to bear anything, I said I must go. I'd get a cab to the airport and hopefully catch her before she got a flight for Spain. I'd make her my agent. It would be like a marriage, my creativity, her personality. She'd never be able to leave me if she had a stake in my success. The present agent was answering the phone as I swept up my photographs roughly and shoved them into the container. A knock on the door. The agent opened it. Elle stood there.

I'd never been so happy, so relieved. I was reclaimed.

'I came to get you,' she said, 'in case you had trouble getting a taxi.'

I rushed towards her, almost hugged her. She stepped towards me smiling, so lovely, and she was mine. The last hour had been an inner earthquake and everything now fell back into place. I was so pleased I let Elle do the talking and just sat watching her, silent. What a difference between her and the English woman. Elle, so dazzling, she took the light from the room, and the woman was left in ever-deepening darkness, a mere rag beside this exquisitely designed stylish creature who would stand out in a million. The talk wound in and out, through neighbourhoods, restaurants, shops, hotels, and resulted in the agent remembering she had a secret and special sanctuary on the hotel roof. She took us up some back stairs and through a fire door, on to a quiet flat space dotted with trees in tubs, a swimming pool in the middle.

There were a few people lying on chairs on the sunny side and a waiter brought drinks from a health bar. The agent explained that as hardly anyone knew about this place it was always quiet. We sat in the shade and the talk turned to business. Elle was interested in the client list and what fees the agent demanded. After ordering vitamin cocktails the agent went back to her room to get some information Elle wanted. At last, I took her hand, squeezed it, kissed it. I was so glad she was in the world.

'Don't accept this agent. She's nothing. She needs you. You certainly don't need her. You're on your way now. You need an exclusive agency. Casper will know one. You need New York, Paris, London, Rome.'

I said I wanted her to be my agent. For always.

As she replied her eyes, avoiding mine, took in the last sunbather across the pool, a big-breasted, voluptuous, dark-tanned girl, mouth half open, wanton expression, soaking up the sun. Elle's eyes stayed on her just a fraction before moving back to me and in that moment it was as though the girl was viewed through a lens, pulled into sharp focus until she was absolutely clear and totally revealed. Her white bikini top barely covered her breasts and the material covering her lower hips was stretched to snapping point. As though aware of the gaze, excited by Elle's attention, she started to move one leg to and fro, opening her thighs, expressing and offering her whole body, and dark pubic hairs became visible at the edge of the white strip of material. As though compelled to, she suddenly sat up and took off her bikini top, releasing opulent breasts that she joggled provocatively. She swished back her long curly hair so her body was totally exposed and then lay back on the sun bed, legs open, wide and careless. Elle's eyes rejoined mine.

'I couldn't do that, but thank you.'

'Why not, Elle?'

'I couldn't be anyone's anything. Certainly not an agent.'

The agent offered us a place in the sun, but Elle said she disliked sunbathing.

'Aging?' said the agent.

'Depends who's doing it.' Elle glanced, one quick glance at the near-naked girl opposite. She was lolling open and wanton, made for sex. 'It suits some people.'

The talk went back to deals and percentages, exposure, build-up, and I could see the agent was irritated. Who was Elle and where was she coming from? At least Elle knew where the agent was coming from – too unknown, too cheap.

'I don't think Catherine should make a decision at this time.' Elle brought the meeting to an end. It seemed to me that she dared another look at the sunbather.

The agent said, 'She soaks up the sun, that girl. What a tan!'

As though in response the girl sat up and smeared oil on her breasts. I was sure Elle wanted to do that for her, caress with oil that responsive body. I was filled with what I came to understand – intense jealousy.

'What's your answer, Catherine?' asked the agent.

I looked at Elle.

'Catherine shouldn't make a decision.'

The agent turned to me. 'Is this what you think?'

Elle opened the fire door and, without a backward glance, hurried down the stairs. I was relieved she didn't look back beyond me to the poolside.

The agent asked me to stop for a moment and opened the door of her suite. I looked at Elle. 'She'll wait.' The agent went in ahead of me, leaving the door open. Elle shrugged and leaned against the wall. 'She'll try to persuade you, but you've made your decision.'

I said I'd collect my photographs and went to the table. The agent gave me a card.

'In case you change your mind. I think you're making a mistake. It's not just self-interest.'

And for the first time since I'd arrived her face came into focus, and was in the room, in my mind. 'You've not got a track record and you need building, not frightening, to success.' Then she said that I shouldn't be influenced by people who weren't even in the business.

'But Elle knows Casper and is arranging for him to finance a short film I'll shoot and –'

'She'll be lucky.'

'She doesn't need luck. She knows him. I told you.'

'Well, let's see if she gets him to back her picture.' She put the documents she was carrying on the table, suddenly tired. I said goodbye and started to leave.

'She's a killer,' and she closed the door.

Elle ran with me down to the street and held my hand. It turned out to be a lovely afternoon and a lovelier evening.

17

High, joyous hours, higher than anything I'd known. I was up beyond safety, nourishment, sleep, even thought. The exhilaration, too much for my body, needed to be met with a sexual wildness, unimaginable caresses which would finally satisfy the craving for joy and I'd return, perhaps not to peace of mind, but at least to myself. I was burnt out, ecstatic, exhausted, my senses shot, and it was all inflamed further by her seducing presence.

She felt something of the same, her eyes, how they gleamed when she saw me, told me that. The lovemaking would be fierce, brutal, stricken with cries like the ones I'd heard on summer days from open windows, when I'd say, 'Show-off bastards. It's just pretending.' My body was in a rage to be with her and I didn't hear anything anyone said, but ran mindlessly to where she was, needing to be squeezed in her thin strong arms.

She aroused me beyond sense with a single glance, the beauty of her face setting off wave after wave of longing, her smile, which I could never capture, tearing at my sad heart. I'd known her before, before forever began. I was shot, fixed, blown, filled with craving only she could assuage.

I told James things were taking longer than expected.

'You sound strange. Different.'

I blamed any change he might have noticed on jet lag.

'No. You sound the way you did when you came back from Spain that first time.'

After meeting her. Yes, I remembered that. I said I'd be back in a week. He didn't like it and he didn't understand my tone.

I was too excited and tried to calm down in the bar with a Diet Coke and a string of cautionary thoughts. I must not lose James. I must not hurt him.

I waited for her, my entire being one aching hollow. I embraced her, trying to find the right proximity that didn't draw attention to our femaleness, our matching organs.

'My, you are chaste,' she said.

She was passive apart from the controlling, drugged hugs, and that surprised me.

It felt odd holding a woman but I did it thinking, which partner am I? She told me gay relationships were not defined in that way, like heterosexual ones. But I still felt the pressure of her breasts as I held her, which in my terms made me the man.

*

The next day, or was it the one after, the agent phoned with a deal. An almost-forgotten Hollywood actor had seen the spread on Star and his wife and liked the way I shot an old face. I was offered a reasonable fee to make his life, his presence, seem essential and compelling. She arranged the meeting at the hotel suite to sort out contractual details and Elle said she'd drive me. She didn't get out of the car as she usually did, blew a kiss for luck, and left to do some shopping. I didn't like the creepy, tingling feeling in the back of my legs. Fear? I liked being with her. The price? I did not like being without her.

The agent asked me to agree the deal with the magazine and sign the contracts which, as I never read contracts, took less than two minutes.

'You should always go through each clause, otherwise how do you know what you're getting into?'

I thought she was becoming boring again, but I had to admit I didn't look at things or measure them up because I didn't know how to. I couldn't locate much common sense or sense of consequences in myself so, when faced with a dilemma, I stayed too far away or jumped blindly in, neither action attended by rational thought. Of course, that's what I'd done with Elle.

'How's your friend getting on with Casper Shulz? Has she got backing?' she asked coolly, knowing she hadn't.

I hadn't wanted to think about that because when looking at Elle's strange make-up – rich man's mistress, attentive stepmother, lover of women, well-born society hostess, alluring party girl – I might have to add 'liar'. Casper Shulz was probably just show-off, the cheap coin of status I'd seen her use with the staff on the plane, the clerk at the hotel, the movie star Jewel in the foyer. How she'd bragged that if I was too meek to go for it, she could arrange a session with her. What had happened to that boast?

I was too occupied being with her to think of working, of dealing with Casper or a movie star, but this was why we were in Hollywood.

'There's a lot of strange people around the movie business.'

'Strange?' I didn't like that description.

'They come in with an idea, a name, a fortune, a promise. The façade is good and they waste a lot of time. Movies attract them. The empty pocket punters.'

'Have you one in mind?' I waited for her to actually say Elle's name.

'One? I see a hundred a week, and your friend doesn't have the feel of someone seriously making films.'

'This is Elle's first film, provoked by meeting me, by wanting to take my work further.'

'Your work takes you further. You don't need a pretend impresario.' She shuffled the contracts into an envelope.

A scalding rush of humiliation kept me silent, playground painful, right there from a childhood I could never handle. It turned to anger. I longed for effective words to assassinate this bullying thug with her deadly common sense which hid, of course, a touch of truth. She had common sense enough. She'd been born with it and paraded it as a virtue. It killed off joy as far as I was concerned, and I told her my personal life was my own and let's keep to business. But I realised I had to go back to London at some point, my life was with people like this agent, and this stolen time was just a lovely bubble. Perhaps Elle was forever blowing bubbles.

The coffee arrived and she suggested we take it up to the roof and get some peace in that secret place before driving to the photographic session in Malibu. Before I reached the roof I remembered the dark sunbathing temptress and looked for her immediately on the far side of the pool. She wasn't there and at this hour it was in shadow, deserted. A few bathers were at the far end ganged up in the merciless glare. The agent was pointing to some sun chairs, and there she was in blazing sun that bleached her white sharkskin bathing suit, her body shifting as though restless or aroused, and then I saw someone else. Elle stood in shade opposite the girl. For a moment I thought it wasn't her, but a man, slim and rather romantic in the white shirt and perfectly arranged silk scarf, but that posture belonged to just one person. The way she held her head, the absolute stillness, identifiable anywhere. The agent was saying something about a sun chair or a table and chair, and Elle materialised beside me. It was a shock. Her presence had all the atmosphere of infidelity, betrayal, pain. She was fully dressed and out of place on this roof reserved for leisure.

'What are you doing here?'
'Sunbathing.' She was never short of an answer.
'But you don't like the sun.'
She half laughed. 'Perhaps I'm trying.'
'So why are you here?'
'It's a quiet place. Peaceful.'

Not once did she look at the girl on the sun bed and her eyes stayed on mine, but I knew the minute I turned to go those eyes would snap back to the dark luscious body, gaze at it, she'd gorge herself on it until it filled her up. The girl lifted her head and the breasts swelled up dangerously, like balloons about to burst. She was looking for her admirer. Dark eyes, slightly curving, black curly hair, full pouting mouth. She looked spoilt and sexually greedy and I thought she'd had a lot of men, could get anyone she wanted, was bored with conquest and wanted to try a woman.

The agent finished her coffee and it was time to go. Immediately, I asked Elle to come with us. The agent objected and unusually, so did Elle.

'I'm not going.'

They both laughed, said I was childish. I still wouldn't go. The agent couldn't be bothered with all this and started for the stairs. The girl slid down the bathing suit and caressed herself with oil. Elle still had her back to her but I felt she was aware of the girl's actions and resented being stopped from watching. She was deprived of this oil-smearing ritual and getting impatient.

'I'll wait up here till you get back.'

'Yes, I bet you will,' I said, my voice a low hiss.

'I'll sit and read the papers.' And she pulled out a chair at a nearby table and sat down. A tree in a tub obscured her view of the girl.

'So you won't come?' I was horrified by how abandoned I felt.

'I'll be in the way.'

'When has that been a problem for you?'

'Look, the film guy might pay too much attention to me and it'll ruin everything.'

She opened the wad of beloved newspapers, the newsprint sickly smelling in the heat. The agent, impatient, was calling for me to hurry. I hurtled down the stairs, full of black pain, looking into a future without Elle. What was I doing taking photographs of a spoilt stranger, miles away on a rich people's beach? I ran back up the stairs and Elle was no longer at the table. She was in her original position, opposite the girl. Wild with jealousy, wilder perhaps than the sex-packed rival on the bed, I rushed to Elle full of accusations, threats. They remained unsaid. Instead I mumbled, 'What do you find so fascinating that you have to stand here like a statue?'

Her tawny eyes turned to me, very level and not friendly.

'Don't let her see you behaving so crazily. And tidy your hair.'

Was this a criticism?

'I'm watching the smog down on the coast.'

I couldn't believe what I'd heard.

'It should lift by now.'

I didn't speak because I was unsure what would come out. She pointed. 'Now you can see Marina del Rey.'

Lies, all lies. I wanted to strike her. Then the girl stood up and even the habitual sunbathers, obsessed with their own shapes and sizes, had to acknowledge those breasts. They were enormous, jutting, and designed for pleasure. She shook out her towel, making the most of that, stroked it into place on the baking bed, then wobbled and nuzzled on to her back, thighs open. It seemed to me that, as Elle allowed herself one small glimpse, the thighs moved in lustful response.

Fuck the smog! The girl! That's why she was here.

Jealousy did what seduction could not, and, as soon as I was back from the coast, I rushed her into the hotel bedroom ready to do anything sexually to keep her. I'd spent hours pointing my eyes and my camera at faces old, young, indifferent, but all I'd seen was the girl on her back on the sun bed, and Elle on top of her, writhing together through lewd scenes. I tore off my clothes and pressed against her and eventually her hand lifted and held my buttocks and I could feel the rings hard on my skin. Those slender hands and arms filled up with a hard male strength as she jerked my hips against hers and pulled me down with her on to the bed and her lips moved against my neck, teeth bit along my ear and then she was on top of me. I saw the voluptuous girl again and this provoked a rush of erotic thoughts. Did Elle hold the same image? I wanted to rid her of that. I suggested blatant pleasures she could give me and her hand reached between my legs, fingers probing and I heard, 'Oh yes.' I wanted to see her face, how it was when aroused. Looking up, I saw only her eyes. There was something wrong there. I was looking at her eyes but saw, in each, a corridor leading backwards, and the physical structure of each eye seemed to change, expand and, in some places, contract to allow the corridor to be there. It was like a cervix changing during birth. The corridors terrified me. They were minute, leading from the pupil backwards, perfectly designed, definitely corridors. The excitement snapped off and I sat up cold, alarmed. That was the end of that.

*

It was her idea to get a miniature camera for use in night locations, public and private. She'd seen a shop near the agent's hotel and wanted me to approve the purchase. However discreet the instrument, it would still need a flash and she was disappointed. Money could not buy the kind of private apparatus she was looking for, the kind that recorded intimate moments, leaving the subjects innocently ignorant.

'I hate all that bright shock. Everyone blinking and crazy looking.'

'But we have to get some kind of agreement from those shocked and blinking strangers if we're going to photograph them close up.'

'Why?'

She was now treading in the delicate area between using people's lives without permission and pushing for exceptional reality that had to be unaware and unposed. I found intrusion was not something she was prepared to understand, not when it came to other people.

'What do they care?' She couldn't sound mocking enough.

'Identifiable and on someone else's film, they care.'

'How crazy you are.' It was one of the first times she left the sustained charm layer and became energised. 'What do you think the press do? It is 1985. Haven't you heard of telescopic lenses? What's all this conscience? No wonder you haven't got anywhere.'

'Is snooping on people getting somewhere?'

'Snooping? This is our film we're talking about. We need night locations, night people, research for the script.'

The sales assistant, guessing incorrectly the kind of film we were trying to make, listed the absolute essentials for a porn movie. He had the same effect on her as the prissy receptionist in the hotel.

'All these words. What's the matter with you? I'm trying to decide whether to buy a camera.'

'You will have to light the set.' He thought he knew what he was talking about and wanted her to see it. 'It's called day for night. You'll be depending on close-ups.'

She covered her ears in mock horror and turned to me. 'We need to show Casper something. It'll strengthen the outline if we have slides.'

I chose to believe her. There was no reason why I shouldn't.

'If you don't want flash I'll use a camera with wide aperture and fast film, and a slow developing process. But I'll only get what I see.'

'You won't get detail and, if I'm guessing right, that's what you ladies need.' The assistant was still talking about a sex film.

Before she could turn on him I said, 'If the faces are in darkness I'll get nothing. If there's a bit of light I can use that.'

'No, not good enough. The pictures have to be visible. I want to see them so I need light. And it certainly isn't in this shop.' Insultingly, she pushed the camera so it slid towards him. 'Too old-fashioned, like the photographer. I'm not spending money on that.' And she left the shop on those well-shod fast feet. Technology had let her down.

As I was buying film and a new lens she rapped on the window and signalled she'd be back in five minutes. Old-fashioned flash, old-fashioned morals – she had to walk those off.

'She's the sort who'll get into trouble with celluloid.' The assistant had not liked her. Once again I wanted to defend her and tell him to keep his opinions to himself. Instead I laughed uncertainly.

'Oh, she likes trouble. She handles it.'

Could I?

'I've seen her around,' he said. 'Maybe in a magazine.'

Everyone had seen her around and I understood they responded to her in a direct, one-to-one, personal way, and I was not in the picture. They didn't care if I was with her, not with her. They didn't want my view, they had their own.

As I waited outside the shop I realised the film was a device to get away from Mia and to keep me by making my work seem valuable. Twenty minutes passed and she still wasn't back so, as the shop was near the agent's hotel, I called round to see her. She was busy and I stayed in the foyer and phoned James.

'How's it going?' was replaced by, 'When are you coming back?'

I talked about the night film and that was a short conversation, and then on impulse mentioned Elle's eyes becoming strange. The corridors leading back from the pupils. I didn't mention the position I was in when I saw them.

'Contact lenses,' he said.

I was so relieved! They'd reflected some light from the window, the path outside, or something in the mirror, the floor leading to the door.

The agent was still busy so I phoned the camera shop, left a message for Elle for when she returned, and went upstairs to the pool. The stairway was cool with an air of restfulness and stepping on to the roof into a disconcerting, dusty heat and blazing yellow smog sky was a shock. I had to pause and blink sun out of my eyes and there, almost a mirage, only yards away, was Elle, standing in exactly the same place opposite the lolling girl. The sight of her alarmed me. There was something predatory about her presence; worse, it was frightening in its rigidity and intensity of purpose. Yes, for a moment I was going to run for it. Did I want to be part of this strangeness? But she saw me and the smile was full on as she came towards me. I expected an explanation but didn't get one, so asked why she was there.

'It's peaceful.'

'I thought you wanted to sunbathe? Wasn't that it last time?'

'I like peace.' Her tone had an edge. No more questions.

She'd left the shop on impulse, I was sure of it. Straight up to the roof and, drink in hand, she could be taken for a hotel client. Of course she'd checked first to make sure the girl was there. During that time on the roof, to confirm my suspicions, I tried to get her to sit in other places from which she could not see the girl, but she always found a reason to move and somehow end up in the same position. Then I saw the girl's eyes meet hers in a look of complicity. They would meet somewhere in this hotel, in some almost public spot. Elle would do with her what had not been attempted with me. No awkward, slow undressing for this girl. No sugary hug that kept her still. And they'd want it again, the torrid exchange, the coarse hot talk. The agent, now beside me, asked what was wrong.

I'd leave on the morning plane. The girl had mislaid her suntan lotion and a spoilt brown hand felt lazily around the bed. Elle, up like a shot, retrieved the bottle and, laughing, placed it between the slippery tanned fingers. No, I'd get the night flight.

The talk moved to and fro between filming at night, scriptwriters, permission for locations, and I waited for the girl to leave because Elle would make some excuse and follow her. She'd get her into the utility cupboard, where they kept spare oranges and plastic cups, and make love to her, against her, hands filled with those huge breasts.

'Will you do the first draft script?' The agent was talking to me.

I proposed a brief outline, all the time thinking of that dark girl, her lips, her pubic hair, her ripe flesh sweating, writhing and crying out with climaxes that Elle would hush with a crushing kiss. And if Elle's eyes had corridors and her embrace a strange anaesthetic effect, the girl wouldn't care. What Elle got out of it I wasn't sure. Her excitement would be quiet, its outcome discreet. Power. She'd get that of course. Afterwards, they'd slop amongst the tumbled fruit and Elle would smooth back her hair and step daintily from the cupboard and the girl would struggle into one of her many minute bikini bottoms, wipe the sweat still dripping from her breasts and she'd reach over and, using her towel, wipe some telltale mark from Elle's face, and the idea of that hurt more than anything.

'The outline sounds unusual,' concluded the agent.

I smoothed back my hair.

I thought – now I'm gay.

18

Walking by the ocean, the fog lifted and my inner hurt lifted too. All of a sudden I was happy. I stopped to watch as Elle skimmed flat stones across the water and had the same feeling as when I'd first seen her walking over the hill. She was so known, part of a familiar life I couldn't identify. When had it happened? Where? Rubbing wet mud from her legs she turned and saw something in my face she liked and, as though responding to my thoughts, whispered, 'But you're mine.' She put an arm around my waist as we walked at the water's edge and now it was a high hopeful time, joyous and free as I'd once felt years ago when I didn't know such happiness would have to be paid for in pain.

'We have to be together,' she said and I laughed with pure pleasure. Everything was all right and always would be. She added, 'I always knew I'd meet you.' I asked why.

'Because Mia told me.'

I was slightly less happy. 'Is she psychic or what?'

'You are the one person who could take me away.'

'Is that what you think?'

'I don't do anything so I'd go for somebody who did. That's what she said. A talent in the way you see things. A ragged life on the edge.'

'But you will do something. You'll do this film with me.'

'Exactly.'

And it occurred to me that although we had talked about locations, scripts and wide aperture we hadn't actually met with reality, the backer, Casper Shulz. I didn't really care about the film. It was a pretext. She was all I cared about.

'We have to do the film, Catherine. It's the one thing that's ours.'

We sat on the beach and the waves with lacy edges delicately touched our feet.

I phoned James discreetly from the lobby downstairs and let him think the film was happening. I didn't like lying to him and kept the calls short. She phoned Mia from our room and kept the calls long. Whatever I was doing, reading, bathing, preparing the script, waiting, the conversations droned on relentlessly, the incomprehensible words seeming to crawl over me like insects. Before she picked the phone up for the next round I'd ask if she'd been speaking to Mia. She shrugged, then agreed.

'Why do you let the calls be so long?'

'Because they can't be short.' She picked up the *LA Times* and would have hidden behind the pages but remembered she had to call Olav. His was the second most called number on the gigantic bill that, bent over with laughter, she carried up to the room, its sheets escaping and fluttering out of her arms.

'One-hundred-and-thirty pages, even for me that's a bit much.'

She wouldn't let me see the final amount.

'How will you pay for it?'

'Oh, I'll send it to Olav.' Still laughing, she let this huge broken nest of paper drop on to the bed where it twittered and shuddered as though full of small creatures. Looking at it admiringly, she said, 'It's the second biggest phone bill I've ever had. Take a photograph of it.'

I heard the name Dag many times. It turned out to be her stepson. She was lying across the bed plaiting my hair as I told her how I'd shoot the film. She was becoming interested, absorbed and the hair-plaiting slowed and again the phone rang and again I could hear Mia's harsh shout, laughter this time and I waited for this strange language to include the words, 'I can't talk now,' and bring the call to an end. This did not happen and she became as involved in the story Mia was recounting as she had been in my proposal for making the film. Mia's story had two central figures, Lily and Serge, and I had the feeling they had shared a drunken and scandalous evening. In any case, it was more interesting than what I'd been telling her, so I chose another way of dealing with the rejection and shut myself in the bathroom where I washed my face, my hair and re-applied make-up. If she wanted to hear about the rest of the film she'd have to come into the bathroom and ask me. I dried my hair and did the yoga breathing exercises that should keep me sane. I decided to walk through Bel Air and all of this would show her not only how I felt about Mia's calls but what I was going to do about it. I opened the bathroom door. She wasn't sitting by the window reading a newspaper as I expected, or writing a letter or hanging up the latest batch of Rodeo Drive clothes or watching television, instead she was sitting amongst the bunched-up pillows, phone to her ear, speaking in that special intimate way, and I knew it was the same conversation. Forty minutes later she was still talking about Serge. I got my bag and jacket and opened the door. This she would not allow and I waited for the phone call to finally end. If she'd noticed my actions they'd meant nothing to her so I closed the door and came back into the room. Forget Bel Air, I'd go to London. What a terrible mistake this alliance had been, painful, wasteful, emotionally dangerous. I opened the cupboard noisily, took out my clothes and slung them on the bed. I climbed on a chair to lift down the travel bag. She'd notice that. Although my packing was angry and final, her conversation with Mia continued with no change in her voice, no concern or hurry. I could see her in the mirror, so beautiful, so desirable. She was everything I'd ever wanted without knowing of this everything's existence before I'd met her. No, meeting her introduced me to everything I'd ever wanted. I'd still leave. I wanted, though, to make a satisfactory exit, let her know how badly she behaved, make her suffer. I let the travel bag leave my hand and drop to the floor and, finally, with a few words of farewell that I'd begun to recognise, she brought the conversation to an end. She looked at me, her eyes a mean green, and laughed.

'So dramatic, my God.'

'It's as though you want to include your ex-mistress, have her present in this room.' My voice was shaking. I was so jealous of Mia, so threatened during these long, exclusive conversations. Yet again I told her I found it painful. She decided on a physical solution and, kicking my bag to one side, took me in her arms, patching up all the pain.

'You must want me very much to be so jealous.' Even this small moment of calculated conciliation was interrupted by the tweet of the phone – it had begun to sound like a caged bird – and Mia was back again, she'd apparently forgotten a detail from the Serge/Lily saga. Of course I would not leave, and the phone calls were apparently the price I'd have to pay. Again I said I didn't like it, how could I know from this unknown language what she was going to do? Mia was obviously trying to get her back and between one moment and the next, Elle could get up and go. It often sounded as though she was fighting for her right to stay away. Her tone had started to become varied as she showed surprise, mock disbelief, anger, amusement, and I could sense she was in the grip of the girl's needs, complaints, thoughts, suggestions, one of which was probably, 'Come back to Spain.'

'What can you expect? I've lived with her for years. We have things to say.'

'But you left her to be with me.' How I hoped that was true.

'But I can't just drop her. She's ill.'

'What if she comes here?'

'She'll hate the rooms.' So it was a possibility.

'Is she coming here?'

'She hasn't mentioned it.'

'But you want her here?' I was trying to be cunning and paying a high price for that with a nervous heart. I couldn't wait for the answer, couldn't bear it, so carried on talking. 'Can't you wait until after we've done the film to have her back?'

For once she didn't say anything.

I took hold of her hand, knowing that, if she left me, the pain would be unendurable. Not today, don't go today, said my heart. It'll be okay tomorrow. Go then, said my mind. I'll do anything if you stay. Heart and mind together now. I wasn't aware I was gripping her hand and she bent back my fingers and pulled away.

'So you do want her here?'

'Not particularly. I want to be with you.'

So I would live.

'What does she think we're doing?'

'Making a film. I've told her she'll have a part.'

'Let's get on with it then. I'll do the script. We don't need a scriptwriter at this stage.' We did, but I didn't want anyone else around. Even casual people had a way of turning into rivals.

I asked her to make calls to Mia somewhere else. Then the phone rang and she almost answered it. Quickly, I said, 'I am in love with you. That's why it hurts.'

'But that's wonderful. Let's celebrate that instead of this inquisition.' And she jumped up and took me to an exclusive restaurant, one of Olav's favourites.

I did wonder if we'd meet Casper Shulz, if she even knew him. For all I knew he was sitting in this very restaurant, unknown to both of us.

19

She was absolutely of the moment, sometimes joyous and free and then she'd escape from that sustained poise and become a young urchin, jumping up and catching the branch of a low tree and swinging until she turned over and fell without fear. She had enough in her to be in the moment and didn't need things or plans or projections. I didn't know anyone like that.

I said, 'You don't have any fear, do you?'

She didn't know what it was except she didn't like it when she saw it in other people. And she'd sometimes bring the tomboy act into smart restaurants and play teasing games. It was good show-off stuff, but it was always with waiters.

We lived a playful, expensive life and I tried to get to know her but I was, I realised, always taken off track by some distraction or embrace which smothered difficult questions. I managed to pull away from those quick, strong little hands.

'But you sleep with men.'

'Only when I have to.'

'You slept with Mia.'

She hesitated slightly. 'Not exactly.'

'And you want to again.' I thought I was being cunning, that I'd trapped her into truthfulness.

'She's too ill.'

'You did once. Wanted her.'

'Well, there must have been something. Let's go to that new French place.' She wanted to see if Elizabeth Taylor did go there.

'You wanted that girl by the pool.'

She made a careful gesture of innocence. 'Pool girl?'

'The tanned, mostly naked girl on the sun bed. The one you stared at for ages. That girl. Remember?' I waited for her to remember.

'I can't recall any girl.'

I was astounded.

'You do recall the pool on the roof?'

'Of course.'

'And you stared at the girl. You went back to see her several times.'

She laughed.

'You do remember the girl.'

She shook her head, so I described her.

'It seems as though you saw more of her than I did.' Teasing now, she said, 'Don't accuse me of what you want to do yourself. Should I be jealous?'

'Elle, you looked at that girl and you found reasons to go up on to that roof to pick her up. Did you? You wanted to.'

'If there was a sunbathing girl she made such a small impression on me I don't remember her.'

'You're lying.'

And we were into our first disagreement. She wasn't worried about being called a liar and she tried to off-load her attraction to the girl on me. To her, the pool area was a blur of muscled people tanned an ugly brown, with silly trees in tubs, showy vitamin cocktails and unexpected peace.

'You were, and possibly are, fixated on that girl. You were picking her up right in front of me.'

She put her lipstick on with a quick, greasy, sightless dash and was going out.

'If you just admitted you fancied her … It's this denial I can't bear. I tell you the truth.' And now there was a worse truth. She cared so little for me she didn't even care that I called her a liar.

'The truth seems to be that you're excited by a curvaceous sunbather and want to accuse me of what you want to do – handle breasts. Was that it?'

'Did you go off with her?'

'But, Catherine, I'm with you.'

'But you left Mia for me. Rather quickly, I must say. What's to stop the same thing happening with the sunbather?'

'I see I'll have to wear blinkers going out with you.'

'Don't wear your contact lenses.'

'But I don't wear contact lenses.'

So the corridors in her eyes could not be so easily explained. 'Didn't you wear them a week or so ago?'

She quickly knotted a silk scarf. 'Now it's getting late. Instead of the Orangerie we'll go to Musso's because I know you like it. Or Barney's

Beanery.' And she slipped her feet into the soft moccasins and was well shod.

She came close to adjust my jacket collar and I quickly glanced at her eyes. They looked all right. No corridors from this angle.

Later, after she'd jived to Fifties music in Barney's Beanery and was photographed by a Hollywood paper and much admired by the diners, she became careless, even open, her personality not dissimilar from the physicality of the girl of the sun bed.

I said, 'At least you keep your skin good. It comes out radiant in photographs. The girl by the pool with all that tan would turn out a bad brown and flat.'

'Unless she was wearing her white sharkskin bikini.'

Oh, so she'd noticed that.

'But her voice. She was so common.'

*

When Elle was asleep I looked for photographs of the girl. I expected to find extravagances of lewdness, the two of them filmed by a camera positioned at the end of the bed, timed to go off as they reached the first climax. I didn't find any photographs. Her diary was small and contained only a few appointments, written in Russian. And then I found the address book, smaller than a gift in a Christmas cracker. I was sure it would contain a new entry, discernible by fresh ink or pencil, maybe an Italian name or an initial with an LA number. But there was nothing. I was sure Elle had followed her into some public room or cubicle, the changing room perhaps, and they'd done all and more of what I imagined there. And I was sure a camera came into it because Elle was so interested in cameras these days. It would have taken place spontaneously while I was at the beach on the photographic assignment, or when she drove off for a hair appointment or to play golf.

'What are you looking for?'

'Go back to sleep. You're dreaming.' And I snapped off the light and quickly lay beside her.

'My diary, my phone book. You *are* a Sherlock Holmes.'

I didn't answer. I pretended I'd been sleeping all the time. There was no monopoly on deception. I was surprised by how few possessions she had, how they revealed nothing about her.

*

The attraction was still there when she looked at me and we would have been lovers by now if it had not been for the strangeness of her eyes, those corridors in the pupils leading backwards that I'd seen so clearly on that crucial night when it had seemed right to give in. Her love showed itself in the drugged embraces, which were less frequent. She paid me compliments from offside.

'You've got such lovely breasts. Casper will like those.'

'What about you?'

I knew only too well my place in relationships, a fragile one. I existed in that splinter between the ecstasy at the beginning and the first hint of repetition, terrifying in my case. I was a beggar on Love Street and got brightly coloured crumbs but no real nourishment. About committed habitual relations I had no idea: about grown-up domesticity not a clue. I started well in the ecstasy, was good at novelty and ended without choice as the roll call of daily responsibility began. I thought it was to do with the man. I had not met the right one, the charismatic, challenging, hard-to-get one, recognised and powerful, the guy on the white horse – I'd make that work. This prestigious person would rescue me from the glue of infatuation and carry me into a constantly renewing intimacy of which I could not tire.

I made do in that splinter of ecstasy but it was slim pickings. The pain as I was replaced by a mature, life handling partner was torturing. I knew it, but it didn't mean I could do anything about it.

Now I was with a woman in an unconsummated relationship with endless challenges and rivals, yet perhaps already that dreadful everyday intimacy had begun into which I could put little or nothing, and she was disappointed and bored and wanting her old partner back. I'd mostly survived on a dangerous optimism which assured me I'd meet the right partner somewhere my work was recognised, and I a star, and here I was allowing what should be only a dalliance to break my heart. I couldn't bear to lose her.

20

She started to look after me, perhaps she always had, and she wanted to be of service, part of my world. Her very look said I was valuable and worth being alive to know and love. As I wrote the night film script, she'd come quietly into the room with a favourite drink or soup or something new she thought I'd like. 'I saw these biscuits and thought of you. They remind me of you when you smile,' she laughed. I looked at the pale ovals and couldn't see it myself but made a show of delight and she brushed the crumbs from my face with a silk chiffon scarf, just purchased, of a colour and shape I'd always wanted. 'It's for you,' she said, winding it round my neck. I felt hugged and warm, soothed, with an even bigger inner hug that need never stop, that came from her absolute approval of me, her unconditional love. It occurred to me that this was some kind of mothering I had never had and I began to wonder what exactly I had received from my mother. My early years were spent in a state of separation. My mother was often ill and I was looked after by relatives I scarcely knew. When present, she was often distant and self-absorbed. I grew up in an isolation which I'd always believed was good and helped me to be creative and free of attachments. I could be the Bohemian existentialist I wanted to be. I'd had the experience of freedom and adventure, and the price had been no close ties to draw me back into a safety I distrusted. So this honey pot of total enveloping love was a state I had not reckoned with.

She offered me another biscuit. 'I made them promise to re-open the shop if you like them enough.'

I liked them. I'd like anything because I loved this caring treatment. As I finished yet another segment of the script she stroked my hair and quickly placed a new sheet in front of me. Respectfully, she sat watching as I wrote and became part of the work, of my life, of me.

I tried to make my voice interesting and keep the energy of the plot. She offered few comments and little criticism and I was made aware how limited her receptiveness was. Did she like the characters? How about dislike? Was she really satisfied with the points that even I knew were weak? She said they were fine so I started to explain why they were perhaps less than adequate and again she stopped me. 'It's all fine. Don't let's be too clever. I never finished school.'

She'd run my bath and watch me lying in the foaming water and be ready to wrap me in a soft, warmed towel. That's how it was those days – being enfolded in a heated, soft, safe covering. She was the lover, mother, husband, companion, guardian angel I'd never had and had thought I could do without.

She'd do anything for me but was it enough for her? She said, 'I love watching you. That's all I want.' There was no need for anyone else. We were enough for each other. And, for the first time, I was enough for myself. The ambitious, restless career mattered less. I was in the now. And it carried on day after day, so good even I trusted in its continuation. Why would something so good not continue? This wellbeing made me serene, but she was its source and when she was absent, so was the wellbeing. And I'd wait, a little jagged, unable to be at ease. It reminded me of my bad addict days. I spent as little time apart from her as possible, and didn't see my old friend Jack, who lived in the Hollywood hills writing movie scripts, or have lunch with the agent in West Hollywood. I thought Elle would get bored eventually, but it was apparent I was still all she wanted. The phone calls continued but she made less of them and even they seemed further away. To show her love she'd make little changes to my appearance. My hair was a problem because it kept falling forward so in the end she arranged it up, off my face, in a clasp. Laughing, she took away my red lipstick. 'Street girls wear that.' As we edited the first draft of the script I waited for her input. I wanted her to be involved but, again, she made little comment, offered no ideas, had few criticisms. Once we moved on to draft two, the biscuits were replaced by small savouries, and my lipstick had vanished and I looked plainer with my new hairstyle, but that no longer mattered because we were joined and she was enough for the outer world. She had enough beauty, style and lipstick for both of us. And I was – whatever I now was. One thing – I was getting what Mia had got, and more. Yes, I'd replaced Mia.

There were no shadows. I had to really try to find just one fault. She had no sense of humour.

21

It started – the row – because I drank coffee. No, it really began because I had not complimented her driving skill.

'My driving is musical. No bumps.'

I suppose I agreed.

'Then why don't you tell me?'

'I didn't know you needed compliments.'

'Need? I take care, driving you. You could at least appreciate it.'

I tried to avoid possible but, as yet, unimaginable unpleasantness by saying I didn't know anything about driving. I realised it was cowardly.

'You're self-centred.'

Even the day was grey. We'd been together three weeks and she'd driven me every day. Why should this come up now?

'You're just used to rough men bumping you from place to place. What do you know about smooth treatment?'

So I agreed that she was musical in her driving style and then laughed. Musical? Was she having me on? She was not laughing as we pulled into Musso's on Hollywood Boulevard. So musical was the word and this was serious. 'Okay, it's musical. I thought you were taking the piss.'

I was hungry, enjoyed the deli food and couldn't order enough. It was going to be a good day. At last the jet lag exhaustion had gone. And that's when she pointed to the coffee.

'D'you know what that does to you?'

I thought I did.

'It coats your stomach. It's poison.'

'I like it.' And I drank some more because it seemed the natural thing to do.

She smacked the table hard, her eyes ice-cold, her face pink in two blotches either side of her nose like badly applied rouge. Her face was not as it usually was, but on a slant and shaky as though the whole lot could slide down like the result of some bad plastic surgery, and she'd be lost forever. I quickly put down the cup. In the weeks we'd been together I'd been happy, miserable, scared, jealous, confused. Now I was going to be hurt.

'I'm telling you from a good heart. Don't drink it.'

And I realised this wasn't a minor criticism, a point of view, a bad moment. This was a row. I told her why I liked coffee and how I didn't drink that much and I felt ridiculous about justifying it. This wasn't our usual kind of conversation, not remotely.

'But you don't sleep deeply. That's just it. It stays in your body.'

I told her this was ridiculous. It was something out of *Alice in Wonderland*. Distorted, unreal. I just wanted her to come back and be Elle, powerful, distinctive, not falling apart over a cup of coffee.

It mattered to her, the coffee drinking. It was either that or the fact I didn't heed her advice. It was part of not applauding the musical driving. I had a choice. I could stick with the coffee or give in and stop a habit I liked for no reason that I could see. I chose the coffee but it didn't taste as good as it had.

She smacked down her water glass and got the attention of the next table. I dropped my knife and fork, no longer hungry.

'You ordered far too much. No wonder you can't finish it. What a pigsty, this table.'

I couldn't believe it, this sudden criticism from someone who loved me, who had just held me in her arms before leaving the hotel.

'I can't eat because you're being so disagreeable. If I saw the point –'

'But I'm telling you the point.'

'But I don't get palpitations or – oh, this is too ridiculous.'

She'd gone.

I ran after her and the waiter ran after me with the bill. I discovered how little money I had on me or, come to that, in the bank. She was sitting in the car, its engine running.

'Look, if it really upsets you, Elle –'

'It's your attitude,' and she shoved the gears unmusically, her mouth brutal.

The agent had set up a meeting with a PR department in a major studio and on the way I talked optimistically of what this connection could do for our film. She didn't answer. It was the first time since I'd known her that she'd withdrawn into silence. I felt churned up, too hot, and even my clothes were coming apart. Nothing did up properly or stayed where it should and there was a gap between my skirt and blouse. I asked her to stop at a coffee shop on the way.

'What for?'

'Coffee.' I was trying to turn it into a joke.

She didn't react. I needed a cold drink before the meeting because my mouth was dry. No, I needed to speak to her and get this unusual problem sorted out. I was in a strange place where even the rules I'd had to take for granted lately did not apply. I was frightened of the change in her. In this mood she could leave. Unthinkable. I tried to take her hand.

She shook to a stop by the coffee shop and turned to stare at me. 'We're only going in if you promise me you won't drink coffee.'

I actually thought she was joking. If I allowed myself one laugh it would become a gale of mirth, shaking, hysterical.

'It's just a habit. Have you no willpower?' She was stern, unyielding. Not a joke in sight.

We sat at the counter and the waitress placed glasses of iced water in front of us. Elle shoved hers back at the waitress. 'I didn't ask for ice. And none for her,' meaning me.

'So, what's wrong with ice? This is getting strange, Elle.'

'It's not strange. It's strange for your digestion. It's a shock to the system. You don't know what kind of water they use. It's full of germs.'

She was a million miles away from the urchin who jumped up and caught the branch of a tree, spun round in the air, not caring where she fell. She ordered a fruit juice which she didn't want and I took fresh orange. Then I ordered a coffee because it was all too silly and I needed it before the meeting. I needed my assertiveness back more than the caffeine.

'But you promised me.' She was almost pale. 'Are you a liar? If you drink it I'll leave you.'

I held the mug of coffee halfway between my mouth and the counter. This was an infringement of my rights.

'Why can't you take friendly advice?' She was watching the mug. 'Open up. You're closed and stubborn.'

I hadn't gone through what I had to accept this. There had been too many seriously bad times not picking up a drink to give in to this silliness. It occurred to me then she was behaving so unusually because she'd had a row with Mia, and was taking out her anger on me. I drank the coffee in one go and when I put the mug down she had gone.

The pale car was speeding out of the parking space as I ran screaming towards it. She had to stop at the roadside to let a truck pass, and I got in front of the bonnet, yelling and clawing at the window, amazed at the same time that I could behave like this. Her eyes, I could see, were dark and lethal as gun barrels. I think she'd have run me over. We had the attention of the coffee shop and passers-by, but she didn't stop the engine. A couple came towards us and watched – and this was Hollywood, so it must have been good. I heard a new burst of traffic approaching that would block her and ran to the side of the car, grappling with the door. She sped on before I'd got properly in, the door still open. Screaming, I finally fell, courtesy of gravity, into the seat, panting, half-crying, utterly humiliated. I still hadn't closed the door properly as we arrived at the studio entrance.

'I'm not going in.'

'Don't be ridiculous.' And now she laughed. 'Surely you don't retreat just because you're found out.'

'Found out?'

'You lied to me. You're a liar. And you try and hide it with all this crazy drama.'

'Lied?' I was perplexed, on top of being scared, petrified, half-mad.

'You drank coffee, and you can't hide in drama, so you retreat. It doesn't affect me. If you cancel, you're just punishing yourself.'

My clothes were bedraggled, my top sweat-stained. That was the good bit. My inside was ripped with pain and confusion. Why? Was all this my fault? Was she just in a bad mood? So far I hadn't seen one. Was this what they were like? I was shaking, my voice uneven.

'Lied about what?'

She sighed, exasperated, reached across and pushed open the door. 'Get out.'

'It's Mia, isn't it? You've had a row. She wants you back.'

Arrogant, hard, she gestured at the door. 'You'd better go in while they still make movies.'

*

I don't remember much about the meeting or what was agreed. Elle had given me her tan silk jacket to hide my riffraff clothes and the woman admired the jacket, but not me. That was one meeting I should have avoided.

When I came out she was in a better mood, her smile was back, as always, full on, and we drove into the Hollywood hills and called on my friend Jack. He was typing on an old manual typewriter in his run-down redwood shack, which hung on the edge of a canyon surrounded by coyotes. He was also surrounded by superstars in their grand houses but he preferred the coyotes. While racoons ran noisily in his roof and other unseen creatures gnawed under the floor, he showed us a book about the Russian Revolution on which he was basing his latest script. I could see he was very taken with Elle, and she angled it so she got his attention, and I didn't mind because she was my love. But I did think Jack, whom I'd known for years, could have torn himself away to at least ask what and how I was doing. Right now, the answer to both questions would be 'lousy'. She brought out qualities in him I'd never seen. They played a game of verbal ping-pong with sexual undertones, which, surprisingly, she did not lose. Later he phoned and I asked what he thought of her. 'Oh, marvellous,' was his reply.

About him, she said, 'He's smoking himself to death. He's ruining the membranes in his nose. There's no mucous.' She was certainly against oral pleasures that day.

I suggested an early dinner at an Italian restaurant in the hills frequented by the Hollywood élite. I wanted to impress her. Also, I was smarting and jealous after the interlude with Jack and I wanted her to see that people, even famous ones – hopefully – recognise me. We drove around the canyon but couldn't find the restaurant or the way out of the canyon, and I could see she didn't like to be anywhere near failure, especially her own. I tried to suggest another direction, but, losing face and her temper with it, she told me to shut up. I felt the relationship was as terminal as Jack's house, on the very edge of the canyon. One tremor would do it. I clung on with meek directions.

'Why can't you just sleep or something? It's because you're so rattled I keep losing the way. Mia always went to sleep in the car.'

It was a slap in the face and my turn to sulk. Of course she'd use her partially departed mistress as ammunition. I looked out at the glorious evening full of hurt and asked how the day had gone so wrong. But the day wasn't finished, as I soon found out when we arrived at another Italian restaurant, a lesser establishment in Marina del Rey. It was empty, expensive and I disliked it from the start. I couldn't bear the painted chairs and the overlaid tables, and said we should leave.

'But you've been demanding an Italian restaurant for the last two hours, making me drive round and round looking for somewhere that doesn't exist.'

'It does.'

'And now we're in an actual place, not an aberration in your head, and you want to leave.'

'I've eaten there several times.'

'But you don't know the name or the street. I drove over every inch of ground in those hills. If it was there I couldn't fail to find it. You made it up.'

I decided to get a cab to take me up there and call when I arrived. It was somewhere off Mulholland and Coldwater. Then I thought, maybe it's closed down.

There was nothing on the vast menu that looked trustworthy, and I ordered the simplest spaghetti with plain tomato sauce. I asked if the sauce was fresh or came out of a tin. The waiter said, 'Sure.' I nudged her to leave but she sighed and ordered minestrone soup.

'We have a very good house wine.'

'I don't drink.' At least I got that right.

The place was still empty and she in a distant mood. I didn't want a dessert and said I couldn't drink tea after Italian food. I waited, and then suggested I'd have a coffee, a weak one.

'Do what you like.'

I filled up with a thousand unshed tears, hurting, betrayed, I tried to tell her.

'I was only trying to help you, help you obviously don't want, Catherine.'

I'd hardly lifted the coffee cup when she jabbed with horror at the sleeve of the tan silk jacket.

'Oh, my God.' She stared, her eyes wider than I'd seen them, and I was ready for anything. Was there a tarantula hanging on to the cuff? Had I cut myself, my wrist? That could be next. Somehow, a sad clumsiness had lowered my arm too near the spaghetti plate and the generously shaped sleeve had dipped into the scarlet sauce. I grabbed a napkin, plunged it in water and started to rub at the offending stain.

'Don't,' she cried. 'Don't you dare make it worse.'

She grappled the jacket off my body and laid it reverently across the table. The waiter suggested we try salt. She suggested he bring the bill.

'There's a cleaner's near the hotel, it might just be open.' And she ran to the car carrying the jacket like an injured animal. 'It'll never be the same.'

I was helpless and humiliated. It was a horrific day. But underneath the pain was the thought: it's only a jacket. It's not a person, it's not me, the person she's supposed to love. She goes on as though the jacket is her lover and I am punished for a mistake I would never mean to make. If she really loved me she'd smother her disappointment over the jacket and be glad and grateful to be with me. It became a pattern – under the pain, a commentary that kept me alive.

The jacket was returned to the hotel hours later, wrapped in layered white tissue paper, giving it a respectful demise. The note attached read, 'Everything that could be done has been done. Twice. Sorry Ma'am.' The sauce stains on the sleeve looked like a map of Asia and in other circumstances would have made me laugh. I thought they were much improved and a cause for optimism, but not for a perfectionist. She looked at the sleeve briefly, then threw the jacket to me. 'It's yours.' Then she sat on the bed, her back to me, and started a long Russian phone call.

'I'm sorry, Elle.'

She did not acknowledge me and I laid the jacket back in its papery grave and covered its wounded arm with the white tissue paper. Then I walked out.

It was a beautiful soft night with a light breeze from the south as I paced backwards and forwards like a chained animal on the path near the main entrance. She could very well leave me. Could I leave her? I'd given my love, my very self. How could a jacket come before that? I got an occasional swift glance from the sane on their way out or in, and I deserved them, these glances which they chucked like cheap coins to a beggar. I found I couldn't go out of the gate, could not leave here because my absence, meagre and pointless in itself, would give opportunity for an absence which would be effective and possibly devastating. I realised I'd looked for an identity for her and now I had it. She was a lady who did not like stains.

Eventually, she found me sitting on the entrance step, head in hands, so unhappy I didn't care. She did.

'Get up. Don't let people see you like this.' She took the compact out of my bag, opened it and put it in front of my face. Tears blackened by mascara had made more stains, my lipstick had left my lips some time ago and was smeared under my nose. 'Sort it out.'

And she walked off amongst the trees into darkness, knowing I'd follow. I followed.

'You don't have to mope around with that long face and greasy hair. You look like a grey cloth.'

So I told her how I felt, the pain, the disappointment. She didn't care about that.

'Why didn't you wash your hair before you came down here? How can you sit on the step looking like this? It's a top Bel Air hotel, not a youth hostel.'

'You don't care about me.' Could it be true? I waited for her to disagree. 'How can a stained sleeve mean so much that you have to punish me? Why?'

'It was my jacket. You shouldn't have borrowed it if you can't take care of it.'

All the things that she'd so liked about me were now against me. I was no longer her child or the untidy artist, beyond the usual restrictions of society.

'What's a jacket, Elle? We're together.' When that obviously didn't mean too much, I added, 'I thought we shared our clothes. We share everything else.' I had worn her silk trousers and she my cashmere black shawl.

'I hate stains.'

'But you have twenty jackets.'

'Don't touch my clothes again.'

'I'll replace it. I'll buy you a new one.'

'You couldn't afford it.'

What were we really arguing about? I hadn't taken care of something that was hers, therefore showing I didn't take care of her? Or was she trying to find an excuse to go back to Mia?

'You're such a sight sitting on those steps. What do people think? They know you're with me, for God's sake.'

I wasn't hearing this. She had hurt me bitterly because of an action that surely was not important and, instead of comforting the pain, filling me with love, she now introduced an equally shallow issue, my untidy, stained grief, visible in a public place.

'Do these people you don't know,' I waved a hand at the assortment of hotel and staff by the entrance, 'mean more to you than me?'

'Oh, do cheer up. You must be getting your period. Yes, that's it. Now we'll go dancing.'

I tried to take her in my arms, I tried for one of those hugs that would numb all this, but she pulled away and off to the car. 'But I'm hurt because you've hurt me,' I shouted.

She turned hostile now. 'Surely you don't have to show the world you're in a bad mood. Snap out of it. Smile. Dance.'

She started the engine. I was a million miles from dancing.

'I don't give a shit about these people.' I was shouting again. 'I care about you and me and right now we're in trouble. All because of a few tomato stains. I said I'm sorry. How many times do I have to say it?'

'People are watching.'

'God, you're shallow.'

We went dancing and she was back as my – was it ally? Conspirator? Almost lover? She held my hand discreetly and rearranged my hair publicly. It had just been a bad day. That was all.

22

Whenever I woke up in the night she was awake. She lay there, not stirring, breathing lightly. Sometimes she'd be moving by the bed.

'What are you doing?'

'Getting some water. What else?'

I never heard her sleeping deeply or snoring or making sounds. She was as contained unconscious as she was when awake.

The mornings were still nice and friendly and she'd plan the day, a happy carefree one in which Casper Shulz and work did not occur. Breakfast was wheeled in and I now hesitated about the coffee, but she made no comment. She'd place the single flower from the trolley vase in my hair and blow a kiss. Then the interminable phone conversation in an unknown language began, its meaning impenetrable.

I'd shower, exercise, get the cameras loaded and the film ready for development. Her latest batch of cleaning would be hung in the closet and the maid would restock the bar. I think it was the sight of the miniature champagne bottle being slid into the fridge that provoked the thought – Jesus, what exactly does all this cost? The champagne bottle was hardly a big item but it sent a chill through me, as icy as the white, glistening receptacle it was going into.

The phone rang and I waited on the balcony. I took photographs, poured another coffee. The phone rang again.

'It's for you.'

I expected Jack. It was James.

'When are you coming back?'

'Look, as soon as I can. How is everything?'

'But you've been away four weeks.' He was very angry.

'Four? Three.'

'Four.'

Was it? Where had the extra week gone?

'I'll be back.' And, with insecure promises, I hung up. I was sure it was three weeks. I supposed it was being in love that made time, with her, disappear.

She was trying on a new jacket that had been altered to allow for longer sleeves.

'I hate sleeves that aren't quite long enough. Olav, for all his money, has suits made with sleeves that are too short. They're up to here.' She sliced a hand across a forearm. 'He's so mean. He's even mean to himself. Those little sleeves. How Mia laughs at them. And you don't have to talk to James like that.'

At first I didn't understand.

'Being so submissive. Why don't you tell him you're having a good time?'

I felt emotion like a huge wave leap inside me. Was it rage? Hurt? Humiliation? The result was anger.

'Don't listen in to my personal calls. Do I listen to yours?' The wave was huge, like the one in the Japanese painting which rose sky-high and would come crashing down, destroying everything. That wave was the end of the world. 'Do I criticise what you say on the phone?' Of course I didn't. To start with, I couldn't understand it.

'You're just a cloth when you speak to him. Men hate that.' She turned round. 'Do you like this jacket?'

If only I'd had an opened jar of tomato sauce. We'd been in the room too long. I choked on anger as I asked where we would have lunch. Yes, I would just chuck the sauce at her, and I imagined her standing there with scarlet, dripping sleeves. And then I noticed something quite irrelevant; she never wore red.

And then came the row. It began logically enough.

'I should phone James and speak in Polish for half an hour. How would you like it?' Heart thumping, I sat on the bed. 'You don't give us a chance.' She got the car keys and her minimal daily possessions. 'You're going back to her.' She sighed and swept back her hair. 'Well, how do I know you're not? She ruined that day in the hills. You're fighting with her to stay here. You did quarrel, didn't you?' She didn't answer. 'Hidden in that foreign dialogue? How can I tell? She's going to have her revenge.'

'Possibly.'

I didn't like her agreeing. What exactly would Mia do?

'Are you going to stay with me?' I felt the blood leave my face.

'She understands I need to do something,' and with that she'd reached the door.

'What about me? You never question how I feel. I'm just there, part of your world. Oh, I should be so lucky. I'm just there.'

She laughed and I was ready to hit her.

'You just do what you want. I'm not even part of it.'

'Drop that gloom bird, grey cloth shit. Who'll notice you like that?'

'They certainly notice you. Showing off to the plane staff about who I'd photographed. How cheap can you get?'

She laughed again, cynically this time. She was showing me it wasn't a row, just weakness on my part.

'You need to show yourself off. If you won't, I will. No wonder you're nowhere.'

'The rudeness to the guy in reception here. Is that being somewhere?'

'How is that a problem?' she said, roughly.

'It embarrassed me.'

'You embarrass easy.' She blew out her lips, couldn't be contemptuous enough. 'D'you think I want a little closet shrimp like him running my life? You're too thin-skinned.'

'You didn't ask how I felt about it, if I wanted that scene. You were out of order.'

'Mia would understand.'

I knew she'd say that.

'You just use me. You're pretending to make this film. It's got about as much reality as a photographic assignment with that movie star, Jewel. Remember her? In the foyer?'

'Of course.'

'Remember how you said you'd get Jewel to agree to be photographed?'

'Sure.'

'You put out a rough, cheap scene and you don't care what it does to me. Mia might understand it, but are you sure she can take it?'

'Mia's not a frightened little English half-star.'

'So why does she scream the place down and get the police at the door? Doesn't sound like someone who can take a lot.'

The only reaction she made was to walk to the window. In itself that was nothing, but the walk was too sustained and purposeful and didn't belong with anything else she did or was. It scared me. I realised I'd gone too far.

'Who told you?' Her voice was calm. This wasn't a row for her, yet.

I didn't care. I was going. I knew that.

'All the people in earshot.'

'You do mean the village, of course.'

'How many other places does she scream in?'

'Lily. That's who told you.'

Again I got my travelling bag down and stuffed it with clothes. 'It's just bullshit, all of it. There's no Casper Shulz.' I snapped the bag shut. 'I'm off.'

'Not when you're seeing Casper.'

'How many times have I heard that?'

She pointed down towards the main entrance, her finger long and jabbing. 'He's just getting out of his car.'

23

Casper Shulz's car was like a plane on wheels, silver with white and blue patterns where it reflected the sky. He was big and tanned with small, black sunglasses that showed only the reflections of what he was possibly seeing. He was off-hand, spoke German, and ignored me. Elle was the one he wanted to see. For my sake she tried to keep the conversation in English and then went off with him to play golf. Later, she told me he'd agreed to pay development costs and he'd find a distributor. He also wanted casting approval and would pay for a star.

I realised she hadn't given him my script and he hadn't asked for it. She fell back on the bed and kicked off her shoes. I wondered if she'd slept with him.

'I bring you good news and even that doesn't cheer you up.'

'I don't like being left out.'

'Oh, come on. Your trouble – you didn't have an older sister. Well, let's see if the next appointment makes you happier.'

The movie star, Jewel, was actually in the bar waiting, and Elle went straight up to her and started talking. The conversation was short and lively and caught every eye. At one point, Jewel looked over to me and smiled, but, for some reason, when I tried to join them, Elle shook her head very slightly and I knew to stay away. The barman brought me a Coke, two men collected the movie star and Elle stopped at a corner table and became involved in another, even livelier discussion. When she came to me, her cheeks were flaming.

'They're Russian, that group. But from Gdansk. That's not quite Moscow.' I noticed how, when under stress, her cheeks changed colour and those two patches appeared like overdone rouge.

'And her?'

'Oh, she'll do it. We'll set it up for Wednesday.' Her casual air was astounding. 'But she wants her PR there and her lighting man, and she has the final decision on what contacts are sent out and in fact wants all contacts and negatives handed over.'

Out of all of it I didn't feel good about the lighting man. But why pick on him when the deal was so impossible?

'Well, you're only just starting,' she said, airily, and, although I was such a novice, she took me across to show me off to the Russians from Gdansk.

I didn't like Casper Shulz but I didn't tell the agent in West Hollywood. Or that he'd ignored me. I found myself sitting in her hotel suite again, needing advice on the movie star's staff being too present at Wednesday's session and how much interference I could allow. She was waiting to hear something that made sense of her prediction that the night film would never happen. Otherwise she might as well stop being an agent.

'Is Casper Shulz asking for an option?'

'On?'

'The script of course.'

I didn't know, and returned to the more pressing subject of shooting Jewel.

'I don't believe that either,' said the agent.

I told her how Jewel was actually in the bar waiting for Elle and Elle went straight up and talked to her.

'I don't believe it,' she said again.

'But I saw Elle discussing the deal with her.'

'Saw. Did you hear it?'

Now I thought about it, I hadn't.

'They could have been talking about the weather.'

'You have it in for Elle so whatever I say –' I was beginning to dislike her. She was making my already questionable security doubtful.

'Jewel won't act in that film, if that's what you're thinking,' she said with satisfaction. She'd found something to be right about. I assured her it had never even been considered.

'She's got talking to Jewel on some pretext. Some remark about Tolstoy or something.'

'But she's offered me the deal.'

'Elle offered you the deal, but she knew you wouldn't do it. Not with those restrictions.'

Then I remembered the actress had looked at me and smiled. What else was Elle offering her?

'Okay, I will photograph her on Wednesday.' And I got up to go.

'You can't accept those conditions. And they don't expect to use your photographs and you won't get agreement to use them yourself, so what's the point? Elle knew you won't go for it. She just got talking to Jewel. Even stars have lonely moments and she made it look like a much bigger thing.'

And I remembered the quick, negative hand movement as I approached.

And then she used a nasty word to describe Elle. 'Psychopath. That's what they do. Get near to an important person and make a show of it to get some status. And they lie about what was said. Who can prove otherwise?'

'Why?'

'Power.'

'What is a psychopath?'

'You should know. You're living with one.'

I thought I should get home to James.

'I might still say yes to Wednesday.'

'Waste of time.'

'But what if the actress did say yes?'

She hesitated. 'She's one of the most photographed women in the world. They were talking about something else, I promise you.'

'But what if –'

'Then they're doing a favour for someone. Maybe.'

'I'll find out Wednesday.'

She walked down with me to the entrance and I thought about the roof and the sunbather we'd quarrelled about.

'Is she still up there? By the pool? That Mediterranean-looking girl?'

'No. She's disappeared.'

I thought disappeared was a big word.

'A couple of people came to ask for her. She was gone between a night and a day.'

*

I asked when I'd do the photo session because I was going to challenge her.

Calmly, she said, 'I told you. Wednesday.'

'And she really is all right about it?'

'She is. Are you?'

'How did you get to her, Elle?'

'I want you to get ahead. Didn't I hear you say you can't have people around? That doesn't sound like you're all right about the session.'

'I'm fine.'

'By the way, she has to be photographed out of doors and they choose the locations.'

'I'll do it,' I said simply.

'That's fine then.' And she went on eating the snapper and salad. She didn't seem to have a problem. She talked about Casper and how he'd come from a fishing family in the north of Finland.

'Why speak German?'

'His mother is German. You *are* a Sherlock Holmes!'

Then she described how he'd made a first fortune selling paint door-to-door. It seemed a mundane thing to do but Finland in the old days was under-populated and had been frequently ignored by the rest of the world. Things taken for granted in trendier countries were a novelty there. 'No one had seen a door-to-door paint salesman. I remember the first pizza. I think he had something to do with that as well. He educated himself, got a place at university, started a pharmaceutical company and made a second fortune selling pills. He started marrying society heiresses and entertainers.' She listed them. All the time I wondered, how had she convinced that A-list movie star to wait for her in the bar? And how did she sell me? I even wondered if it was the movie star at all, but someone who looked like her. But why go to all that trouble to make me feel good? Or was it to prove Elle had power and meant what she said? She delivered.

'Then he got bored and started climbing mountains and was the first to balloon over Everest. And now he's planning to walk across a desert in China.' She said he was over seventy, and I had to agree he looked good for seventy.

'By the way, they'll only agree to your photographing Jewel if it's cloudy weather. She doesn't look good in bright sunshine. It casts too many shadows.'

In a city of constant sun, how could I do it?

'How did you get to her? I don't remember you saying.'

'I persuaded her you could bring out a new quality in her. They like that. I said her photographs always make her so available. Also of course I spent a lot of time walking around the hotel with Casper. No one's so rich and so up they don't need more money. And by the way, they want a special lens and no close-ups.'

24

As the days went by Elle was still impatient and angry if I didn't let her touch me in public. It was as though she could make a show for the street but nothing much happened in the bedroom. She left me alone and, in the end, I asked if she actually wanted to be my lover.

'You know I do.'

I told her it wasn't so much the homosexual aspects of lovemaking that held me back, but small oddnesses. I told her the truth because that was what had been decided at the beginning. Our love would be based on truth. The truth was her eyes had once had strange corridors leading back endlessly and the hug was anaesthetic and strangely sweet. It was how I imagined poison, but I didn't add that.

An expression I hadn't seen before changed her face, eyes stricken, not at ease, but she recovered quickly. She tapped me under the chin. 'You're just trying to find reasons not to do it. You'll be wanting it one day, sure I can give you pleasure, and that will be that.' Then she asked if I had sex with James.

'Rarely.'

'There you are. You're supposed to be with a woman.'

And then I told her how I could never keep a sexual relationship going for long. 'I seem to be childish and turn the guy into a mother.'

'At least this time you got it right.'

But she wasn't a mother. A stepmother was quite a different thing. I asked if she'd wanted a child.

'It just didn't come my way. But I've got Dag, my stepson, and he's closer to me than a natural child.' She sprayed her hair with styling mist, smoothed it back and wanted to go out. The motherhood story was at an end and I thought a lot was left unsaid.

'I love being with you, Catherine,' and she put her arm through mine as we walked down to the foyer. The manager, smiling, opened the door for us.

'Have a good day.' It was a day of smiles.

It was a superb day, the sort I remembered from my childhood, brilliant sky with friendly, pure white clouds, a soft scented breeze. Out of sheer pleasure, she stopped at the first shop and bought me a green silk waistcoat.

'If we get this blue sky on Wednesday, you'll be out of luck.' She sounded completely truthful. How wrong could that malicious agent get? 'You'll wear the waistcoat with a dark shirt.' She held up another waistcoat against my chest. 'D'you want it as well?'

She tried on a shirt and cap but in the end bought only the waistcoat. She always knew exactly what she wanted. As she handed over the credit card she had a good idea. 'Let's go down to the marina, hire a boat, have a picnic.'

'Anything else, ma'am?'

She shook her head and the card was placed on the machine. It didn't just bounce. It seemed to jump and fly up in the air like a bird escaping from a cage. At first she laughed and tried to catch it. It fluttered out of reach and lay on the counter on its back, dead.

The assistant blamed herself immediately. 'I'm so sorry, ma'am. It seems there's something wrong. Have you another card?'

Elle spent a full minute looking at the card lying flat and lifeless on the counter. I felt her head was full of thoughts. Then she brushed it away like a dead insect. She took out another card from the small wallet, one I'd seen her use to hire the car. She was unusually silent as the shop assistant muttered suggestions for this imperfect sale. Perhaps passing through the airport check too many times? The scanner often rendered cards ineffective. 'I can see you travel a lot, ma'am.'

The second, less extravagant-looking card paused on the machine and I could see Elle's eyes watching it dully. For the first time she was unnerved. It didn't fly about like the other one, just lay there and became extinct. She produced a third. This one didn't just lie there or fly, it virtually exploded. Elle turned to me.

'You pay for it.'

I didn't want the waistcoat, but I didn't want her to be embarrassed. I agreed with the assistant that going through security checks at airports was murder on cards. Mine stayed alive and I walked out with the waistcoat, which cost nearly half of what I'd made on my one assignment in Hollywood.

'What's the problem exactly?' I asked once we got outside. Not answering, she walked swiftly back to the hotel. 'Are we going to get the boat?' I didn't believe there was a real problem; I thought the cards must have failed because of some hiccup in the system. She walked with sustained rage to the room and went straight to the phone.

'They've cut the line.' The message button was blinking scarlet. She lay down on the bed and the phone rang. 'Don't answer it,' she said and put an arm across her eyes.

'There is a problem,' I said, as part of it, the manager, came knocking on the door.

'Don't let him in. Let me think,' she said, harshly.

But he was inside already, the passkey in his hand. He looked at her as though he'd been saving up for this moment from the day he first saw her.

'Your credit just ran out, Miss von Zoelen.'

She sat up. 'Did I give you permission to walk into this room? I don't remember it.'

'What other arrangement are you going to make?'

Coldly, she said, 'When I've decided I'll let you know.'

'Your credit ran out at 11.50 and it's gone noon, so you owe for the cost of the room until noon tomorrow, and the cost of the items in the mini-bar –'

'Oh, do shut up.'

'Your credit stopping was very sudden.' He sounded almost in awe.

'Get back to your office and reconnect this phone.'

He had a lovely time telling her he would not, it was against the rules, and if she didn't reinstate her credit line she must leave the hotel. First she must pay the nightly rate and again he said it was after noon. She turned to me.

'Is he a talking clock?'

'You can no longer use the services in the hotel.'

Finally she got rid of him and turned to me. 'Can you pick up this bill?'

One night here was more than I spent in a week in London. I agreed immediately and asked how else I could help. She felt in her pockets for money.

'Go and pay and we'll get out of here. We'll go to the cheap hotel where your agent friend stays, in West Hollywood.'

'Oh no,' I said, immediately thinking of the sunbather.

'Phone her to get us a room. She must be there on a special rate. Use your credit card for the booking. You'll have to use the phone downstairs. I'll pay you back.'

I didn't think my credit card extended that far, but I'd rather have slept on the beach than be in a room below that heaving, heavy-titted rival roasting on the roof. Then I remembered she'd disappeared. With my luck she could as easily reappear.

'I'm going to find a phone and make some calls. Pack your stuff.'

I'd had plenty of practice at that. She was gone an hour while I folded and rolled the extravagance of clothes – I now needed an extra travel bag. How I disliked the waistcoat, its shrill green reminding me of jealousy! And of course I knew who was behind the crisis. Mia had not got her way and now had her revenge.

Disapproving staff entered insolently and took the champagne from the bar and the luxury basket from the bathroom. The maid, suspecting she would never be tipped, started to strip the bed.

She came back, cheeks inflamed beyond red, and said we'd get a taxi to the West Hollywood hotel. Immediately, I asked what had happened to the credit line.

'One or two little problems. Nothing I can't sort out.' Skilfully, she packed her things in less than five minutes.

'It's Mia, isn't it? Because you won't go back.'

'Never mind the cause. I have to deal with the result.' She lifted the phone to call for a porter but it was still not connected. 'Go down and pay, and ask them to send a porter. Call a taxi.'

'Taxi? Why not the car?'

'Oh, there's a stop on that.'

So I had a good idea. 'Casper. Development money.'

'He's for just here, Catherine. My problem is everywhere else.'

'Why can't you tell me what's happened? I am with you, after all.'

'It's unusual. Let's leave it at that.'

*

We got out of there and the prissy clerk allowed himself a laugh which I thought I'd hear in my grave. In retrospect, I should have let her make the long calls to Mia even longer.

The first thing she did at the new hotel was get on the phone. Politely, I asked her to keep it minimal, as my credit card could easily resemble hers. I considered asking James for money, but then I remembered the mortgage repayment promise. Wasn't that why I was here? Again I asked if Casper could pay up the development money now.

'Casper's abroad.'

'But if he agreed –'

'His lawyer has to draw up the contract. That can take weeks.' And she got back on the phone, nuzzled the mouthpiece with long foreign words. I went up to the roof to check who was there and not there. When I came down she said, 'Change of plan. We're to fly to Washington. Let's go.'

Her stepson, Dag, was in Washington.

*

The driver took the freeway to the airport although she told him to dip down by Marina del Rey. He wasn't speaking English, didn't understand it, until she thumped the back of his window. He turned surly and rough.

'D'you want to drive this hack, lady?'

'D'you want the police to put you over the line? You're illegal. Go down Doheny and take a left, then all the way to the coast.'

Sighing, he turned and did as she said.

'Does it really matter?' I asked. 'Compared with everything else?'

She started on him again because he was going too slow. 'Put your foot on it and keep it on.'

25

She checked into a five-star hotel in Washington and said that the President of the United States had stayed here. I asked what was wrong with the White House?

'Before he moved in. When he was President-elect.'

The porter slipped the key card into the lock and opened the heavy door on to real luxury. It was the grandest hotel I'd been in or imagined. She waved at the bouquets. 'Take them out. My friend is allergic.'

'I'm not.'

'You look as though you could be.'

She took a sparkling water from the fridge and went straight to the phone. I stopped her.

'Can we sort out what's happening? I'm in this too.'

'Mia's cleaned me out.'

I sat beside her on the bed.

'She's emptied the bank accounts.'

'Why?' I didn't need to ask that. 'Is she furious with me?'

'She's furious with me. At some tender moment I must have been very weak, because I made the accounts in our joint names.'

Again I asked why.

'In case anything happened to me. She'd get nothing.' She sighed. 'My sweet ex-husband and his family would see to that.'

'But what about Olav? Doesn't he keep you?'

'He's pulled the plug too. She's gone to him with a sad story. They're smoking me out, trying to get me to go home.'

'Does Olav have to listen to Mia?' I couldn't put what I'd seen of her together with a multimillionaire who never stopped travelling and had his suits made with too short sleeves.

'He's found out I'm with you. Casper probably told him. And he's got a soft spot for Mia.'

It all pointed one way – towards parting. I was exhausted, close to tears.

'I'm going to see Dag.' And she picked up the phone at last. 'You wait here and rest and then we'll go out to dinner.'

'But aren't we going back to LA?'

'Doesn't look like it right now.'

'But what about the session with Jewel and –'

She couldn't shrug big enough. 'Hack work. Waste of your talent. You don't need to take their photographs. You need them in front of the camera doing your film.'

'Will you have to go back to Spain then?' My heart sank faster than the evening sun.

'I'll sort out Olav. He'll be all right. He's just got his head in a muddle. Emotions are not his thing. I must call Dag.'

Finally she dialled a number and had a silky conversation with her financial saviour. After a whirlwind of preparation she still wasn't ready. The shoes didn't match the jacket. She wasn't sure if she would wear a skirt. For a short ten minutes she had a crisis of outer identity.

'He likes me feminine but sporty. Most men like me sporty.' She tried on several scarves, a shirt. I offered her the green waistcoat which had announced our impending disaster. She slicked back her hair, lit a long brown cigarette, and opened the door. 'Oh, give me a hundred. Just till I sort it out with him.' She looked in the mirror and took off the scarf. I didn't have quite a hundred dollars. 'Get some room service, all you want. Use the phone. We'll go out to dinner.' She blew a kiss and was gone.

It was perhaps a mistake, but I phoned Mia because I disliked the feeling of helplessness, hanging around waiting, unable to do my part in putting things right. After all, it was my life too. She sounded shakier than I'd heard before. I wanted to explain we were going to do the short film and she would be in it but I didn't get that far.

'This is between Ellie and me.' Her voice was smoked out, she had difficulty breathing.

'How can we do this film if the money –'

'Catherine, I told you before, you don't understand. Get out of it.'

So I got angry and told her she was a jealous, vengeful bitch and Elle was mine.

'Then pay for it,' she said, sarcastically, and hung up.

I phoned back immediately, but she didn't answer, so I phoned Lily who was thrilled by the new liaison. She was also shaking, but from excitement.

'You did go off with her, didn't you? The whole village has been taking bets on it –'

'We're working together.'

'Of course, of course.'

'Making a film, Lily, we've got backing.' And I mentioned Casper Shulz.

'I've seen him. He's been here.'

So I mentioned Jewel. I knew she hadn't been there.

'I do miss you. You livened up the place, from the very moment you came here. It's like you turned a switch on. I could tell there was something that first evening between you and her, but I never thought you'd run off together.'

'What's Mia been doing?'

'Living it up. That huge round bath filled with bubbles and men and her in the middle with champagne and strawberries. And he came down, the old man.'

'Olav?'

'Very concerned looking.'

'When?'

'Two nights ago: maybe three. I don't know what she did to him but he wasn't in the mood for bubbles and baths, I can tell you. I saw him leave. He looked ten years older. Serge got the grocer's shop, by the way.'

I said I was pleased. Then I remembered to ask who was behind it financially.

'Who do you think? Madame.'

There were various calls from men with Russian and French accents and they left names, numbers, and then Mia rang. I asked how she got the number.

'Ellie gave it to me.'

So they were already talking and, not only that, on good terms.

'You don't need to ring,' I told her, 'I'll sort this out.'

She laughed, the sound awash with drink and pills.

'There are other ways to make films. Like getting backing from a studio –'

'Poor Catherine.'

'I did work before I met Elle, you know. We'll do this film.' And I described something poor and honest while catching sight of my surroundings, which were not poor and possibly not honest. So Mia was back. Had she ever gone?

I lay waiting for this rich-poor lover I could not live without. I seemed to exist in an opera these days: very high, ecstatic, or the opposite. I wasn't sure I could handle the low notes. I should phone James. I should tell the agent in West Hollywood I'd left. So I phoned Mia again and tried to placate her, to persuade her to give back the money, to let me go on living.

She cut through that with, 'You can't have Ellie.'

Had I, in all this extravagant froth, said I wanted her?

Three hours later, Elle romped into the suite.

'Get ready, quick! He hates to be kept waiting.'

I jumped up and put my arms around her, holding her. 'If you go anywhere, promise I can come with you.' I would have the affair with her now, the wedding night, the gay virginity offered and taken, but she was after more mundane things, and also in a hurry.

I'd do anything to be with her.

'Cancel him. See him tomorrow.'

Cut and dried, she replied, 'Try this on,' and chucked over the green waistcoat. Had she heard even a word I'd said? I asked how long we were staying there.

'How do I know?' She sat on the bed. 'Maybe we'll go to New York with Dag. A lot of my friends are there. It'll be clubs and parties –'

The last thing I wanted. 'But can we go back to LA and to the film?'

'Of course we can. We must.' She got the script out of the bag. 'Let's give it to Dag for his opinion.'

'Why Dag? You should have given it to Casper. Surely that would have been more sensible in the circumstances?'

'Casper doesn't read anything. Hasn't time.'

If I didn't get back to LA we wouldn't do this film and we'd be separated. I was determined to go back. 'I can ask my friend Lou for a loan. She's doing well. There's a book of her photography –'

Then she got a good idea – for her. 'Let's do it in New York. That's a city.'

And I wasn't sure any more that she cared about this film, had ever cared. Work was not what this was about. The only question – why was she with me?

26

Dag greeted me with great formality. It was dislike at first sight for both of us. After an initial assessing look, he dismissed me. After that, his restless eyes roved the room, making sure nothing was missed that he could use. I found him arrogant and disappointing. I wasn't what he'd expected.

He was weak. Even in that dark room filled with the late-night fun élite of Washington, his character was obvious. If I were studying him for a portrait session, I'd say he was degenerate and the weakness had always been there and that no amount of money or acquired power could get rid of it. A stylish crowd pushed towards our table and greeted him. A live band took care of the entertainment and killed off any chance of conversation. The food was indiscernible and, to make sure we knew we'd eaten something, it was covered in chilli paste.

Elle played up to him, amused him, agreed with him, teased him, flattered him. Was she mad? I decided she was playing up to him for his connections or to get back at his father. Then I knew it was for money and I wondered where her huge personal inherited fortune had gone.

She did try to build me up and at least she kept everything in English and even gave him the script which his long pale hands had hardly the strength to hold.

'So you met Jewel?' He was amused and spoke as though he knew her personally. 'Did you,' he paused and remembered I was present, 'go around with her?' This was not how he intended to conclude his question. He ruffled through the script's pages as though shuffling cards, and let it fall from his fingers on to the table.

'Are you going to read it?' I asked.

'What? In a nightclub?' He made a lot of the laugh.

'I meant, do you intend to read it?' That wasn't what I wanted to say. He was making me inadequate and very ordinary. I wanted to say, 'Piss off. Give it back.'

And then he started a story about Mia dancing naked across the tables in Cannes.

'God, she's incredible! What a body! There's nobody like her when she's on form. She got them so high they were up on the tables with her. I must ring her. Is she in Helsinki?'

'At the house.' Her tone was flat and gave nothing away.

His eyes dwelt on a black girl in a white sequin dress that covered her body like a skin. 'She'll be fun.' Elle turned quickly and looked at her. He slithered up until he was standing and Elle stroked his silk trousers.

'Let's pick her up,' he said, 'and really go clubbing. We can go smart or slum. Your choice. Oh, look, I like her,' and he waved languidly at a green-haired waif in the doorway. 'We'll have her as well.' He liked a lot of people, but not me.

I grabbed back the script and Elle nudged me and with a head movement indicated that I put it back.

'It's the only copy,' I lied.

'She'll never have an only copy,' he said, insolently.

Turning to Elle I stuck to the lie. 'I must photocopy it. I'll give it to Dag tomorrow.'

'Perhaps she thinks I'm not up to the job of making a critical assessment of that piece of work.' As he moved from the table he said, ' "Oh, the toil we lost and the spoil we lost and the excellent things we planned, belong to the woman who didn't know why, and now we know she never knew why and did not understand." ' He waited to see what I made of it. 'Rudyard Kipling, in case you didn't know.' I didn't know. 'I got a first in literature. I'd better quote something better, but with less immediate point. "What might have been and what has been, point to one end, which is always present. Footfalls echo in the memory, down the passage which we did not take, towards the door we never opened, into the rose garden." T.S. Eliot.' His voice was cutting and precise, however much he drank.

He went over to the green-haired waif and picked her up, and I told Elle I wanted to leave and she must come with me. She shrugged.

'Impossible.'

'But he hates me.'

'Don't be silly. He's just jealous.'

'Of?'

'He can see I'm mad about you.'

'Are you?'

'You must know that.' And she stroked my cheek, her expression sensual, irresistible, and I felt a leap of erotic response. The next moment, I was in her arms and inside her embrace and her lips moved hard against my neck. I was filled up, made numb. I hadn't had that hug for a time.

As he came back with the girls he ruffled my hair. He'd seen the hug and apparently liked it, his eyes were slits of approval. And it occurred to me that was why she'd done it, to excite him.

'The black one's for you,' he told Elle, 'and Catherine and I will make a threesome with Green.'

I pinched her, pulled her, but she insisted on staying with Dag. 'So he picks up girls for you. Does he watch? Join in?' I had to stay with her, which meant staying with him, and the rest of the night was taken up with clubs and more girls, dancing, drugs and drink. As we left the final club, Dag realised it was dawn. He looked at the distant sunrise as though afraid of it.

'Jesus. I've got to start work in two hours.'

'Well, let's go on somewhere else,' said Elle. 'There's no point stopping now.'

He hesitated, then got into his car, a baby version of Casper's, and drove with difficulty. 'Christ, if they catch me.'

'You've got diplomatic immunity,' she reminded him.

'Not from my father. Good old Stephan.'

I asked where he worked and she told me the Finnish Embassy.

He found a run-down place in the bad area. I was still on Coca-Cola and switched to mineral water. They switched to vodka and Coke and he rolled a spliff.

'We should have Mia here,' he said. 'She lives in the moment and she makes the moment last.'

'Yes, I love that about Mia,' she said.

I couldn't believe it and sat, not important to anyone, not wanted and never would be again. I was aborted out of life in that moment. That's what a moment could mean to me.

'What I really need is –' and he mimed snorting coke. 'That'll sober me up.' And he looked around for a supplier, his face pale and shadowed. Elle looked as immaculate as she had when we'd started out. Her face was glowing and wholesome like an apple, the best apple in the barrel. He lifted the script from the bag.

'I'll read it today.'

'Perhaps you're too clever. I thought you'd got a first in political science, not literature.'

'I got a first in literature at Oxford, and then a first in political science at Johns Hopkins.'

'And you've also got a first in life-building,' she said, holding his dank hands. 'That's what you are. A life-builder.' And she didn't even look pissed.

I had a coffee but exhaustion made me quit the game and I went back to the hotel and fell across the bed, passed out in every part of me, except the one deep piercing point of consciousness that insomniacs have to suffer. I felt so earthbound and ordinary. That's how they made me feel. I couldn't move and the maid hovered round me at first, thinking I was dead.

Elle came back much later and closed the curtains quietly, hoping I was asleep.

'You've been screwing with that black girl.'

'Jesus.' She fell on the bed.

'He finds girls for you, doesn't he?'

She patted me. 'Everyone's so jealous.'

'Where's your money?' Now I could sit up.

'Oh, don't start a drama now.'

'The money from your anarchic Russian grandmother. Remember her?' She was falling asleep. I shook her.

'It's tied up. It takes a bit of time to get it.'

I'd take her money and make the film. I'd use her. That's what I'd do. It didn't take away the love or the pain of that love.

*

'The time. Shit. What time is it?'

I could hear her voice but I was in a black place with no light, no boundary, no hope.

'I have to meet Dag. He's downstairs waiting for me. Where's the light?'

There was no light and never would be. The blackness was beyond measure or limit and, having once known light, I longed for it, but wouldn't it be preferable to accept the dark, forget the light and so be spared pain? As though in answer, a shaft of light pierced the dark and my eyes were open. I realised they'd been open all the time, it was just that the place I'd been in was black beyond redemption. Was it simply a hotel room with the curtains closed and night outside?

'It's the ball tonight. I'm Dag's guest.'

A rushing sound in my ears. Wings? Water? She'd got the bedside light on and it streamed into the interminable dark and turned it bright, and I was now in a safe place with the bad experiences part of dreams given over to memory, to be forgotten.

'Elle, I've got this rushing thing in my ears.'

She was cleaning her teeth, clacking along the rail of her clothes, and trying to listen to her messages.

'What shall I wear? It's after ten. It has to be long. Royalty will be there. I'm Dag's partner and I'll be presented, but I know them anyway.'

What day was it? What had happened to the day? I felt cold. A rushing sensation filled my head. I was Dag's guest in a hotel once frequented by a US president. That did nothing for any of it.

'Am I supposed to come as well?'

She hesitated. I was not.

'I don't want to be left alone.' And I didn't.

'You don't have to shout.'

'But I can't hear.' I sat forward on the bed, my hands pressed against my ears. Everything in my head was black and mournful and not normal, racing towards catastrophe. 'I've got this rushing feeling –'

'Exhaustion. A virus. Stay in bed.' She couldn't think of anything else and carried on dressing.

'Am I ill? Is that it?'

She shrugged. She didn't go much for illness.

'Then stay with me, Elle.'

'What am I supposed to do? Put on a nurse's uniform and sit around a bedside, and miss Dag's ball? He's arranged it.'

The words were mean and probably meant to hurt, but the voice saying them was, as always, colourless, a tawdry voice. It reminded me of an artificial flower, false and dusty.

'Look, I'll phone you,' and she went on about room service and the endless calls I could make. I could even go out and see Washington. The phone rang and she spoke joyfully in German.

'Casper's come to get me. Would you believe it? He's held up his trip just for me.'

I knew once she had been thrilled by me. The novelty had worn off. She drank from the mineral water bottle and took some headache pills.

'D'you want a coffee? A hot drink?' It was incomprehensible to me that someone could spend all night drinking, most of the day sleeping it off, and then jerk awake in shock with a hangover and hurry off into the night on a sip of water. Well, yes, I'd done it, but only to the off-licence for more drink.

'You should know I don't drink coffee.'

This was the first time she was going to leave me. This was a big change, the beginning of separation, and all because Mia stole the money. Outside forces, not us, had made the rift.

She changed clothes again, swearing in Russian, and I now got it, reality. I was no longer the most important person in her world. She was no longer in love with me. How did I get out of the country, passion, depression and possible near-collapse? I lay back on the bed and the wings in my ears beat in protest. I understood how rich, aged husbands feel, who, having given everything to their young adored wives, have to watch them leave on a pretext for a night of sin and face the loneliness, the rejection that money can't save them from, then death.

Finally dressed, she impulsively lay on top of me and kissed my cheek. I needed the nearness and clung to her.

'It was a good time, wasn't it?' she said. 'Dag can certainly have a good time and share it. That's what I love about him.'

'Love?'

'He's a life-builder.' And she put her arms around me and squeezed. Then the phone rang and she jumped up, took an apple, bit into it, grabbed a jacket and with a wave of her hand, the whole apple stuck in her mouth, was gone.

Survival. First pray for strength, then drink water, order a hot drink, some food, get washed, get on the next plane to London. Pray for sanity. Drink and drugs had put me here many times and I knew the routine, but I wasn't as young-muscled as I used to be.

I phoned Jack in LA and he said, 'She's a killer. You'll never win with her. Never.'

'What shall I do?'

'Get out.' He paused. 'If you can.'

I asked what he meant. I didn't like the sound of it.

'Get out now. Go to the airport.'

'I haven't the strength.'

'Everyone's got that last drop left to get to an airport. We can all do that.' And he talked me through it, packing the bag, putting the cab expense on her hotel bill, getting cash, also on her bill from the front desk, for the travel expenses, food, taxi in London. 'Phone James. He might meet you.'

'I'm booked for tomorrow.'

'Go now or you'll never leave.' His voice was rusted from cigarette smoke. 'Don't leave a note.'

Her face, its beauty, stabbed into my consciousness until it was all I could see. I wouldn't leave. I'd see her one more time.

'I'll go tomorrow.'

'Too late. But okay. Order a meal, then another one, a better one, and put on some music, something calm and rational – Bach. There you are. Pack quickly. Then I'd watch some TV. It'll get you through the night.' He was worried I'd drink.

'Why is she doing this? She's ruining everything good we had.' The advertisement for Coca-Cola kept winking on and off opposite the hotel and I was afraid to think another thought, it was too scary to allow, so I kept on talking. 'Is it because we haven't done the film and she's disappointed? Did she think I had more influence? Is that it?'

He laughed, and paid for it with several minutes of coughing. 'Don't start being deceitful. Not to yourself. You've always been honest and you need to rely on that. You know she can't make a movie.'

'But she's the producer.'

'No, honey. You know what she is.'

I didn't. I said she was an heiress.

'She's a working girl.'

The thought I'd tried to avoid presented itself, and I saw myself walking across the floor towards the winking Coke sign and just going on towards it, up to the window and continuing through the air towards the lighted sign. Did I want to kill myself? Jump from a window? Could pain take me that far? I wasn't going to really leap across space and hold on to the sign, be part of 'Drink Cola' blinking colourfully. No, I'd walk sustained and without sense of space or touch, like sleep walking, and the floor and the space outside the window would be the same. What the hell had that impulse been about? And I remembered how she walked with sustained power, frightening in its intensity, to a window in the LA hotel when I said something that upset her. Not part of anything.

Jack was still talking me through the next minute.

'I'm not a lesbian, Jack.'

'Does it matter?'

'But I'm in love with her. If I have sex with her will I only get turned on by women, or what?'

'It's not about that.'

'I don't want to be gay. What do you mean, it's not about that?'

'If she wanted you sexually you'd have been had by now. She's not into that. She wants power.'

If I just tried to make love to her, would that keep her? I'd try and get it over with. She'd come in and –

'Make sure you win, Cathy. That means don't lose to her.'

And I knew what I'd do.
Cinderella got to the ball.

*

She was sitting in the noisy banqueting room in the far corner and her eyes lifted as I walked through the forest of tables to get to her, the plain clothes security guard behind me, the official one in uniform watching from the entrance. It was a formal affair in this gracious building – not the White House, but good enough. Her eyes met mine and I sensed her disquiet. She hadn't expected this. Then she smiled and was as she should be.

'What a surprise.' She got up and reached out for me to join her and Dag asked for another chair. I was introduced to Casper again, a senator from Wisconsin and various foreign and American important people that I forgot as soon as I saw them. They were finishing dessert and I accepted a mousse.

'I didn't call you,' she said, 'because it's so boring. So many speeches.'

Casper asked her to dance and she got up and, hidden from the group, whispered, 'How the fuck did you get in?'

'I told them I was your lover. You've got plenty of company, they said.'

'Smile and don't do that grey cloth jealous act ...' In turn she smiled at the guests and told them how famous I was in photography, and I'd heard it all before on the plane to LA. If only I could stop loving her.

I watched her dancing and saw that a lot of other people watched her too. She was superbly confident, but it didn't stop there. She had a touch of danger and could take it further. She didn't just want to be admired, that was too easy. She wanted – what did someone who had everything want? I almost had the answer when Dag spoke.

'You're good at getting into places.'

I looked at his pale eyes, turquoise in this light, and had nothing to say.

'They've got security here, after all.'

'I said I was with you. And it was a matter of life and death.'

'Well, it would be,' he said simply. 'They came and asked me if you could come in, and I said yes.'

For some reason I thanked him.

Elle and Casper were now the centre of attention and the other dancers were applauding their display of tap-dancing. She wanted to confront reality, the normal, that was what she did, travel to the existence beyond ...

'He must have had lessons with Fred Astaire. Well, he's old enough,' said Dag. 'He'll bust open that sheep cell-filled heart if he tries to keep up with her.'

The tap-dancing speeded up and became jitterbug and the band fitted in with this impromptu performance.

'She goes to the edge,' I said to myself.

Dag heard and said, 'She doesn't go to the edge. She is the edge.'

The applause was all she could want, and Casper bowed, thinking it was over and tried not to flop into the nearest chair. But she was doing the charleston, fast beyond belief, and I hurried across to Casper to ask him to dance. I was determined to be at least a part of this. If he knew me he didn't show it, and stood with the others to watch Elle. She got a roar of approval and someone important approached her and took her hand, and they started to waltz together. It was Cinderella after all, I thought, as the audience moved forward for a better look, photographers got busy and then Casper pushed past me to get near her and trod on my foot roughly. I cried out but, oblivious, he stayed, his foot still heavily on mine, and he seemed to stamp all over me before shoving in front to reach Elle and be part of her success. All the while I expected the huge double doors of the banqueting room to sweep open, and something horrible to come in. Something so awful I couldn't imagine it. She was off in a swirl of distinguished partners while I was waiting for this dark thing to come. As I left, I caught a glimpse of her face, composed and not even perspiring as she was held in the arms of a young prince.

27

James said, 'You look terrible.'

Coming round the hedge, up the untidy path to the front door, was like coming down from a sacred mountain that I'd never find again, into the grey rough of everyday. The colours seemed duller than I remembered, and the smells were more acrid and nauseous.

James opened the door, his face a pale thin dart in the gloom, and Daisy jumped into my arms. There were more boxes of books in the hall and the dust was thicker. He leaned forward to kiss me and I made sure his lips missed mine and met my cheek.

'No. You look tragic.' He put the kettle on and then smiled, warm and pleased. 'It's good to see you, Cathy.'

And I remembered when I'd loved him. It was a good, true smile, his eyes bright and challenging. His smiles grew out of pleasure. James knew all about excitement and how to arouse. Even in my exhausted state, I could see how attractive he was, and other people saw it too. They'd be fighting to stand in my shoes if I didn't do something about it. Was I mad? Play the wife, don't lose him, I told myself.

He gave me strong, black coffee and I thought of that other coffee in the deli, that fatal day when Elle and I had our first quarrel. As an atonement for my disastrous self-will, I asked him to water the coffee down and add milk. I asked if there'd been any calls, and then I told him there could be no improvement in the mortgage deficit for now.

'I rather got that impression.'

My head was tumbling with images, scraps of conversation, bitter sorrow. I'd had my stab at enchantment and failed. Now I'd have to get by on a photographer's nightmare – weddings.

I left the table and went upstairs to lie down.

'Are you limping?' he asked.

My foot was swollen and cut from Casper's brutal stampede to be Elle's next partner. I soaked a flannel with cold water, wiped it over my face and lay on the bed, the flannel cooling my head, too exhausted to move. The wings were still rustling in my ears but I heard James's feet softly coming up the stairs and, as I listened, I understood I had been one thing and now I was quite another.

*

I worked on my marriage and when Elle came into my thoughts I blotted her out. I murdered her a thousand times by denying her existence. For the next few weeks I gave my marriage the best I had.

James's life had changed very little since my arrival. He filled his time from the moment he got up with private activities – writing, reading, walking the dog on the Heath, tutorials. He was available to his students whenever they needed him and he was kind to them, almost motherly. His life was simple, ordered, and he chose frugality. Left alone, he always had a good day and I was surprised he could feel so good on so little. He tried to achieve a state of balance, especially with me. When I first asked if he loved me, he'd said, 'More than you realise.'

'A lot? A little?'

'Enough.'

He came into a room and brought calm. It was almost medicinal. His voice was soft and distinct, without affectation, not even any American influence in spite of the years he'd spent there. It was a classless, seductive voice.

Now I worked on my marriage by giving him time. I dressed up, made up, went with him to his favourite café on the Finchley Road, frequented by mid-European refugees from the late Thirties and Forties, or to the Czech club in West Hampstead, or to see old films at the Everyman cinema. Evenings with his university friends that I used to avoid so I could go and photograph the city became part of my life. Some people said I'd never seemed better. I played the game. And I photographed weddings. I walked and talked and listened and cleaned, cooked, shopped and thought I was going mad. I wanted to die. And she'd surface in my mind and I'd plead with God to take her away, to roll back time so I had never set eyes on her. Give me back yesterday and I'd never have climbed the evil hill of that fortress village in Spain. There was one moment when I might have gone too near the railway bridge. The pain was unmerciful. Yes, I was drawn to that solution but for the dog, Daisy, the whimper she made, and the way her eyes stayed on mine.

Then James wanted me physically and I hugged him, but unlike her hugs they didn't keep him still. I was beyond caring about 'intimate', too intimate, 'platonic'. Those were old worries, times had changed and I was now gay. I joined with him in the act which had once been so pleasurable but I couldn't fool James. He was a sexual and intuitive person. He was good at sex, he knew what he was getting, and he was getting no-show with me. I understood it would be a matter of time before he discovered my non-appearance in my body, which seemed to be present with his, and then he'd find a proper partner, the life partner who didn't fade out after six months, the sort I could never be and dreaded.

Whatever I'd done, however I felt, I knew to keep it from him. Again he asked about my weeks in the States and I promised I'd get around to it, and filled his hands with photographs to be going on with.

'And what about Elle?'

There was no reaction in the world that could hide the pain.

'Oh, she's still there.' If only he hadn't said her name.

'Have you quarrelled with her?'

The kitchen offered generous ways of escape. The soup was boiling, a wasp was at the window, Daisy wanted to go out, come in, a fly was on the bread. I chose a glass of water and, drinking it, muttered something, and got out of there.

I didn't notice the localised pain in my foot too much. The injury from Casper's roughness had not healed and it leaked and swelled, and that was unusual. I was a quick healer.

My friend Lou asked me to her exhibition, a crowded successful affair – I thought how much Elle would have liked it. Lou's work was complex and clever, image superimposed on image endlessly, and each print selling at the top of the market range. She complained about the gallery, their commission, lack of commitment, the inferior reproductions, lousy wine. I'd heard it all before and part of Lou's creative journey was to cast off the safe and suffer until she found the new. I would have thought she'd understand my situation. It was at this private view that I discovered I had to keep sitting down.

'You look wiped out. Shadows under your eyes.'

I hadn't seen her since I'd gone to meet Elle and Mia in the Hampshire hotel. We agreed it was over three months ago.

'I hear you went away with a strange and elegant Russian lady.'

She'd got that from James. I pretended someone was calling me and ran out into the street. She came after me and took my hand. 'You're so changed. I know what it is. You're pregnant.'

I half ran up to Regent's Park and sat huddled on a bench in the dark. What should I do? Could I go on living like this? Could I dissolve the deep, dark aching inside me? Was I actress enough to make a performance of reality for James daily until I was recovered enough to be the role? Elle hadn't phoned me because she didn't want me. If she wanted something, she got it. Jack had seen that.

When I got home I asked immediately, 'Any calls?'

'No.' James was sitting out of sight, by the dog basket. 'But we should have a talk.'

*

The next day, Lou came to see me.

'How do I tell my husband I'm gay?'

Lou moved along the battered sofa so Daisy could have her place. It had been the refuge for so many animals in the past and was scratched, gnawed, stained and almost refurbished with a network of old dog and cat hairs that no amount of hoovering removed.

'He doesn't want to know,' she said.

I agreed. He'd built a wall of denial behind which he hid, so allowing our marriage to continue. The luxury of having it out with me meant separation. The night before, his invitation to talk had been limited by my refusal to include the USA. What had I really been doing? I gave him the script. Yes, Dag was right about that. I would never have just one copy. He'd read it quickly and tried to pretend it was interesting. Then he admitted he knew nothing about that kind of structure. Did I?

'He hopes it will go away.'

Lou watched me with a solemnity I had not seen before. 'You're not gay, Cathy. It's an unexpected infatuation.'

Her soft, dark, curly hair was piled up on top of her head and some had broken free and hung down and over her ears, casual and stylish. That's how Lou was, by nature or design. Her pale, milky skin glowed as though lit from within and I fleetingly wondered why her beauty meant so little and Elle's so much. I remembered every little thing about Elle. I'd known Lou for years and hadn't really acknowledged she was beautiful.

'At least it's not a man,' she said. 'He won't mind it as much.'

I'd considered that.

'Some men get quite a buzz from a woman who's been with another woman.'

I didn't know.

'So it's not going to be a marriage-breaker.'

But it was. It wasn't about a buzz or titillating women. I was in love.

'You look good,' I told her.

'I wish I could say the same about you. That woman has put all your lights out. You're a shadow. You don't belong there, Catherine.'

We sat in silence and she wrung her hands as though washing them, and I recalled Dag's hands and realised they were bloodless.

'What are you going to do?'

'Get away of course.'

'That's a funny thing to say.'

I didn't know what she meant.

'Your answer could have been, "I'll never see her again," or, "I'll go back to her," or, "I'll go to a shrink." You sound as though you're a captive.'

'I meant get away from the situation of course.' And I stood up and wished I hadn't. I felt weak and hung on to the sofa, waiting for it to pass. 'I haven't slept with her, if that's what you're thinking.' I was surprised how much I needed to defend my heterosexual identity. I did not want to be a lesbian or associated with that orientation. But I loved a woman, was changed by her. Here I was, half dead, while she flounced around Washington or Spain or the Arctic Circle.

'I don't think gays have a very good time of it. There's a lot of pain. Gay women are very jealous. It's very intense because they're running on the same energy, female energy. There's more absorption with heterosexuals.'

'I would have slept with her, but something unusual, more unusual, happened.' I told her about the eyes and seeing corridors, the corridors of a grand house, now I came to think of it.

'You don't want to be gay. That's why you thought you saw them.'

'I had seen them, unfortunately. Nothing to do with thought.' Then I told her about the movie star, Jewel, and the deal. I asked if it sounded real.

'She was seen talking to her. Who knows about what? You didn't hear it.'

'But Elle offered me the deal.'

'Knowing you wouldn't go for it. And then you both left town all of a sudden.'

'She wouldn't make all that up just for me. Jumping credit cards, thrown out of the hotel. She'd have made some excuse.'

'Ask Jewel's agent, or her personal manager. Phone, saying you're sorry you couldn't do the session and would like the opportunity if Jewel comes to Europe.'

Why hadn't I thought of that?

'Now let's look at the photographs.' That was the real business and, as she studied them and criticised and occasionally approved of the shots of LA, I sat on the sofa and yet I was walking along corridors endlessly, for eternity.

28

The movie star's agent was too grand to speak to me directly and I was passed to an assistant who didn't know anything about photo sessions with Jewel, and less about me. She'd have to look into it. What newspaper or magazine did I work for? When she knew I was on my own and virtually unknown she almost flung the phone away and didn't ring back. So I tried the lesser agent in West Hollywood who assured me I'd do better trying to photograph ghosts, it would have more reality, and then offered to place some of the work I'd done in LA if I sent her the contacts. Then Lou rang Jewel's agent and, hearing her name, the organisation opened up enough for the PA to get back to her.

'Two Wednesdays ago? Exterior shots?' She didn't know anything about it. And Jewel would never negotiate her photographic sessions.

'That's one session that will forever be a mystery.' Casually, Lou offered me a small commission at a dance rehearsal, saying she didn't have time herself. She never let her kindness show.

I went to the doctor who looked at my untreated foot and gave me a cream to apply and antibiotics if things did not improve. I told him about the rushing deafness in my ears. That, he said, was a virus. The exhaustion? The aftermath of the virus. He pulled down my eyelids, took my blood pressure, listened to my heart and said that if I should be pregnant it wouldn't show on a test yet.

I walked with Daisy on Hampstead Heath. All around, the full trees whispering in a wind from the south, on this beautiful wistful day I could only feel separated from. But in my mind I was walking along the corridors of an old house. Perfect corridors that went on forever.

I'd been back fifteen days and everything was as it should be except I wasn't in it. I was there, and yet not there. I considered phoning the hotel in Washington, the house in Spain. I could call Lily but knew she'd give me bad news. Then I had a dream more real than reality.

We were lying in the hotel room in Washington as we had before she left for the ball. And she jumped up, took an apple and ran downstairs.

'Wait for me,' I cried and ran after her. 'I can be ready. I look good enough.'

I caught her at the hotel entrance and from the way she looked at me I knew I was far from good enough. I realised I had curlers in my hair and half my face was covered in a face mask.

'Go and get ready,' she said.

'Can I come with you?'

She looked towards the door and I saw a shadow that I thought was Casper's. 'I have to go,' and she ran towards it.

'But where are you going?'

And she told me a name.

'But where's that?'

'It's a well-known restaurant. The best. Anyone will tell you how to get there.'

And she turned, her strong teeth biting into the large apple, and I thought she was going to wait for me. I sped back to the room and in this dream that was more vivid than reality, got ready so fast I was applying my lipstick while running down to the foyer. She was gone. I asked the doorman where the restaurant was and he called a taxi. I made the driver forget the speed limits and within minutes we arrived at a low building with many small, lighted windows.

'I'll wait for you,' he said.

I told him he didn't have to.

'Oh yes. It's not the sort of place for you.'

I asked why not.

'Not for a woman like you, and on her own.'

As I opened the door I realised it wasn't Casper she was with, but Mia.

She'd deceived me. She was still with Mia, and they were here in this dangerous place. I went in expecting a brothel but here were well-behaved, elegant and successful people quietly eating. The tables were filled and I looked immediately for Mia's long gold hair.

The maître d' approached with the same alarm as the taxi-driver. 'This is not the right place for you, Madam.'

I told him I was looking for Elle. He didn't know her. I described her. It didn't bring his memory back. So I described Mia's hair.

'Oh yes, I might have seen them earlier but they're not here now.'

Not believing him, I looked around and started to move between the tables. Close-up, the clients were even more wealthy and stylish as they ate small portions of French haute cuisine on huge china plates. The maître d' grabbed me back as though he wanted to protect the clients' privacy. 'You can't come in here.'

'But she was here.'

'They've gone.'

'But she only arrived a few minutes ago. She left the hotel just before me.'

He shrugged. What could he do?

'Where have they gone?'

'I wouldn't know that, Madam,' and he encouraged me to the doorway.

I didn't believe it. She was still here with Mia. I could feel them, just a shadow away. In the dream I tried to run into the midst of the unconcerned diners, but again he got hold of me.

'You don't want to be mixed up with them. They're not your sort.'

'Why?'

'You're too good.'

Again I felt the pain of losing her. And then I knew she was around the back. There would be private rooms, of course. I looked as though I was leaving and he misjudged my limpness and let go of me. I turned and rushed amongst the diners along the oval of the room and around into the other half of the oval. This was the back and I expected private rooms and kitchens. I was in a strange area, this matching oval of the dining room, and I curved around it and discovered a maze of lavatories. Some of them were ornate, perched on pedestals, with wooden seats. Others were grand like thrones and mounted on a flight of mosaic steps. Some were ordinary, small, plastic toilets with broken seats, and each one was in a cubicle. The cubicles were interlocking and seemingly endless. I pushed a half-open door. Inside was a regal room, faded and peeling, with a lavatory at the far end. Along the walls were a selection of doors, and I tried them. Each contained a lavatory and an entrance into yet another lavatory. This huge white area was silent and deserted and all the lavatories were filthy. Some of them were overflowing, others had shit smeared on the walls. Repulsed, and frightened, I ran through this kingdom of interlocking cubicles until I'd completed the oval and was back at the entrance of the smart dining room. I sped past the maître d' and flung myself into the taxi.

'You shouldn't have gone there,' said the driver. 'You are in shock.'

I told him to go to all the restaurants, clubs, piano bars, smart and slumming, as Dag would say. That restaurant was like two sides of a coin. What did the lavatories remind me of? Tombstones. Sepulchres. Plastic gravestones. All desecrated.

The dream changed and I was no longer in a taxi but running through the night in scented fresh air. And I sped even faster and leapt, legs pedalling, into the air. I knew that of course I could fly. And I batted my arms fiercely and pedalled those legs with all my strength to keep up to fight gravity, and it was like struggling to stay up in water and not go down and drown, and I started to keep my place just above the ground. My legs circled faster, arms grappled fiercer, and I quickly pushed down on the air with my hands and lifted myself an inch higher, and now I could rise, dog-paddle style, up, house-high into the air. Of course I knew how to do it. Of course I could fly. I'd just forgotten. Now, going up, I felt triumphant, happy, and I could trust my arms to keep me up and I flapped them and stretched my legs out straight behind me, my body horizontal. I was swimming between high buildings and rising up into the sunset and then the city spread out below me, hotels, clubs, traffic, and I could hear police sirens, singing, mobile phones, and now I could wave my arms as wings and it was easier the higher I went. Soon I was soaring and could join my arms over my head to make an arrow and point in a new direction, up, right, left. I rose into dark mauve sky and the stars were huge yellow jellyfish. I needed nothing and I swirled and dived, dancing in the sky, knowing pure freedom and joy. I was flying across an ocean and there was land in the distance. I saw a hill, and on top of it, an ancient city I recognised. It was the immortal Spanish city that I loved, where I'd once been so happy. That was what would bring me back down. I had to make a decision to stay up and be free, or go down and have sensual earthly happiness. I swooped down because I believed I could always go back up. After all, I knew how to fly. It was night-time in this place and, between stone buildings, I dropped in the empty cobbled street near the cathedral. I landed with precision. I brushed myself down and started to walk as normally as possible, as though I hadn't done that miraculous journey. I felt exhilarated, I'd danced with the angels. And a voice said, 'Always remember, you can fly.'

29

I thought he'd say, 'It's a man, isn't it?' I was prepared for that. Or, 'We'll have to let the house go for something smaller and more realistic.' Or else, 'You don't fancy me any more. I'm no longer adored and I've joined the multitudes of plain human beings that you don't fancy.'

'You have to trust, Cathy, that I will look after what I love. I took you on.'

And I thought all the surprises came from Russians.

'But –' and of all the 'buts', I nearly chose sex.

He said, 'You've done very well. You gave up.' He meant the drink. 'I'll look after you.'

'I'm not a very promising partner, James. Nothing lasts with me for long. Perhaps I can't grow up.'

And he went inside and made dinner.

A part of me was still young, almost childish sometimes, and it was this that he loved – occasional glimpses of innocence and spontaneity, but he kept his appreciation to himself. He said later that, in his experience, when a woman discovered what appealed to a lover she started to improve on it and so ruin it. That night he said I moved beautifully, with grace, my smile gave me beauty. He liked my thinness. I was out of reach. Maybe he liked that too. Marriage, like everything else, was about dying and renewal, exhalation, inhalation. It seemed he would not leave me.

And then the phone rang. It was 3 a.m. and she said, 'I'm flying now. I'm coming to get you.'

'No.'

'You can't deny what we have.'

'I won't let you in.'

'Oh, I'll get in.'

It seemed incredible that all this suffering and pain was caused by a person with such an insignificant voice.

'I'm on TWA from Washington.' A lifeless sound, and rigid. And then the goodbye in Italian, so common.

*

'If she's coming anyway you may as well meet her full on.'

I'd waited until after 7 a.m., then gone to Lou and woken her up.

'I'll take you to the airport.'

I thought Lou possibly wanted to see what this enigmatic and stylish Russian woman was like. She splashed her face with water, put the kettle on.

'But should I see her?'

'Oh, that's another question. But then you wouldn't be here. You'd have told James and he'd have stopped her getting in the house. Or you'd have gone away. Or both. You could go away. I'll drive you to a hotel in the country. Think about it.'

She got dressed as she made the tea.

'It's over three weeks.' I didn't want to see her but I longed to look at her. I didn't want to receive another pang of pain but I'd die for the chance to be held in her arms.

'We'll drive to the airport and maybe pass it and into the country. You decide.'

Lou was a confident driver, but not 'musical'. 'There's hotels further out.'

Didn't I know! With my luck I'd end up in the one she'd shared with Mia.

'I've been treated like shit. I want to see her. I think we should turn back. But if I saw her just once. Yet I'm owed an explanation. Three weeks and not even a call. What if something happened to her?' I hadn't thought of that. I changed my mind, my motives, my personality, my existence. Lou said, on that drive, I was the definitive study of ambivalence.

'You see two sides? You'd be so lucky. Seven.'

She stopped at the terminal but didn't park.

'Don't you want to –' I paused and couldn't quite say, 'see her.'

'I think it's something you'd better do alone.' And she started the engine.

A moment of fright now.

'Look, I'll just see her come through arrivals. Just a glimpse. Then I'll leave. Could you wait for me?' I looked round for a suitable place.

But Lou drove off and I was relieved to be alone as she was relieved to be free of me. The plane had landed and I waited with a hundred others for the passengers to appear.

'It'll take forty minutes,' said the man beside me. 'They haven't put the luggage on the belt.'

'Why not?' a woman asked.

'Because there aren't any free, as usual.'

The automatic doors opened unexpectedly and she was there. She stood looking out at the crowd, like a competitor in a beauty contest. Her hair had been done and was shaped like a pear. She had no luggage and carried a smart plastic bag. I didn't wave. I couldn't move. I would have run. And she chose me from the hundred viewers and bestowed upon me the full, lovely smile that didn't grow like James's from an honest pleasure but was full-sized and immediate and possibly a means of defence, the way some animals showed their teeth as a warning. She came towards me and I suppose I didn't respond because she nudged me.

'That's a tired little face. And not even a greeting. Aren't you at least glad to see me?' Her voice was hard and edgy and her hair was middle-class, attending-charity-galas hair. She laughed. 'I had it done just for you and you don't like it.'

I actually did not know what to do with her. Automatically, I said, 'Let's have a coffee,' and started towards the stall by *Arrivals*. There had been a dozen questions but when I looked into her eyes there were none. She took my hand greedily, dug her nails in, drew blood. 'I've been thinking about you all the time on that flight. How I want you.'

'What about on the ground? Not so ardent then.'

She stroked my face and I felt a surge of hot, unwelcome excitement.

'Let's go to a hotel,' I said. Was I mad? I could no longer trust myself. 'First I need to talk to you.' I turned away from her eyes, freed my hand, remembered the struggle to be without her.

'Hotel first. After that, we'll have even more to talk about.' And she lifted my hand and licked up the blood. 'Kiss to make it better.'

She went, lighthearted, to the exit and whistled up a passing cab. The driver was impressed by her whistle. It was something to hear. 'Do it again,' he said. And she really whistled this time and got the attention of hordes of travellers. Cheekily, she returned their stares and jumped into the cab.

'The nearest hotel.'

He asked what price, what standard? She was in a light free mood and didn't care. So he chose the Sheraton, which gave him a fare.

This was not what I wanted at all. Here I was back in her control, with no say in anything. I told the driver to go into London. I'd decided to go home.

'Ignore her,' she said. 'Jet lag.'

And I did look like the one who'd been over-travelling.

*

She could hardly wait to get into the room before getting hold of me. She kicked the door shut sharply, lifting up her foot behind her like a horse.

'You're not going to deny me. I've waited for this.' And she got her leg between mine and held me tight and tough. 'It's not something you can pick and choose.' And she swept me on to the bed and I was crushed in the beginning of a hug, and her greedy hands found chaste places to stroke, my hair, my cheek, and she told me how she'd missed me and I told her once again that she'd have to take over the sexual act and do it, and again I handed over all control. The hug was sweet. I felt blessed. Afterwards, I told her how it felt and I couldn't understand how she did not seem to feel this sweetness.

She pulled my head close to her mouth and whispered, 'It's a lovely feeling instead of being just sexual. Only lovely people feel that.'

'Aren't you lovely?'

'No, I'm sexual and bad.'

And I wanted to find out how bad but she sat up straight. 'There's no time.'

And she got up and smoothed back the pruned hair as though what had taken place had satisfied her, and I lay dishevelled but sexually untouched and wondered what it could be. Did she, amongst the muttered words, manage a discreet orgasm, words over-romantic and nice, love-talk from a reader of *Woman's Own* magazine, hardly the stuff of sexual climax. She opened the plastic bag and threw me a carton. Inside, a large size perfume which she'd got on the plane. The present provoked an uncomfortable thought. What was she going to do for money? I almost asked where her luggage was, but it seemed too boring a question for her. Instead I asked where she was going in such a rush.

'Going?'

'You said there's no time.'

'I have to get the plane for Toulouse.'

Electrocuted by panic, I stayed clamped to the bed. She undressed and turned on the shower. 'Come and get under with me. It's so cool.'

And I had to wait until that water and splashing stopped to ask, 'Why are you going?'

'Because I have to sort out things down there.' And she stroked her body with a silky cream. 'Do it for me.'

I struggled up and moved my hands to and fro across her back, over her legs and her delicate feet like hooves. She lifted my sweater and filled her hands with cream and wiped it over my breasts. 'I've so missed you.'

The body moisturising session had all the elements of an erotic encounter, yet she was chaste and her love showed itself in owning me rather than having me. I was hers, full-time, without stop. No up and down and separation provided by a sexual act.

'I will come back and get you.'
And I filled up with life again.

*

Back at the airport she changed money and gave it to me. 'About three hundred pounds. It comes to what you spent on the LA hotel.' She gave me another hundred. 'That's for the waistcoat.'

'Why didn't you call me?' I asked.

'Why did you run away?'

'What have you been doing?'

'Surely I'm the one with questions.'

'You slept with him.'

'Him?' She was almost amused.

'Casper. Dag. And those guys you danced with. That prince –'

'Not him. Them. Get your pronouns right. D'you want more money? Excuse me, I should have asked.'

'No …'

'How many times have I heard you say you're married? I honoured that.'

'When did you honour anything?'

She laughed.

'Did you sleep with them?'

'But I'm crazy about you. But it's very difficult.' She looked at the boarding times, hoping to escape. 'I have to sort it out with Mia. When I've done that –' She looked at me.

I wanted to say, 'Don't go.' I wanted to ask questions. I remained silent and that disconcerted her.

'After all, I just left her in the middle of absolutely nowhere. And she's hit the drink again. She's ill.' Then she looked at me so beautifully I wished she could be eternally my lover, my life partner. I'd go to the ends of existence with her. 'But I will come back, Catherine.' I still didn't, couldn't answer. 'You could meet me somewhere. Monaco. You can always fly.'

Remember you can fly. It set off a definite echo. 'Why did you say that?'

'Because you don't drive.'

She was about to go and I believed I'd never see her again. What was more important – where she'd been, or where she was going? Tears running down my face, I asked if she loved me. She turned and enfolded me in a joyous hug, full of feeling, normal, and we clung together. Her arms leaving my body must be how dying feels.

'Ciao.' And she was gone.

*

I took the photographs of the dance rehearsal for Lou. The wound on my foot not healing sent me back to the doctor and I remembered I was exhausted. He took blood, sent it away for tests, remembered the pregnancy possibility and asked for a urine sample. Lou arranged a meeting with a publisher because she thought I should do a book of Night in the City. Black and white. Big format, eighty pages. The publisher was interested in Lou, not me, so Lou suggested writing the introduction. She was going to keep this on the boil. He said it would be too expensive. He was really saying I wasn't well-known enough. He'd let her know.

We had coffee in Camden Town and she said she'd introduce me to a top photographic agency. 'And I'm going to take your stuff to Magnum.' That was all she could manage for my career. I, the person, was even unluckier. 'That woman has changed you. Depolarised you. You were pointing north and now it's south. A big chemical change.'

I told her about the foot not healing.

'It should be stress and emotional stuff, but it's like you've been through some elemental shock and you're physically different. Some scanner into a different world. There's a big shadow over you.' And she suggested going to a spiritual healer, a tarot reader, a church.

In the end I went to my London agent with my portfolio of LA photographs. She told me they were building in Canary Wharf and described skyscrapers.

'Do those. We'll get you a commission from one of the supplements.' She'd left out the important word 'try'; she'd 'try' to get a commission. I hadn't been so unlucky for months. In the meantime, weddings.

To make money, James took on a summer course at the university and considered doing an exchange lectureship with a professor in Munich. He asked me to go with him. We ate in the garden which was wild, unkempt and one of the areas of marital battle. I'd tried, with the help of a gardener, to create a garden with a rose arbour. Weeds had been pulled up. James had come flying out of the house.

'What are you doing? Leave them.'

The gardener had explained they were weeds. James had thrown him out. 'I want no more intrusion in this garden.'

I'd been so full of rage I couldn't speak at all, and hadn't since on that subject. It could grow until it came into the house for all I cared. It was about then I stopped bothering so much about the inside.

Now I told him my rate for weddings had gone up and I might have a spread on Canary Wharf. 'It's a city of glass.'

He was looking at me uneasily. 'You've gone again. You're just not here.'

I hoped I'd been there earlier when I cooked the dinner. The fish we were eating looked all right.

'You're like an animal responding to a call that only you can hear. It's from some presence that only you can see. To us the presence looks harmless as it stands amongst us. It's all right, we say. And the poor animal shivers.'

He'd been talking to Lou. All this animal talk was his way of finding out if I was running off with a woman. Yet there was something familiar about the story. Something I'd heard about or dreamed. Having a good idea who the animal was and how I fitted the part a little better than he thought, I was alarmed.

'What is the presence?'

'A hunter.' He finished the fish and Daisy stood on her hind legs and placed her front paws on the table. The fishbone was a disappointment and she got down. He said, 'She's not to do that.'

'What does the hunter do?'

'Stalks the animal, I suppose.' He dipped his bread in olive oil.

'Why do you say it's a presence if it's an obvious figure that strides about in full view?'

'We take it for granted, but the animal knows better.'

And the moon came up full and he made Turkish coffee and found a box of Turkish Delight. I knew he talked differently to me, more simply than to his students.

I told him I had four hundred pounds from the US for work I'd done there, and put Elle's money on the table. Altogether it was a good evening.

*

I was in the darkroom with the July weddings and he said I had a phone call. The speed with which I went to the phone assured me I had not got over my infatuation, not one bit of it. I believed it was Elle. The GP spoke in a quiet voice and said I wasn't pregnant but there were some changes in my blood structure, the platelets, I think he said. It was only slight, but he was making an appointment for me at the hospital. I asked if it was serious.

'It sometimes happens if you've taken antibiotics for a long period.'

I'd taken a lot of things for long periods in my life, but not antibiotics. Although the injury to my foot had happened over a month ago it had not properly healed. It would seem, as Lou suggested, that I'd gone through some change. I phoned her but she was off to a mixed exhibition in Edinburgh, where her work was being offered at superlative prices.

'It's part of the Festival. I'm flying up for one night.'

Her recent prize hadn't done her prices any harm. I wondered how her work would evolve from the superimposed images. I didn't see where they could go, except to become overblown and pretentious, but that could be jealousy. As she went up, so I went down. I hadn't got the Canary Wharf commission, the West Hollywood agent hadn't moved the latest photographs of LA that she'd asked for, and I hadn't got the book deal. As long as people went on getting married! I wondered how my friendship with Lou would be if I ever became successful.

All of a sudden I wanted to phone Elle, needed to speak to her. I needed just one piece of magic. I could go a long way on that. I dialled the number of the house in Spain, then hung up. So I tried Lily.

'They're back together. Serge saw them walking down the hill this morning. She looks terrible.'

'Elle?'

'Of course not. She went completely crazy the other night. Elle had just arrived back.'

'Did they have a row?'

'Mia tried to jump out of the window. Then Olav came down and he wasn't allowed in. Madame wouldn't open the gate and told him to fuck off. She asked Serge to take him back to the airport. He spent the night in the old place where you stayed. The two-star one was full.' Then she whispered, 'I can't say any more because I think Serge has come in and he doesn't like me talking about her.'

'How's the shop?'

'Business is up but he works hard. She bought the shop and put up the start money.'

'So he works for her as well?'

'In other ways, yes. Little ways.'

'Are they going to stay together, Lily?' She knew I meant Elle and the Princess.

Her voice got lower. 'Looks like it.'

I stayed sitting on the sofa with Daisy. If just one thing would go right. If I could take the perfect photograph of Kentish Town, of the railway bridge, the Assembly House pub with its nineteenth-century glass, fug of fumes from traffic, the white doors in Leverton Street behind which the middle-class professionals protected their sanity from the council clients, mad, drunk, rapacious and murderous, further along.

So I picked up my cameras and went out to do the only thing I could – take photographs.

30

The phone was in the kitchen and James's friends were shouting, Daisy barking, Lou yelling at me because we'd started another game of mahjong and again I'd laid the four East Winds. I was always lucky with East. Then the phone rang. How could I always get the East Winds like that? They could not get over it. Or believe it. Was it synchronicity? Was there such a thing? Jung liked the idea.

I took the phone out into the passage as soon as I heard her voice. She would ring at a time when the impossible was being challenged. She sounded tired and flat.

'I'm having a terrible time. I've had to be with her day and night. And now her mother's coming here. It can't be worse. The mother blames me for day turning to night. At least she tries to.'

'Come here. I'll look after you.' Did I say that?

'How can you?'

I told her how good I was at looking after people.

'I'm not people.'

'No, you're the person I love.'

'I love the way you say "person". Say it again.'

They called me from the kitchen. 'Come on, East.'

'Come now, Elle. Just get a plane.'

She did hesitate.

'I can't leave her like this. She's in shock.'

'Get a doctor and then get out of there.'

'I've had no sleep.' She did sound reduced. 'I'm afraid she might do something. I've hidden the pills. I'm going to get her back to acting. That's what she did, and she was good at it, so some people say. I'll revive the scholarship she had.'

'Where will she do this acting?'

'Finland. Denmark. I'll get her started and then secure her a place in the main theatre. Small parts.'

'Who'll pay for that? Olav?'

She paused.

'Has he been to see her?'

More silence. Then a small, 'Yes.'

The guests wrenched the door open and wanted me back in the game. I shoved it shut with my foot and didn't notice the pain.

'You've got guests.'

'Not really.'

'You're having a good time.'

'Not remotely.'

'Nor am I. It's this village that's done her in. She's got nothing to work at here. She did the house and that ended, so she did it again.'

'Is Olav angry with you?'

'Why?'

'For being away,' I said, quietly.

'He blames me for Mia not using her talent. So does her mother. So does Dag. And the National Theatre. The whole of Finland will blame me.'

'Where were you for those three weeks after I left? You didn't get around to telling me.'

'No, I didn't. I was with Dag in New York. And I had big problems with Olav. The shit hit the fan at the bank. And I had to sort Mia out as best I could, and show I was alone.'

'That's already an awful lot of reasons for three weeks' silence.'

She laughed. 'Yes, it is. I was going out with Casper and we partied, and day just followed day.'

I felt a panic, deep down, like an approaching earthquake. 'Which one is true?'

'Both.'

I heard a horrible noise, full of rage.

'What's that?'

'Her. I have to go.'

'I miss you,' I said.

'I miss you and I love you.' The phone was cut.

*

She called from Toulouse airport and I said I'd arrange a hotel.

'I want to be with you.'

'You will be. We'll stay –'

'In your house.'

So she had no money.

'You could stay in this house?' Things were worse than I thought.

'Of course. It's where you live.'

I should have said I must ask James first, but she arranged to take a taxi from Heathrow.

I told James she'd stay for a couple of nights and tried not to look happy. And then I thought, where will she sleep? Where will I sleep?

She came into the house like a child on an enforced vacation, sweet-faced and going to make the best of it. It was the last thing I expected. She wore a mustard coloured duffel coat and her face was brown, with rosy apple cheeks, and the point on the hood made her more vulnerable, added to the childishness. She looked sweet, and that was something I never thought I'd see. Daisy licked her hand and James came in and greeted her and I think was surprised by her seeming lack of sophistication. I quickly brushed off the best chair but she sat on the dog-haired sofa with Daisy. I noticed there was little luggage, one travel bag at most, so would she stay? While I made a hot drink they talked about politics and it was obvious her opinions came from a quick scan of the morning papers and stopped there. They were, however, in opposition to his. Then the money market got a turn. What would the US do about the dollar? Then he swung back to our trip to LA and caught her out.

'So you're making this film in black and white?'

She agreed.

'But it will never be distributed.'

Careful now, she waited for him to tell her why.

'Television companies won't buy black and white. That's why everything's in colour.'

I cut in to save her and said it would be sepia.

She said, 'I don't pay too much heed to what's happening right now. Things change.'

Elle was born without a rule book. Who'd said that? Was it Dag? More importantly, she knew the men who could perhaps change corporate opinion. Colour could become old-fashioned.

He took his coffee and leaned against the sink, swiftly looking her up from top to toe without seeming to. I wished he'd leave. I couldn't bear the two of them together. It became out of my control. She asked about his work, couldn't do more than a couple of questions on that, and praised his domestic anarchy. She added a smile on that one. It got her nowhere. He was one of the men she wasn't going to affect. Almost amused, he waited for her to try another tack. He was thinking – she uses tired old tricks. I knew him. He'd be bored by her and see her as little as possible and wouldn't mind her staying, as long as she didn't interfere with his life. We'd had all kinds staying in that house.

She was looking at his feet and I thought she categorised his sandals as left-wing and hated them.

I suggested a walk and she put up the duffel coat hood again and it stuck up in a point at a different angle and did look appealing. It even got to him.

Outside, arm in arm towards the Heath, happy. She took Daisy.

'It's got an atmosphere, your house.'

I thought she sounded approving and wondered what she meant. I didn't ask.

*

We sat by the pond and the late sun made the water golden and in the distance the line of poplar trees waved like broomsticks sweeping the dead air. The late afternoon traffic was puffing on East Heath Road. I wanted her to like the Heath, see the best of it. I wanted her to like Hampstead, and there was some 'best', although it wasn't a village any more. She would not like Kentish Town and at all costs must be kept out of Camden Town. I needed her to like something so she'd stay. We were happy and close and I was full of plans and places to take her, so I had to ask, 'What did you do during those three weeks?'

'I had to survive. It's like a man going to war. Mia would understand.'

I didn't get much out of that answer. 'You could have rung.' And the sky darkened the pond as though in warning.

'I would only have wanted you with me and it wasn't possible. You have to trust me.'

That answer was worse. 'Did Mia fly out to Washington?'

'How could she? Mia is ill.'

'That's now. What about a month ago?'

'No, she did not.' Said with conviction. 'I had things to do. Why ruin this moment?'

Good question, but I'd had three terrible weeks which I wasn't sure I'd survive.

'I love being with you,' and she took my hand, and I believed her. I didn't think she bothered with lies, just omissions. 'Can we go dancing?'

I thought she'd like barefoot boogie, which had just started, and jazz in Soho. I asked what was going to happen to Mia.

'She'll go back with her mother to Helsinki. She'll go on with her studies so she joins her life up where she left it seven years ago. Those years spent with me removed as though by surgery.'

I told her the creative need was apparently the one you should never suppress. That's what I'd heard, anyway. It did all kinds of harm. You could manage without other things like sex, self-esteem, even food, but don't deny creative expression. She thought what I said did apply to Mia, and that sticking her in that village had been a terrible mistake. Once back performing she'd start recovering.

'Unlike Dag and Olav, I didn't think she was that good. But she'd do a wonderful one-woman show. And she's so outrageous and gets away with it.' She was full of sudden praise for her possibly former lover, and it occurred to me she was sending her back because she was tired of her.

'What will happen to the house?'

'That isn't sick. A cleaner looks after that.'

'Was it hard to leave her?'

'I suppose it was.' And she played with Daisy and I thought she would cry, but, surprisingly, there were no tears but more smiles, and I thought she'd taken it very well.

'You must be strong to go through all this.'

'There's no point taking a gloomy view.'

And I asked about Jewel. I might as well get all the mysteries, if not solved, at least aired.

'My, you are still a Sherlock Holmes. How many more of these inquisitions are there?'

'The Spanish say, when the bullfighter's in the ring, let all the bulls come out. Her agent doesn't know anything about that session you arranged.'

'I'm guilty of some things, but not an agent's ignorance. I don't talk to agents. Just the clients.'

'She said Jewel would never arrange her own photo session.' That was my trump card.

'She didn't. I did.'

'But no one knows anything about it, Elle.'

'I told you already, those actresses should be in front of your camera working in your film. Don't play with their silly egos asking to take their photograph.'

I seemed to remember it had been her idea. 'But what's happened to the film?'

'Forget it for now. What you need is status.'

So I told her about the publishing deal Lou was trying to get me.

'Oh, forget all that. What you need is an exhibition.'

*

She cooked a Russian speciality. Fish pie, potato pancakes and porridge with cumin spice. 'I used to do this in the summer when we'd stay on our island, every Finn has a summerhouse. We spend the winter longing for summer.'

'A short summer,' said James. He did his best with the food. She was not a very good cook.

'We go in June and clean up the summerhouse, repaint everything, repair the boat, clean the engine, and then on the longest day have a party outside. We go on boats from island to island. It's light nearly all night. We cook outside on a grill.' She described a frugal outdoor life which was more or less the same whether you were royalty or paupers.

There was tension between them, not surprisingly, as she was nervous of him and he knew I wanted her. The conversation had nothing to do with what was really going on. He asked about the food, and as that was not something he cared about, I knew we were about to be in trouble.

'At five o'clock we have our main meal.'

I thought he said, 'No lunch? And leave my fucking wife alone.'

'What?' I sounded alarmed.

He looked at me, vaguely interested. She seemed all right. Maybe he hadn't said it.

'What did you say?' I insisted.

She cut in with 'Breakfast is usually bread, a block of cheese you slice. At midday you have a sandwich, which …' She trailed off.

'What happens after the five o'clock meal?' he asked.

'Nothing.'

'Oh, shut it,' I screamed, jumping up from the table. They went on talking about food. I sat in the garden. I could still hear their conversation. James asked about drink.

'We have many alcoholics,' she said.

'Let's go for a walk, anything,' I shouted.

But he had to go on talking about alcohol and Lutheranism until he got bored.

He got a neighbour to make a fourth at mahjong and I lost, didn't even see an East Wind. Someone won and I knew I could never spend another evening like that. There was a moment when she smiled right into my eyes and it almost took my breath away, it almost burned me. He noticed.

Bedtime and I kept putting it off. I'd given her a small room on the top floor with a single bed. It was the opposite of the hotel suite in Washington and I had to remind myself it was clean. It was also a long way away from James.

He seemed to hang around with unnecessary talk about Russo-Finnish matters, and I suggested he go to bed as he had to get up so early and Elle and I needed to work on the film script. Instead he went out into the garden and she and I had a neutral conversation about photography. He was now the enemy.

'Come and see the darkroom.' That got her upstairs, away from him. Just being with her – I was too alive. I turned on the light and showed her the different processes of development, at the same time whispering solutions for the night hours.

'I'll go to bed with him and –'

'I wish you wouldn't. I dread it.'

'When he's asleep I'll come up to you.' What if he woke up? 'No, I'll sleep downstairs.' I sometimes fell asleep on the sofa.

She pulled me to her and the need between us, from one to the other, only hours of lovemaking might satisfy. I could hear her heart crashing against mine, and I was frightened the door would open and he'd come in. Just then, the door was punched and shaken and we leapt apart and started talking about photography. I went to the door and casually opened it and Daisy sat outside staring at me. I suspected James had come up, the dog following, and, seeing the door was shut, had gone away.

I went back to the kitchen, made a hot drink and innocently called him to join us. I showed her the prints of the area I'd taken on my last dreadful day. James came in from the garden and made me jump. I was prepared to be jumpy. He put his arm around me and it was like an assault.

'I'm going to take Elle up to the top of the Heath. The view over London at night is –' There were many words for that view, but I didn't have them.

'You're to come to bed,' he said, 'or have you forgotten you have a hospital appointment for exhaustion?'

*

I promised myself personally that I would never spend another night like that one. Over and over I said, 'You will not go through this again.' I understood how animals on heat felt and I needed to be with her in the single bed, sure that enough time had elapsed for us to consummate the affair successfully. I didn't so much imagine sexual caresses as be their recipient while they were paraded through my night-time head, more defenceless and raw than during the daylight hours. I tried to slide out of the bed and go to her but his arm tightened around me and towards dawn he got on top of me. But the act was with her and drew from me a long shuddering response, any sound of which I suppressed, pushing my face into the pillow, and I knew she knew and I could see her eyes yellow like headlights at the end of the bed.

'We're going to Munich,' he said. 'On that lectureship exchange.'

*

It was being with the mother I'd never had, close and protected by the lover I'd never expected, laughing with the ally, the conspirator I didn't know, holding hands with the friend I'd never encountered. She was the one my soul loved and I hadn't known she'd even existed. Some spiritual force had put us together and we fitted better than a hand in a glove. She was my soul mate and I lit candles in churches and thanked God for her presence. We were inseparable and now there were no phone calls to keep us apart, no terrible, unexpected criticism to break my heart. It was all as it should be in God's world. Yes, I thanked God for this union. All I had to do was keep it from James and the rest of the ordinary world. I did wonder if Mia would suddenly show up. I would.

Elle was happy in the house, the atmosphere calmed her and she became less powerful and more easy-going. She became helpful and did cleaning and tidying and cooking. The rough aspects of Camden Town were taken in her stride as she shopped at Marks & Spencer's and got the bus back. She liked to go with me while I photographed weddings or social occasions. 'I'll sit here and wait for you. Just know I'm thinking about you, and take those pictures for me.'

We walked with Daisy on the Heath and I felt serene, complete. It felt as if I was in a meringue, soft and without needs on the inside, moulded and sweet from love on the outside. I was a new person. Complete. And I loved her pointed duffel coat hood, her smile, her rosy cheeks, her beautiful golden neck, her slim pointed feet. The only problem was James. He made this closeness be on loan like a library book that had to be returned before it was even properly read. It was obvious she felt good in the house, the house soothed her and she loved Daisy, and so it went on day after day and there was no reason for it to end. She could live as frugally as James and she could live in my life and it was enough.

'All I want is to be with you.'

Yes, the night-times were there, when we forked off into separate worlds and lay sleepless and I would find her downstairs in the garden or making a hot drink.

'What are you doing?'

'Looking at the night.'

Later, James gave me a ticket. 'Munich in two weeks.'

She came with me to the hospital and the doctor was amazed at how my chemical make-up had changed since the GP had done the tests. 'It's like another person. Quite extraordinary.' So he took more blood and noted that the injury on my foot had not really healed.

She told me to forget doctors.

'They keep searching around until they find something and it's never the right thing. The lab must have got it wrong. You just need an exhibition.' And she distrusted fame and success. 'It's who you know. And who will pay for the work, and if the powerful ones support you, the others feel they must or they have to ask the terrible question, "Have I missed the point?" '

I was rather keen on talent and excellence myself. And originality.

'Oh, you've got all that,' she said, 'for nothing. There'd be no point otherwise. But you need approval, like your friend.' She'd seen Lou's work and thought it pretentious. 'Except you're better than her, but she's worked it. She won't last.' Critics were people Casper Shulz had to approve of, or they didn't last. For her, pure power was all that mattered.

She helped with the weddings, in the darkroom, taking London pictures at night. She played mahjong with James's friends and cooked blinis and fish pie and got on with everybody, charmed them, except James.

'How long is she going to stay?'

I told him she was setting up an exhibition. I just had to do the work.

'What exactly does she do?'

I didn't know. She was just Elle.

He obviously did not believe she was going to produce something for me and save the mortgage crisis. What moneyed person lived in the anarchy and discomfort of his house?

Dinners at his colleagues' houses could be an ordeal. I always felt excluded. The conversation, academic and critical, meant I stayed silent. I brought Elle with me to the dinner given by James's head of department for a visiting professor at UCLA. He was immediately taken with Elle. So was the head of department. They gravitated towards her as surely as Casper had at the ball in Washington, and she smiled and had the right retorts, even asked some of the right questions. They almost fought to sit next to her at dinner. Yes, I was jealous and later accused her of having always to be in the centre.

'I don't have to be. I am. I can walk into a room and the most powerful man there will automatically seek me out.'

I couldn't have looked too pleased.

'Oh, don't sulk. You live in an interior world. You're a creative person. The external show doesn't bother you.'

Why did they come to her? Because she was a working girl, as Jack had said?

'I've always been successful with men,' she said.

So I asked why.

'Because I think like a man. I'm one of them, I talk their language. They can't bear those silly, cosmetic, self-indulgent women. They don't know how to relate to them.'

It was at the professor's dinner that I did see something unusual, Elle out of her depth. I don't think she felt any better than I did.

The focus had swung round to James's interest in Henry James and I'd managed one round of that conversation. The professor praised James and quoted a passage from memory. ' "Henry James despised Dickens –" '

'Tried to,' cut in James.

' "He said Dickens was just fragments, details, rotten architecture but wonderful gargoyles." I remember you wrote that.'

'Orwell, actually,' said James.

And then the head of department's young wife added, '*Hard Times* and *The Europeans* were both moral fables. Henry James might have dismissed Dickens' influence, but would he have written *The Europeans* without *Hard Times*?' Her voice grated, the laugh was worse. She glared round the table.

'Oh, look who's been to school,' said Elle.

'He was a great entertainer, Dickens,' said the American professor. 'But I wouldn't use "moral fable" to describe any of his work. Would you?'

For a horrible moment I thought he was asking Elle. Before confusion set in James replied, 'Henry James didn't think so. But he was disillusioned with the English. He had believed the English offered the ideal way of life.'

'He's not the only one to be fooled,' said Elle.

'At that time there was considerable confusion between American and English viewpoints,' said the glaring woman.

'There is considerable confusion around this table,' said Elle. 'You'd better believe me.'

I took her outside. She asked, 'Who is this guy Henry James they keep talking about?'

31

She changed the kitchen and made space on the table and got new eating bowls for Daisy. She washed clothes, cleaned shelves, brushed the dog, talked to neighbours. I never thought I'd see her do these activities and was amazed how flexible she was, that she could join in. She bought flowers from the stall by the station and placed them in the kitchen.

'What are these?' asked James disagreeably.

'Flowers.'

'Come here,' and he pulled me out of possible earshot. 'Get rid of them.

I hate cut flowers.' And then he saw the weeds she'd pulled up lying on the path like dead friends. And the new plates she'd bought from Habitat. As he stared at them I knew her days were numbered.

'She's trying to thank us for letting her be here.'

'She's hiding out.'

I told him he was stupid. He didn't like that.

'James, the house suits her. Don't fuss. And we're doing the exhibition.'

'Don't bullshit.' He collected the plates, fast as though he was doing a juggling act. 'Get rid of them.' He accosted her in the doorway as she was coming back with the dog. She took the dog for walks at least twice a day and suddenly I knew it was to make phone calls. He told her about the plates, the flowers, the weeds and how he wanted things left alone. And he'd be going to Munich with me for two weeks.

'Then I'll look after Daisy.'

'I've already made an arrangement.'

She went past him upstairs, different to how I'd ever seen her, slumped and strangely defeated. Her hand on the cool soft polished wood of the banister left no trace, although it was a hot day.

I found her sitting on the floor in the corner of the bedroom, head on her knees. I thought she'd been crying.

'I've had a lovely time here,' and she lifted her face, eyes quite dry.

'It will go on,' I promised her.

'Oh no. He doesn't want it. It suits me here,' she laughed. 'Whoever would have thought that? It's like the house is a loving parent. It reminds me of my childhood before – before …'

'I'm going to talk to him. It's my house too. I'm not going to Munich.'

And then she got up and mocked him, the way he'd wrung his hands about the plates, and it wasn't easy to watch. There was something insistent and cruel about her performance.

'He'll go and we'll stay.'

She looked at me as though I had the solution and for the first time since I'd met her I was the one in charge. 'It'll be all right. You see.'

'Sometimes you're so free, Catherine. Carefree. That's what I love about you.'

I went down the three flights to the kitchen to tell him I wouldn't be going to Munich but her mimicking James, as she had the waiters, jarred. This was my husband, sometimes precious and valued, and she seemed to have no sense of that and her attitude was rough. There was no respect, but I'd never associate her with something like that. On the other hand, he wasn't putting what I wanted first or even last. He just wanted her out. I was somewhere between the two and I'd better find out where that was.

Before I even spoke he said, 'I told you, I look after what I love. I want her out of here.'

I started again about the exhibition and he cut through that as he had before and would no doubt again. He didn't keep his voice down and I was afraid she'd hear from the open bedroom window. I gestured for him to come inside but he stayed under his tree in the garden and made it clear she was no longer welcome in his house. I suggested a walk to talk this over. He suggested she be out by the evening.

'But why?'

He looked at me, face pale, eyes blazing. 'Because there's something wrong here and it's going to blow up.' He flip-flopped to the front door in the sandals I knew she loathed. Her men did not wear sandals. I followed him.

'I want her to stay.'

'Cathy, trust me. Move her out.'

I followed him to the path. He said he had to hurry to his reading group.

'I am not happy with this. In fact, I want to talk about it. You've had friends stay for months.'

'Friends.' He pointed back at the house. 'Is she a friend?'

'A companion.' My heart was breaking, voice shaking. I knew not to go too far from the truth. 'I've never had family.'

'And you still haven't.'

'But what is it you've got against her?'

He looked down as though the answer was on the dirty pavement. 'She's on the way to making big trouble.'

'But she's always nice and sweet to you.'

'She is not nice or sweet.' He couldn't listen to any more. He walked off. At that moment, the front door slammed shut in a breeze I hadn't felt and I was left on the pavement without keys. I shouted to him but he didn't turn round. I rang the bell, Elle did not answer. I called through the letterbox. Nothing. After several minutes of this I went to a neighbour and rang my house. The phone was engaged. I was now into a bad situation so I phoned Lou.

'You've certainly been keeping the *femme fatale* to yourself. She is stylish. She's got style.'

'How do you know?'

'I saw you in the street but I didn't cut in. I felt not to. The way she holds her head. That walk. She's got something. A star.'

'Not in James's house.' And I told her what was going on.

'He's on to it.'

'He won't talk. Talks about things blowing up.'
'What are you going to do?'
'That's what I'm asking you.'
'Move her to a bedsit –'
I'd already thought of that. I wasn't sure she even had bedsit money. 'Can I borrow money if I have to?'
'Yes.' Lou didn't even hesitate.

Back at the house a lot of banging and calling finally brought Elle to the door. She was smiling. She'd heard the knocking, all of it, from the beginning, but said nothing.

'Have you been sleeping, Elle?'
'I could have been.'
'Did anyone ring?'
'No.'

Two lies. One to go. 'Did you ring anyone?'
'No.'

'Well, it's funny because I phoned from a neighbour and the line was busy.'

'I can't worry about the British phone network's inefficiency.'

She was withdrawn and smiling and we made some lunch. I told her how much I wanted to be with her. She patted Daisy and said that was fine. She'd heard all he'd said and knew she had to go, yet showed only calm and strength. She took things well.

We chose the contacts I should enlarge and what kind of mount the photographs should have. She'd seen a gallery in Piccadilly, but I thought it was aiming too high too soon. Amazingly, she'd already drawn up the guest list. If no one else saw my work, the crowned heads of at least three countries would have their fill. I did wonder if she was mad, a mental state of exaggeration. So, exasperated, she ticked the royal members Casper and Olav knew.

'These people like sport, especially sailing. And Olav has the boats. Casper has the horses. And you've got the guest list.'

She said October was the ideal month but I doubted if a gallery at that level would have space just like that in a couple of months' time. A process had taken place in me while working with her that removed doubt and ambivalence. I would not leave her. I would fight to keep her here in this house and, if necessary, would leave with her. I knew it was the right decision because a sense of peace, more serenity, filled the kitchen. You could almost lie against it. It was like thick cream. Everything was going to be all right.

And then the phone rang. It had a different sound from all the other hundreds of times it had rung, a lonely mournful singular sound. And I didn't answer it and she went towards it and I said 'Don't,' but she snatched up the receiver, listened and then spoke in Russian and soon I knew it was Mia on the line.

That call, the first swallow, announcing change but not summer in this case, heralded the fact that the outside world was now inside. I waited for the call to end and I waited a long time, so I made some tea and sat outside under what had looked earlier like 'his' tree. Was the decision mine? How many players were there? Three had seemed plenty. Now there were four. She came out expecting no change and offered to pour me another cup.

'Why did you lie about not using the phone earlier?'

'All right, I had to phone Mia. I have my life too. It doesn't stop because I'm here, or rather thrown out of here.'

'How dare you give her this number? How could you let her ruin everything after all we've said?'

'My God, you're a better actress than her. All that energy, drama.'

'You bitch.' And I wished I could slap her.

'You must be getting your period.'

'Fuck off.'

'Definitely. I knew there was something with that long face, and stirring him up.'

'How dare you deny me the right to have feelings? How dare you degrade them to some chemical state?'

'That's what it is. You're changed chemically.'

'You say this every time to get off the hook. You don't want to admit you're wrong. You've never, ever said sorry.'

She laughed, mockingly. 'You should see yourself. If that isn't chemical, what is? You're going into the menopause.'

And this statement she repeated whenever trouble arose. Periods, menopause, chemical distress.

'But you started it, Elle.'

'No, Catherine. You stir me up to get my anger because you need to let all this out. You want to have your blowout.'

It sounded an ugly experience and one I hoped never to have. 'Just so you get it straight about James, he wants you out. I'm trying to keep you in. Is that stirring him up?'

'You stir him up with all your drama so he reacts. If you were calm none of this would happen.'

I was on another planet, in another reality altogether.

'And the way you suck up to him. God, it's something to see.'

I couldn't believe this.

She mimicked me offering him a hot drink. 'How can you treat him like that? Who is he? Some bookworm with no money, all tied up with some dead guy, James. He's not even a man. Those sandals, those ugly toes sticking out. He's a gutter communist. The worst sort. "Would you like your coffee now?" ' she mocked.

I'd decided this relationship should be based on truth, at least on my part. I explained I was perhaps over-nice to him to make up for the fact I had my lover in the house.

'What's the good of that? Creeping around with hot drinks. Tell him the truth. Come out with it. A lot of men like it with two women.'

I still didn't slap her face. Yet.

'At least he's not a liar. He doesn't bullshit about what he can do for me. All that build-up with Jewel. My friend Lou found out they knew nothing about it. Even the agent in West Hollywood said you're a power maniac.' That wasn't the word, but it would do.

'D'you want to speak to her?'

'Why should I? I've already got an agent.'

'Jewel.' Looking at her watch she went to the phone and dialled long distance. It was answered and she asked for Jewel and yes, I was now interested and silenced. She said her name, Elle von Zoelen, and, after a short wait, a breathless voice was speaking. She'd rushed to the phone. Elle gestured for me to hold the phone and speak. I wouldn't.

'Jewel, I've got the English photographer here. I'm standing in her kitchen in London. She wants to say how sorry she was not to do that Wednesday session, but we had to leave in a hurry for Washington. I'm going to put her on.'

And she held out the phone as though it was a baton in the Olympics and I must take it or else let down a custom that had gone on for hundreds of years. I said I was sorry and repeated Elle's words.

'Yes, well, another time.'

'But there seemed to be a lot of stipulations.'

'Not really. What are stipulations?'

'Conditions.'

'I like the lighting man around even on day shots. And I know what I need to get a picture across. I've spent long enough on it.'

I agreed with her and asked why she was willing to work with me. Had she seen my work?

Elle was sighing now. Was I on the wrong track?

'No, Elle talked you up to me. If Eliane von Zoelen says you're a good idea, you're a good idea. She says I need something fresh.'

'I did try to apologise to your agent and PR people but they didn't know anything about it.'

'They just handle the money things. As far as I know Elle wasn't buying these pictures and getting someone to place them. If she decided to do that we'd have filled the agent in or some of my other guys.'

Total power and support, that's what I was talking to. Was she ever down? Depressed? Frightened?

Elle swept the phone out of my hand. 'If they won't let you do that movie you go to Casper. You can always get him through his New York office or Dag.' She hung up.

My first thought was what Lou would say – that it wasn't Jewel at all. But I knew the voice. It was husky with a funny catch in the middle notes and the laugh was hers – no one laughed that low at thirty.

'What film won't they let her do?'

'Oh, it's about a blues singer who supposedly murdered her husband and was in love with a male movie star in the Fifties. Jewel would sing those songs but they don't want her to sing. And secondly, they don't want her playing a woman they consider "bad image". She was gay, got the dead husband's fortune and loved this film actor, who was also gay. And she had a drink problem. It sounds like an everyday thing for the general public but the studios are timid. They think for their public. They're mice trying to roar like lions. They remind me of your husband.'

'You didn't know her when we saw her that first day in the foyer. The day we arrived.'

'I met her in the bar and she thought she'd seen me. A lot of people think that. And I mentioned Casper in the first breath and she knew of him so I was all right to talk to. And then she'd been to one of Dag's parties for a politician. He held it on top of a volcano. Flew everybody out by Concorde. He promised them it would erupt at any time, so live it up. It erupted the next week.'

'You didn't tell me.'

'Tell you?' She was amazed. 'I spent the next days getting you that deal.'

'Was she on her own in the bar?'

'No. With a group of people, but I can handle groups.'

'So you got to know her. All that, and advice on the movies she should make.'

'Well, yes. Although she wants to be the most famous star in the world, she has a real problem about being recognised constantly in public. She can never be a private person again. She can't do the things you and I and everyone else do, and suddenly that anonymity seemed like a luxury. So I proposed ways of handling that.'

'Ways?'

'If I go out and everyone thinks I'm Garbo, then all she has to do is go out and be a member of the general public. It's all a question of attitude and make-up and disguise. Decide who you're going to be.'

'So she listens to you.'

'So far. And you have to change your attitude and make the gallery deserve you and not the other way round.'

And we got on with the photograph selection and it was sort of all right between us. I felt stunned and needed to talk to someone other than the cause of my disturbance.

'Why d'you want her to make a film of that gay singer? I take it it was your idea.'

'Oh, definitely. Because it's right for her. Her next move.'

'D'you like being a Svengali? That's what you are, of course.'

'Oh, no. I'm more than that.'

And somehow, because of her big-headedness, she'd given something away that she didn't mean to, and she bit her bottom lip and looked uneasy. Her eyes clicked up to mine to see if I'd reacted and they were pale, frightened eyes. I went on with the work and looked as though I hadn't noticed, and what that actually was I didn't know.

And then the phone rang, and then again the phone rang.

32

Mia was back on the phone and she spoke intimately into the mouthpiece as though I'd suddenly learned Russian. I moved the tray of food back in from the garden, put the juice back in the fridge and sat on the back step. James still hadn't returned. Too agitated to sit there, I went into the kitchen and took the food out of the oven, the juice out of the fridge, and set the table in the garden. She was still on the phone. I sat, looking at the fishcakes as they cooled, hearing her voice giving love to someone else. All this without a drink. Yes, I was thinking back to those days and a drink would certainly be called for on this occasion and the many I'd gone through in the States. The call lasted an hour and four minutes and she came into the garden ready to eat.

'That looks good,' Elle said to the collapsed, congealed fishcakes.

'It's all ruined. You've ruined it.'

'But life goes on, Catherine. I'm part of it.'

'One hour and four minutes part of it ...' And then I couldn't speak, was unable to finish the sentence. I'd seen that before in a woman who'd been battered. She couldn't finish anything because she didn't have the confidence. Her husband had seen to that. Remembering her, I made myself complete the sentence even though it didn't make sense. She had ruined the lovely days we'd spent together, the harmony. She said she'd had to help Mia, who was trying to get money out of Olav. She had to tell her how to do it. That's the story I got.

'It's about as elusive as the three weeks you spent wherever without calling me.'

The phone rang again. I told her not to answer it.

'I have to.' And she left the half-eaten cold fishcake and went in for another marathon advice session on how to shake money out of Olav. I felt cold and twisted inside. She'd have to leave. When she finally got off that phone I'd book her a room in the Post House Hotel. I called to her to hang up. I had my husband to consider. He'd show up next.

I remembered when I'd loved him. James loved youth, and I remembered the day after our first night. We were at an academic lunch in Oxford and I was tense and there was no opening for me at that gathering. I sat quietly. And then James looked at me briefly and smiled, a little private smile. He was remembering the night.

'You make me feel –'

'What?'

'Something I thought I'd lost for good. Young.'

Now he was just someone in the kitchen.

'I'll have to ring her back. I'll pay for it,' she shouted. The kitchen was in half darkness. And then I saw a rectangle of grey twilight as the front door was opened. The rectangle was closed into darkness as the door was shut and he was in the house. He would have gone straight upstairs.

I used to think James knew about consistency. Because he was grown-up he'd protect our happiness as he would me, but the damage of my past was apparently too big, as were my dreams of freedom and a star's life in Hollywood. I could never settle or be content.

He'd been lightly built and fast moving with good reflexes. His face unaggressively tanned, eyes black and challenging. He'd seemed composed, courteous, but I knew it was a front for something wilder.

I passed through the kitchen filled with Russian words and went upstairs to find him. 'It seems she's going back.' I thought it was a lie.

He was sprawled on the bed watching television.

'She's right-wing. That's why you don't like her.'

'I can't talk to her,' he said.

'Because she doesn't know anything about Henry James.'

'She doesn't know about anything.'

'Oh come on, James. That's not true.'

'She's just shrewd. How long is she going to be here?'

With relief I realised that meant he did not expect her to leave now.

'She did get that session with the movie star. I spoke to her myself so she does do things that seem improbable. So she could get the exhibition organised. She's found a gallery.'

'How much longer is she going to be on that phone because I'm waiting for a call?'

As I went down the stairs he shouted, 'Get her off that phone.'

In the kitchen I spoke loudly. 'Hang up because James is waiting for a call.' She took no notice. I pinched her. She fought me off effortlessly, still talking. I tried to cut her off but she defended the phone. Worked up now, I went back upstairs and told him she wouldn't be long. Cold, I took the first jacket and went downstairs. I had trouble putting it on. In the lighted kitchen I saw it was the jacket with the tomato sauce stains. I tore it off and went into the garden and beat it against the table. I lashed it against the tree, the earth. I was beating it to death. And then I heard her laughter.

'And you try to tell me people say I'm disturbed. What are you doing with that jacket?' She got it off the fence. 'You are a strange person.' She sat in the kitchen and ate an apple.

I was going to say she couldn't use James's phone like that but she wasn't worried about him. Then she leapt up as though stung. I ran forward to swipe at whatever insect it was. 'Are you all right, Elle?'

She dropped a piece of apple on her silk blouse. She was ahead of me into the bright light, stretching out the blouse, peering at the juicy wet mark.

'It isn't too bad.'

Why did I involve myself in these stain catastrophes? For her it was too bad and even I could hear my remarks were weakly placating. Silly optimism, she did not want.

'Get me the salt and that tissue. Get out of here. You make it worse.' And she tore off the blouse and spread it out over a chair and made the visible invisible.

I sat in the garden for the thirtieth time that day at a disadvantage, and wondered what it was about stains that so disturbed her. I'd not remembered meeting anyone like that. Obviously it was a sign of perfection or the need for it.

She came out wrapped in a towel and wanted to know the nearest good cleaner. In this area that was a contradiction in terms. I was about to say it's been a terrible day, but the phone rang. I told her not to answer it because it could be James's call. He shouted from the window, 'Elle, phone.'

'It's your fault I dropped that apple. You're just stirring me up. You keep doing it.' Angry with me, but pleasant as hell on the phone. After several minutes he called from the window.

'Get her off that phone.'

She came into the garden with the damaged blouse, which had been washed and rolled in a towel. Stains for her were like disease.

'I've got to go away,' she said, simply.

I panicked. First I said, 'Oh no.' And then, 'Can I come with you?'

She didn't even hesitate. 'I'd love that.'

Then she looked at me fully with warmth, but I saw it was all on the surface. That's what charm was. Wonderful for other people. A chemical covering that had nothing to do with the inside of its possessor.

She kissed the dog. 'I'll miss you.'

33

Olav had some of his money offshore. I wondered if Elle had set up the trip to the island because James was being so difficult. She might like the unusual, but not this threesome.

'That was a quick decision, I must say. Between one call and the next.'

She half-smiled. 'But I have to see Olav. I think it's time we had a little talk.' She had the same expression as when the credit card jumped. She laughed and I sensed fear, a long way down, too far down. It was as though she was scared of what was happening in her. It was easier on the surface.

'Does it worry you seeing him?' And now the fear was quite closed off, the smile full on, defensive.

Although there was no money she bought club class tickets. The plane was full and she didn't get the seats she wanted, and that got the same reaction as a stain. She started giving me advice as soon as we took off.

'We have to buy you clothes. You'll have to dress up and talk about your photo-sessions with the old guy in Spain. Forget the one in the States, he won't have heard of him. And mention Jewel. He knows who she is. Don't go on about your career struggle. He's heard all that thousands of times. And your husband's a professor, not a teacher.'

I realised I was her ambassador. I now had my identity.

I'd lost the one I had thirty-six thousand feet down in Kentish Town. James's reaction to my leaving was such that I had to blot it out to survive. I asked for another Coke. She suddenly turned.

'Why d'you keep drinking that stuff?'

'Why? Is this a philosophical question?'

'You don't need it. It's greed.'

'I want it.'

'Want? Your wants are ugly.' We were back in the deli in LA with the coffee.

'Okay, I won't have it.'

'It makes you fat. You want what's bad for you. I want someone at their best. The best they can be. I don't want sugary flesh.'

She hadn't heard what I said or it made no difference.

The cabin crew came round with the tea and poured some in her cup. She shook a hand out. 'I didn't ask for that.'

The girl, realising her error, lifted the teapot too quickly and a drop splashed on to Elle's cup and sent several resulting splashes on to her chest. It was like some scientific experiment in a horror movie. She cried out as she saw the extent of the stains on the plain pale green silk shirt and fortunately multicoloured silk chiffon scarf. The trouble that resulted was big enough for the main crew member to be at our side. Elle went for the jugular and there was no calming her. She was off and I shrank into the seat, needing invisibility.

They brought ice and clothes-cleaning sticks and potions and royal champagne. They flopped a form under her nose – they'd pay for the cleaning, they'd pay for her life. Her eyes sought out the teapot-bearer and she went for her, only her. The teapot tilted and I got some on my leg. I did try not to scream. The teapot was removed and the girl taken away.

'I'll never ever travel with your company again.' And she mentioned the name of the chairman. 'D'you know him?'

The head of the cabin crew did not.

'You will,' she promised him. 'He's going to hear about this. I want the girl's name.'

'But it was an accident, Madam.'

'Oh no,' said Elle. 'She's been trouble from the start. I asked her when I got on for champagne, and I am paying club class –'

'But the rules –'

'If I was a man I'd have got it. She'd give a man a glass of champagne. Oh, definitely.'

We had every eye in the cabin on us.

'All those girls want is to pick up businessmen. They don't spill drinks on them, I notice.'

I nudged her to shut up.

'They just smile and do anything for them. But if a woman asks for something all you get is this –' and she imitated the girl's pudding face.

'If you have a complaint, Madam –'

'If?' She laughed sardonically. 'Put that in the plural.'

And then he said the wrong thing. 'Please fill in the complaints form.'

She assured him she was not on a flight to write a time and motion study for their company. No wonder other companies did better. With staff like him what could she expect? Expletives were used and she mocked the girl with the teapot and I knew he was at the limit of his training and the best thing he could do was disappear in the direction of the drinks trolley. I was in such a state of tension my stomach muscles were jammed against my spine and my legs numb. I pleaded with her to stop. From the corner of my eye I could see the other travellers ganging up together against her but they were not yet prepared to take her on.

She was like the north wind the Arctic dwellers dreaded. It had to blow itself out, this wildness, and then she'd be all right again. I wasn't going to explain this to the enemies.

The one in charge left the rule book behind and offered her some fairytale help – 'Immediate private lounge treatment on arrival, help with the stained clothes, her luggage would be collected' – he ran out of promises and went towards the flight deck. I hoped he wasn't going to unload this problem on the pilot. All we needed now was a patch of rockiness at the controls.

The man behind us had let his opinions become too loud and she turned on the offensive. They snarled, two Rottweilers, and she won. Her cheeks were flaming but my insides were redder. I was blushing with shame and nerves from my toes up. I asked her to calm down and drink the champagne, and I kept hearing James's voice. Of course she's not helping you. She utilises your life.

'I hate this,' I hissed. So she turned back to the man and went another round.

'Who asked you to let your wolf out?'

He told her he didn't accept expletives.

'Then don't fucking listen to other people's business.' She was fearless, unstoppable and possibly unbeatable. The head stewardess brought Elle a piece of news.

'The girl who spilled the tea is down the back of the plane, crying her eyes out.' She waited for Elle to be sorry.

'So what? If you don't train your staff properly, is it my business?'

I understood during the journey that Elle was trouble. Big trouble. She covered herself with a silk quilt of sustained one-tone calm, controlled, I realised, to the point of breakdown. The price, these huge outbursts of rudeness and anger triggered by some meaningless occurrence. The stains on her scarf merely added another colour to the existing ones and those on her shirt had faded to pale patches with curly edges like skin disease.

Before we landed she gave me some advice. 'Don't listen to the old man. Mia's filled him with some fancy ideas.'

'Because I stopped the phone calls?'

'A mixture of jealousies. You women are steeped in it.'

The car waiting for us was a long, huge chauffeur-driven job with a bar, a phone and a present on the seat, 'To my darling one.' The smile was back as she got in next to me and patted my leg.

'This is one of the largest Mercedes in the world.' She picked up the present and read the label. 'He hasn't put my name on it in case he has to use it for someone else. Cheap trick.' She tossed the present on to another seat and poured a drink. 'You've got the grey cloth look. Cheer up. We're going into a bright smart place. There's no room for grey cloths.'

So I brought up the matter of the dripping teapot and the ensuing drama, thirty-six thousand feet up.

'I hate that sort of thing. I can't be part of it because you won't let me. I'm there but I'm not able to do anything for you, the situation or myself. You say shut up. You ignore me. You make me mute. I can't go on.'

She knocked on the driver's window. 'Stop.' He pulled over, she opened my door.

'Get out.'

I panicked instantly. 'I can't.'

So she pushed me out onto the busy road, slammed the door shut, and the car sped off. I scrambled to safety. I sat on the verge, just missing the wheels of a passing airport bus. My first thought – she'll come back because this is illogical. My second thought, it's my fault, I'm too sensitive. My third thought, I shouldn't be here at all.

The air was fresh and there was plenty of greenery. If I wasn't stuck on a verge I could like this place. I stood up and waited for her to come back. She'd have to because that car held all my belongings, passport, credit card, cameras. I hopped from foot to foot, the nerves creeping up my legs, stinging like electric shocks, chilling my solar plexus, overheating my head. I was frightened, a frightened child, all of the abuse tearing at the grazes of the distant past, under which unhealed wounds waited. Somewhere back there I'd been frightened nearly to death by circumstances over which I had no control. All to do with my mother, the war, being abandoned. I didn't want to bring what should remain back there into the present, which had enough problems of its own. My philosophy was to move on and by change and new challenges grow, so the horror of that past had less hold.

I remained like a scarecrow at the side of this island road and I tried to reach her by thought. Come back. I'll never criticise you again. I'd make a speech, a poem of atonement, and eventually the car did come softly, expensively up to my dirty toes and the driver got out, opened the door, and there she was, sleek and composed in the cool gloom, and I fell on to the seat and said, 'Fucking evil wretch,' and the poem was all forgotten. Then I became aware it wasn't just her and me, but a third person occupied the opposite seat.

'This is Olav.' And she laughed. 'The English have a funny way of greeting. It's a send-up.'

'And I thought I liked the British humour,' said Olav in a quiet, modulated, accentless voice that had spoken in boardrooms and conferences throughout the world. He was international, a conformist and old enough to allow himself some rare specialities, one of which was the ice queen who sat opposite him. Yes, he had the short economy sleeves that Mia sneered at, in an otherwise exquisitely made suit of the particular blue wealthy men elect to wear. I'd seen photographs of gatherings of these men, including Swiss bankers, in this expensive blue which confirmed their status and became the uniform of their unofficial club. He was healthy, meticulous and accessible, and that was a surprise.

'Perhaps we kept you waiting too long. Elle had to pick me up. She said you had something to do, but what you found to do on the side of the road I can't imagine.' He poured me a glass of sparkling water.

'You had something to do,' she muttered. 'To pull yourself together. So smile.'

He knew. He knew about her temper, her rash acts, my dependence on her, the infatuation, the hopelessness.

'I heard you photograph old men. You'd better give me a shot.' He was in his late seventies but could have been fifty. 'We're going to my house, south of the capital. That,' he pointed, 'is the golf course.'

The car ate up the road and was doing sixty as though it was standing still, and was the first calm action I'd been involved in for days. He pointed to a house on a hill.

'That's mine.'

And higher up to what looked like a church. 'That's mine as well. ' He stabbed a finger at a line of boats. 'Mine.'

There was a lot of 'my' on the journey. She, I noticed, said nothing. Then he smiled and I was looking at a rat. He clapped his hands and placed them on her knees as though warming them. 'She is a beautifully made woman.' And I thought he was going to say, And she's mine.

'She's classy, outrageous and she's mine.'

She gave him a lovely smile, the usual one, but with a tilt of her head. She'd be back on the payroll.

He finally got his hands off her lap. I was so jealous, outraged, I thought I'd throw up. He didn't miss my discomfort and poured me another drink.

'I love Olav,' and she turned to me and winked. It was a wicked wink, one she could have made use of with the cabin crew on the plane. Was she going to sleep with him? Why hadn't that occurred to me?

We turned into a town like a picture postcard lit by a kind sun. Everything was picturesque and harmless. Not a drunk or beggar in sight. This was a rich man's town, nothing here to frighten or depress him. He pointed at all of it with one panoramic sweep. 'Mine. All mine.' Even the people.

A private cemetery, he remarked, contained the grave of an associate and brought tears to his eyes. Elle kneaded his arm.

'He's not gone far, Olav. Only from sight.'

'I don't believe all that,' he said. 'When you're gone, you're gone.'

'Oh, you'd be surprised what there is,' she said, lightly. 'Fairy stories don't even touch it.'

'I just believe in nature. There's no good thinking about a god.' He looked at me as though I could think otherwise. 'A man-made concept because scared people need one. I believe in nature. Nature has its own intelligence and will go on long after we're extinct. I'll be buried in the earth and my return, if at all, will be as a plant.'

'Darling, we'll know it's you and see you're watered.' I'd never heard her use that tone before.

'What will happen to all this when I go?'

And I thought of just the money concealed on this island. My mind couldn't even encompass the rest.

The main house was kept in the original style. Frugal, furnished to facilitate his life, it was a bachelor residence; everything was clean, uncompromising, masculine. He described himself as a seaman and liked to live alone.

'I spent months at a time on boats in my youth. For all my business I'm still that person.'

His bedroom was sparse with a single bed and gym next door. He enjoyed being tough and challenged. Two sea-going boats waited in the harbour and he navigated those himself. The office was the heart of this simple house and clocks showed the time across the globe and machines whirred and clicked, making him even more money in offices worldwide.

The only concession to a social life was an upright piano, and in this drawing room, which could seat seventy, he liked to give musical evenings. He especially liked a singer to be accompanied on this piano. There were many photographs of his boats, his grandchild and his deceased wife, Maria, but none of Elle.

Once in the house she melted and flattered his ideas and opinions, laughed at his smallest joke – they were all small – insisted he recite his favourite poems. She'd have him singing at the piano next.

'Come on, Olav,' she cried, 'sing Catherine your songs.' She opened the piano lid and led him to the stool. I tried to be friendly to him but I was so furious with her, I had to get out. She showed me my bedroom.

The minute she was away from him her face dropped. 'God, he's hard work. What do you think of him?'

'He reminds me of the devil but performs in reverse. Instead of "All this can be yours," as in the grand temptation, he says "All of this is mine but be nice and you can get some."'

'What's the devil got to do with it?'

'Just that what happened is similar to the temptation of Christ.'

'Why do you talk about that?' She was irritated.

'Maybe all that greedy gathering of everything is bad. And when it's used to tempt you away from good, then it's evil.'

'Evil? It doesn't exist. This is where you sleep.' She seemed upset. Were the notions of good and evil too naïve for her smart life? I thought it was something deeper.

'Where's your bedroom?'

'Next to his.'

The fury was now rage and I wanted to strangle her.

'You're going to sleep with him.'

'He never lets anyone sleep. Certainly not with him. In the old days you might be called into his room. He liked it first thing in the morning.'

'I hate you, Elle.' And I got my hands around her throat. Her strong arms did some kind of karate movement and smashed at my wrists, and my murderous hands flew from her neck. She chose to laugh and pulled me onto the bed.

'Such fierce little hands. My, my!'

I hated her because she'd murdered my love and I could imagine squeezing that handsome neck, but the resulting limp, heavy, lifeless body gave me no satisfaction and a dead body was inconvenient. I wanted her alive and suffering.

'I told you all that anger doesn't agree with you,' she said, sweetly.

'You are going to sleep with him.' I couldn't bear the pain and I lay on my side and howled like a wolf.

'If sorting out this money nightmare means I have to do it, too bad. You'll just have to take it.'

Stunned, robbed of life, I stopped howling and lay motionless.

She clicked fingers in front of my lifeless face.

They've kept dinner waiting for us so we'll have to go up. Be quick. Smile. Look happy in his company. He hates a gloomy face. And by the way, don't mention Dag. He doesn't like him.'

The meal was simple. Whatever he had back there was certainly not a cook. He asked about my husband and I managed a description of his work and wondered what the hell I'd do about him. Was he now ex-husband? I was tight-faced and certainly not smiling and he asked how we'd met, Elle and me, he meant. I had trouble with that one and, after a lot of nudging my leg, Elle took over. She arranged for me to photograph Olav in the morning and had already chosen a location. He pretended to be shy. I thought I'd be dead by then.

He asked to be alone with Elle as they had things to discuss, and I walked out on to the rocks above the harbour. I looked down at that possibility of death and hoped she could see me and worry. The sudden cold drove me in, and for a man who only liked smiles he wasn't doing too well. His face was sunk in shadows, his eyes when meeting mine were tortured.

'Where have you been? To a funeral?' she said. 'You look like you're still at one.' She gestured that I should smile.

I asked to use the phone.

'Who to?' she said, promptly, and set about lighting the fire. The sun was quite gone and an aggressive moon was pressing against the window.

'It does look near,' agreed Olav. 'I don't like a full moon.' And he added, 'Any more.'

His eyes were not the eyes I'd seen at dinner. I thought she'd sorted the money thing all right, asked for far too much.

*

In the morning it seemed he didn't want his photograph taken after all.

Elle said, 'He wants us to leave. Come on. He'll drive us to the airport.' She turned and spoke fiercely and he paled and kept saying a word I supposed was No. The housekeeper carried the plates away, her face surly. Elle packed for us in two minutes and we were in the car within five. I caught sight of the housekeeper and she was looking at Elle and her expression was one I'd not forget. Loathing or more. She was muttering prayers or curses, and made the sign of the cross.

This time down the hill there was no 'mine' or 'my' or waving at his territory.

*

The taxi was driving through forest black and empty for miles. It cut down a narrow path and there before us was a lake surrounded by banks of trees. The water was silver and dark where it reflected the grey sky. It was a mournful, unwelcoming place. Elle got out joyfully and ran to the water. 'Isn't it beautiful? This is a secret place. I don't think people know about it.' She mimicked Olav. 'All mine, mine, mine.'

Birds, large and black, circled above her, swooping in as though to welcome her. I shrank back, glad the taxi was waiting.

They screeched, seemingly excited, and I could hear the beat of strong wings. She stood, arms lifted, welcoming the lake, the birds, and then she took off her clothes, dived in and swam.

The taxi driver watched me and I was even scared of him. The place was too mournful and, even worse, spiritually desolate. I wanted to get out of there.

And she swooped out of the water in a great spray and frightened us. She came out of the lake naked and strong, and then I knew what she was. More than human, an element that had to pretend to be one of us, an element which had more joy than we did, and perhaps more evil.

Elle nudged me. 'Wake up. You're having a nightmare.' Another one? The plane came in to land.

34

Sitting by the Hampstead pond she told me about her mother.

'She had this sadness right from the beginning. That of course was being married to him, but I didn't know it then. She was creative but never got the chance to do anything. He, my father, killed all that off, and she finished the job for him by getting ill. Ended on a life support system in a white room – for some reason it had bars on the windows – she couldn't even move in the bed. But she didn't die. It went on for years. All that was left of her were her eyes. That's the only way she could communicate, by her eyes. She couldn't touch me –'

'How old were you?'

'Six when she got ill. They promised me it wouldn't be for long. I thought they meant her coming home. They meant the end. But she couldn't die. When I was thirteen she made it clear she wanted me to finish it for her. I pulled the plug and then went out dancing with Stephan von Zoelen. That was quite a day. All these dreadful commonplace women live on forever ... that's when I knew there was no justice.'

I had absolutely nothing, not one word to say.

She looked at the pond. 'It's nice how the sun ripples on the water. Nice and tame. But it's not as splendid as my lake.'

'Didn't you want children of your own?' I said, eventually.

'I can't have children.'

'Why not?'

'Oh, it wouldn't be right.' And she jumped and got Daisy out of the water and dried and hugged her.

'I've just remembered my mother's nickname for me. By the way, did you photograph the cemetery in my village? You said you were going to.'

'With the desecrated grave?'

'That's rubbish.'

For some reason I said no. The undeveloped reel was still in the darkroom.

*

She was confident she could go on staying in the house although I told her we should make other arrangements. For a start I couldn't handle the threesome. She said she looked forward to being there, and it was the down-to-earth atmosphere, its sense of freedom she seemed to like. I did not look forward to James's reaction one little bit and told her it was unlikely we could stay.

'But we're doing your exhibition. We need the darkroom.' She assured me the smart gallery in Piccadilly would find space for my work in October. Having seen what she could do with a top movie star I kept my doubts to myself. October anyway was far too soon and I'd need time to set it up, get the publicity. I'd also need new work.

'Get on with it then. I'll help you.'

She was upstairs watching television when James came in and saw her coat over the chair.

'I don't want that woman in this house.'

'I'll talk to her.'

'I'll talk to her, you mean.' And full of rage he started for the stairs.

I grabbed at him. 'I'm the one who needs to talk. It's my house too, James.'

He lost his temper exceptionally and shouted at me, ripping through the business of the suspect lesbian love to the real problem, the dereliction of our marriage. We had no intimacy, trust, togetherness, money. And now to bring my lover into the house ...

'But she's not my lover,' and I found I was crying.

James said we had to go to marital therapy, and from the safety of that process decide what to do. Another person was not going to come in and decide for us. He'd found a therapist and wanted to arrange a meeting. 'If you don't like him we can go to someone at the Tavistock, who –'

'I told you. The sex thing for me never lasts.'

'Sex has nothing to do with it. The problems are much deeper. Sex is the last thing to go.' He tried to tell me about damage limitation, and I'd had enough. I knew he must be a fuck-up dude to live with me and this was the truth. We could go to a dozen shrinks, it wouldn't make it any better. I could keep a sort of routine and be calm, I could take photographs and wanted to do marvellous work. I wanted fame and applause. I could be a good friend, I hoped. But I wanted the new, the exciting, Hollywood, the adrenalin, the night, the fix. Day-to-day living with the same person – where was that? Of course, it would die with her, but I never saw where the fuse would blow.

'You need treatment.'

I didn't need treatment. I needed remaking. So he used the argument that I was his wife.

I screamed at him and he slapped me, which brought her to the kitchen. He told her instantly to leave. 'This is between me and Cathy.'

'You don't have to let the whole street know,' I shouted.

'Leave this house now,' he told her and he held my arm tight as he said it.

She was going to reply but something in his manner, the absolute defence of his property, including me, made her hesitate. It was more than that. He represented a terrible judicial authority which, if necessary, called upon inexhaustible energy and rightness to continue its cause. You only achieve that authority by education, qualification and spiritual integrity – states so foreign to her she couldn't even think about them. He contested everything in a quiet, modulated voice.

'You have to go, Elle.'

She ran upstairs and I got away from him and went after her, and on the second landing she bent and somehow aged, sort of scuttled into a room, all crouched over and looking terrifying. This was no longer Elle. She scuttled like some huge, pale old spider running for cover. And, quite breathless now, I arrived at the room and for a moment it seemed empty and then I saw her, crouched on the floor by the bed. I was about to go towards her but there was something not right about the way she was. The sun cast shadows across her and the wall, like bars – the room her mother had been trapped in – something long and imprisoning. But it was only the sun, I told myself.

'I don't want to go.' She sounded frightened.

'You don't have to. It's my house too.'

'I've felt safe here. It was the same feeling as the summerhouse when my mother was there. Yes, I feel well here.'

The leaves stirred by the wind outside made a tinkling like tiny bells.

'I don't want to be thrown out.'

I promised she wouldn't be. I could see it was vital that did not happen.

'I was thrown out of the summerhouse when my father brought the mistresses to stay. Sent somewhere really awful. He was a tyrant but they all admired him. He was such a great doctor. They told me I was a liar.' She looked more normal and wasn't in a barred room at all. It was just a trick of the sunlight.

'But it was never the same when my mother had gone.' She burrowed her face in her hands like a child so I couldn't hear what she said. It sounded like, 'I can't be thrown out.'

I wanted to comfort her, put my arms round her, hold her, but it was as though she was a different person. Broken and down. I knew all about that. I didn't immediately associate it with Elle. But it was more than that. Somehow I couldn't look at her. She was not mine to touch.

'It was all cold in the summer for me after that.' Her voice was hard and flat.

James was sitting in the garden. I told him I needed to work in the darkroom. He wouldn't hear of it.

'But the house is half mine. She stays.'

'Sit down.'

I refused. 'We're doing this exhibition together in October. I need the exhibition, so –'

'She has a certain fixedness of purpose that is disquieting.' He looked up at me, eyes hard. 'She has a Napoleon complex. She's self-willed to the point of … the psychiatrists have a name for it. Give the therapist a try.'

'What, for her, you mean?'

'For us.'

'I'm in love with her.' There was our marriage over.

'Some people say being in love is a mental illness. It has all the symptoms. I don't give it a very good time in my teaching.'

'Let her stay.'

'Not a chance.'

'Then I go with her.'

He did try to reach out for me, but I'd gone.

35

She moved us into an unfurnished flat above the pond with a view across Hampstead Heath and nearby the cafés and shops of South End Green. I hadn't ever been installed in such an idyllic place and it was the beginning of a happy if expensive time. There was just one cloud in the over-bright sky. She chose all the furniture and furnishings herself. When I asked to be at least part of the process she became impatient.

'Oh, don't be silly. What do you know about it? This is the start of a big career for you. Let's get you a background.'

I thought she loved me because I felt this unconditional love without limit, in which I was able to be myself, a new self, one so far not experienced.

The first thing we did when we got in was to turn the music up and dance: we danced through the empty rooms and, still dancing, she opened champagne and offered me the bottle, and my blood went cold and the dance for me was over.

'I forgot,' she said, and drank from the bottle. 'I was having such a good time.'

While a darkroom was being installed I could work at Lou's studio. This, at the end of August, meant I had six weeks until the opening of the supposed one-woman show. Nothing about it was real and I waited till she was out to phone the gallery in Piccadilly. I sat down heavily for this call. There wasn't space this year, next year or no year. I had to prove myself on a level of excellence which would bring them to me. They wouldn't even look at my portfolio. They did ask who my agent was, and I started to mention the name of the London one, but hung up in the middle of yet more dismissal.

Elle came in with flowers, various bottles of mineral water and numerous sheets of mounting paper.

'I thought we should decide what mounts you want before we go to the framers. Lou is right. The best one is in Finsbury Park.'

I sat in the kitchen, a light open-plan space with polished pale floorboards, and told her the truth. There was no show and never would be.

'Why are you always so negative?' The red spots of colour I dreaded appeared on her cheeks. 'Did you mention Casper?'

'Of course not.'

She picked up the nearest phone and restored herself to good humour as she spoke. While she continued on the phone I had to admire the simplicity of the apartment. A pale soft yellow wall-to-wall carpet in the living room, and even paler sofas and armchairs. Plenty of mirrors and glass. A low glass table held glass sculptures, an ashtray. It was as light as could be to join the sky which filled the windows. The rooms were coloured by the sun which appeared both in the morning and the end of the day in the far windows. On rainy days, it was like drowning at sea – she preferred those days. The glass reflected the essence of the pond below. It was a cavern of the ephemeral, inviting change, unexpected moods, reminding me of a kaleidoscope. She had furnished it well and, looking at it, I could see there was no place for Daisy and was silenced by what I'd left. These pangs, and there were many of them, missing life over there in the dark and the dust, had to be blotted out.

She came off the phone and asked why I wasn't getting the mounts sorted out. I waited.

'Of course there's space.'

'Not when I rang.'

'There is when you mention Casper Shulz. You haven't got the main gallery. You've got one side room and the downstairs, but good enough.'

'How?'

'How? He's made a suitable arrangement, which means he's either bought enough of their main exhibition in advance, or he's made an offer for it to be continued elsewhere advantageously. He's obviously guaranteed you selling. Now we have to know how many frames we get on their walls, and what sizes.'

Was I pleased? No. I'd get there by some unexpected route which had nothing to do with who I was, or the quality of the work. She didn't like my silence. 'I told you, it all comes down to money. I have to do the invitations now. Casper suggested touring the exhibition. Germany, Scandinavia, Paris, the States, Japan. If you do well enough, solo, otherwise with two other photographers.'

'I prefer that.' I didn't say it sounded more honest.

'Not necessarily. He's already got his newspaper editor friends receptive, and if they're difficult he goes to the newspaper owners. Don't look so betrayed. You must have learned that look from James. This is life. It's stage-managed. We make our own luck. Nothing just happens.'

'I could be putting loo paper on those walls.'

'We could. But you are good. You're going through a crisis of confidence.'

'How will he get his investment back?'

'Oh, he'll speculate on your work.'

I wasn't mad about 'speculate'.

'He'll get it on to the market, get the price up, and then he'll sell. And then you'll do a book. He'll own the rights. And then the film. We'll have to sign something over to him.'

'Why is he doing it?'

'Because I'm crazy about you.'

'He doesn't know that.'

'No. He's crazy about me.' She laughed so I knew it was a joke. 'Can't you just trust it?'

'Truthfully, no.'

*

Lou helped me mount the sixteen pictures and changed the frames. She was in awe of Elle, fascinated by her, almost shy. Elle gave her an initial dollop of charm and then treated her like the scrubwoman. She even had her varnishing the wooden floor in the apartment.

The gallery priced my work too high. Casper might be beyond wealth, but he understood prices.

'You won't sell to them if you're robbing them.'

He still wore the small, dark, menacing sunglasses and directed all his advice and opinions to Elle. If he liked my work he didn't say so, but he decided how to sell it. His old selling paint door-to-door skills came in handy. 'We'll promote its simplicity. And that means it has to be really good.' He was still talking to Elle, so she'd pass it on to me. Half of the photographs were not, in his opinion, up to standard. People didn't want art, but cheering up or being excited. I asked why he didn't speak to me and she said, 'Because you're just The Talent.'

I wanted to see the gallery to decide where and how to hang the work. She wouldn't hear of it.

'We do that, Casper and I. You just go and take a few more railway stations at night. Do another of the one with the gas lamps and the fading Fifties poster.'

I reminded her I had a hospital appointment.

'You don't have time for that. Or time to be ill. Go and lie in hospital once the exhibition is over.' I agreed with that.

Casper's organisation got behind it and the show was ready in a week, the preview filled comfortably with real buyers, A-list socialites and a few critics. How, I wondered, would Casper control them?

'If they don't write it up optimistically, and we only need one good line, the editor won't put it in the paper. But they've already been given a hint and after all you are new talent and they'll go some way to supporting that.'

I asked Lou for her absolute opinion.

'Your work is raw and sometimes it works. But you're unripe and they're pushing you too fast. They've got money all right, but they don't know what they're doing. They're inventing a career, and you won't have "legs".'

'Meaning?'

'You won't last on your own. He's given you far too big a gallery. But you must believe in your work. Sometimes it's powerful and super-real, marvellous in atmosphere. You've got some way to go, technically. You're a documentary photographer and you don't repeat yourself.' She named a top portrait photographer and said I was the opposite of her. 'She always does the same picture, whatever she shoots. So you don't see the subject, you see her.'

'What I want to know is, will the viewers realise they're being manipulated and will they accept it?'

She couldn't think of it like that. It was the sort of moral argument that – she nearly said – James would handle. If she had a criticism, I was a bit too lucky.

'Take my advice and photograph those views from Primrose Hill and the moon over the city. Shoot from low down so you include the hill. You get things no one else can. You sort of coax it out of the night. Do a set. You'll sell them. They'll buy them for their offices. Dentists will take them. You'll sell those, every last one, because it's their city. Don't go for low cafés and alleyways any more, because they'll find those derivative even if they're not. Get that fairytale atmosphere.'

She became so enthusiastic I felt able to ask what she thought of Elle.

'Never met anyone like her. Goes too far. But some men like it. She'll take them further than they know how to go. She's dangerous. She's into danger. But I wouldn't have thought she was gay.'

And I had to agree that she wasn't into female sex. Quite the opposite. She was almost prudish.

'You're excited by her because she's both man and woman. Who wouldn't go for a taste of that given the chance? I'd love to take her photograph.'

'So would I.' It was the one thing she wouldn't allow.

Elle bought me a dress for the preview and I hated it. It was wildly wrong, depressing, and made me depressed because it made me ordinary.

'Oh, you'll never be that.' She was still willing to laugh. 'Just trust me.'

'I need to wear black.'

'You're not fifteen. Casper and I know what we're doing. You've got to stop all that Bohemian-on-the-edge business. You're in the real world now. These money people – they mustn't be frightened of you. Smile, look them in the eye, be normal. That's what they want.'

I no longer wanted to be there. I tried to tell her she'd got everything the wrong way round.

She poured me a glass of lemonade. 'And you're not to keep eating between meals. You eat all wrong and you'll get fat.'

I explained these were my meals. I had no time to sit down.

'The dress starts you off in the way you're meant to go on. I've got a beautician coming round to do your make-up. I'll do your hair.'

'Oh, this is too much.'

'Do it the Kentish Town way, then. But where did that get you?'

So I decided to do it her way, just for one night. But it wasn't the preview I'd wanted. I had tried to see James, but he'd only accept my presence if it was in a therapist's room. I invited him to the preview.

'Not a chance. It's her show.'

I told him how much she believed in my work.

'She knows nothing about it.'

'You're too angry to talk to.'

'She utilises your life.'

'You keep saying that.'

'She uses you and takes you over, for her benefit. What has she ever done? She can't get it for herself. She has to get it from others. She's a life-stealer. I don't want to talk to you again unless you agree to get help.'

'Tough love. What do you want?'

'I want peace,' he whispered. It sounded chilling and put an end to any more discussion.

*

I wore the dress and she wore the suit, and she didn't need me. They gravitated towards her and she tried to include me, because that's why we were all here at this exclusive evening.

'I want you to talk to him. Go on.' She pushed me towards some chubby money guy, her fingers gripping and digging into my arm. And then on to the next target and she wheeled me across the room like a pram with a spoke missing. 'Tell him you love the night. Tell him why you printed twelve. Say you would love to photograph his wife.' Her fingers were dry sticks. 'And Casper's friend, don't look now, wants you to do a portrait of his wife. Remember to smile. And carry a glass of champagne, for heaven's sake, or they'll think there's something wrong with you.' I understood how Mia had gone mad.

And these people, so rich, were such a disappointment. I wanted them to have freedom and glamour and be more adventurous and exciting. I kept seeing Olav waving at the island. Mine, All mine. And the emptiness was frightening. I didn't know it would be like this. And she went on shoving people into groups and couples, and I thought of how James took hold of someone in his sensuous and giving way: the happiness we had shared still lingered in that house, which he said he could not afford and would now sell. Of course I had a six-month fuse with guys. I was obviously latently homosexual. It was still a shock.

Casper's soft, groomed voice could be heard from every point of the room as he sprayed out the names of his associates that kept him at number one. Of course they'd buy the stuff on the walls. They snatched it up like Kleenex tissues. They'd buy used paper bags if it'd please him. So he did the deals and the show was a sell-out.

'The dots are going up,' said Lou.

'I couldn't give Jack-shit,' and I walked out, and she would have followed but there were potential collectors for her work too, and I understood that. I kept hearing her saying my work would grace dentists' surgeries. Hers didn't.

I didn't know anyone at the preview except Lou. When Elle had heard who I intended to invite she'd had a seizure of rage. 'You can't put those people in the same room as Casper Shulz. They'll wear those hideous sandals and have ugly toes sticking out, like your ex-husband.'

And I gave in, but I'd only do it once.

36

It wasn't until after New Year 1986 that we really settled into the Hampstead flat. Casper had sent the exhibition to five capitals where he was familiar with the money network and we had been travelling over three months. There were long posters of views of Primrose Hill and night over the city with a high moon. I even saw one in a café in Paris. The critics were not as kind as Casper expected and preferred the subjects he had not chosen. I had put an earlier photograph of a café in Kentish Town just by the door, and they all focused on that.

'So what?' said Casper. 'Who's ever heard of a critic? Name one. Even a dead one.'

He wanted me let loose in Paris at night.

'Get those railway stations. And get on a train and take stuff of the suburbs, the lighted windows in the houses by the line. Mysterious. Nostalgic. You're good on that. Everyone wants to know the drama behind the lighted window.'

He spoke to me direct now because I'd made enough money for him. He wanted the Pantheon at sunrise to be used as a logo for one of his companies. Meanwhile, the book, *Night in London*, was being published and we were due to go back before Christmas. Then he remembered Venice, and we took the night train from Paris, and he planned to sell fifty sets of prints. He was wise enough, in this city of major art, not to go for an exhibition. I found the much-adored Italian port deeply disappointing. It had been looked at to the point of exhaustion. There was nothing I could find to photograph except the floods, the decaying walls, the hypnotised tourists, and Casper did not want that. So they got me to photograph birds flying above the lagoon, with Venice in the background. It was Elle's idea and something about the scene with birds and water resonated with the dismal aching sadness I'd dreamed on the plane.

'It's too gloomy,' said Casper, and wanted bright, light shots at the milky white beginning of dawn, with just one tall sail boat appearing, and he chose one with red sails that came like a knife through the white mist. They did prints, posters, postcards of that, and it was their biggest seller. But Casper hadn't finished with Venice and wanted St Mark's Square, Harry's Bar, the palazzos, the churches, and I couldn't do it.

'You can.' Elle's nails bit into my arm.

And I did it. But this would be the last time.

Back in London, the flat looked fresh and filled with flowers. She'd engaged a cleaner to keep it immaculate and alive for our return. I fell back onto the pale sofa to read my post and she rushed across to place another cushion under my head, took off my shoes, made me some tea, couldn't do enough. The phone started up. Maybe it had never stopped, and there was plenty of Russian energy.

'Casper says they're lining up to be photographed. The movie stars, the rock stars. There's a Hollywood wedding-of-the-year he's booked you to do. It's scheduled for February. An eight-page supplement. They're offering enough, but he's trying for more. He says you're one of the hottest, if not *the* hottest photographer around. You get to call the shots.'

And I heard it all, and I'd been through it all but I didn't believe any of it. It had happened. I was there. I tried to tell her. Was that a mistake!

'But that's what fame is, okay? It's quick. How d'you want it? Slow? You've got enough money to keep you for two years.'

'How d'you work that out?' I was on to that one. Casper's arithmetic and mine were different. His eight only looked like my eight.

'How do I work it out? Casper does it. You're not going to start that Sherlock Holmes stuff with money. If it wasn't for me you wouldn't have a dime. I don't know what you'd do without me. So come on. Cheer up. We'll go out and eat.'

We always went out and ate. We'd done nothing else for five months. I still tried to talk to her honestly but I'd begun to see it was a foolish exercise. It might be what I wanted, but she wanted approval. No, worse, flattery. Yes, I was in a lousy mood and depressed. And I clung to her before going out for yet another meal, and tried to revive the heat, the passion, even the hug.

It never lasted for me. Of course, that's why she'd chosen me.

*

In the mornings we worked on the text for the book and in the afternoons she took a siesta and wanted me enfolded in her arms. At night, we went out taking photographs and dancing in the clubs. There was never any sex and I wondered who she had it with. I thought it might be Casper. He was old and tired, clapped out and sagging, but he perked up when she appeared. She brought him to heel, made him swallow vitamin pills and have silicone shots for his lips.

'What d'you mean, you want it natural?' she said. 'It's an unnatural world.' And he fawned on her and she gave him the occasional pat on the head. No, I didn't think it was Casper.

Of course she didn't want sex. She mainlined on power and control and something I couldn't quite define, but that was more intimate than those two. She started to arrange the party for the London book, the flights to the States for the Hollywood wedding. She'd opened a bank account in London and had the rest offshore. When Casper paid her she invested it for me.

'Will we buy something?' I asked.

Touching on the future like that was a shaky business. Her eyes moved around uncertainly.

'Buy something?' She didn't know what I meant. We were always buying many things.

'A home?'

'But I have one. Let's see –'

Did I have one? James was still in London as far as I knew. The phone was always on answer service.

'Is Mia still in Spain?'

'She'd better be, or the old man will pull the mat from under me. He pays that mortgage and those loans, a small peseta at a time.'

I asked about Mia's plans for Helsinki and the theatre.

'They weren't her plans, but mine. She'll have to stay down there till Olav settles down. And she's not well enough to do all that challenging performing stuff. She can go to the theatre school in the spring.' She started making party lists and shopping lists, and I said I'd go out and see Lou.

'See Lou?' She put the pen down. 'That's a hell of a way to show gratitude. After all I've done for you.'

'I meant just call in.'

She didn't respond, so I asked if she wanted to come too.

'I do not. I think you've gone way past Lou.'

And I thought, okay, for now. I'll see her tomorrow.

And she carried on with the lists and I just sat on the pale sofa, looking at the egg-yolk-yellow carpet. And I felt torn inside.

'Why d'you have that grey cloth face? Go and do something.' Her face was brutal. I stood up, determined not to fight with her. 'Let's go and eat.' And I started for the door. We went to the Italian restaurant although I wanted to go to the Chinese. Then I said I was sorry for suggesting that impromptu visit to Lou. It was thoughtless. I wasn't sorry at all, but wanted to get back our closeness. She didn't acknowledge the apology and we ate in silence. I felt depression, anticlimax, sadness like a lift coming down, and me inside it. I couldn't bear the wrongness between us. I wanted, needed, that sweet all-encompassing love. I tried talking about our travels. There was nothing to talk about. I knew, but I wasn't going to tell her, that the exhibitions had made no dent in the world of photography. The film had better be good, which meant she and Casper had to keep out of it. Otherwise I had no future. I asked if she wanted to go back and play cards. I'd taught her a game she seemed to like. Again she didn't answer and when we got back to the flat she went straight to the television. So I asked what was wrong.

Again no answer, so I said I'd go shopping. I gathered my chequebook, bag, coat and scarf, and got as far as the door.

'Don't expect me to be here when you come back.'

Stabbed by fear, I writhed to a halt. I hadn't heard that. Yes, I had heard that.

'Look, let's talk.' I got myself into the nearest chair and as I sat down I felt the heaviness of my body. I felt glued to that seat, ready for what was to come. 'If I've done anything to upset you –' I told her how I couldn't live without her and I'd do anything for her. 'Is it because we don't have sex?'

'Jesus.' She was up on that one and looking dangerous. 'That's all you think about. Giving yourself to men. And what do you get out of it? You just let them use you. "Let me suck your cock. Come on, punish me. It's so big. Fill me up." ' And she mocked the sexual gyrations. I had, during the open and honest moments of our travels, felt close enough to tell her of some of my encounters. Perhaps I'd been trying to excite her. To give myself totally to her. Past, present, fantasies.

'You're just a grey cloth. Okay, go and have a man. Have twenty. But don't come crawling to me when you've nothing left. I took you out of that dusthole with that anal creature. You've had no upbringing. No mothering. You're a wreck, everybody can see it. What are you doing with that loser, they ask me. I have to defend you.'

Filled with rage, I fought back and lost. She got her leather jacket and walked out, slamming the door.

I sat there maybe half a minute. It was unbearable. I couldn't have done a whole minute. Up off that chair, running down the stairs, down the street, calling her, shouting, crying. Abandoned? Unthinkable.

'I'll do anything, but don't leave me.'

She hailed a taxi and tried to escape, but it was taken and she got me instead. And I made her walk on to the Heath and I said, 'Sorry, sorry,' but what it was about I had no idea.

'But you have these mood-swings. You're sick. I've seen it for months. At least that anal reptile is right about that.'

Again, defending myself, I said, 'But I'm upset because you upset me.'

'No, no, no.' She couldn't scoff enough. 'You want the pain. You want me to hurt you. And you don't let up until I do.'

This sounded all wrong. It sounded like a hell of an ugly scene, new to me.

'I don't recognise this, Elle.'

'Of course not. You're in it. It's denial. You want me to punish you. You turn me into an angry person.'

'But all I wanted was to call on Lou.'

'There you go again.' Cheeks blazing. 'You can't leave it alone. You're starting again.'

'Why can't you fucking listen to me, you bitch?' And I lost any control I might have had, and screamed at her.

'If you go on like this I'm leaving.'

'Then fucking leave.'

And she did. Good, I thought. And watched her go. And again I couldn't bear it and ran, heart pumping, towards her. This time she got a cab.

I crossed the street on stiff, clicking legs. What had I done? Lost the only person I'd ever really loved. I passed the pub where I'd drunk a million times but the thought of a drink didn't occur to me. I had to survive. I'd played this one before. Three years old? Fourteen? Hollywood? I'd go. It had always been the answer. I had the money. Five thousand in the current account. I'd go now and buy a ticket. I'd get some shoes, a coat, make-up, books. I gave myself licence to have anything I wanted because I could afford it. There was plenty more where the five thousand came from. And I walked up Rosslyn Hill, eyeing the clothes shops. Yes, I could have anything in the street. The odd thing, I didn't want anything.

She'd gone. I thought my heart was breaking there and then, like a dropped cup.

I thought it better to return to the flat and wait for her to ring or come back. Once inside, I walked to and fro, praying for her to come through the door and hug me, and all would be well again. Whatever I'd done, and I was unclear exactly what it was, I'd never repeat it. I'd expunge it from my pattern of human activities.

The phone rang and I grabbed it like a life raft. Lily said, 'I've been worried about you. Are you all right?'

'Yes. No.'

'I talked to one of the village women. You asked me what they thought. They think she is a figure that brings epidemics, the plague. But they'd find anything. They just don't like her. Especially what she's done to Mia.'

I asked how she was.

'Never goes out. Wasting away. Won't eat. Serge tries to feed her. He keeps the villagers out. I think she's got a wasting disease. He's over there now.' She took a drink.

I recalled in LA how Elle looked from the hotel roof down to the beach, looking at the sunbathing girl.

'She's not to be feared,' said Lily. 'D'you know what she is? A house-wife.' She hung up.

Elle was filled with bad, strong elements, the north wind, swirling and wild, bigger than her. How could this little housewife who cooked badly be filled with this power? Perhaps it wasn't part of her? Did it pass through her? The necessary camouflage – huge charm.

I paced up and down the yellow carpet, my legs shaking with fear, breathless, and the afternoon was gone. Was it that I hadn't been altogether happy about the exhibitions? I had shown some temperament, which Lou would certainly have done, because my work was threatened. I hadn't wanted the softening of approach, the dentists queuing up for sunsets. I wanted to phone Lou, but didn't want the line to be occupied and so miss Elle's call. The darkness was suddenly unwelcome and there was a faint, foul smell. James was right. I should see a shrink.

I didn't hear the key turning but suddenly there was light.

'Can't you even put the lights on?' And then she gave a terrible shout and rushed to the carpet and I jumped back, thinking she was about to hit me. She bent down and looked at the yellow wool, mourned it, almost wept over it. And there, indisputably, were footprints clogged with dog shit. I ran for a cloth and bucket.

'Leave it. Only you could do this. I told you, always take your shoes off.'

I didn't bother saying sorry. The only thing was to kill myself. These were stains on a scale beyond anything she'd dealt with. I watched dully as she cleaned the rug, her movements staccato and brittle. She pushed past me for fresh water and I suggested we get a cleaning service in, and then the phone rang and I went to answer it.

'Leave it.'

She lifted the receiver but whoever it was had hung up. Quickly her fingers sped through the numbers for call return. The caller had withheld their number.

'Well, well. Who are you expecting a call from? Mr Right?'

She was off again, raging at me, tearing at me, and I'd had enough and I realised I had the fruit knife in my hand and I went towards her, gathering strength from the rage, the injustice, the absolute murder of my love. I was Clint Eastwood on a horse, facing ten killers. And the knife was at her throat and I thanked God that's where it stayed. 'Don't ever speak to me like that again.' And I backed away, put the knife down and went into the bedroom.

I sat on the bed and realised there had been no fear in her eyes. Nothing. Although it had scared the life out of me, the knife business hadn't bothered her. And I realised it was the first day that I hadn't taken a photograph and this was my favourite time of year.

Around midnight I crept into the main room where the washed carpet was drying. Elle was lying on the sofa, her duffel coat over her head. Softly, I asked if she was asleep. I pulled gently at the coat and asked if she wanted anything.

'Out of this hell,' she said, roughly.

'I'm sorry. I shouldn't have gone into it.' And there I was, sorry, sorry, sorry again. Yet I'd fight to the death to save one of my convictions, beliefs. What should I do? Fight her? And, if she cries and leaves, not feel guilty? Or lash myself and crawl in filth and say, 'Look what you've done to me. Feel guilty. Be sorry?' Should I kill myself?

'Can we talk about it?' This was becoming my theme tune.

'You're sick. And you're making me sick. You're in this SM scene which you obviously had with your mother, and with James. Oh yes, you did, you did. And I don't want to be in it.'

Again I felt the stirring of pain and humiliation. This was unjust. She knew nothing about my mother. I hated the insults to myself and those I loved, especially James.

'You've had no discipline in your life. It's all you! You!' And on she went until I felt like a formless bit of muck, lower than the shit I'd accidentally trodden in. And I sat crouched over, head in my hands, wanting her to see she'd done me in, how hurt I was. But she got up, flung shut the door and went to bed.

This became the pattern. She attacked me and I retaliated and she hurt me. I fought back. I drew blood and she retreated and sometimes broke and cried. But then I felt guilty and tried to rescue her. I hated the forced separation between us. I wanted it back the way it was before.

On this particular night, after I'd sat until my legs were numb, I went to the bedroom and lay beside her, not bothering to undress or wash. I seemed to sleep and was somehow connected to her – not the hug, which rarely happened any more, but I felt pressure on my body as though she was lying on me.

'You're stopping me breathing. Get off,' I said and opened my eyes. And she wasn't there at all, and there were long, dark lidless eyes like insects all around the bed and a scuttling sound in my ears.

'But I'm not lying on you.' Her voice now.

'Can you see them? Eyes?'

She put the light on and they were gone. 'I was asleep,' she said.

I was sure she hadn't been in the bed, but over by the window. The pillow wasn't dented, nor the duvet moved.

'You haven't been to bed.'

'I was looking out at the Heath.'

'But it isn't that way. It's behind us.'

And there was a tight feeling in the room, as though there wasn't enough space for us.

The next day I got out while she was on the phone and left a note saying I'd gone for a walk. I ran to Lou's studio and told her about the eyes.

'They're black, opaque, long, lidless eyes. The sort the ancient Egyptians painted.' I drew one, and she said it looked like the cover of a book about an extraterrestrial being. The eyes stretched right across the face and she thought they belonged to aliens. Her cleaner said it was the evil eye. Lou asked what Elle thought about it.

'You have told her?'

'Not a chance. She brings some funny atmospheres.'

'Brings? Not creates?'

'They don't come out of her. She sort of introduces them.'

'You don't sound as if you're in love.'

'What do I do about these eyes?'

'Photograph them. You'll have to use flash. You'll probably get red eye, so use a filter.' And then she realised what she'd said, and laughed.

The cleaner said the eyes were not those of aliens because they would let in too much light.

'These eyes need to be this size because they're in a dark place where there's hardly any light.'

Lou talked about my success, how amazing it was, and all the time I knew it had been contrived, and I also knew I must get back. I could not be absent like this. The price was too high. I asked Lou not to mention my visit.

I used the opportunity to phone James and he answered and seemed pleased to hear from me. I said I had money and would like to give him my share of the mortgage.

'We need to talk about that.'

'Please don't sell it.' Sudden fear. There were now all varieties of that emotion. Sudden was the worst. Should I run back to him? Could I? Was it too late? I asked if I could see him, now.

'I'd rather not, Cathy.'

'But you've seen my photographs?'

'Here and there.'

I wanted to know what he thought. When he didn't say anything I asked him again.

'Do your own work.'

'It never got anywhere, James.'

'You can now.'

'I take it you don't like what you've seen.'

'It's populist. It's crap. It sells.'

I asked about Daisy and hung up. I wondered if the deal going to the shrink was still on. Had he got someone else?

But these were minor problems compared with what waited for me in the apartment. Unusually, she was not on the phone, which gave her too much time on her hands.

'You didn't go for a walk. You went to that friend of yours.'

For a moment I considered lying. 'Yes, I did. I started for a walk, and then –'

She smacked the table, enraged. 'Why be so two-faced, deceiving me?'

'But she's my friend.'

'Did you see her or not?'

'Yes.'

'Then why, when I called her, did she say you hadn't?'

'I hadn't then.' I felt about five years old.

'She tries to break us up. She criticises the work. I don't want her in our lives. Okay?'

It wasn't okay. 'I could say the same about all these people you phone.'

'They're my world. Do I have to give my life up to be with you? Is that what you want?'

I sat down, my stomach tight, rigid. These days of abuse, so unexpected, undeserved. I felt like crying. I had to get the strength to fight back. I couldn't allow this assault on my freedom, my status as a human being. I fought back. She did better. I gave in and went to hide in the bed. I couldn't tolerate the injustice, so back I went into the fight. Though I should have got a gold star for trying, I didn't win. I went back to bed, longing for her to come and hold me, and promise it was all right, that this had been a terrible life accident. She did not come. After a while I went and sat on the sofa and looked at the stained carpet, which was not the same yellow, not by several shades of brown, and she started weeping, a high unpleasant sound. I couldn't bear it, and thought we should both go to shrinks. She ended in bed, distressed beyond redemption. No photographs got done that day.

Apologies, I discovered, were a huge mistake but I still went on with those. Perhaps because I felt sorry. Sorry was a luxury! I was desperate. If anyone rang for me I found it difficult to speak. It was Yes and No, and they said I sounded strange. My agent asked if I was all right. I said, Fine. And Elle listened from wherever she was in the apartment, and sometimes I thought even outside the apartment.

Lou did ring, and cut through Elle's defence. I believed it was she who used the withheld number service.

'At least tell her you're doing well,' Elle screamed. 'Have you no loyalty?'

The worst part was my sitting heavily in for a session of sorting it out. I needed justice. I got further into the forest of fear. She turned my words upside down, inside out. It was an *Alice in Wonderland*, tricky territory. I was hurt. I was right. And she'd done it.

She said I drew this aggression out of her for my own pleasure. She talked about her rage as though it was a huge phallic symbol she was proud of. Sitting more heavily, I'd say, 'But can't you see I called Lou because she's my friend, and we talk about photography?'

'No. You see Lou to upset me and start off this next round of my anger because you want it.'

'So what do I do about seeing her?'

'You just say nicely, Elle, would you mind if I called round and had a chat with Lou? It's this thing behind my back. You don't need Lou. We're going to America. You're a star. The dullest star I've ever seen. Cheer up.'

'You're twisting it.'

'No wonder James couldn't stand you.'

This had me off the chair and reaching for the fruit knife. She got it first. I felt soaked with unshed tears on the inside and lay flat out on the carpet, trying to cry.

'If you could see yourself. I should take a photograph of that. And you say you're not sick.'

No photography got done that day, or the next. And yet I still had something like love for her.

She arranged the publishing party for the end of April and booked the restaurant. The invitation cards were sent out.

'You don't need that agent,' she said, and tore up the envelope. 'What has she ever done for you?'

I said her outbursts of rage were not right and suggested she was under strain. That was the polite term.

'Only with you,' she said, simply. 'They don't happen with anyone else.'

And suddenly she relaxed and was smiling Elle again, and it was like a summer's day and we turned up the music and danced and she didn't refer to the bad times, just said once, 'I so miss my lake at this time of year.' But it was winter.

37

The phone rang late in February and as she was asleep I answered it. Olav said, 'I need to speak to Elle.' As far as I knew he hadn't been phoning her at all since their row on the island.

'She's asleep. It's six o'clock.'

'Wake her up.'

'Is it that urgent?'

'Mia's taken an overdose.'

Shocked, I said, 'Is she –?'

He didn't know. He sounded bleak. Her mother had phoned him with the news. I said it was kinder to let me wake Elle and tell her. 'It will be a terrible shock.'

'I doubt it,' he said, drily. 'Put her on.'

'Why did she do it?'

'There are some things she can't live with.'

And Elle's hand, glittering with rings, streaked out and grasped the phone.

'What now?' she said. Then came a torrent of Finnish. I waited for signs of shock. I tried to hold her hand. Eventually she hung up. 'If she dies –' and I was sure she said, 'I lose the house.'

I made tea for her and added honey. Reluctantly she phoned the hospital.

'She's not dead. He's as over-reactive as you. You'd get on well together.'

'God, you're nasty.'

She looked up, eyes hard. No sign of worry there. Yes, she did take things well. And yet – I began to question her reactions. Did she take things well, or simply not care?

'It's because I won't go and see her. She's been trying this on for weeks. It gets nowhere with me. That's why I'm not going to the hospital. She has to learn.'

I was so relieved. I needed her like a drug. An emotional drug. I only had to see her face smiling to feel eased. I wanted only her, more and more of her. Being with her was like drinking absinthe. Seventy per cent proof. High beyond intoxication, into another realm.

We had a routine which made sure the day was used well. Food shopping, making meals, washing up, walking, card games, television and no photography. I felt I had to fight for that time, to be on my own, to concentrate, to be allowed to go out and do the work. And yet she wasn't stopping me. The idea had been placed in my mind during the terrible rows.

What did I think about Mia's desire not to live? I recalled her eyes that first evening outside the village bar as she carried her cat. How much brutality had she received? I felt sorry for her and frightened for myself. And, catching sight of my reflected face unexpectedly, I saw something of that pain in my eyes.

*

The luggage was chosen, one case each and new clothes wrapped in tissue. The cameras were placed by the door. The bell rang and, automatically, I went to open the door.

'Don't,' Elle said ferociously, peering through the curtains. 'It's Lou.'

Relieved, I again went to open the door.

'It would be nice if she phoned first. Don't let her in. I'm not having people just dropping by when it suits them.'

'But she's not people –'

More ringing, more angry hand gestures. I did not know what to do. A visitor – such an unusual occurrence. Elle went on with the packing. Then the phone rang and I made sure I answered it. Lou said, 'What's wrong with your bell?' Hearing my voice and my nebulous reply, she said, 'What's wrong?' I said nothing special and hung up.

'What have you done with the ashtray?'

It took a moment to realise she was asking about the huge glass ashtray which seemed to always rest on the low glass table. I explained I had taken it into the bedroom because I had some grapes I wanted to eat.

'How dare you move it? If you move something, you put it back. I don't want to live in James's squat.'

And she'd seemed so safe and happy. I couldn't believe it.

'I like things kept in their place. I only like them that way. You're stirring me up because you want the anger.'

And then I was out of the door and gone.

*

The psychotherapist told me I was not in a love affair, but a co-dependent, eclipsing dependency where I was the victim and Elle the perpetrator. He seemed to applaud my story as a classic case. I was thankful James was not hearing this, but somewhere in the street buying me a Coca-Cola. The therapist said this kind of liaison was usually between a man and woman and was considered a modern phenomenon. It had, however, been active for centuries and was still little understood. The prognosis was not hopeful; usually the victim, with too few boundaries and too much need for closeness, would attract the perpetrator who needed to control and punish. The perpetrator had great charm but no self-esteem or self-value, and by an act of abuse and violation diminished the victim, who this way allowed the perpetrator to snatch at some sort of power.

It usually began with criticism and so, feeling I had nothing to lose, I recounted the coffee-drinking incident in the LA deli.

'And then you stopped drinking coffee and the criticism moved on to something else. The perpetrator always blames the victim for his or her hurtful behaviour. You asked for it. You deserve it.'

I couldn't believe that the unique pattern of Elle's and my relationship was duplicated in unhappy homes all over the globe.

'She can be terribly angry and upset, and then someone phones or comes into the room and she is smiling. She turns on a sixpence.'

He explained how doctors would be called to homes where the perpetrator husband was behaving violently. He'd be acting dangerously one moment, but as soon as he heard the knock on the door, he'd be charming and smiling, transformed. And while the wife sat there, bruised and at the end of herself, the perpetrator would confide how disturbed she was, how in need of help, and he'd be most persuasive.

'But doctors know what they're looking at. Most of them are not deceived.'

He said I was in a diseased relationship for which there was no cure, usually leading to serious injury, even murder or suicide. The only answer was for the victim to escape to a safe place and start again with a new identity. Alternatively, an injunction was brought against the perpetrator. Usually the perpetrator would not desist until a new victim was found. I was hoping for another solution. There was one. The perpetrator could have treatment.

'But they rarely do. They're usually in denial.'

I told him about the Hollywood agent's description of Elle as a psychopath. As the therapist didn't know Elle, professional etiquette made him refrain from labelling her, so I asked him to describe a psychopath. It seemed they were born with some steps of the ladder missing. Needing to control, they did not feel guilt or remorse. They had no conscience.

So perhaps Elle taking the bad knocks so well was just a question of not having more usual reactions in her make-up. She had not felt sad about

Mia. She did not miss Daisy. Or Olav. I wasn't sure about her mother. Perhaps living in the moment was the only place she could be.

He wanted to understand why I was a victim, had no boundaries, carried inside me a wounded child who wanted the world to mother and heal.

'It's a dangerous habit,' he assured me, 'looking for that kind of fixing.'

'What shall I do?'

'That's what I'll help you with.' He said I needed three sessions a week, starting now. The American trip must be cancelled. The violence would get worse, however safe she seemed. The dangerous dynamic only increased. 'You allow her to batter you because it's a situation you've already experienced.'

I admitted my mother was difficult and resorted to anger, but nothing on this scale. And I thought I was depressed when I'd arrived in the room ...

I had a coffee with James and asked what he wanted to do. He didn't know.

'It's the money thing,' I said. 'It's always been that. That's why I went off with her. To earn enough to keep that mortgage.'

'You've learned self-justification from her, I see.'

'Do you still want to be married to me?' I asked.

'Only if it can be a marriage. At least be in with a chance.' He told me he loved me, and I remembered him saying – I look after what I love.

So I asked him what to do. I didn't know where I was. Married, unmarried, gay, victim, famous. He said I was a child and should give the therapist a try.

So I did what I always did, took photographs. It was my answer to the problem.

*

I phoned Lily because I wanted to hear what exactly Mia was going to do and what was planned for her. I really wanted to find out why I was so uneasy. The oddness of corridors in a would-be lover's eyes had grown considerably.

Lily didn't know much about Mia and I thought Serge had censored all conversation. She said she'd seen my photographs in newspapers and was honoured to know me. When was I going to visit? 'She was here recently.'

'She?'

'Elle.'

'Where?'

'Here. So I thought you might have come too.'
'When?'
'Three, no four days ago.'
'But that's impossible. We're here.'
'But I saw her here. She was wearing that dark yellow coat with a hood. A duffel coat.'
'What time?'
'Evening. It was getting dark.'
'It must have been someone else,' I insisted.
'Walking up the hill towards her house.'
'Someone her size wearing the same coat.'
'Yes,' said Lily, doubtfully, 'but I think I saw her face.'

I went through the clothes in the cupboard and in the case. There was no duffel coat. I went through her pockets. No used stub of a ticket to Spain. I phoned Lily again, because I realised she'd been drunk.

'Did you speak to Elle?'
'I was going to. But she looked – different.'
'How?'
'I don't know. Old. Not her. Pale. It could have been her.'
'Were you coming back from the bar?'
'Obviously, if I was going downhill, I was going to the bar.'
'It couldn't have been Elle. Had you been to a party?'
'I don't go to parties to do my drinking.' She wanted to say something else, but changed her mind.

When I next saw Elle in a good mood I asked about the duffel coat. I said I wanted to wear it.

'That would be difficult.'
'Why? Is it lost?' How I hoped it was.
'No, it's at the cleaner's. It got some dust on the front.'

Dust? No dust in that flat. Or on the Heath. Plenty in Les Frontières. I was silent.

38

The London summer was hot and she wanted to go back to Helsinki.
'Where will we stay?'
'I have to go alone.'

Inner nightmare flares of panic stopped me breathing. The next question was why, so I asked it and she said she had to talk to Dag. The Mia drama had made more trouble.

So I suggested taking photographs. She wasn't keen on that.

'I just can't bear to be without you.'

'Family obligations matter. You don't have a family so how can you know?'

The next question was how long. And she came up with a believable package that I thought was half true. Dag came into it again. Our film.

'Maybe I should spend the time going to the shrink then.'

'Shrink?'

What a mistake. Hadn't I learned anything? You don't feed wild animals small children with cut knees that smell of blood. You give them containable, unexciting nourishment.

'What the fuck do you mean?' Berserk now, she screamed, 'Shrink!' The word shrink must in some language somewhere mean murder. That's how she made it sound. She ran at me like a bull and shook me violently. Eventually I fought back, it took a lot of time. I didn't fight a woman, I didn't fight, I had no instincts. But I was doing my best in a tired way, too tired to do damage, too frightened to kill.

'Okay, okay.' I got free, held out my arms for peace. She lunged again and pulled my arms, my hair. It was a sustained damage. She didn't slap, punch or kick but pulled and squeezed and if I was grateful for anything it was that. But not for long. She punched me in the chest. And I still didn't feel any fear. Even then I wanted to be with her, the Elle I'd first loved.

And then Jack walked in.

It took her longer than spinning on a sixpence to pull round from that one.

'How dare you just walk in.' She glared at him. 'Get out.'

'Don't be so bloody silly.' He looked at my arm. 'Are you all right?'

He came fully into the room and stuck his well-travelled bag on the pale sofa. In spite of the state I was in, I wanted to move it.

'Of course I can come in,' and he picked up broken glass ornaments on the table. Of all the things going on I wanted to move his bag. Did I now see life as she did? Keep the sofa clean. Dirty travel bags out in the passage. It looked like a huge dark ape sitting there. I nudged him to move it. He went to the sink, wet a cloth and pressed it on my arm. I was dripping blood. Then he rolled a cigarette and lit it.

'How did you get in?' She tried not to sound rough.

'Your door's open.'

She wanted to slam the still open front door, but shut it gracefully. She moved a hand through her hair and bit her lower lip, checked her clothes. Yes, the shirt was pulled out of the trousers.

'Could I have a cup of coffee? I've been travelling all night.' And he sat next to his bag on the sofa. I didn't move. 'I know I've come at the wrong time, but your neighbours downstairs were in the hall, wondering what was going on and should they call the cops? So maybe I'm not such a bad guest, eh?'

She couldn't think of a thing to say.

'I did ring the bell. You didn't hear it. I could hear the screams up the street.'

Screams? Had I been screaming? She poured herself a large glass of wine.

'Catherine hasn't been well. She's in the care of the hospital. Something has to be done.'

Would he be on her side or, like the doctors from the past, not be deceived?

'I hate people busting in. How did you get in? Credit card?' she asked.

He laughed, a smoker's hacking choke. 'Oh, so you're familiar with that. A nice lady like you? No, the usual way. Just ordinary keys in the lock. You left them in the door.'

Of course, in all of this she hadn't got the rest of the shopping inside. She brought it in and I saw the yellow duffel coat in a cleaner's bag. It had a note printed on the cellophane. 'Stains: we have done our best to remove the stains on this article, but regret that we have not been entirely successful. Further efforts could cause irreparable damage.'

*

Jack made the coffee and she told him how Casper was arranging exhibitions for me in the Far East. It was the first I'd heard about it. I'd understood Casper was counting the profits from my work so far before going any further. The book of photographs had done well in the first days after publication from his intensive promotion, but it didn't have legs. The public did not pick it up. He was planning a deal with a chain and I'd go on a signing tour across the UK maybe. I got the feeling he was flogging a dead horse or tins of dry paint, and he knew it. Other exhibitions were happening with recognised, mature photographers and my impact was submerged in the applause and acceptance of their work. I couldn't go on doing pretty work.

Jack talked about his film in Holland, that's why he hadn't seen us in the States. This meant nothing to Elle and her eyes were not just glazed but closing, and her brain had stopped at the word 'Dutch'. He saw the futility of more conversation. I was still standing by the wall. He got up, said he had friends to see. 'If I get stuck, can I sleep on the sofa?'

The idea almost made me laugh. She murmured something and watched him. He was a match for her. He took my hand and walked me to the door.

'Come on. She'll let you go. I want to walk to the tube with you.'

I turned to her. He pulled me. 'She knows I won't take you away.' And he looked at her, even through her, and thought he recognised what he saw.

Outside, he took me straight on to the Heath. He was carrying his bag so the sofa story was over. We sat on the grass behind some trees. I was reluctant, worried because she would be watching, and she didn't like spontaneous acts. And time not accounted for met with lethal punishment.

'The first time I saw her I knew it was war and I was going to have to fight with her or like her. I'd have won the fight but I wouldn't have seen you again. She's a killer.'

'Oh, you'll never win with her. Forget it.'

'You should have left her strutting round that silly village.'

'I can't keep anything from her, yet I can't be honest with her. She denies me existence.'

'There's not room for the two of you. Not as equals. Not enough air for you both. So she'll do you in and think nothing of it.'

'She loves me.'

'What a silly idea. She's got the same excitement about you as a cat with a mouse before the kill. When you've got no more life that she can draw on she'll leave.'

I said I had to go back. She *might* leave. A quick, snatched bit of luggage, and then off.

I entered the flat nervously and although she wasn't in the room, it seemed filled with her presence. I didn't like the look of the mustard-coloured duffel coat. The way it lay over the chair, like an old skin. I stayed still, watching it, making sure it was just a coat. It was all that was needed to announce her power, its existence in this apartment. I felt she was alive in the gleam of the mirrors. She was hidden amongst the curtains.

There was a green shadow in the room, hovering there, pure evil. I watched it dissolve. I quickly looked behind me, dreaded to see her standing there. I'd prefer an angry approach to that sustained by standing with those glowing yellow eyes. What were they seeing? What did they want?

And then I was tired of the fear, of the constant adjustments I had to make to this tyrant with steps of her ladder missing. I turned and walked purposefully into the bedroom, where she stood looking in a mirror which reflected the living room, and would have caught me. The feeling of being caught was right.

'I'm sick and tired of running around you and your ego. You're a psychopath. Go and get treatment. You're evil. You –' And I tried to describe how she'd smothered my creative instinct to produce dandified works for her shallow friends, to promote herself. She lived by proxy, utilising my life. Nothing was worse than smothering the creative impulse. Hadn't I said that about Mia?

And she turned and her face was the same but there was a change, a greyness perhaps, an aura around her of darkness, the opposite of Jesus's halo. And I cut short the attack because I was dealing with something I didn't understand, well out of my range. Mia had been right. I didn't understand what I was in.

I backed away and decided to run for it, all the time keeping my eyes on her, and her eyes glowed most horribly and she charged towards me and I thought, if I scream loud enough they'll get the police. Then I thought, what can the police do?

*

I'd been thrown, blown across the room, and was lying against the wainscoting, which was also pale yellow. I thought the painter hadn't done such a good job in all areas because the paint was dotted on the wall and had stained the legs of the bed. I sat up, expecting to be injured, and looked at the closed bedroom door, which I knew was locked. I looked at the window and stood up. My exit from there might look like suicide. Then I sat on the bed and prayed bits of prayers half remembered from schooldays. I looked at my hands. My wedding ring was no longer there and I couldn't remember when I'd taken that off. This felt momentous, like the end of the Jazz Age, the middle of the Depression, the beginning of the Bubonic Plague. I sat for quite a long time wondering how to get out of the apartment. Then I got up and opened the door. She was watching television. It seemed to be evening.

'I didn't want it to end like this.' I was firm and decided. I was to be reckoned with. She paid no attention. 'I went into it with love, and it would still be like that, but this happens.' I emphasised 'this'. It included everything bad since the deli scene in LA. 'Do you see that you should have treatment?'

I was very nice and sat on the sofa and did feel genuine compassion for her. I wasn't scared because, although rough, my prayers were those of a repentant sufferer. I felt a state of grace did exist, that good, like evil, was an entity, a reality, and I wanted the good. Whether she'd heard it all before and was tired of it I don't know, because she turned, uncaring, and said, 'Which shrink is James taking you to?' And we were on a different spiritual plane altogether.

I don't know how I hit the floor again. It felt as though some reverse force had expelled me against the wall. She looked the same but her eyes were very still. I was frightened for myself and now for James. I did not want him in this. So I lied. There was no shrink, never had been. I'd never seen one. I mentioned it because it could be a good idea – for me and her. What did she think?

'That you're a fucking liar, and I'll get you. And James.'

Several spiritual levels lower I wanted to kill her. Full to bursting with rage, I ascended from the sofa.

'I'm going to make some changes.' And I got my bag, cameras, some odd, mad possessions, my shoes, and went to the door.

'I'm getting my own place.'

*

I walked along the road. I was gone. Free. Out of it. A woman with choices. I'd phone James. Everyone had to be phoned now before visiting. I'd taken on that habit. I'd go into hiding, a new name. I'd take the photographs I wanted to take and see the shrink. I got as far as the Classic Cinema in South End Green, all on my own, grown-up, the wounded child quiet inside me, and I turned to get on the bus for Kentish Town and, between one thought and the next, there was blackness, purgatory. All of it and worse. I never wanted to feel that again. If this pain was the price for leaving her, there was no choice. As though on an elastic band I was pulled back to the flat, up the stairs and into the lemon yellow stained room. She was watching television.

'I'm sorry, Elle. I'll never say that again.'

'You'll never see that smoking, trouble-making American again either. Or James.'

'Okay.' I sat down, back in her life.

39

Dag was staying in the house in Spain and needed, it seemed, some item to do with the décor which could only be found in an English village. He gave Elle specific directions and, keeping to the outside lane, she arrived at a medieval high street in less than an hour. I asked again what she was looking for and she said absently, 'The blacksmith.'

'Why?'

'Dag needs something – a heavy hasp.' She looked at a map.

'I don't think there are many blacksmiths left.'

She slammed out of the car, switched on her smile as she asked directions from passers-by. Next she went to a phone box and came back more irritated.

'I've obviously been told the wrong place and now Dag isn't in.'

She drove to the next village and asked more questions. Frustrated now, she got back in the car.

'It's all gone wrong because you're here. I shouldn't have let you come.' She looked at me, hated me.

'Can you get this hasp in London?'

'Oh, shut up.'

We ended up in the local supermarket buying the week's food.

The road leading to the motorway back to London was winding, narrow with blind curves and, she said, extremely dangerous.

'People drive as though theirs is the only car on the road. But it's not just them that will end up having an accident; they'll involve me too.' Her eyes were hard.

'Fancy coming all the way here to get the week's shopping.' I thought I was making a joke.

The car jolted and almost stopped with a grinding and screeching of gears and brakes, and fumes, acrid and hot, rose up from the floor. And then, like something in a fairground, it sped forward, twisted and writhed, its back wheels lifting like a bucking horse. I added my screams to the squeal of the wheels. And I realised it wasn't a technical breakdown, just her in a bad mood. She wasn't showing any feelings, but the car was doing it for her.

'Get out and walk back with your week's shopping,' and she reached over to the door handle.

'Never! Fuck you,' I yelled.

Passing vehicles almost scraped the car's sides as they tried to manoeuvre round her madness. She was going to kill us both. As unhappy as I was, suddenly, for some inexplicable reason, I wanted to live. It surprised me.

She manhandled the gears and the car bumped along the road, a metal catastrophe glinting in the sun, broken, dying, and then it took off, finally free, beyond gears, brakes and engine parts, into that metal heaven for vehicles, and in its joy it passed everything on the road and we were doing eighty and she wasn't even looking.

I, selfishly inclined to live, pleaded with her.

'So what if I die? So what?' And she brought death nearer by swerving into a U-turn only a lunatic would navigate. I gave her reasons to live. We'd missed love and found tyranny. I said I was sorry. No. Heartbroken.

'You will be,' she promised me.

I said I'd give her anything. She had total power because she could drive and I couldn't. She pushed the car up to ninety and only luck, destiny and the law of averages got it around the bend to shudder to a stop where anything could hit it. It had simply given up, committed suicide all on its own.

'Get it forward. Forward,' I screamed.

A lorry passed us, just, but took the side mirror with it. The driver's horn was loud and his voice, 'Fuck you, lady,' curled like smoke so we could hear it long after the sound of the horn had gone.

She was furious because she'd messed up on the blacksmith visit and could never be in the wrong. I was awash with tears, sweat and spit on the outside and dry with terror on the inside. What if something just hit us and I didn't die, just lay mangled in agony? I could imagine it, the awesome near-deaths I'd experience in her company.

She didn't want to kill herself after all. I was wrong about that. She was tougher, oh much tougher than little commonplace roadside extinctions. She drove to a lay-by quite musically and got out. She'd just wanted to kill me.

Sightlessly, I got out and an overtaking car nearly took the door off. I told her I was sorry I'd met her, sorry I'd been born. Then I remembered my self-respect and said I'd willingly be responsible for my share in our emotional downfall and look into it, change it, and this brought a yellow gleam to her eyes, a bestial toughening of the features.

'I've had enough. Finally you've done it. You've cracked me up,' she said.

I suggested a walk in the adjoining field. 'Let's discuss what we should do.'

We'd been doing nothing else for hours, days. She plunged off into the grass.

'You had to do it, you couldn't let go until you'd finally broken me,' she cried. I ran after her.

And there I was, angry again, defending my sanity, my right to life. And, there she was, her face was blood-filled, hands like claws, harming my arm, my face. And I was crying again and she was running and somewhere, in the sensible, little-used part of me, I registered the fact we were miles from London, and that only she drove. And possibly the car no longer worked.

'Come back, Elle.' And she ran into the distance. She could move, I'd give her that. I told her in that field that I hated her, her arrogance and wilfulness, brutality, always had. I shouted and fought and all I wanted was to be held by her. Let the love come back, the care, the union. We had been two allies trespassing on a rather special path and the togetherness gave a certain safety. But we weren't together any more. I walked to the car and stood uselessly. The feelings raged, tugged through me till I thought my own body was going to do the job for me now and end it. My heart thundered, blood flooded inside my ears and I thought how insufficient words were to give expression to these feelings, hers and mine. We were reduced to fault-finding, threats, recriminations, whereas the pain – more the agony – needed operatic language to do it justice, this experience which would change my life for good.

Blind with need, I ran back into the field and there she was, sitting like a stump in the grass and I tried to hold her, to get back that which was lost. It had been something so powerful and lovely it should be rejoiced over, not murdered in a turmoil of rage and hate. My hands couldn't hold the soft fabric of her sleeves, her hair seemed cropped and unavailable, hands tucked away. Everything was out of reach. I told her we had a chance. She trampled that to death. I told her I hated her, it was finished, and as I tried to think of a real punishment that would affect her, I saw the sun slanting into the car and thought of all the food on the back seat, going off. Such a trivial consideration might perhaps keep me sane.

I realised in that field that love, so valuable, so precious, could be so easily lost and not recovered. It might be a gift given and taken away by a superior spiritual force and, when it was gone, it left two recipients stranded.

A line of sheep in the field opposite had gathered at the wire fence and were watching us. Thirty pairs of unblinking eyes. God, we were an unexpected entertainment. It beat eating grass. Another untidy fight, and she got to the car. The only good thing about that day was the car started and then she drove blind and thoughtless, and she wanted the death climax to come, not from her, but from outside, so her veneer of perfection was not stained. An accident would do it.

I realised two things that day. There was only place for one of us in the scheme of things. We both couldn't be there. Only one of us could have the role of a woman alive and working. Yet we were two. Because there was no space, we eclipsed each other.

She had the solution. She stopped for dinner in Beaconsfield and ordered half a bottle of wine, which she drank quickly. We were beyond speaking. Then, unusually, she ordered a liqueur and held up the balloon glass of orange fire. She held it out to me and I could see the lights twinkling in the silky liquid. I could smell the pungent orange and I could almost taste the many layers of experience one sip would provide. And I knew, on taking a sip, all this pain would be relieved. She was smiling over the glass and I remembered the woman in the painting by Gustav Klimt, mocking, dangerous, evil. Mia's drama teacher had seen that.

'Taste it,' she said.

'I don't drink.'

'But that was years ago. How can you be an alcoholic? You don't drink.' She pushed the glass under my nose. 'One sip. To join me in a sensation I like.'

I walked out.

She wanted me dead. That was the solution, for two are too many in a role for one. That was one day out in the country I would not describe to my friends.

40

I could see pale late summer sunlight glittering on the pond, people walking dogs across the Heath. They seemed so near yet impossible to reach, people in a painting. At least the light is honest, not deceptive or too full of a beauty that should not be trusted. Elle was right about that. I remembered when I could walk so lightly across that thin grass. Who'd think it would be considered a luxury? That freedom I had for nothing and didn't even see as such?

I've been in this room for one day, maybe two. Yesterday (was it yesterday?) she charged at me like a hard-muscled beast, her face unrecognisable, contorted with rage. The mixture of fear and honesty on my part I could see even then was a mistake.

Restlessly I walk from the window overlooking the Heath to the ones over the street with its canopy of trees. I close the curtains and can see without being seen. She's not out there but she could be out there. I should go out for the things I need. Again I go to the door but don't touch it. I look at it, however, and recognise the locks are not locked, there are no bolts or bars. She's not in the room but it seems as though she's more present than if she were actually here. I have given myself a talking-to, and of course I can walk out. Just go down the carpeted stairs, open the front door, follow the curve of the road made private by trees. Of course I can, but she'd know where to, and to whom, and I'd be so – only one word for it – punished. What if I just flit like a ghost under the shadow of those trees which lead to a normal street where I might have normal ideas again? She'd find a punitive twist in that. She never gets it wrong, is never short of an answer.

I avoid the mirror. The bruises are visible but nothing compared with the damage inside, in my mind, heart, that's where hell is. I pass the precisely arranged furniture, everything expensive and rigidly in position, yet it seems as though I'm in a poor place. The antique influence, muted luxury, doesn't even reach me. I'm in hell, inside and out.

The room is all of a sudden filled with a blaze of lemon light and I wonder if I've reached that point, so isolated and endangered, when people who are about to die before their time receive a masterly spiritual revelation which comforts and assures them that everything will be all right, but not just yet. I wait with added unease for the lemon light to do something I'm not sure I can handle, but it settles into a blob on the table like a custard tart, like those I used to buy round the corner in the baker's, cooked fresh daily, but that was back then, when I was I, and with my husband.

The sun's down and I'm very cold. They told me, the people I phoned on the helpline, that I should get out. I must have sounded as though I was locked in, and that she was just around the doorway waiting for me to make a foolish move. Of course I'm in prison. That's it.

The phone rings. Jack asks if I'm all right. I cut him off quick because it occurs to me the phone is bugged. It just made sense. Her being there when she wasn't.

*

A noise inside the house. Click of the front door. Her well-shod devil's feet climbing the stairs? Tiny feet, so innocent-looking. Terror makes me pick up the first thing, which happens to be a salt pot. My body assures me my state is more than terror. We've gone beyond that, my body and me. Heart pounding, sweating, suddenly sickly, I sit down. I stand up. I move to the window. A tree branch knocks the glass pane sharply. I jump and drop the salt pot. She's all around. Even the trees warn me. But she doesn't come in.

Of course, I should have got up from the low wall outside the locals' bar in the south of France before she even started over the hill. I should have taken the first plane out of Toulouse. To Latvia if necessary. But there

I was carelessly, more, foolishly, just there, all accessible for what was to come. No defences. I didn't even think I needed any. I got into something I didn't know, for which I had no life-map, and thought it was experience, would lead to growth, make me a better, no, a great, photographer. How I sneered at caution. But I realise it's useless keeping on second-guessing everything.

Her coat, with its expensive leather trimming, lies correctly on the chair. It does instead of her, reminding me – reminding me of what? That she rules. That's the nicest way to put it.

Did I have a destiny that I've somehow veered off, so suffering a life accident, my present upturned, future uncertain? Do I have to claw my way back to that original destiny?

She stole my freedom. I'm wrong. She murdered my freedom. She came from an unimaginable state, bound in ruthless rigidity, designed to kill off the exuberant, the soft, the carefree, all this disguised by glossy-lipped smiles, confident and long-lasting, which did instead of friendliness. Charm covered the rest.

I had no protection. Protection? I couldn't acknowledge the word. I watched out crossing roads, checked the door at night, didn't cross knives, took the pill. The protection I actually needed wasn't a modern commodity. Faith would have provided it, but I only paid lip service to God. Then. I thought He was only to be found in churches. I thought being free and open was the best I could be. I didn't know any better. I gambolled joyous and innocent in a colourful life without boundaries. Of course the darkness came in.

I'd heard of the hostage becoming so dependent on the abductor that she or he would in the end go to the abductor for everything, even comfort. That made sense because the abductor was all there was. My case was different. I was kidnapped from my life in broad daylight, in front of a group of people who had no idea what was happening. How could they know I was the victim and she the perpetrator? The crime invisible, my screams those of a ghost unheard. I was working surely enough, seen to be doing things. Not too much laughter any more. Not when she was present.

In every town, every country we visited, the handcuffs were on and sometimes a gag, the odd touch of torture, made sure it all stayed in place. To make sure I was suitably confused she blamed me for not sparkling to advantage. Where was my wit? Did I have to be a grey cloth?

There are friends I could ring but strangely I can't think of one. I could go out and walk in the fading light. I could do a few things, but she is just a thought away and she wants me inside. She prefers the inner world of this room, not diversion or solace.

I get off the bed and walk around the two rooms. That's acceptable. I know how an abandoned dog feels. I look out of the window. I look with longing at the street. I could just go down the stairs and never come back. Everything in me likes that idea. I could have done it, maybe, a month ago or the month before that.

Her eyes, her eyes are all around me. She's busy in every corner of the room. She sees the act before it's conceived. She sniffs up the thought before it is even in existence, sniffs it up and snuffs it out. I think of her life purpose – she was born to do me in.

Of course people didn't see it. There I was, making my living, cooking food, taking planes, trains, cars. I was a normal person, well, not quite. When was I ever normal? Am I grieving now for a false past as well as everything else? People thought I was lucky. Wrong. I was a prisoner. They hadn't seen the abduction, didn't see the persecution. And when they did have the slightest suspicion of something unusual she quickly disguised it or told them I was a moody, hormonal person suffering from depression. If they replied that they had never noticed it before, she countered by suggesting an early menopause. If that didn't go down she blamed my 'terrible childhood'. She blamed what she did to me on my parental upbringing, and then on me.

I fought back, tooth and claw, against the injustice. Friends saw it and because they cared for me, couldn't bear it. They understood the lunacy of going against her.

'Get away,' they said. And, when I couldn't, they did. For good.

I'm in prison all right, its bars not visible but more actual than the usual kind. I could no more leave this room than – be happy. Again I look down to the street. Yes, suddenly it seems a long way down. She's brought me to this. The prison bars are seen on occasion, when the light falls at a certain hour.

As Jack said, I should have left her strutting about in the frontier village.

*

Still she doesn't come.

I was almost at the top of my profession, the photographer they suddenly all wanted. Was it a year ago? I'm so ill, so scared, I couldn't even look at anyone, let alone hold a camera. I was beginning to be recognised and, my God, I'd worked for it. I could just make a friendly phone call. But my voice, it's so down, and I can't hide it. I can't reach out for help from anyone. I can't speak about this, not ever. No one must see me like this.

She hasn't come in. All those noises, just tricks to see if I can still take it. She's switched on some point in me, the me beyond the parts I know, beyond mere emotions or the responses I've developed since birth. This point, I think, belongs to the spirit. She's shifted the prison cell technique directly on to me so that I imprison myself. I do what she did, only better. It's as though she's inside my head. It's more acute and distressing than if she were here in the flesh.

I've opened the window, just to be part of the world. Yes, I could just walk along that curving street, but then she'd accuse me of behaving provocatively, behind her back, perhaps preferring my freedom. Freedom. Always the issue. She's made it clear she'll never let me go. In case that should sound like an empty threat she's given it substance. She'll ruin me and has told me how. Of course there is one way out. Real out. I don't want anyone finding anything.

I've thought about it. A boat out to sea, and then pills and champagne. But, as my old and now forbidden friend Jack says, it's a hard thing to do, to kill yourself. I thought he meant the decision. He meant the execution. Don't bungle it.

Jack, the last friend. But she doesn't know I still contact him. I could phone him but I don't want him in this. I don't want to give him all the pain that she'll bring down on him, just for knowing me.

Before she ran out, face blazing – was it only yesterday? – she said I'd ruined her looks, her life joy, her bank account. No, that came first. And I think she mentioned vivacity. She's very fond of descriptive nouns, rather fond of herself actually. Vivacity. Yes, that's gone. I'd ruined her optimism, taken away her light. She was now a dark, near-spent thing, old and lamentable. I'd done that. Actually, I'd like to claw her to death.

I grab her elegant coat and lash it against the door, fling it on the floor.

I should never have made that call to the helpline. She'll trace it. A man passes below, sees me and looks right through me. Do I exist? I don't like the way it looks down there, below the window. It seems a long way down. I haven't noticed that before. The next thought is not allowed. The one after that follows, with blatant obviousness. I should kill her.

It won't go on like this. I sense, with chilling horror, that life will not permit it, and I will be obliged to take an original action to break the bonds, dissolve the bars, rid the fear.

It comes down to this. Her. Or me.

41

They had me laid out and ready for some tests, and the cubicle was small and the chair piled with my clothes. Jack came in with an unlighted cigarette between his lips.

'I don't know all the technical terms, but it's as though something takes your energy,' he said. 'It seems these levels can go seriously low and your blood composition changes.'

'Is it leukemia?'

'They didn't tell me.' And he gave a hospital-visitor's smile.

'If I get out of all this I'm going to take the photographs I really want to do.'

'That's good news to me. Get your clothes on now and we'll go and do it.' He paused, remembering what he'd heard from the doctor. 'But I think you'd better let them do whatever they do. I'd better get out of here, or they'll start on me next. I look worse than you do. They thought I was the patient.'

'Jack, can you – get hold of her?'

'I'd rather not.'

'I don't think she's away.' I hadn't seen her for a week.

I was dehydrated, so they put me on a drip and gave me a bedpan in case I needed to pee. Nurses came and went, and then Elle came in with the same unwavering smile, and I was blessed. I felt a swoop of sugary pleasure, awesome relief. It wasn't a church blessing, not even Harrods brand. It was Woolworth's version but it would do. It was what went with Elle.

'God, I hate the smell of hospitals,' she said. Then she sat and held my hand.

The doctor came back and reminded me I'd been offered innumerable opportunities which I'd not been prudent enough to accept. He stressed 'prudent' and gave Elle the same sort of glance he'd given Jack. She didn't look like next of kin either.

'Who is your actual nearest family member? We need your next of kin.'

'I don't have any.'

The nurse came in with a tray to take blood and, as the needle went in, Elle moved her head sharply and looked at the wall, jumping her foot up and down.

I asked if she was all right.

'Of course,' she said. Her small voice couldn't do justice to the obvious excitement. The nurse asked if she was going to faint. 'How do I know? That's your job.'

How I wished she wouldn't start a Rottweiler scene here. I thought she should have said nothing after the first smile.

'Why get involved with hospitals?' she asked, roughly. 'Did they kidnap you?'

'I hadn't eaten anything for some time. When I went out to get some milk I had a sort of turn, so I went into Casualty.'

She couldn't look scathing enough. 'Get well because Casper's got a wonderful thing set up in Japan.'

'When?'

'Spring.'

We were still in September. Spring seemed a long way off.

'It all went wrong with that coffee in the LA deli.'

'It does so much harm to your system. And to those around you. Your vibration is stirred up. The caffeine stays in your body. I'm very close to you. I get it too. I'd rather you didn't drink it.'

The fear was back. I saw that the good moments were only puddles in a desert, and soon they'd be mirages.

*

Jack sat in the overgrown garden of the old house, peeling potatoes. 'He's letting me stay here. It's great.' He jumped up and got me a chair. 'What are they going to do?'

'A biopsy here and there.'

'Soon?'

'Very. I talked them into letting me go for a couple of days, and promised to go back.'

'But you couldn't find her?'

I thought she'd run away to Dag. She hated illness.

Daisy came into the garden, but wouldn't let me touch her. I'd been away too long.

'She's sulking,' Jack said. 'She'll get over it.'

'Will James?'

He shrugged. 'I love it here.'

I'd let all the bad in the world happen to me because I had no boundaries and I saw that, if you didn't have a belief and state it as part of your life, then things got in that weren't wholesome. She was predatory, and lived off me. She was away now and could not know I was in forbidden territory. She'd included my film script in her luggage.

'Well, it is mine. You wrote it for me, remember?'
'Ours.'
'The cost of that trip makes it mine.'
'Olav's money.'
'I earned it.' And she was gone.

*

Going along the road with James, into the therapist's house, up the stairs, into that chair, talking about the childhood and the inability to grow up, I knew she was watching. She could see into my mind. I could see the irony of the situation, sitting opposite a good therapist while he investigated my emotional state, telling him everything but not this. I couldn't mention it, even to Jack. Not the long-distance seeing.

Walking back along the street James said, 'Why d'you keep turning round?'

'Do I?'

I asked what we should do. I was really asking if we could be back together. He said it needed time and work.

'With the therapist, you mean?'

'And ourselves.'

I went back up to the darkroom. I just couldn't go on feeling terrible. I had to accept that I'd left James, and quite rightly he wasn't taking me back.

The photograph I took of Jack in the garden was one of the best things I'd done. Lou was so pleased she showed it to her gallery, and they said they would include it in their next mixed show. Now I'd really started.

Elle didn't ring and I didn't know where she was. I asked James if I could stay at the house and the answer was hard for him.

'I'd rather not, because I still think you'll go back to her.'

I went back into the flat and hated it. I decided to get my own place and asked Jack to help me look.

'But she'll come back, and it will be the same.'

'No. I'm bound to win in my own home.'

'Wrong.'

*

They gave me a pre-med, but the exploratory operation was going to be delayed, so I just lay, half out of it, with time to think, plenty of time because I couldn't do anything else. I'd so wanted to phone her, to creep into her arms, to plead with her for comfort and softness, but I kept it down in the depths of my being – that's where it belonged. Occasionally it splashed up and blacked my thoughts with an ink of unholy sadness, inner skid row. I'd done the outer one. This was worse. I'd never tell anyone, not even her. I had to become separate, able to exist in my own being, complete. Maybe I wasn't meant to have relationships at all. If I could get up I would, however, phone her. Except I didn't know where to reach her and she certainly wasn't trying to reach me. But of course she'd know what I was doing.

James put some flowers in a bottle. 'They're going to do a biopsy on your spleen and liver.'

I closed my eyes and remembered her coming over the hill in the high village and it was as though I'd slipped through time into another reality. She was a galleon in full sail and her shoes clicked rhythmically on the stones and the sound had been familiar. 22 September 1984. She'd slipped into the small space between Lily and me on the low wall outside the bar, and smiled right into my eyes. She wasn't afraid of closeness, I knew her, had known her all my life. The Spanish say if you meet a person you think you've known in another life, cross yourself, say your prayers and run.

What was it she said? 'It's beautiful here but as beautiful as it is, so it is bad. You have to distrust beauty sometimes. We learn that here.' She'd sat, her elbows on her knees like a young boy. 'It might suit you here because you're paradoxical.'

She was in the village now. I was sure of it.

And the other side of the spinning on a sixpence – her mother dying, only her eyes showing Elle she was loved. And she'd seen dreary, worthless women go on living, but that gracious spirit had to die. Did I come under 'dreary'? The grey cloth. Of course, she paid me back for being alive – although the way things were going in here, that could change.

And I kept hearing the therapist saying, 'You can't fix her.'

'What's the answer?'

'You must cut off from her. Don't reach out. Contain your need.'

'When was your last period?' the nurse asked.

Of course, she didn't have periods. I'd never seen her having a period. Was she in the menopause? She talked about hormones, hers and mine, but I'd seen no sign of bleeding. She never left a smell when she went to the lavatory. That was a quick, neat action. She was never ill or complained of malaise. Everything about her was dry.

Un-nice things happened around Elle. And I knew I must protect James. Then I passed into greyness.

*

Dag said, 'Come on a bender with me. You're bigger than your craving. Why live small?'

I promised him it didn't work like that. Things got massive as you neared death. We were by the lake I knew only from my dreams.

Dag kicked out the last of the fire and walked on into the trees. Something had stirred the water up and it rippled like black oil heavily against greasy, green, fungus-covered rocks. A high wind moaned through the trees. I saw Dag on the other side of the lake walking in a flapping black coat. He seemed to gather all the shadows around him and I found myself saying, 'I believe in God.' When he got closer I saw it wasn't a coat at all, just darkness. I was full of half-remembered prayers.

'Do you believe in evil?' I asked.

'I don't believe. I know it exists. You'd better know it too. These days people excuse it, call it sickness. They're sick. It's a commodity like colour, noise, energy. Evil doesn't want to be excused. Doff your cap to it if it should come your way.'

'And Elle?' I asked.

'But she's a mistress of the unnatural.'

She was calling and we hadn't heard her. What had she heard?

He said quietly, 'You certainly go where most people fear to put their feet.'

*

I came round from the anaesthetic with a longing to go into the darkroom. I could hear her voice. 'You can't get away from me in there.' It was a dirty voice, as though she'd been eating dirt.

Jack stayed with me in the flat, which was getting a lived-in look. Stains, ash, ashtray moved, flowers in the wrong place and dying. He did the shopping, cooking, and brought me books.

'D'you want a real drink?'

I shook my head.

'You've really given up?'

'There's nowhere in me for a drink to hide.'

'The other stuff too? You're strong.'

'I'm free.'

He laughed and poured me a coffee. 'Life's a cage. Freedom? You're just shaking the bars.'

I got over the small operation quicker than I should, and went to the therapist, not so much for myself but because I needed to know more about Elle.

She surrounded herself with highly charged, deceptive charm that held the viewer's attention. Camouflage was her speciality. I'd tried to know her by asking questions. My intuition would have been a better instrument. I asked the therapist about stains. Why were they so terrible?

'Because she's an obsessional, controlling person and can only survive in that way. Stains damage her world. The stains could get inside her. She needs perfect control outside to try and make safe the inside.'

I told him about her absolute stillness, the sustained movement, the sudden purposeful walk when there was no apparent need, and how it had become frightening. She belonged in a horror film. And I got frightened there and then. Of course she would know about this conversation. And my words slowed and I would not go back there. He gave me a list of what was wrong with me. Add paranoia. And again I knew I must protect James.

I'd found a studio in Kentish Town and would move my stuff out of the flat the following weekend. As I cleared out what was no longer needed I opened her clothes cupboards. I thought there might be some of my shoes in a box. Her clothes, hanging in a certain way that made me stop, looked limp, but as though they could come alive. There was something evil about them, as though they were full of ill-will and disease. And, as I stood there, an insect flew out from amongst the silk and I jumped back and closed the doors. Perhaps it was better not to look as though I'd moved out. Leave a few precious things behind. One day she'd come back. James had said it. 'She'll be back.' And then Jack started, and Lou. 'When Elle comes back.' I'd move out with the minimum, just what I'd come in with.

42

I was buying spaghetti from the Italian shop when I heard a voice behind me. 'I bet you're frightened. In case I find out what you've been up to.' And I thought it was her and spun round but it was just a couple of lovers and she was teasing him with a scary voice.

I stopped at the vegetable shop before walking back to the flat. It would be my last dinner and tomorrow, after breakfast, I'd leave. And I went in and flung the food on the table and filled the kettle and turned on some music. I chopped the garlic, peeled the tomatoes, and then I turned round. There was something different about the place. It was tidy. I turned everything off and went slowly to the bedroom. She was lying straight out on the bed, dressed in the mustard duffel coat, her feet turned up. Shit, she was dead. Then the eyes turned and, if her mother's held love, these held the opposite. They were deadly.

I told her she'd frightened me. And I was immediately guilty. Frightened and guilty. And she sat up with an unvarying smile. It was 10 September and she'd been away over a month.

Quickly I told her about the biopsy. Gave her stuff she could feel sorry about. Except she didn't. 'And what did they find?' Soft voice and something in her eyes. Fear. She was frightened.

I had to handle this to my advantage, and use her fear of what might happen to me. Was that why she'd run away?

'What do you expect them to find, Elle?'

She was ill at ease, concerned.

'Why didn't you let me know you were here, Elle?'

'Because I needed to lie down. I wasn't recovered after my journey.'

It seemed it had been a long one.

'You didn't come and see me in the hospital.'

'No!'

'Scared?'

She looked down and bit her lower lip. 'I suppose I thought you might die.'

She didn't use 'afraid' or 'scared' or 'guilty', but then psychopaths don't feel.

She said she'd been staying at her lake and had found money to make the night film in Finland. 'It's quite something, I can tell you.'

As she ate the spaghetti she warmed up. 'I thought we should direct it together. Dag has thought up changes in the script. I need to be a director.'

'You're always looking for an identity.'

She didn't like that. 'Dag thinks it's a good idea.'

I told her about the studio I'd rented but didn't have the courage to say I was moving out. She said it was a good idea, and we could give up this flat and move to Finland.

*

James came round early because I'd forgotten to phone him. I suggested going for a coffee and he understood she was back.

'No, I'm staying here.' He sat at the table. He was silent and I wasn't sure what to do. She appeared in the doorway and said hello.

'She's coming with me,' he said.

'I hate these early morning domestic dramas. They're always dreary because your sugar levels are low. Have some breakfast, and then start.'

'Get your stuff,' he said to me.

'What are you in such a hurry about? I thought she was an established photographer about to do a film. Since when does that happen in your house?'

'Let her go, Elle.' He didn't look at her.

'I'm not stopping her.'

'Oh, but you are.'

'What's she going to do? Exist in a little studio while you make up your mind if you want her back in that house you can't afford?'

'I love you.' He looked at me. So did she.

'Forget him. He's the past. Your future's with me.'

'Can't we talk this through?' I said. Then to James, 'Talk to her.'

'She's beyond communication.'

And I knew if I went with him, something indefinable and bad would happen. She'd never let him get away with it.

'I'm staying with Elle for now.'

'After all you've been through.' His eyes were bright and hard, like diamonds. 'And come through. And won. And you should end up with that.' He gestured over his shoulder to her and dropped his head into his hands.

43

I had to know what to do and how to do it, and it had to be effective. Timing was vital. I got out the undeveloped reel of film from my first visit to the village. It contained shots of the desecrated grave.

When I came in she was watching television.

'Your note said evening. A long evening. Isn't this night?'

'That's right, Elle. I've been night-shooting.'

'A letter came from the hospital. I opened it in case of something urgent.'

I wanted to say, 'I wish you hadn't,' but nothing came out.

'You've got a malfunction of the spleen.'

I still didn't speak.

'My, my. You do keep yourself to yourself. I remember when that was different. You couldn't wait to get your hands on me.'

'The spleen. That's to do with blood.'

I looked at her and she looked at me. And then she went to bed.

*

It was agreed with Dag that we shoot the film now, before the winter light, and we sat making lists of what was needed. To say I was half-hearted would be an overstatement. I wasn't even hearing the lists. This was a photographic occasion where I would not be present.

'Do the film,' she said. 'Don't listen to the doctors. They always exaggerate.'

I was self-contained with difficulty, and occasional fear surged through me, rabid and mad fear I felt she could smell. We planned the trip to Finland as we had the others and she went shopping.

'I'm getting my hair cut in the West End. Is there anything you want?'

I gave her a difficult list and anticipated she'd be away some hours.

I got the darkroom ready and took the reel of film showing the desecrated grave. I put the film through the processes, filled the trays and left one negative in the developing liquid. I left it for four minutes and then hung it up to dry. I put the light behind it and could see clearly the broken tombstone and above the hole in the earth a shadow. I dropped it back in the liquid and blew it up further. I pinned it on the line and got the others into the trays and out for quick drying. I was frightened, excited – there was a black shape taking form now, more than a shadow. I pinned up the last two, and suddenly the darkroom door opened and the light was turned on, and she stood there smiling and the prints were ruined.

'You know you must never put the light on when I'm developing a reel of film. Are you mad?'

'I'm sorry. I forgot.' She came forward and I lurched away, but she just looked at the films flapping in the draught, and empty. 'Oh, what a shame,' she said. 'But I really think this going back to your old style is a mistake. How many of those would you sell? Not too many, as I remember it. I couldn't go to the West End without you. I was worried about that hospital letter.'

I left them hanging there, ruined. The moonlit open grave and broken stone, and something that the camera might have caught that should not be seen.

*

She had her hair dyed platinum blonde. How it changed her! She was ice-cold like an Alfred Hitchcock heroine. How he'd have liked her! Even her smile was chilling.

I got to the airport and then said I felt weak. The letter from the hospital backed up my excuse. 'You go on and I'll follow.'

She stroked my face, and the rings hurt. 'Poor little thing. You tried being inquisitor, and then you thought you could be my contestant.'

Blood cold now, spleen galloping, say nothing. Not a lot to say. Let her get on that plane. Oddly, there were moments still, when she touched my hand and looked at me, when I felt a return of love or perhaps the memory of that love. I felt empty but was filled, not by God's grace, but by old love for her.

44

Lily collected me from the railway station and suggested walking up the hill. She looked fatter while I was thinner. The other changes, at least on my side, were much more significant. The sleepless journey on the night train had given me time to think. My worst enemy was myself and my compulsion to go back to her, even now. My best help was Lily and the prayers I'd learned.

She led me up the hill and a voice inside me started up, 'Remember you can fly.' I was frightened, but I was tired of the fear. She pointed to the house, which looked sombre and dark even in the sunlight, and was gone.

Surprisingly, the door was open and the gate no longer there. It looked squatted. The hallway was disused and musty, no longer the scrupulously clean dwelling of a perfectionist. A stray, thin, orange dog sniffed at the door. The stairs were dirty with earth. Stains on the tiles, the walls. She'd go beyond psychopathic if she saw what had happened to the grand room which had been her work of art. Even the furniture, I remembered, had been sculpted from the floor. Big shock here. Yes, there had been strange, sculptured mounds, joined to the walls, the floor. They were torn open now, and dirt and dust was everywhere as though there had been some explosion. Had a household earthquake occurred in Ms von Zoelen's premises? Had her very controlling perfectionism been stretched too far and blown up? I looked into the huge apertures, earth-filled, smelling worse than a lavatory. Had Mia gone crazy in revenge and destroyed everything?

And then a rustle behind me – it would be one of those laughing birds, perched on the open windowsill. Dag stood there, dressed in silk. He seemed shy, found out.

'You don't want to be in here.' He waited.

'Is she here? Elle?'

He decided she wasn't. 'No, I just popped down to see Mia.'

I was so tired of lies, of being kept on the outside. 'What is all this?'

'I guess she's changing the house again. The workmen ... Come and sit in the garden.'

I stayed in the devastated room. 'She's going to love this.'

He laughed. A little, drained laugh.

And there, lying on the terrace, was the sunbathing girl from the hotel roof in LA. So I'd been right about her involvement with Elle.

He giggled. 'Poor Olav. He'll never be the same. What a shock for him. He thought he knew everything. And I myself always thought everything was so dull.' He tried to encourage me to the door and I turned and ran upstairs. I could smell the honey scent of the hug, like a perfume. Of course, she was here.

And I walked along corridors through the endless apartments, a haven of corridors, and I'd seen them inwardly for so long, the corridors of the old, grand house that had started in her eyes.

She was against the wall at the end of the last corridor, the platinum hair making her surely a star, even now. Something in her posture showed me she was afraid. Tired of deceits that had seemed like truth, I walked without hesitation to where she was. We looked one to the other and her eyes were scared.

She said, 'I had to come here because they're doing the house yet again. And the builders –'

'Were you always like this?' I asked. 'It's not...'

'It is,' she said. 'Too late.'

A barred shadow fell across her face and I remembered how she had spoken of the room where she had set her mother free, her rage at the loss of that presence – the loving, the beloved gone, leaving a space for fleshy, boring housewives to fill. Of course, she hated women.

'I'm going,' I told her.

'Too late. Where can you go?' And she smiled. 'You're an addict,' she said.

'You can get out of it too.' In spite of it all, I wanted to rescue her. 'I'll look after you, Elle.'

And somewhere a long way back in innocence, she wanted to come with me. I could see that. The way her face softened, the eyes expressive. No smile now. And I pitied her and held out my hand towards her, and she shrivelled backwards, eyes changing, as though she was frightened of the changes happening inside her.

'So you're my confessor after all.'

'It's better to be forgiven on this side of life, Elle. That's what I understand. You can't hate enough, change people enough, deform them out of all recognition.'

'You're an odd confessor. You're making my confession for me.'

'Did you love me?' I backed along the corridor, not sure of anything.

'I did once,' she said. And she started towards me. 'A kiss before going?'

And I was drawn towards her as I always had been, and her eyes changed.

'You always were a Goody Two Shoes.' The eyes full of corridors, closing, opening like the shutters of an old camera, and they fluttered and lengthened and were lidless, long and dark like insects, dead eyes, earth-filled eyes from out of the grave.

And I ran.

I leave, and she has nowhere to direct that extreme violence, the brutal attacks, the battering. She'll turn it on herself, thrusting inward, all gnashing and ripping, her joints grind, breath screams, huge tides inside her rise and dash against her fragile skin. Her eyes glare yellow in the unwanted daylight. The insides of her ears beat with the sound of rising tides. She will implode, the inside, a violent wreckage, will dry like dust. The outside, an old pale creature immobile in death. Yes, she will murder herself. All I have to do is remove my life from hers. She will feed off herself, eat herself to death, violate herself and when the huge tides of blood dry she will wither and die.

Is she innocent?

The sunbathing girl was by the open front door.

'I used to take ecstasy. But I learned that to go for the real good stuff you have to be so bad.'

Dag was there and I tried to run between them. 'It's okay,' he said, 'she's not with Elle. She's with me.' The gate to the street was still unblocked.

'I have to go.'

Builders surprised me as they carried buckets of cement into the house.

'How many times has that been done?' said Dag.

I was amazed to be able to leave intact, light-hearted. I was free. And, as in the dream, I did have the feeling I'd started to fly. Yes, I ran to the hill and I could start the dog paddle that kept me up in spite of gravity. I was free of the obsession, of fear. I could start my life again.

I walked down the hill and a group sat outside the bar. I looked for Lily, or René or Claudette. Even Serge. I wanted to tell them I felt so free. I was about to walk on, but I felt the urge to have one last look at this bar I would not visit again.

I came out with a glass, and a woman was sitting on the low wall opposite the grocer's shop. I slid into the space beside her, almost touching her. I was surprised how easy I was with people. How close I could get. I looked right into her eyes and smiled, and could see her responding excitement.

'Do you live here?' she asked, shyly.

'It's a beautiful village. But as it is beautiful, so it is bad,' I said. 'We learn that here.'

'That doesn't sound like a compliment.' Her eyes couldn't leave my face.

'So we distrust beauty here.'

And the woman was intrigued and blushing, and the hands of the clock in the square were at 8.50 p.m. and the date was 22 September 1984.